Keri Arthur
Award for U
Contemporary
Reviewers'
by trad

Visit Keri Arthur online:
www.keriarthur.com
www.facebook.com/AuthorKeriArthur
www.twitter.com/kezarthur

Praise for Keri Arthur:

'Keri Arthur's imagination and energy infuse
everything she writes with zest'
Charlaine Harris, bestselling author of
Dead Until Dark

'Keri Arthur is one of the best supernatural
romance writers in the world'
Harriet Klausner

'Keeps you spellbound and mesmerized on every page.
Absolutely perfect!'
FreshFiction.com

Keri Arthur
FIREBORN
A Souls of Fire novel

piatkus

PIATKUS

First published in the US in 2014 by Signet Select
an imprint of New American Library
a division of Penguin Group (USA) Inc.
First published in Great Britain in 2014 by Piatkus

A CIP catalogue record for this book
is available from the British Library.

ISBN 978-0-349-40415-8

Printed and bound by CPI (UK) Ltd, Croydon, CR0 4YY

Papers used by Piatkus are from well-managed forests
and other responsible sources.

MIX
Paper from
responsible sources
FSC www.fsc.org FSC® C104740

Piatkus
An imprint of
Little, Brown Book Group
100 Victoria Embankment
London EC4Y 0DY

An Hachette UK Company
www.hachette.co.uk

www.piatkus.co.uk

FIREBORN

I'd like to thank my wonderful editor, Danielle, the copy editors who make sense of my Aussie English, and Tony Mauro for the fabulous U.S. cover. I love, love, love it!

Extraspecial thanks to Miriam, the Lulus, and my lovely daughter, Kasey, for their support over the past (crazy) year.

CHAPTER 1

All of us dream.

Some of us even have pleasant dreams.

My dreams might have been few and far between, but they were never, ever pleasant. But worse than that, they always came true.

Over the course of my many lifetimes, I'd tried to interfere, to alter fate's path and prevent the death I'd seen, but I'd learned the hard way that there were often serious consequences for both the victim and myself.

Which was why the flesh down my spine was twisted and marred. I'd pulled a kid from a burning car, saving her life but leaving us both disfigured. Fire may be mine to control and devour, but there'd been too many witnesses and I'd dared not use my powers. It had taken me months to heal, and I'd sworn—yet again—to stop interfering and simply let fate take her natural course. But here I was, out on the streets in the cold, dead hours of the night, trying to keep warm as I waited in the shadows for the man who was slated to die this night.

Because he wasn't just *a* man. He was the man I'd once loved.

I shifted my weight from one foot to the other and tried to keep warm in the confines of the abandoned factory's doorway. Why anyone would even come out by choice on a night like this was beyond me. Melbourne was a great city, but her winters could be hell, and right now it was cold enough to freeze the balls off a mutt—not that there were any mutts about at this particular hour. They apparently had more sense.

The breeze whisked around the parts of my face not protected by my scarf, freezing my skin and making it feel like I was breathing ice.

Of course, I *did* have other ways to keep warm. I was a phoenix—a spirit born from the ashes of flame—and fire was both my heritage and my soul. But even if I couldn't sense anyone close by, I was reluctant to flame. Vampires and werewolves might have outed themselves during the peak of Hollywood's love affair with all things paranormal, but the rest of us preferred to remain hidden. Humanity on the whole might have taken the existence of weres and vamps better than any of us had expected, but there were still far too many who believed nonhumans provided an unacceptable risk to their existence. Even on crappy nights like this, it wasn't unusual to have hunting parties roaming the streets, looking for easy paranormal targets. While my kind rarely provided any sort of threat, I wasn't human, and that made me as much a target for their hate as vamps and weres.

Even the man who'd once claimed to love me was not immune to such hate.

Pain stirred, distant and ghostly, but never, ever forgotten, no matter how hard I tried. Samuel Turner had made it all too clear what he thought of my "type." Five years might have passed, but I doubted time would have changed his view that the only good monster was a dead one.

And yet here I was, attempting to save his stupid ass.

The roar of a car engine rode across the silence. For a moment the dream raised its head, and I saw again the flashes of metal out of the car window, the red-cloaked faces, the blood and brain matter dripping down brick as Sam's lifeless body slumped to the wet pavement. My stomach heaved and I closed my eyes, sucking in air and fighting the feeling of inevitability.

Death would *not* claim his soul tonight.

I wouldn't let her.

Against the distant roar of that engine came the sound of steady steps from the left of the intersection up ahead. He was walking toward the corner and the death that awaited him there.

I stepped out of the shadows. The glow of the streetlights did little to break up the night, leaving the surrounding buildings to darkness and imagination. The ever-growing rumble of the car approaching from the right didn't quite drown out the steady sound of footsteps, but perhaps it only seemed that way because I was so attuned to it. To what was about to happen.

I walked forward, avoiding the puddles of light and keeping to the darker shadows. The air was thick with the growing sense of doom and the rising ice of hell.

Death waited on the other side of the street, her dark rags billowing and her face impassive.

The growling of the car's engine swept closer. Lights broke across the darkness, the twin beams of brightness spotlighting the graffiti that colored an otherwise bleak and unforgiving cityscape.

This area of Brooklyn was Melbourne's dirty little secret, one definitely *not* mentioned in the flashy advertising that hailed the city as the "it" holiday destination. It was a mix of heavy industrial and run-down tenements, and it housed the underbelly of society—the dregs, the forgotten, the dangerous. Over the past few years, it had become so bad that the wise avoided it and the newspapers had given up reporting about it. Hell, even the cops feared to tread the streets alone here. These days they did little more than patrol the perimeter in a vague attempt to stop the violence from spilling over into neighboring areas.

So why the hell was Sam right here in the middle of Brooklyn's dark heart?

I had no idea and, right now, with Death so close, it hardly mattered.

I neared the fatal intersection and time slowed to a crawl. A deadly, dangerous crawl.

The Commodore's black nose eased into the intersection from the right. Windows slid down smoothly, and the long black barrels of the rifles I'd seen in my dream appeared. Behind them, half-hidden in the darkness of the car's interior, red hoods billowed.

Be fast, my inner voice whispered, *or die.*

Death stepped forward, eager to claim her soul. I took a deep, shuddering breath and flexed my fingers.

Sam appeared past the end of the building and stepped toward the place of his death. The air recoiled as the bullets were fired. There was no sound. *Silencers.*

I lunged forward, grabbed his arm, and yanked him hard enough sideways to unbalance us both. Something sliced across my upper arm, and pain flared as I hit the pavement. My breath whooshed loudly from my lungs, but it didn't cover the sound of the unworldly scream of anger. Knowing what was coming, I desperately twisted around, flames erupting from my fingertips. They met the sweeping, icy scythe of Death, melting it before it could reach my flesh. Then they melted *her*, sending her back to the frigid realms of hell.

The car screeched to a halt farther down the street, the sound echoing sharply across the darkness. I scrambled to my feet. The danger wasn't over yet. He could still die, and we needed to get out of here—*fast*. I spun, only to find myself facing a gun.

"What the—" Blue eyes met mine and recognition flashed. "Red! What the *fuck* are you doing here?"

There was no warmth in his voice, despite the use of my nickname.

"In case it has escaped your notice," I snapped, trying to concentrate on the danger and the need to be gone rather than on how good he damn well looked, "someone just tried to blow your brains out—although it *is* debatable whether you actually have brains. Now move, because they haven't finished yet."

He opened his mouth, as ready as ever to argue, then glanced past me. The weapon shifted fractionally, and he pulled the trigger. As the bullet burned past my ear, I twisted around. A red-cloaked body lay on the ground five feet away, the hood no longer covering his features. His face was gaunt, emaciated, and there was a thick black scar on his right cheek that ended in a hook. It looked like Death's scythe.

The footsteps coming toward us at rapid speed said there were another four to deal with. Sam's hand clamped my wrist; then he was pulling me forward.

"We won't outrun them," I said, even as we tried to do just that.

"I know." Sam's voice was grim. Dark.

Sexy.

I batted the thought away and risked another glance over my shoulder. They'd rounded the corner and were now so close I could see their gaunt features, their scars, and the red of their eyes.

Fear shuddered through me. Whatever these things were, they *weren't* human.

"We need somewhere to hide." I scanned the buildings around us somewhat desperately. Broken windows, shattered brickwork, and rot abounded. Nothing offered the sort of fortress we so desperately needed right now.

"I *know*." He yanked me to the right, just about pulling my arm out of the socket in the process. We pounded down a small lane that smelled of piss and decay, our footsteps echoing across the night. It was a sound that spoke of desperation.

The red cloaks were quiet. Eerily quiet.

A metal door appeared out of the shadows. Sam paused long enough to fling it open, then thrust me inside and followed, slamming the door shut and then shoving home several thick bolts.

Just in time.

Something hit the other side of the door, the force of it enough to dent the metal and make me jump back in fright. Fire flicked across my fingertips, an instinctive reaction I quickly doused as Sam turned around.

"*That* won't help." His voice was grim, but it still held echoes of the distaste that had dominated his tone all those years ago. "We need to get upstairs. *Now*," he added, as the door shuddered under another impact.

He brushed past me and disappeared into the gloom of the cavernous building. I unraveled the scarf from around my face and hastily followed. "What the hell are those things? And why do they want to kill you?"

"Long story." He reached a grimy set of stairs and took them two at a time. The metal groaned under his weight, but the sound was smothered by another hit to the door. This time, something broke.

"Hurry," he added rather unnecessarily.

I galloped after him, my feet barely even hitting the metal. We ran down a corridor, stirring the dust that clung to everything until the air was thick and difficult to breathe. From downstairs came a metallic crash—the door coming off its hinges and smashing to the concrete.

They were in. They were coming.

Fear leapt up my throat, and this time the flames that danced across my fingertips would not be quenched. The red-gold flickers lit the darkness, lending the decay and dirt that surrounded us an odd sort of warmth.

Sam went through another doorway and hit a switch on the way through. Light flooded the space, revealing a long, rectangular room. In the left corner, as far away from the door as possible, was a rudimentary living area. Hanging from the ceiling on thick metal cables was a ring of lights that bathed the space in surreal violet light.

"Don't tell me you live here," I said as I followed Sam across the room.

He snorted. "No. This is merely a safe house. One of five we have in this area."

The problems in this area were obviously far worse than anyone was admitting if cops now needed safe houses. Or maybe it was simply a development linked to the appearance of the red cloaks. Certainly I hadn't come across anything like them before, and I'd been around for centuries. "Will the UV lighting stop those things?"

He glanced at me. "You can see that?"

"Yes." I said it tartly, my gaze on his, searching for the distaste and the hate. Seeing neither. "I'm not human, remember?"

He grunted and looked away. Hurt stirred again, the embers refusing to die, even five years down the track.

"UV stops them." He paused, then added, "Most of the time."

"Oh, that's a comfort," I muttered, the flames across my fingers dousing as I thrust a hand through my hair. "What the hell are they, then? Vampires? They're the only nonhumans I can think of affected by UV."

And they certainly hadn't *looked* like vampires. Most vamps tended to look and act human, except for the necessity to drink blood and avoid sunlight. None that I'd met had red eyes or weird scars on their cheeks—not even the psycho ones who killed for the pure pleasure of it.

"They're a type of vampire."

He pulled out a rack filled with crossbows, shotguns, and machine pistols from under the bed, then waved a hand toward it, silently offering me one of the weapons. I hesitated, then shook my head. I had my own weapon, and it was more powerful than any bullet.

"You'll regret it."

But he shrugged and began to load shells into a

pump-action shotgun. There was little other sound. The red cloaks might be on their way up, but they remained eerily quiet.

I rubbed my arms, felt the sticky warmth, and glanced down. The red cloak's bullet had done little more than wing me, but it bled profusely. If they *were* a type of vampire, then the wound—or rather the blood—would call to them.

"That blood might call to more than just those red cloaks," he added, obviously noticing my actions. "There're some bandages in the drawer of the table holding the coffeepot. Use them."

I walked over to the drawer. "I doubt there's anything worse than those red cloaks out on the streets at the moment."

He glanced at me, expression unreadable. "Then you'd be wrong."

I frowned, but opened the drawer and found a tube of antiseptic along with the bandages. As medical kits went, it was pretty basic, but I guess it was better than nothing. I applied both, then moved to stand in the middle of the UV circle, close enough to Sam that his aftershave—a rich mix of woody, earthy scents and musk—teased my nostrils and stirred memories to life. I thrust them away and crossed my arms.

"How can these things be a type of vampire?" I asked, voice a little sharper than necessary. "Either you are or you aren't. There's not really an in-between state, unless you're in the process of turning from human to vamp."

And those things in the cloaks were neither dead *nor* turning.

"It's a long story," he said. "And one I'd rather not go into right now."

"Then at least tell me what they're called."

"We've nicknamed them red cloaks. What they call themselves is anyone's guess." His shoulder brushed mine as he turned, and a tremor ran down my body. I hadn't felt this man's touch for five years, but my senses remembered it. Remembered the joy it had once given me.

"So why are they after you?"

His short, sharp laugh sent a shiver down my spine. It was the sound of a man who'd seen too much, been through too much, and it made me wonder just what the hell had happened to him in the last five years.

"They hunt me because I've vowed to kill as many of the bastards as I can."

The chance to ask any more questions was temporarily cut off as the red cloaks ran through the door. They were so damn fast that they were halfway across the room before Sam could even get a shot off. I took a step back, my fingers aflame, the yellow-white light flaring oddly against the violet.

The front one ran at Sam with outstretched fingers, revealing nails that were grotesque talons ready to rip and tear. The red cloak hit the UV light, and instantly his skin began to blacken and burn. The stench was horrific, clogging the air and making my stomach churn, but he didn't seem to notice, let alone care. He just kept on running.

The others were close behind.

Sam fired. The bullet hit the center of the first red cloak's forehead, and the back of his head exploded, spraying those behind him with flesh and bone and brain matter.

He fell. The others leapt over him, their skin aflame and not caring one damn bit.

Which was obviously why Sam had said my own flame wouldn't help.

He fired again. Another red cloak went down. He tried to fire a third time, but the creature was too close, too fast. It battered him aside and kept on running.

It wanted *me*, not Sam. As I'd feared, the blood was calling to them.

I backpedaled fast, raised my hands, and released my fire. A maelstrom of heat rose before me, hitting the creature hard, briefly halting his progress and adding to the flames already consuming him.

My backside hit wood. The table. As the creature pushed through the flames, I scrambled over the top of it, then thrust it into the creature's gut. He screamed, the sound one of frustration rather than pain, and clawed at the air, trying to strike me with arms that dripped flames and flesh onto the surface of the table.

The *wooden* table.

As another shot boomed across the stinking, burning darkness, I lunged for the nearest table leg. I gripped it tight, then heaved with all my might. I might be only five foot four, but I wasn't human and I had a whole lot of strength behind me. The leg sheared free—and just in time.

The creature leapt at me. I twisted around and swung the leg with all my might. It smashed into the creature's head, caving in his side and battering him back across the table.

A final gunshot rang out, and the rest of the creature's head went spraying across the darkness. His body hit the concrete with a splat and slid past the glow of the UV, burning brightly in the deeper shadows crowding the room beyond.

I scrambled upright and held the leg at the ready. But there were no more fiery forms left to fight. We were safe.

For several seconds I did nothing more than stare at the remnants still being consumed by the UV's fire. The rank, bitter smell turned my stomach, and the air was thick with the smoke of them. Soon there was little left other than ash, and even that broke down into nothingness.

I lowered my hands and turned my gaze to the man I'd come here to rescue. "What the hell is going on here, Sam?"

He put the safety on the gun, then tossed it on the bed and stalked toward me. "Did they bite you? Scratch you?"

I frowned. "No—"

He grabbed my arms, his skin so cool against mine. It hadn't always been that way. Once, his flesh had matched mine for heat and urgency, especially when we were making love— I stopped the thought in its tracks. It never paid to live in the past. I knew that from long experience.

"Are you sure?" He turned my hands over and then grabbed my face with his oh-so-cool fingers, turning it one way and then another. There was concern in the blue of his eyes. Fear, even.

For *me*.

It made that stupid part of me deep inside want to dance, and *that* annoyed me even more than his nonanswers.

"I'm fine." I jerked away from his touch and stepped back. "But you really need to tell me what the hell is going on here."

He snorted and spun away, walking across to the coffeemaker. He poured two cups without asking, then walked back and handed the chip-free one to me.

"This, I'm afraid, has become the epicenter of hell on earth." His voice was as grim as his expression.

"Which is about as far from an answer as you can get," I snapped, then took a sip of coffee. I hated coffee—especially when it was thick and bitter—and he knew that. But he didn't seem to care and, right then, neither did I. I just needed something warm to ease the growing chill from my flesh. The immediate danger to Sam might be over, but there was still something *very* wrong. With this situation, and with this man. "What the hell were those things if not vampires?"

He studied me for a moment, his expression

closed. "Officially they're known as the red plague, but, as I said, we call them red cloaks. They're humans infected by a virus nicknamed Crimson Death. It can be transmitted via a scratch or a bite."

"So if they wound you, you become just like them?"

A bleak darkness I didn't understand stirred through the depths of his blue eyes. "If you're human or vampire, yes."

I frowned. "Why just humans and vampires? Why not other races?"

"It may *yet* affect other races. There are some shifters who seem to be immune as long as they change shape immediately after being wounded, but this doesn't hold true in all cases. More than that?" He shrugged. "The virus is too new to be really certain of anything."

Which certainly explained why he'd examined me so quickly for wounds. Although given I could take fire form and literally burn away any drug or virus in my system, it was doubtful *this* virus would have any effect.

"So you've been assigned to some sort of task force to hunt down and kill these things?"

Again he shrugged. "Something like that."

Annoyance swirled, but I shoved it back down. It wouldn't get me anywhere—he'd always been something of a closed shop when it came to his work as a detective. I guess that was one thing that *hadn't* changed. "Is this virus a natural development or a lab-born one?"

"Lab born."

"Who in their right mind would want to create this sort of virus?"

"They didn't mean to create it. It's a by-product of sorts." He took a sip of his coffee, his gaze still on mine. There was little in it to give away what he was thinking, but it oddly reminded me of the look vampires got when they were holding themselves under tight control. He added, "They were actually trying to pin down the enzymes that turn human flesh into vampire and make them immortal."

"Why the hell would anyone want to be immortal? Or near immortal? It sucks. Just ask the vampires."

A smile, brief and bitter, twisted his features. "Humankind has a long history in chasing immortality. I doubt the testimony of vampires—many of whom are unbelievably rich thanks to that near immortality—would convince them otherwise."

"More fool them," I muttered. Living forever had its drawbacks. As did rebirth, which was basically what vampires went through to become near immortal. But then, humans rarely considered the side effects when they chased a dream.

I took another drink of coffee and shuddered at the tarlike aftertaste. How long had this stuff been brewing? I walked across to the small sink and dumped the remainder of it down the drain, then turned to face him again. "How did this virus get loose? This sort of research would have been top secret, and that usually comes with strict operational conditions."

"It did. Does. Unfortunately, one scientist decided

to test a promising serum on himself after what appeared to be successful trials on lab rats. No one realized what he'd done until *after* he went crazy and, by that time, the genie was out of the bottle."

And on the streets, obviously. "How come there's been no public warning about this? Surely people have a right to know—"

"Yeah, great idea," he cut in harshly. "Warn the general population a virus that turns people into insane, vampirelike beings has been unleashed. Can you imagine the hysteria that would cause?"

And I guess it wouldn't do a whole lot of good to the image of actual vampires, either. It would also, no doubt, lead to an influx of recruits to the many gangs dedicated to wiping the stain of nonhumanity from Earth.

I studied him for a moment. For all the information he was giving me, I had an odd sense that he wasn't telling me everything. "The red cloaks who were chasing you acted as one, and with a purpose. That speaks of a hive-type mentality rather than insanity to me."

He shrugged. "The virus doesn't *always* lead to insanity, and not everyone who is infected actually survives. Those who do, do so with varying degrees of change and sanity."

I frowned. "How widespread is this virus? Because if tonight is any example, there's more than just a *few* surviving it."

"About sixty percent of those infected die. So far, the virus is mostly confined to this area. We suspect there's about one hundred or so cloaks."

Which to me sounded like a serious outbreak. It also explained the patrols around this area. They weren't keeping the peace—they were keeping people *out* and the red cloaks *in*. "And everyone who survives the virus is infectious?"

"Yes."

It was just one word, but it was said with such bitterness and anger that my eyebrows rose. "Did someone close to you get infected? Is that why you swore to hunt them all down?"

He smiled, but it wasn't a pleasant thing to behold. Far from it. "You could say that. Remember my brother?"

I remembered him, all right—he wasn't only the first child his mom had been able to carry to full term after a long series of miscarriages, but the firstborn *son*. And, as such, had never really been denied anything. He'd grown up accustomed to getting what he wanted, and I'd barely even begun my relationship with Sam when he'd decided what he wanted was *me*. He certainly hadn't been happy about being rejected. Sam, as far as I knew, was not aware that his older brother had tried to seduce me, although there had been a definite cooling in their relationship afterward.

"Of course I remember Luke—but what has he got to do with anything?"

"He was one of the first victims of a red cloak attack in Brooklyn."

If he'd been living in Brooklyn, it could only mean he'd truly immersed himself in the life of criminality he'd been dabbling with when I'd known him.

"Oh god. I'm sorry, Sam. Is he okay? Did he survive?" I half reached out to touch his arm, then stilled the motion when I saw the bitter anger in his expression. It was aimed at himself rather than at me, and it all but screamed comfort was *not* something he wanted right now.

"Luke survived the virus, but his sanity didn't." The fury in Sam's eyes grew, but it was entwined with guilt and a deeper, darker emotion I couldn't define. But it was one that scared the hell out of me. "I was the one who took him down, Red."

No wonder he seemed surrounded by a haze of darkness and dangerous emotion—he'd been forced to shoot his own damn *brother*. "Sam, I'm sorry."

This time I *did* touch his arm, but he shook it off violently. "Don't be. He's far better off dead than—" He cut the rest of the sentence off and half shrugged. Like it didn't matter, when it obviously did.

"When did all this happen?"

"A little over a year ago."

And he'd changed greatly in that year, I thought, though I suspected the cause was far more than just the stress of Luke's death. "How the hell could something like this be kept a secret for so damn long?"

"Trust me, you wouldn't want to know."

A chill went through me. It wasn't so much the

words, but the way he said them and the flatness in his eyes. I had no doubt those words were a warning of death, but even so, I couldn't help saying, "And what, exactly, does that mean?"

"It means you tell no one about tonight, or it could have disastrous consequences. For you and for them."

And there it was, I thought bitterly. Fate's kick in the gut. When would I ever learn to stop interfering with the natural course of events?

Sam stalked over to the bed, placing the shotgun in its slot and then picking up a regulation .40-caliber Glock semiauto pistol—a partner to the one he already carried. "We need to get out of here."

"But I want to know—"

I stopped as his gaze pinned me and, with sudden, sad clarity, I realized there was very little left of the man I'd known in those rich blue depths. Only shadows and bitterness. I might have saved him tonight, but the reality was I'd been about twelve months too late. This was nothing more than a replica. He might look the same, he might smell the same, but he held none of the fierce joy of life that had once called to me like flame to a moth. This man's world had become one of ashes and darkness, and it was not a place where I wanted to linger.

"Let's go," he said.

"Don't bother, Sam."

He briefly looked confused. It was the second real expression I'd seen—the first being that moment of surprise when he'd realized who'd saved him. "What do you mean?"

I walked across to him. Ashes or not, he still resembled the man I'd never get over—not in this lifetime, anyway—and it was hard not to lean into him. Hard not to give in to the desire to kiss him good-bye, just one more time.

"I'm one of them, remember?" Bitterness crept into my voice. "One of the monsters. And I'm more than capable of looking after myself."

He snorted softly, the sound harsh. "Not in this damn area, and maybe not against the—"

"I got in here without harm," I cut in, voice as cold as his, "and I'll damn well get out the same way."

"Fine." He stepped aside and waved me forward with the barrel of the gun. "Be my guest."

I looked at him for a moment longer, then walked toward the door. But as I neared it, I hesitated and turned around. "I don't know what has happened to you, Sam Turner, but I'm mighty glad you're no longer in my life."

And with that lie lingering in the air, I left him to his bitterness and shadows and went home.

CHAPTER 2

The harsh sound of the alarm's buzzer woke me just over six hours later. I opened a bleary eye and glared at the alarm balefully, but it didn't take the hint and mute of its own accord. I slapped the stop button, then rolled onto my back with a groan. The already-tangled sheets twisted around me further, tugging free from the bed to expose my toes to the cool morning air.

But cold toes were the least of my worries, because my arm still hurt and I felt like shit. I had fallen into bed not long after two, but sleep had been elusive and my dreams were filled with blue eyes that were far too shadowed and filled with death. Death that would step my way if I wasn't very careful.

Despite the warning the dreams had contained, the desire to find out what had happened to Sam rose like a ghost, insubstantial and fleeting. I shoved it back in its box. Dreams aside, I couldn't afford any sort of curiosity about either him or the red cloaks. He'd made it abundantly clear what would happen if I did.

And why would I bother anyway? He'd told

me long ago that he wanted me out of his life forever, and nothing I'd seen last night indicated
he'd changed his mind. I was still a monster in his
eyes, still someone he believed should be dead
rather than living and breathing the same air as
him.

I don't know why I'd hoped for anything else.

I flung my good arm over my eyes, not ready to
get up and face the world just yet. In the city
streets far below our apartment, trams rattled and
groaned, and the gentle hum of traffic mingled
with the harsh cry of the gulls circling the nearby
quay. A gentle breeze stirred past my toes, chilling
them even further. Rory had obviously left the
balcony doors open again.

I couldn't hear him in the kitchen, though, and
I should have, given he was on morning shift at
the fire station.

I tugged the sheets away from my limbs and
climbed out of bed. The cool air hit my skin like
ice. I shivered and grabbed a dressing gown, pulling it on as I walked across the hall to Rory's
room. As I suspected, he was still asleep, sprawled
naked and belly down on his bed, the blankets
covering his butt and little else. But the air in his
room held little of the chill that had greeted me,
meaning he was in a deep enough sleep that caution had fallen by the wayside and instinct had
taken over. He was radiating enough heat to
warm not just his body, but the entire room.

"Hey!" I lightly kicked the foot hanging off the
end of the bed. "Time to get ready for work."

He didn't respond, so I kicked the foot again. This time he muttered something I suspected wasn't polite. I grinned and kicked him a little harder. He grunted, and this time the muttering was definitely a word. "Bitch," to be precise.

"You're on morning shift, remember, and your captain *did* warn you last week not to be late again."

He rolled over onto his back, and the rest of the blankets slipped from the bed onto the floor. He worked out in the gym and ran around the nearby Tan Track—a 3.8-kilometer stone aggregate track around the beautiful Botanic Gardens—so he was slender but well toned, with long, lean legs, a flat stomach, broad shoulders, and well-defined arms.

And he was, I noticed with amusement, more than a little horny this morning.

I walked around the bed and flung open the curtains. Sunlight flooded the room, turning his red hair—which was a feature of all phoenixes— to copper and highlighting the dust and the mess. One thing Rory had never been was tidy.

"Fuck," he muttered, his deep voice gravelly and harsh as he flung up an arm to shield his eyes. "That's just cruel."

"I thought you liked your job."

"I do, but—"

"The only butt I want," I said, unreasonably cheered by the fact that I wasn't alone in feeling shitty, "is yours climbing out of that bed and into a shower pronto."

A devilish light began to gleam in the warm amber depths of his eyes. "I've got a better idea."

My grin grew, but before I could actually react, he lunged forward, grabbed my arm, and dragged me down onto the bed beside him. For good measure, he threw a leg over the top of mine to prevent me from escaping, though I hadn't actually tried.

"How about you and I waste a little time and energy?" he murmured, as he tugged at the dressing gown's sash.

"How about you try to keep this job a little longer than six months," I said wryly, even as I gave in to temptation and let my fingers play over his well-defined arms. It would only encourage him, but the fires within hungered for closeness, warmth, and caring—no doubt to counter the cold darkness I'd faced last night.

"They won't sack me." His expression became distracted as the sash came undone. "I'm too good a fireman, and they know it."

He slipped a hand underneath the silky material and traced a line along the length of my hip with one heated finger, skimming the scars as tenderly as the rest of me. My breathing hitched a little and the pulse of excitement grew. But as much as I wanted to give in, I didn't. Not only because he actually *liked* this job, but because he also liked the people he worked with, and it was the first time in the four years since Jody—his human fiancée—died that he'd actually cared about anything or anyone beyond those in our immediate circle. Despite his current nonchalance, I knew it would hit him hard if he was fired.

So I ignored those deliciously trailing fingertips and slapped his arm. "Enough. Go take a shower. A very *cold* shower."

His gaze rose to mine, and a reluctant grin stretched his kissable lips. "You, my darling girl, are going to be the death of me."

"Actually," I said primly, "I believe I already have been. Two lifetimes ago, in fact."

"Three," he muttered; then, with a groan, he released me and climbed off the bed. "Fair warning, sweet Emberly. I intend to pick up where I left off once I get home tonight."

"And I shall be naked and waiting." I watched him walk into his en suite. Rory and I had been friends and lovers ever since we'd been teenagers, which was so many centuries ago now I could barely even remember them. He was my life partner, the spirit I was fated to be with forever, and the only man I could ever have children with. But we were not, and never had been, in love.

It was said that at the very beginning of time, a phoenix spurned the affections of a witch after taking her virginity. In her anger and shame, she cursed us with the inability to love one another, forcing us to forever seek—but never find—emotional completion outside our own race, thus ensuring that we would forever be left with little more than love's bitter ashes, as she had been. I'm not sure I believed the whole witch-curse thing, but it certainly held more than a few grains of truth when it came to phoenixes and love.

As the shower came on, I bounced out of Rory's bed and headed into the kitchen to make us both breakfast. He walked in ten minutes later, dropped a kiss on the back of my neck, then swept up one of the plates of pancakes and headed for the table.

"So, did you manage to save your soul last night?"

I glanced at him sharply, and he gave me a lop-sided smile. "If I can't read the signs by now, Em, something is seriously wrong. So who was it this time?"

Sam's warning shot through my thoughts as I picked up the two steaming mugs and the other plate of pancakes and joined Rory at the table. "No one important. And yes, I did."

His expression indicated he didn't believe the lie, but he let it slide, asking instead, "What's on your agenda for today, then?"

"I don't exactly know." I pushed one of the mugs across to him. "Mark mentioned something about discovering a critical amino acid in the molecules he was studying yesterday, so I daresay he'll be in the lab all day and I'll be transcribing his notes all night."

"Ah, the exciting life of a research assistant," he said, voice dry.

I resisted the urge to point out I wasn't actually a research assistant, even if that was what they'd classified me as. Mark hated interference of any kind, even if it came in the form of help to set up and monitor experiments. After he'd gone through more than a dozen qualified assistants in less than two months, the powers that be at the Chase Medical Research Institute had given up and resorted to employing what amounted to a secretary. Meaning I transcribed his notes and generally ran around after him but otherwise didn't interfere in whatever it was he was doing.

And Rory was right—it wasn't exciting. But I'd done the whole exciting bit the last time around. Right now, all I wanted was something easy.

Besides, this lifetime was supposedly *his* turn to do the dangerous stuff, not mine. Not that *that* had ever stopped me from getting into trouble in previous lifetimes.

"You've never done well coping with a staid and boring life," he added, obviously guessing my thoughts. "And I'm betting you won't last much longer working for that crazy old man."

"They're paying me damn good money to run after that crazy old man, and that makes up for the boring. Besides, for an old guy, he's not bad scenery—he has nice legs and an eminently watchable ass."

"So have you," he said dryly. "He made a play for it yet?"

I snorted softly. "He's old, remember? Besides, I seriously doubt he notices anything not connected to his microscope or his books. Not everyone in this world is as randy as you."

"That he's in his sixties doesn't make him dead

from the waist down—a fact we've both proven over our many years together." He glanced at his watch, then gulped down his coffee and pushed away from the table. "Five minutes to go. I'd better run."

So had I. If I didn't hurry, I'd miss the train. Mark was a man who meticulously planned every minute of his day, and my being late would not only upset his timetable, but turn him into an unreasonable grump for the rest of the day. Although his somewhat unpredictable temper wasn't the only reason I was getting higher pay; he believed I should be available to work whenever *he* wanted me, be that day or night.

Rory kissed my cheek, then headed for the door. Twenty minutes later I ran out of the building and headed for the train. I squeezed out at Footscray Station, then walked down to Byron Street and the big white building that housed the Chase Medical Research Institute.

Ian Grant—the day shift security guard, and a bear of a man with a close-cropped head of gray hair and very little in the way of untattooed skin—gave me a wide grin of greeting as I entered the foyer.

"Hey, Em," he said, "Lady Harriet's office has been trying to contact you for the last twenty minutes. You got your phone off again?"

Harriet Chase had founded the institute some fifty years ago, and it was still one of the biggest privately funded organizations for biological and medical research in Victoria. The old dear was also something of an elitist, hence the not-so-affectionate moniker.

But I had no idea why the hell her office would be chasing me.

I dug my phone out of my purse and, sure enough, there were seven missed calls. I glanced up at Ian. "I gather she's been on the phone to you?"

"Well, it was Abby rather than herself, but she wanted me to get you on the phone the minute you walked in."

Abby was Harriet's overworked but not under-paid assistant. Ian duly picked up the phone and called her, and I suddenly wondered if I was about to get sacked. I couldn't think of any other reason for Lady Harriet's office to be ringing me, especially given she or her staff rarely spoke to anyone less worthy than the heads of the various research departments. Although the security guards did at least get a smile of greeting every morning, which was more than could be said for the rest of us.

"Abby, I have Emberly Pearson here for you." He paused for a moment, then handed the phone across to me. I cleared my throat and said, "Sorry about the missed calls, Abby, but I was on the train and didn't hear—"

"Never mind that now," Abby said, her voice sounding more than a little harassed. Lady Harriet had obviously been in one of her moods this morning. "You need to get over to Professor Balti-more's place. He's due to make a presentation to some investors in half an hour, and he hasn't arrived and he's not answering his phone."

I frowned. It wasn't like Mark to be late, so something had obviously gone wrong. But why was I being asked to fetch him? Granted, I was the one being paid danger money to be his beck-and-call girl, but if this was so urgent, why not send someone else? It wasn't like this place was lacking in research assistants. I said as much to Abby.

"We did send someone else," she said, "but he's not answering the door. You're keyed into his security system, aren't you?"

"Yeah, but—"

"Then go," she cut in. "Make sure you get him back here fast."

She hung up before I could reply. I handed the phone back to Ian. "Well, there goes my peaceful morning."

Ian grinned, his teeth spectacularly white against the inked darkness of his cheeks. "I'd run."

I did. Thankfully, like many of the senior staff at the institute, Mark lived nearby. It saved time traveling back and forth and allowed them to work longer hours. Nothing like being addicted to your job—which was something *I* could never claim. Hell, I couldn't even claim that I'd *liked* many of the things I'd done over the centuries Rory and I had been alive.

Mark's brown brick building came into view. It was a squat, three-story building with vinyl windows that were double-glazed and butt-ugly. They'd been the rage about fifty years ago, and I could only thank the designer gods that the damn things had finally gone out of fashion.

A man with burnished auburn hair and the most amazing pair of emerald-green eyes I'd ever seen exited the building as I approached and, with a wide smile, he held the door open.

"Thanks," I said, even as my steps slowed and my nostrils flared. The heat radiating off him was incredible, and it was all I could do to resist the desire to siphon it away. He *had* to be a fire Fae. No other nonhuman had *that* sort of heat signature.

From what I knew of the Fae, there were four groups, with each group controlling one of nature's fundamental building blocks—earth, wind, fire, and water. This man, as a fire Fae, couldn't actually create fire, but he could shape and control it. All Fae tended to be loners, preferring the solitude of empty countryside to the concrete jungles of this world, and each of them also had a need to be near their element regularly or they would fade away, becoming little more than a sigh on the wind.

While Fae were loners at heart, they were also sensualists, existing to experience sensations both within and without their elements. Fire Fae, in particular, reputedly delighted in introducing innocents to the more seductive pleasures of this world, which was maybe why *this* Fae was here in Melbourne. In a city as big as this, there was a greater chance of finding innocence.

Deep in his bright eyes, recognition flared,

along with curiosity. He might not know exactly what I was, but he sure as hell recognized another being of fire.

"Do you come here often?" His voice was gravelly, sexy as hell, and sounded as if it was coming from somewhere near the vicinity of his rather large boots.

If there was one thing about the Fae that most literature over the years had gotten very wrong, it was their stature. They were neither small nor winged, and the only ones that were ethereal in *any* way were the air Fae.

I smiled. "A couple of times a week, at least."

"Then with any sort of luck, we'll meet again, when I'm not in so much of a hurry." With that, he gave me a nod and walked away.

The urge to chase after him rose, but I resisted the temptation and ran up the stairs to Mark's apartment on the third floor. The hallway was shadowed and cold, the small, ugly windows down the far end doing little to let much heat or light in. Mark's apartment was the second on the left. I leaned on the doorbell and listened to it chime inside. I waited a few minutes, then, when there was no response, flipped up the cover protecting the security system. After I keyed in the code, it scanned my eyes, and the red light switched to green. As security measures went, they were pretty over-the-top, but the institute had insisted on them after the homes of several other professors had been burgled.

The door slid open with a soft *whoosh*. I took three steps inside and stopped, my eyes widening in surprise. The place was a mess. In fact, mess was putting it mildly. The room looked as if it had been turned upside down and given several violent shakes. Furniture was dragged away from walls or upturned, books were scattered all over the carpet, and his precious research papers had been flung everywhere.

What the hell had happened?

"Professor?" I stepped over loose paperwork and around fallen furniture and made my way to the bedroom. The door was closed. I hesitated, then pulled a tissue out of my handbag and used it to turn the door handle to cut any risk of adding my own prints to whatever prints might be there.

"Professor?" I repeated. "You in here?"

Still no answer. I opened the door and warily peeked around the corner. The mess in this room was a mirror of the first; the sheets and blankets were torn from the bed, the mattress flung against one wall, the dresser drawers half-out and their contents strewn across the floor. Someone really had done a number on this place, but where the hell was Mark?

My gaze went to the small en-suite bathroom and I swallowed heavily. But just because it was closed didn't mean he was dead inside—and even if he *was*, it wasn't like I hadn't seen a corpse before.

I forced my feet forward, stepping carefully across the mess, and repeated the tissue process with the en-suite door. The destruction was repeated even here, but Mark wasn't inside.

Relief slithered through me. I swung around, my gaze sweeping the room. Whoever was responsible for this had obviously been looking for something, but what? It wasn't like Mark had a whole lot. He lived and breathed his work, and his apartment held little more than basic facilities and his mountains of leather-bound books. He had money—and plenty of it—but you wouldn't think it looking at either this place or the man himself.

I moved back out into the living area and across to the kitchen. Same result—utter mess and no Mark.

Where the hell was he?

"Emberly?" His voice rose out of the silence behind me. I swung to see him enter the apartment and stop, his brown eyes going wide. "What the hell has been going on?"

His gaze came to mine, his expression almost accusing. I grimaced. "I was about to ask you the same thing, Professor. Ms. Chase sent me over here to find you, as you have a meeting with investors in"—I paused and glanced at my watch—"just over twenty minutes."

"I know. The damn batteries in my watch stopped and I didn't realize the time. I just came back to get my presentation notes." Meaning he'd been breakfasting at the local café again. He raked a hand through his wiry gray hair and added,

"Guess there's no use looking now. I'll have to wing it."

He looked so out of sorts I felt sorry for him. "Do you want me to stay and attempt to clean up? And call the police?"

"That would be extraordinary if you could." He gave the mess a somewhat despairing look. "I wouldn't know where to start."

I smiled. I was used to mess, having shared my many lives with Rory. But for someone as meticulous as Mark, this had to be a harrowing sight. "It's no problem. Just make sure you clear it with Ms. Chase."

He nodded. "Thank you, Emberly. This is very much appreciated."

I shrugged. He gave the mess around me another sweeping, somewhat despairing look, then muttered something under his breath and walked out.

I closed the door, then called the cops and basically did nothing until they arrived. Abby rang to confirm that she'd clocked me in and all I had to do was come back to clock out whatever time I finished. The cops took some pics and my statement, then dusted a couple of items and basically left me to it. They weren't expecting any evidence to lead them to the culprit and neither was I.

By the time five p.m. rolled around, the place was more or less respectable, and the only item I could see missing was his desktop computer. Interestingly, they hadn't found his laptop—it was still safe in its hidden compartment in the desk. I had no idea whether all his paperwork was present, but I left it stacked in piles for him to go through at his leisure. After washing my hands, I picked up my jacket and returned to work.

I found Mark back in the lab. He looked up somewhat distractedly as I entered the secure, sterile environment and blinked a little before recognition surged.

"Emberly," he said, leaning back in his chair. "I had completely forgotten about you and the apartment."

"No problem." I said it wryly, having figured as much. "I tidied everything up as best I could, and I think the only material thing missing is your desktop computer."

"What about the laptop?"

"Still safe in its hidey-hole."

He sighed. "That's all right, then."

I nodded. Not only was most of his important work typed up by me on that laptop, but it was also the computer he used to shift his reports to his cloud service—a procedure only he and I knew about. The desktop was little more than a ruse in the event of a robbery. Or a ransacking, in this case.

"I'm about to go home," I said. "Do you need anything else before I do?"

He reached for the five notebooks teetering on the edge of the table. "I wrote up my notes for both yesterday and today." He glanced at me over the top of his glasses. "You do still have the secure laptop at your place, don't you?"

"Yes."

"Good. I need these transcribed overnight."

Of course he did. I guess it was lucky I had nothing more than a leisurely loving session with Rory planned.

Once I'd stripped off all the protective gear and signed out, I headed home. Rory sent me a text saying he was doing an extra couple of hours and wouldn't be home until nine, so after a shower, I re-dressed in sweatpants and a loose-fitting T-shirt, then pulled out my laptop and started on the notebooks.

By the time nine rolled around, I'd transcribed four of the five notebooks. I saved them onto a USB—Mark's need to be extra careful was somewhat catching—then bounced up and shoved it into the planter box filled with plastic flowers for safekeeping. Once I'd started dinner, I poured myself some red wine and wandered out onto the balcony. A helicopter clattered past, searchlights sweeping the buildings opposite. Light briefly glinted off a round object in a window one up and one across from our apartment, and I snorted softly. The old fart in 61B was obviously using his telescope again, hoping to catch me naked. Of course, it didn't help matters that I *did* periodically walk around sans clothes, but I figured the more he was watching me, the less he was watching other unsuspecting women. And it was certainly no skin off my nose if he got his jollies that way—although that *didn't* mean I hadn't had him checked out to make sure he wasn't anything more than a harmless old man who enjoyed spying.

I finished my wine, went back inside to see how the roast chicken and potatoes were going, and then somewhat reluctantly sat down to transcribe the final notebook. Rory rolled in just as I rose to check our dinner. "Hey," I said, grabbing a pair of tongs so I could turn the potatoes. "You're late."

"Not only late," he said, dumping his bag on the table before coming up behind me. He slid his hands under my T-shirt and snuggled close. His fingers were hot against my belly, his erection like steel against my rear. "But terribly disappointed."

"Oh yeah?" I nudged him away with an elbow, then put the chicken back into the oven. "Why's that?"

"Because you promised to be naked and waiting." He pressed close again and kissed the back of my neck. My skin tingled in response, and desire unfurled within me. "This, clearly, is not the case."

I smiled and drew in the scent of him. He smelled of smoke and flame—aromas that were both delicious and intoxicating to spirits made of fire. "Nakedness happened at six. You're the one who decided he needed to work overtime."

"It got me back into the boss's good books, and *that* was worth the extra hours of frustration."

His fingers moved down my belly and played with the elastic in my sweats. Anticipation curled through me, and my breathing quickened. "Meaning you worked all day with that rod out the front of you? Bet *that* caused some ribbing from the rest of the guys."

He laughed softly. His hands slipped past the elastic, then around to my hips, his fingertips barely brushing soft curls along the way. Pleasure trembled through me.

"Well, the frustration wasn't *that* bad, although we did put out a big warehouse fire." His voice became dreamy. "You should have seen it, Em. Fierce, orange-white flames leaping for the sky. It was beautiful, truly beautiful."

He brushed kisses along the nape of my neck again, and I closed my eyes, enjoying the sensation. "I hope you were careful when you drew them in, Rory."

His hands slid out of my sweats. Disappointment swirled, but only for a moment, because his touch slid under my T-shirt and up toward my breasts. "I was. And, god, it felt *glorious*."

Fire to a phoenix was like chocolate to most women. Totally unnecessary as a fuel source, but sinfully pleasurable all the same. It was a wonder he was controlling himself this well. Had our positions been reversed, I probably would have had my wicked way with him right here in the kitchen, the consequences be damned.

His hands reached my breasts and cupped the weight of them. His skin was so hot it might as well have been flames holding me. It felt good, *so* good.

I licked my lips, then reached back with one hand, sliding it between us until I found the zipper in his jeans. As his clever fingers began to gently pinch and pull my nipples, I slid the zipper down. He wasn't wearing underpants—he rarely did when he was this horny—and his cock came free, thick and hard and pulsing with need. I played my fingers along the length of it, and he groaned.

"Not like this," he murmured, even as his body instinctively pressed harder against mine. "I want the real thing, Em. Flame, not flesh."

And with that, he pulled away, caught my hand in his, and tugged me after him. We all but ran to the apartment's third bedroom, only there was no bed in this room. There was, in fact, no furniture at all. Just four thick, fireproof walls and a bare concrete floor that had been treated with fire retardant.

I kicked the door shut behind us, but the utter blackness of the room didn't hold sway for long. Anticipation danced from his skin, tiny fireflies that spun brightly through the room.

He stopped, then caught my other hand, his amber eyes glowing with heat as he raised my fingers and kissed them gently. "Flame for me," he said. "Please."

I smiled and let the heat rise. Fire erupted between our joined hands, primal and hot. He threw back his head, his nostrils flaring as he sucked in the fierceness of it. His skin began to glow and the heat of it rolled over me, a siren song that was so sweet, so enticing.

"More," he whispered.

I allowed the flames to grow, let the molten fingers reach for the ceiling. He gasped, shuddering, and the delicious waves of heat and desire became more intense, fueling the urge to fully become flame rather than flesh. But not yet. Not just yet.

"Rory," I said, needing more than just the caress of heat and desire.

He responded instantly and erupted into flame. It tore through my body, enticing my own fires to life with such force that it was hard to tell where his flame ended and mine began. This was no caress, no tease. This was a firestorm that ripped through every muscle, every cell, breaking them down and tearing them apart, until our flesh no longer existed and we were nothing but fire.

He was fierce and bright in the darkness, a being that radiated strength and passion and caring. All I could think about, all I wanted, was his heat and energy in and around me. We began to dance, entwine, wrapping the fiery threads of our beings around each other, tighter and tighter, intensifying the pleasure even as it rejuvenated and fed our souls. Soon there was no separation—no him, no me, just the sum of both of us, and oh, it felt glorious.

But this wasn't just sex for us—this was something a whole lot more vital. Phoenix pairs needed to regularly merge flames, or face diminishing—in some cases, even death. And *this* was the reason so many of our relationships had turned to ashes. No matter how much we might love someone else, we could never remain faithful to them. Not if we wanted to live.

The dance went on, burning ever brighter, ever tighter, until it felt as if the threads of our beings would surely snap and implode.

Then everything *did*, and I fell into a storm of feverish, unimaginable bliss.

I'm not entirely sure when I came back to flesh, but it was to the awareness of a distant but determined pager buzzing away madly. I swore softly, but didn't move. In the aftermath of such an intense joining, my legs usually refused to support me. Professor Baltimore could wait for a change.

After several moments the page stopped. I stared into the darkness, listening to Rory's breathing, feeling good and happy and whole.

And yet . . .

And yet, as good as it was between us, I always wanted more. I wanted what Rory and I had *and* an emotional connection. But that wasn't my lot. Not in this lifetime. Not in any future lifetimes. The best I could ever hope for was a man who was willing to share—and men who understood the necessity of my being with Rory were few and far between.

Sam's image rose like a ghost to taunt me. Sam certainly *hadn't* been one of those few. He'd been furious when he'd found out about Rory's presence in my life—furious and betrayed, and justifiably so in many respects. I'd tried to explain what I was and why Rory was so necessary to me, but Sam had refused to listen.

I sighed and rubbed a hand across my eyes. After all this time, you'd think I'd be used to the pain of disappointment. But it never got any easier.

Ever.

Rory eventually rolled onto his side and dropped a kiss on my lips, soft and lingering. "I hope that page wasn't urgent."

I took a deep, shuddery breath that did little to ease my aching heart. "Knowing Mark, he probably just wants coffee."

"Then I better let you go. I know what it's like to suffer caffeine withdrawal." A grin I felt rather than saw teased his lips. "It's almost as bad as sex withdrawal."

"Which is *not* something you suffer very often." Amused, I pushed upright, then walked into the living room and grabbed my handbag, rummaging through it until I found the pager. There was no message, but the little light on the side of the small screen was flashing, which usually meant he wanted to see me but was too busy to tell me why.

I threw the pager back into my bag, then headed into the bathroom for a quick shower. Urgent or not, I wasn't about to head to work smelling of smoke and fire.

"The chicken should be done in another twenty minutes," I said, walking back into the kitchen once I was dressed. "Don't wait up for me—I have no idea how long this is going to take."

He nodded, then wrapped his arms around me and dropped a kiss on the top of my head. "Catch a taxi. Public transport sucks at this hour."

I relaxed against him for a moment, but as the air began to burn all around us again, I pulled away, grabbed my bag and coat, then got the hell out of there before desire got the better of common sense.

I arrived at the institute about twenty minutes later. Lights shone from various windows, including the one Mark usually operated from. I swept my ID card through the slot, then walked across the foyer to the security desk. The guard, a thin man in his mid-forties, watched me impassively from under heavily set brows.

"May I help you?"

I grabbed the sign-in book and nearby pen. "Is Professor Baltimore working in his usual lab tonight? He paged me about half an hour ago."

The guard—Ryan Jenkins, according to his name tag—frowned. "I think the professor left about two hours ago." He paused and checked the other book. "Yep. You can see his signature right there."

He swung it around, then pointed at the appropriate spot. Sure enough, the professor had signed out at 8:52.

I grimaced. Not only had he called me from home, but he'd left the lights on in the lab again. Lady Harriet would not be amused—although she'd hardly say anything to him because he was her top scientist. It would come down to me instead. "Could you arrange for someone to go into his lab and turn the lights off? Her ladyship's got a bee in her bonnet about saving energy of late."

The guard smiled, and it oddly reminded me of a crocodile. All teeth, no sincerity. "Sure will. You need anything else?"

"No, thanks."

I turned and walked out. I could feel the guard's gaze on me the entire time and, for some weird reason, it had chills skating down my spine.

I jogged down the street to Mark's place. From the various apartments on the first two levels came the sounds and smells of life—voices, music, late-night pizza, and even a baby crying. The third floor, however, was shadowed and silent.

I paused, the unease that had lingered after the guard's attention suddenly flaring again. There was only one other tenant on this floor besides Mark, and he was a man in his mid-twenties who was probably out partying, given it was a Friday night. The old woman who'd lived in one of the other apartments had died last week, and the remaining apartment still hadn't been rented out. So it wasn't surprising the floor was hushed.

And yet something felt wrong.

Wrong is better than boring, that inner voice whispered. I flexed my fingers, then walked forward. When I reached his door, I pressed the buzzer. It rang inside, echoing softly. He didn't answer, and there was no other sound to indicate whether he was there or not.

If he was asleep, I *would* resort to violence.

I stepped across to the security panel, entered the code, and had my iris scanned. The door opened. It was dark inside. Real dark. He must have drawn the curtains; otherwise the glow of the streetlights would be filtering in.

I swept my hand across the light switch. Light flared, the sudden harshness making me blink.

And I saw him.

Professor Mark Baltimore wasn't asleep.

He was dead.

CHAPTER 3

He sat on a wooden-backed kitchen chair in the middle of the living room, his hands lashed behind his back and his feet tied to the chair's front legs. His nose had been smashed, and bits of blood and gore had splattered across his face and dribbled down the front of his shirt—which had been torn open, revealing more cuts and bruises. Even his spiky gray hair was matted and dark with blood. They'd really done a number on the poor sod.

But why? What did he have that anyone would want so desperately? Nothing in his molecular research warranted this sort of response—nothing that I could see, anyway. But then, what would I know? I only made his gibberish legible and had no real understanding of what most of it meant. I didn't even understand what type of molecules he was researching. Science had *never* been my forte. Reading illegible writing *was*, and that was the main reason I'd gotten this job—which no longer existed now that he was dead.

I smacked that rather self-centered thought away and dug my phone out of my purse, calling the cops for the second time that day.

As I waited for them to arrive, I dialed the office but got a busy signal. When I also had no luck with Abby's cell number, I left a message, saying she needed to contact me immediately. Hopefully, she'd do so sooner rather than later, because if Lady Harriet found out about the murder via the TV or newspapers, there'd be hell to pay.

Time after that seemed to drag. I tried to ignore the guilt that crawled through me every time I glanced at his body, but had little success. While I knew it was highly unlikely I could have changed the outcome here if I *had* answered the buzzer when it initially went off, there was always going to be that what-if question lingering in my mind.

Although—truth be told—if I *had* gotten here earlier, I might have been found dead alongside my boss. I sometimes dreamed of death, but my own usually came without warning.

The cops eventually arrived. I was questioned, first by the men who'd initially responded and then later by the detective in charge, and it was close to two—yet again—by the time I finally got home. I stripped off my clothes as I walked through the living room, then padded into Rory's darkened bedroom, crawled into his bed, and snuggled into his back.

And promptly went to sleep.

A strange sound woke me. An incessant, annoying noise that just went on and on. I blinked, my mind fuzzy and my body securely cocooned in the warmth of Rory's. Eventually, I realized what the sound was. Someone was downstairs leaning on the intercom buzzer.

"Whoever that is," Rory murmured, "tell them to fuck off. It's still early, for god's sake."

A glance at the clock proved he was right. It was barely seven. But whoever it was apparently wasn't going to take silence for an answer.

I groaned and pulled myself away from the delicious heat of Rory's embrace, then staggered barefoot and naked through the living room. Only I wasn't entirely watching where I was going and I ran shin first into the coffee table, spilling Mark's precious notebooks everywhere in the process.

I cursed fluently and hobbled the rest of the way to the intercom, slapping the button hard and saying, "Whoever the fuck you are, you'd better have a good reason for waking me up at this hour of the goddamn morning."

There was a long silence; then an all-too-familiar voice said, "It's Sam. We need to talk."

Surprise, and perhaps a tiny bit of pleasure, raced through me. "You and I said all there was to be said the other night. I don't want—or need—you in my life."

"Look," he said, voice gravelly and decidedly grim. "I don't want this any more than you do, but you happen to be the only witness to Professor Baltimore's murder—"

"I didn't witness it," I corrected tartly. "I found the body. Big difference."

"And," he continued, like I'd never spoken,

"you worked for the man. You knew him better than anyone else at the institute, apparently, and that makes you a possible key to tracking down his murderer."

"I met the case detectives last night. You're not one of them, so why the hell are you here?"

He hesitated. "This case is no longer being handled by homicide. It's been turned over to us."

"And who, pray tell, is 'us'?"

My voice was every bit as cold as his, but my heart was hammering so hard it felt like it was going to tear out of my chest. And I didn't know whether it was the fear that talking to him could inflame all those barely buried feelings or the half certainty that it would turn them into ashes and blow them away forever.

"That is not something I'm about to explain over an intercom. Let me in, Emberly."

"Never again," I muttered. And the last thing I wanted was memories of him in *this* apartment. When we'd split, I'd either thrown out or gotten rid of every single thing that reminded me of him, and that not only included all the furniture and every gift he'd given me but also the apartment we'd once shared. "I'll come down. Give me five minutes."

I turned around. Rory was standing in the living room doorway, his arms crossed and his expression grim. "Do you want company?"

I hesitated, then shook my head. Sam wasn't dangerous—at least not physically. My mental health was another matter entirely, but that wasn't something Rory could help me deal with. "Go back to bed. I'll join you afterward."

He continued to study me, concern radiating from him in waves. I picked up my old sweat-pants and T-shirt from the floor and dressed, then grabbed my jacket and slung it on. "Honestly," I said, when I finally met his gaze again. "I'll be okay."

He didn't say anything, but his gaze remained on me as I picked up my keys and headed out.

Sam waited to the right of the building's main exit, his arms crossed and his expression closed. The early-morning sunshine gave his black hair an almost blue shine, but his face, like his body, seemed leaner now than it had once been. Certainly his cheekbones looked more defined. More French, I thought, though I knew he could claim that blood only through his mother's grand-mother.

"So," I said, stopping several feet away. The air was crisp and cool and filled with the salty scent of the nearby ocean, but this man's smell seemed to override all that, filling my lungs with his warm, lusciously woody aroma. "I'm here. What do you want?"

"Breakfast." He pointed with his chin to Port-side, the small café several doors down from our building, and, without waiting for me, walked to-ward it.

I trailed after him, tugging up my jacket's zip-per to protect myself from the chilly breeze coming off the sea. *Liar*, that voice inside me whispered. *It's not about the chill; it's about him. About protecting yourself from him.*

That inner voice was altogether *too* smart.

He chose an outside table overlooking the marina and as far away from the other diners as possible. Not that there were many people here. It was seven in the morning, after all, and not even Portside, as popular as it was, started getting really busy until at least nine on the weekends. Had it been a weekday, we wouldn't have gotten a table.

I pulled out a chair and sat down opposite him. He didn't say anything, simply picked up the menu and studied it. Frustration swirled, but so, too, did curiosity, and that—and only that—kept me from leaving.

The waitress came up and gave us a cheery smile. "Are you ready to place your orders yet?"

Sam said, "The breakfast fry-up and black coffee for me, thanks."

The waitress glanced at me, pen poised, so I added, "I'll have the French toast with strawberries and double cream and a Moroccan mint-green tea, thanks."

She nodded. "Any juice?" When both of us shook our heads, she added cheerfully, "Won't be long."

As she disappeared inside the restaurant, I crossed my arms and leaned back in my chair. Leaning on the table would have brought me far too close to him. "So, to repeat my question, what the hell is this all about, Sam?"

"I've already told you why I'm here."

"And I've already given my statement to the police. Everything I could tell you is there."

"Not when there have been further developments."

"Like this case being taken from homicide and given to your unit, whoever your unit actually are?" My voice was dry. "Why is that?"

"Because Baltimore's murder isn't as straightforward as it seems."

"I guessed that the minute I saw him trussed up like a turkey and beaten to death. Just spit it out, for god's sake."

His blue gaze raked me, as sharp as a knife. There was a tension in him I didn't understand, a hunger that was deep, dark, and not *entirely* sexual. My traitorous body nevertheless responded. Damn it, why did he still have the power to affect me so strongly?

Because he is this lifetime's love, that inner voice whispered. *And there is nothing you can do about it but suffer.*

I hated my inner voice sometimes.

"It wasn't only Professor Baltimore who was murdered last night," he said, voice curt. "A security guard by the name of Ryan Jenkins was found dead—and stuffed into the janitors' closet—by the morning relief."

My eyes widened. "I talked to Jenkins last night."

"We know," he said grimly. "At ten eighteen."

I frowned at the odd emphasis he placed on the time. "So why does this seem to be a big deal?"

"Because Ryan Jenkins was apparently murdered between nine and nine thirty. The man you were talking to was *not* Jenkins."

I remembered the unease I'd felt as I'd walked out of the building. Instinct had known something was wrong.

"Meaning I talked to one of the men involved in his death, and you want me to give a description and work up a composite?"

He nodded but didn't say anything as the waitress approached with our drinks. "Your orders shouldn't be much longer," she said and left again.

I opened the lid of the little china teapot to let the water cool a little, then said, "So they killed the guard because they wanted to get something from Mark's office?"

He nodded. "Both the lab and his office were ransacked. We want you to go through those areas as well as his home to see if there's anything missing."

I frowned. "That's going to take all day and half the night. And I seriously doubt—"

"You'll do it, no matter how long it takes." His voice was harsh. Cold. "It has already been cleared with Harriet Chase."

I glared at him for several seconds, annoyed as much at his manner as the order itself. But, truth be told, I probably was the only one who'd have *any* sort of chance of spotting if something had gone missing. It made sense to at least try.

I plonked the little tea bag into the pot and closed the lid. "Have you any idea what they were after?"

He hesitated, his gaze raking me again, as if he was deciding whether I could be trusted or not. And that stung even more than his bitter words had five years ago.

He leaned forward and crossed his arms. It accentuated the muscles in his arms and the broadness of his shoulders. "Your Professor Baltimore was working on a possible cure for the red plague virus."

I blinked. "Really? I knew he was involved in molecular research and was attempting to track down certain amino acids, but I had no idea there was a virus involved. He certainly never called it by that name."

"He wouldn't. For security purposes, it was simply given a number—"

"NSV01A," I cut in, remembering seeing it repeatedly in the notes. When he nodded, I added, "But how did these men know that? I mean, I didn't, and I worked for the man."

"It was kept quiet for the same reason the virus has been kept quiet—we don't want to alarm the public unnecessarily."

"So who knew what he was doing? Because someone must have talked if these men were after his research."

"That we don't know. But as far as I know, only

Harriet Chase was fully aware of what he was doing."

And *that* old battle-ax wasn't about to blab to anyone about a project that could potentially net her billions. "Well, someone else obviously *did* know."

He eyed me severely. "Yeah, you. Or at least, you knew about his notes."

I snorted. "I can't understand half the crap he goes on about in those notes. I'm just there to type it up."

"Doesn't mean you couldn't have mentioned it to someone."

"Meaning I'm both a witness and a suspect? Way to get my cooperation, Sam."

Our meals arrived, and I tucked into my French toast and berries with gusto. But he, I noticed, pushed his meal away before he was half-finished. He picked up his coffee and cradled the mug in his big hands, watching me eat for several minutes. The intensity of his gaze was unnerving.

I scooped up the last of the strawberries, then pushed the plate away with a contented sigh. "What about Mark?"

He blinked. My question had obviously caught him by surprise. "What about him?"

"Well, couldn't he have talked to someone?"

"Who? From what we understand, his work was his life. He had few friends and did little beyond moving between his home and the institute."

"That's not entirely true. He ran regularly with

one of the other professors, and he had breakfast at the café across the road every morning. He was quite friendly with several of the waitresses there."

"Friendly as in lovers?"

I hesitated. "I don't know. I never had reason to ask or care."

"We'll check." He drank some coffee, then said, "Were you and he lovers?"

I bit back a snarky remark and simply said, "No." Snarky remarks, I suspected, would run off his back as quickly as water off a duck's.

He grunted. "Who was his running companion?"

"Professor Jake Haslett."

"Would Baltimore have trusted him enough to mention his research?"

"How the fuck would I know? I ran his research life, not his private one."

He raised an eyebrow, and just for a moment I thought I saw a glimmer of amusement. But it was too quickly lost to the sea of darkness to be really sure. "And you can think of no one else he interacted with on a regular—or even irregular—basis?"

"No." I paused, then added, probably a little too hopefully, "So, can I go now?"

"Not until Rochelle gets here."

I poured my tea, then raised the cup and drew in the rich scent in an attempt to cleanse his smell from my lungs. I might as well have tried to sweep a chimney with a feather. "And who is Rochelle?"

"Our compositor."

That raised my eyebrows. "She's coming here? Why?"

"Because we are a specialist unit working outside regular police boundaries, and we prefer to keep our location secret. It's safer that way."

Which made me wonder what in the hell his unit was doing—other than tracking down and killing those infested with the red plague, that is.

"Then how do I contact you if I discover there's anything missing from the lab, office, or home?"

"You don't. I'll meet you again tonight."

"There are such things as phones, you know." And if he knew where I now lived, he undoubtedly also knew my phone number.

"We avoid using phones unless they are securely scrambled."

Wow, his employers were going to *serious* lengths to protect themselves. "Meaning I'll have to put up with you leaning on my doorbell again?"

He hesitated. "Unless you wish to arrange a meeting time now, then yes."

I drank some more tea and wished I knew what the hell was going on behind his closed blue eyes—although what good it would do me, I had no idea. It wasn't like we could undo the past and the things that had been said.

"Given it's going to take me a good part of the day to go through Mark's things, let's meet at the Magenta," I said. "It's a bar just down the street from Mark's."

He nodded; then his gaze slid past me and he

rose. The smile that touched his lips was warm and welcoming, and it briefly lifted the shadows in his gaze. It was also the first true indication that the Sam of old wasn't entirely lost.

He was just lost to me.

A tall amazonian brushed past me and greeted Sam with a kiss on the cheek that was just a shade more friendly than necessary. And her fingers lingered on his arm as she said, "This is a bitch of an hour to be up. I hope you've ordered me coffee."

She was the same height as Sam—six foot—broad shouldered and muscular, without appearing too much like a bodybuilder. She also emanated a high degree of heat, had thick, strawberry-blond hair that tumbled to her shoulders in waves, and wide, leaf-green-colored eyes. Her clothes were designer.

To say I suddenly felt inadequate in my baggy sweats and old leather coat was something of an understatement.

"I haven't yet," Sam replied. "I wasn't sure how long it would take you to get here, and if there's one thing worse than an early hour, it's cold coffee." Warmth fizzed between them, and it was decidedly sexual in its nature. Lovers, it suggested, not just work companions and friends.

Sam's gaze came to mine again. "Rochelle Harmony, meet Emberly Pearson."

"Emberly," she said, in a voice every bit as cool as Sam's. "A pleasure to meet you."

I shook her offered hand and noted it was a whole lot warmer than his. She was, I realized suddenly, another fire Fae. And maybe *she* was the reason her male counterpart was also here—maybe he was simply waiting for *her* to come into her reproductive period. From what I knew about the Fae, it was a somewhat irregular event that happened only every fifty years or so, and was, in part, the reason why there were so few of them.

She placed a tablet computer on the table and then sat down, firing it up as he placed an order with the waitress.

"Now," she said, unclipping the stylus from the top of the tablet. "Describe him to me."

I did so. She worked on the image as I spoke, and within a remarkably short amount of time, we had a composite that looked like the guard I'd spoken to last night.

"I'll get this out to all operatives and see if we can find a match in the system." She finished the last of her coffee, then glanced at Sam again. "Anything else?"

He shook his head. "I'll meet you back at headquarters."

She nodded, gave me another of those cool smiles, then left. Her scent lingered, all warm exotic spices.

I finished the cooled remnants of my tea, then said, "That it?"

"For now. I'll meet you tonight at the bar—six okay?"

"Uh, no. Not if you want this job done properly. Try something closer to ten."

He nodded, flipped enough cash onto the table

to pay for everything, then rose. "I'll see you tonight."

He walked away, and suddenly the morning seemed a whole lot brighter—another sad reminder that he wasn't the man I'd known. At least around me, anyway.

A glance at my watch revealed it was almost eight thirty. If I didn't get to work ASAP, I'd be meeting him a whole lot later than ten. He obviously had no idea just how much crap Mark kept.

I sighed and headed home. Rory hadn't returned to bed, but then, I hadn't really expected him to.

"What did he want?" he said, gathering me close.

I relaxed into him, enjoying the comfort and peace of his arms for several minutes before actually answering. "Mark was murdered last night, and I found the body."

"Fuck," he said; then, "You okay?"

"I would have been a whole lot better if the case hadn't been handed over to Sam's unit."

He snorted, the sound rumbling through my body. "I told you—someone upstairs is pissed at us in this lifetime."

"It certainly seems that way." I sighed, then added, "I now have to go through everything in Mark's office and apartment to see what's missing."

"You're probably the only one who'd have any chance of knowing, given you were his all-around go-to person." He dropped a kiss on the top of my head. "You'd better leave before my hormones start acting all desperate again."

I grinned, then rose up on my toes to kiss him properly. "Given our love life has been a little hit and miss of late, why don't you see if Rosie's free after work tonight?"

Rosie was a divorcée who worked in the office at the fire station. She and Rory had been friends with benefits for almost three years now, with neither of them expecting or wanting more. I liked Rosie. She was human, but she was good for him, and she understood his loss. Her husband had been murdered two years before Rory's fiancée had been. We still had no idea *why* Jody had been killed and, apparently, neither did the police. Rory was in semiregular contact with the officer who'd been in charge of the case, but there'd been no fresh leads for some time now.

Even my dreams were mute on the subject—not that they ever made an appearance when I actually wanted or needed them.

"*That*," he said heavily, "is a damn good idea."

"Glad I could help." I dropped a quick kiss on his cheek, then spun and headed for the shower.

The search through Mark's office and lab was as tedious and long as I figured it would be, and just as useless. I couldn't see anything missing, but it was hard to be absolutely certain. I stacked the final pieces of paper onto the last of the checked piles, then swept my gaze around the small room. The books he'd cared so much about now sat broken in piles. But at least many of them were salvageable, which was more than could be said about his running trophies. What they thought they'd find in those I had no idea. Hell, even his computers . . .

I stopped suddenly. *His laptop.* Sam's people would have checked whether the institute's system had been compromised, but I doubted they'd have known about either the laptop or the cloud storage Mark cross-copied everything to. Hell, as far as I knew, even Lady Harriet wasn't aware he'd been stashing copies of everything, because he accessed it only from his laptop. I'd once asked him why he was being so secretive about it, and he'd mumbled something about having had research stolen in the past and that this was one way to both ensure its safety and to prove he was the originator.

If someone *was* after his work, then that would be the one place they'd get it all. Although if they had accessed it, why did they then wreck his office, lab, and home?

"One problem at a time," I muttered, then thrust to my feet, grabbed my jacket, and headed back out.

The last rays of the setting sun painted the gathering clouds with streaks of pink and gray. The wind was cool and thick with the promise of rain. I shoved my hands in my pockets and hoped it held off until I made it home tonight—although getting soaked walking home from the train station would certainly cap off a perfectly shitty day.

It didn't take me long to jog to Mark's. I pulled the door open without really looking where I was going and plowed nose-first into a heated chest.

"Ow," I said, instinctively jumping back and then rubbing my nose. "Sorry, I wasn't watching—"

I stopped, suddenly recognizing the grinning man in front of me. It was the emerald-eyed Fae I'd talked to yesterday.

"Meeting in this doorway seems to be our destiny," he said, idly rubbing his chest. Though I'd hit him with some force, I doubted I'd actually done any real damage. He was too muscular—too hard-looking—to be injured by a short woman in a hurry. "How's your nose?"

"Sore, but that's what I get for not looking where I was going." I shrugged, my cheeks heating. Only I very much suspected its cause wasn't embarrassment, but the rather intense way he was watching me. Like I'd suddenly become prey he very much intended to hunt. I might not be an innocent, but—if his expression was anything to go by—he very much intended to explore some of the more sensual pursuits with me.

"Well, I'm afraid it's not entirely your fault." He raised his left hand, revealing a phone. "I was texting rather than looking."

He was also blocking my entry into the building and showed little inclination to move.

"Do you live here?" I asked, more to break the silence than any real need to know.

His gaze dropped to my lips as I spoke, and the

waves of heat rolling from him sharpened abruptly. Desire flared deep within me. Heat—any sort of heat—was a siren call we found hard to resist.

"No. But a friend rents an apartment on the second floor." His gaze scanned me, and it felt like I was standing naked before him. It was a rather pleasant sensation. "You?"

"My boss lives here, but he's a forgetful old sod and I'm always having to retrieve stuff."

He laughed. It was a rich, strong sound that rumbled across my senses and fueled those inner flames. "I've known a few bosses like that. Sounds like you might need a drink to recover."

"Possibly," I said, raising an eyebrow. "Depends on who's offering."

"Ah, of course." He held out his hand. "Jackson Miller, at your service."

"Emberly Pearson."

His big hand enclosed mine, and a tremor ran through me. God, his skin was so deliciously warm it was all I could do not to close my eyes and draw it into me.

"Well, Ms. Pearson, I do think I need to buy you a drink to apologize for my clumsiness." He drew my hand to his lips and lightly kissed my fingers. It felt like a caress of flame. "What are you doing tonight?"

I couldn't help smiling. He was a fast worker, that was for sure.

"Sadly, I'm working tonight."

"Well, *technically*, so am I, but I can always find

time for a pretty lady." He pursed his lips, amusement and desire making his bright eyes glow. "What about breakfast?"

"Breakfast?" I repeated, all sorts of exciting possibilities running through my mind.

"Yeah, breakfast." He paused, his grin widening. "Nothing else, just breakfast. Fae prefer to savor the chase, so the rest will come with our second date."

Second date? I didn't know if I'd survive the first one without at least exploring *some* of his unrestrained heat. But I raised my eyebrows and drawled, "And what if the first date bombs?"

"Given what's burning between us, my sweet, I very much suspect the first date will be hot and heavy and that our second date will be *sooner* rather than later." He took a business card out of his wallet and handed it to me. "Ring me whenever you've finished work, and we'll go from there."

I accepted the card. *Jackson Miller, Miller Engineering*, it read, with a cell number underneath. I tucked it into the top pocket of my jacket. "It could be very late by the time I've finished tonight."

He shrugged and finally stepped to one side. "I'll be awake."

"Then I'll call." With a smile, I brushed past him and made my way up the stairs. His hungry, heavy gaze followed me until I was out of sight.

Damn, but he was *hot*.

I blew out a somewhat shaky breath and tried to pull the scattered remnants of my thoughts together. Work first, then Sam, then pleasure.

Although once upon a time Sam would have been my pleasure, instead of an unknown but sexy fire Fae.

I shoved the thought back into its box. Sam had moved on to the amazonian, and maybe, just maybe, I'd run nose-first into her male counterpart.

I coded myself into Mark's apartment and then ducked under the police tape and went inside. The mess was much the same, only this time there was fingerprinting dust everywhere. I ignored the empty but bloodied chair and walked over to his desk. After feeling around for a couple of seconds, I found the little latch and pressed it. There was a click; then a drawer popped out from the base of the old table. I grabbed the laptop, plonked it down onto the desk, then hit the on button. After a moment, it fired up.

I pulled up the chair and got to work, accessing his network and then entering his cloud site. To discover it was empty. Totally empty.

The bastards had not only *accessed* his site but erased all his files. And the only way they could have done that was via Mark. I wondered how long he'd lasted before he'd given up his secrets. I guess if his battered state was anything to go by, it had been quite a while, and for that I could only admire him. Many a stronger man would have suffered far less before giving in.

I studied the screen for a few moments longer, then clicked back into the activity screen. The information had been accessed at 9:20 and then removed at 3:45 a.m.—hours after Mark had been killed and the institute ransacked. Why? If they'd wanted to ensure they were the sole owners of all his notes, why not erase it immediately?

I didn't know. Probably wouldn't ever know, given Sam wasn't likely to bother me again once I'd handed over all the information I could. And given they apparently had open orders to kill the virus-afflicted, I very much suspected that whoever was behind the professor's death wouldn't exactly be getting his day in court if caught.

I leaned back in the chair and rubbed my eyes for a moment. It had been a long day, and all I really wanted to do was go home and go to sleep before I went to breakfast with a certain Fae. But I needed to complete my task here and get Sam out of my life again, and the sooner I went through the rest of this mess, the better.

With a sigh, I pushed upright and got to it. It was close to eleven by the time I'd finished. I picked up the laptop and left Mark's apartment—hopefully for the final time—then made my way downstairs. The back of my neck began to prickle as I neared the ground floor, and I frowned, glancing around quickly. I couldn't see anyone in the shadows, couldn't feel any body heat, and yet . . . someone was watching me.

And while the sensation might have been nothing more than tiredness and an overactive imagination, I nevertheless hurried out of the building. Only it wasn't just cold, but raining.

"Fantastic," I muttered, shoving the computer under my coat. "Just fucking fantastic."

Shivering, I ran toward the crisp white and pink glow of Magenta's lights.

The sensation of being watched didn't fade.

It grew.

And they were no longer just watching, but following.

CHAPTER 4

I ran on, but all my senses were trained behind me. Whoever it was, they were little more than the occasional whisper of footsteps and a distant shimmer of heat that was too cool to be human.

Vampire.

Fear and panic surged, making my heart race and a cold sweat break out across my skin. I could protect myself better than most, but I'd been attacked by a rogue vamp in a past life, and it was an experience I had no wish to repeat. Legend might suggest a vampire's bite was orgasmic— and they certainly could be—but it was a harrowing, hateful thing when you were an unwilling victim.

And the bastard had killed me, too, simply because he'd caught me off guard and had ripped out my throat before I could fully react. And if a phoenix died before their allotted one-hundred-year span was over, the subsequent rebirth was a wretched, traumatic experience.

I shivered, suddenly thankful Magenta's was close. I raced for the warm pink glow of the bar, slowing only once I'd reached it. A quick glance behind me didn't reveal my follower, but if it *was* a vamp, I wouldn't see him. The bastards were well able to surround themselves in shadows and all but disappear.

At least I was safe for the moment. Whoever it was would hardly make a move in front of so many people.

I shook the rain from my hair, then unzipped my jacket and held the laptop in one hand as I made my way through the crowd hanging around the front of the place, smoking and drinking. Sam wasn't among them. Inside, the music was loud and bass heavy, and the air rich with the warm heat of humans. It took me a few minutes to find Sam, as he'd positioned himself in a rear corner and was half-hidden by the shadows.

He rose as I approached, his gaze scanning me and suddenly sharpening. Just for a moment, his concern washed through me, thick and sharp, and it not only warmed me deep inside, but provided yet another hint that the man I'd once loved was still in there somewhere. Which only made the steely front all that much harder to take. "What's wrong?"

"I'm being followed," I said. "A vampire, by the feel of him—"

He made a disgusted sound and sat back down. "He was supposed to keep out of your damn sight."

I stared at him for a moment; then anger surged. "He's one of *your* people?"

"Yeah."

He motioned me to sit. I ignored him. That odd sense of darkness flared again, sending a shimmer that was part desire, part fear, down my spine.

"Why the hell are your people following *me*? I've been doing all that I can to help you, and this is the thanks I get?"

"Emberly, sit down and *calm* down." His voice held the whip of command. "It's not what it seems."

I snorted in disbelief and shoved the computer at him. "You might want to have your people look at this. It's Mark's laptop, the one we used in the lab to transcribe his notes. We erase the drive regularly, but I'm guessing you'll have someone who can recover data."

"We do." He frowned. "But we searched both the lab and his house thoroughly—where the hell did you find it?"

"He had a special compartment built into the desk." I stripped off my sodden jacket. The shirt underneath was soaked in thick patches that clung to me like a second skin. It was also white and, where it was wet, more than a little see-through— something I couldn't do much about. But it wasn't like he hadn't seen me exposed before. Wasn't like he was even interested.

"So, explain why the hell you're having me followed." I dragged out the chair opposite him and sat down. "Because it certainly smacks of you not trusting me."

"Actually, we don't trust anyone, but in this

particular case, we just don't want you dead. Would you like a coffee? You look cold."

I *was* cold, but I'd be damned if I'd let him do *anything* for me—not even something as simple as getting me a drink. I crossed my arms and said, "All I need is for you to explain that comment."

He grunted. "Think about it; Baltimore is dead, his home and office ransacked, and you're the only link we have to both Baltimore and the false security guard. And if they haven't found what they're after, it's logical to think they'll come after you next."

"But I don't know—"

"*They* don't know that," he cut in brusquely. "Adam will continue to follow you at night, and someone else will shadow you during the day. At least until we know for sure they're not going to snatch you."

I glared at him, though my anger had slithered away faster than rain down a drain. I could hardly argue about what he was doing when it was being done to keep me safe. "You could have at least warned me. I damn near had a heart attack."

He grimaced. "You weren't supposed to know he was there. Most people can't sense vampires when they shadow."

"Well, *I'm* not most people."

"No," he said, voice dark. "You're not."

And *he* would never forget it. God, I needed a coffee. No, what I *really* needed was alcohol. A bucket of it, preferably. But I couldn't be bothered getting up to order anything and I wasn't about to ask him.

So I simply said, "I don't think anything was missing from either the lab or his office, but when I went to his apartment, I booted up the laptop and discovered his stash had been erased."

"His stash?"

I nodded. "Mark backed up all his research in an online cloud service as an additional security measure. Only he and I knew the codes, so that's one of the things they must have beaten out of him."

"What time did they access it?"

"Three forty-five this morning."

"Well after he'd been murdered and everything ransacked."

I nodded again. "Which doesn't make sense. Why do it *after* they'd ransacked? Why not do it before?"

He half shrugged. "Maybe they accessed it only after they hadn't found whatever it was they were looking for elsewhere."

"But all his notes were stored there. All of them—" I stopped suddenly. All except the ones I had, that was.

"What?"

I cleared my throat. "Mark asked me to type up some notes the night he died. I've still got them."

"Fuck. You should have mentioned—"

"I forgot," I snapped. "It's not like I did it deliberately." Not like I wanted his grumpy, forbidding ass in my life any longer than necessary.

And if I kept telling myself that often enough, I might eventually believe it.

Sam grunted. His expression wasn't giving much away, but the darkness in him was stronger, its caress making me shiver and yearn. It almost felt like the aura a vampire used when they wanted to make their blood taking as pleasurable as possible. Not all of them did, of course. Some, like the one who'd killed me, rather enjoyed the taste of fear and panic. But at least the bastard had suffered, because I'd managed to burn a good part of his body before I'd died. Vampires couldn't regenerate ruined flesh any more than a phoenix could—although at least our rebirth *did* give us a fresh, scar-free start.

"Are they still at home?" he asked.

I nodded. "I usually transfer the files across to the institute once I finish transcribing, but I forgot to do that with everything that happened."

"Probably just as well, given they've managed to steal everything else."

"Meaning they *did* get into the institute's system?"

"Yes. Although they only erased Baltimore's notes."

I rubbed my arms, trying to get some warmth into them. Saw his eyes flicker briefly downward and felt my nipples harden.

And wished like hell there was some way to make myself as immune to this man as he was to me.

He leaned back in his chair, his face a mask. "Then we'd better go get them."

"Fuck it, *no*." The words were out of my mouth before I'd even thought about them. "I've just spent the last thirteen hours crawling around floors, stacking papers, and going through books. I've done more than enough for one day. Besides, I have a goddamn date."

He raised an eyebrow, his expression almost mocking. "With the Fae you ran into at the apartment building?"

Anger flared again, and the heat of it touched my cheeks. "What if it is?"

"Given what has been going on in that building, it might be better if you'd wait until he's fully checked out."

I snorted softly. "You lost the right to tell me who I could and couldn't see a long time ago."

"I never *had* that fucking right." His low voice was so cold it felt like I'd been slapped by ice. "Even when we *were* together."

"And *you* never gave me a chance to explain why!"

"Cheating is cheating, Red," he bit back. "End of story."

It wasn't, but it would never matter. It was over between us, and nothing could ever repair the damage, no matter how desperate my foolish heart might be to believe otherwise.

He took a deep breath, and the darkness and anger in him retreated. "Fine. I'll have someone drop by tomorrow morning to collect them."

"Fine," I retorted. "If you need anything else, you know where to find me."

"If we need anything else, someone else can fucking find you." And with that, he rose and walked out.

I released a slow breath, but it didn't do a whole lot to ease the anger and tension that ran through me. What I needed was time in the arms of someone who cared, but Rory was no doubt in Rosie's tender embrace by now. A hot and sexy Fae—even if he was a total stranger—would have to do instead.

I plucked his business card out of my pocket and gave him a call.

"Jackson Miller." His voice was deep and warm, and I closed my eyes in pleasure as he added, "How may I help you?"

"I believe you promised me a drink," I said. "And I'm finding myself in need of one right now."

"Emberly! I wasn't sure if you'd call tonight. I thought I might have scared you off with my straightforwardness."

I laughed softly. "Trust me, a straightforward man will never scare me away. Are you busy?"

"I'm never too busy to have a drink with a pretty lady." He paused. "Where are you?"

"Magenta's. It's just—"

"I know exactly where it is," he cut in cheerfully. "I'll be there in five."

Meaning he was close. Good. I needed to steal some of his warmth. A chill seemed to have settled into my bones, and I couldn't risk flaming in a bar that was packed with humans.

Jackson was as good as his word and appeared

five minutes later, a big, lean man who radiated sexuality and heat. His grin, when his gaze met mine, was easy and delighted, creasing the corners of his green eyes.

"Emberly," he said, and leaned down to drop a kiss on my cheek. Though it was little more than a light brush of lips, the memory of it seemed to linger on my skin, all tingly and warm. "You have no idea how pleased I am to hear from you so soon."

I smiled. "I wasn't sure what you drank, so I haven't ordered anything yet."

"Good, because a lady should never buy a man a drink. Not until the second or third date, anyway."

"I think most ladies would disagree with that," I said dryly, "given it often leads to unwarranted expectations."

"Oh, I have *plenty* of expectations." Mischief sparkled in his eyes. "But as I've already told you, they'll come with our second date. What would you like to drink?"

"Just a chardonnay, thanks."

He nodded and went to get our drinks. On returning, he sat in Sam's recently vacated chair, filling the space with warmth and sunshine rather than moody darkness.

"So," he said, crossing his arms on the table and studying me with an intensity that was different from and yet no less unsettling than Sam's. "Tell me about yourself."

I gave him a vague outline of what I did for a living, then said, "You?"

He half shrugged. "I own an engineering company. We design and develop new industrial machinery to clients' specifications."

"Sounds more exciting than my job."

"It's not. You been in Melbourne long?"

My turn to shrug. "For about nine years now. You?"

"Most of my work is here nowadays, but I do the occasional job in Sydney."

I took a sip of my wine, then said, "So why is a fire Fae working in a city as big as Melbourne?"

He raised his eyebrows. "Why is a phoenix?"

"Change of scenery."

"Same. Of course, it certainly doesn't hurt that there's a female Fae here only a few years away from becoming fertile." That slow, sexy smile appeared again. "And there's certainly more non-Fae possibilities to explore more sensual pastimes with here in the big smoke."

Once again, his expression left me in no doubt that he was hoping to explore some of those sensual pastimes with *me*. Excitement shivered through me. The Fae were, according to Rory, fantastic lovers. He'd been lucky enough to spend some time with one several rebirths ago, but I'd never met one before now.

"So this female—her name wouldn't happen to be Rochelle, would it?"

He shrugged. "I've only caught her scent a few times, and we're not likely to meet until she's ready to reproduce. We Fae are an antisocial lot."

With one another, not with other races, obviously. "So has your pursuit of sin here in the big smoke been a successful endeavor thus far?"

"Yes, though it is never a sin to either enjoy or give enjoyment through sensation and sex." Amusement crinkled the corners of his bright eyes. "Though I do have to say, virgins are a bit thin on the ground these days. Unless, of course, you catch them young, and *that* goes against the moral grain."

"A Fae with morals? I'm shocked!"

He laughed. "Some of us *do* have them. Not many, granted, but some."

The conversation flowed easily from one topic to another, until it felt as if I were talking to a longtime friend rather than a stranger. Hours came and went unnoticed, although the wine was eventually replaced by coffee.

By three, the bar had lost a good half of its patrons, and the raucous, bass-heavy beat had been replaced by more intimate music.

"I guess I'd better go," I said, more than a little regretfully. As much as I enjoyed his company, I was dead on my feet. And if I lingered, we *would* end up in bed together, but I was just as likely to fall asleep as enjoy myself. "Otherwise, this will roll into breakfast and if it does, then breakfast cannot possibly be classified as a second date."

He reached across the table and took my hand in his. He turned it around and, with one finger, lightly traced the outline of my palm and wrist. Desire slammed into me, and breathing with any sort of normality suddenly became impossible.

"I do hope you realize," he said, voice husky and passion burning bright in his eyes, "that I intend to seduce you senseless the next time we meet."

My heart was hammering so hard I swear it was trying to tear out of my chest and leap into his lap. What Rory and I had might be brilliant, but it was also a necessity. While we both enjoyed flesh-on-flesh contact, it was something we indulged in with each other only occasionally. Sam might have accused me of cheating, but I'd been as faithful as I ever could be given the restrictions of my nature, and Rory and I had been strictly flame only.

"If you don't," I replied, keeping my voice low and sexy, "I'll be very disappointed."

His bright smile was filled with promise. "And we wouldn't want you disappointed, would we?"

God, no. "When and where?"

"What about a late brunch? I can pick you up around eleven, if you'd like."

Sam's warning edged its way into my thoughts and I hesitated. *Damn you,* I thought. *You're not going to spoil this.* I wouldn't let him. "That would be lovely."

I gave him my address. He rose, took my hand, and pulled me to my feet. "And now? Can I drive you home?"

I shook my head. "I always prefer to catch a cab home on a first date."

"Then let me walk you down to the cabstand." He picked up my coat and held it out so that I could slip my arms into it. His fingers brushed my breasts as his hands fell away, and delight skittered through me.

"I can smell you," he whispered, as his lips brushed the base of my neck. I closed my eyes, enjoying the sensation. "I can smell your heat and your desire. It intoxicates me, sweet Emberly."

I shivered, torn between the need to be safe and the growing hunger to take what this man offered. His kisses traveled up the side of my neck; then he gently nipped my lobe. A groan escaped. Mine, not his.

"Please," I said, and wasn't entirely sure just what it was I was asking.

He chuckled softly; then he stepped out from behind me, his hand sliding sensually down my back and coming to rest on my backside. His touch was almost hot enough to brand, and the flames inside me shivered and danced in response. "Shall we walk down to the cabstand?"

I wasn't entirely sure I was capable of walking *anywhere*, but I nodded anyway. And the only thing I was capable of thinking was that if he could do *this* to me with a few softly spoken words and some well-placed kisses, then what the hell could he do when he actually set his mind to full seduction?

One thing was sure—I'd find out later today. And I couldn't wait.

The rain had eased outside, but the night was still very cold. Not that I really felt it, protected as I was by the intense, animal-like hunger rolling off the man beside me.

At the stand, he didn't kiss me, as I'd expected, but rather stepped away. He must have caught my surprise, because he gave me a lopsided, totally endearing grin. "Things, I'm afraid to say, are a little knife-edged at the moment."

"A Fae in danger of losing his legendary control?" I said, in mock horror. "Unbelievable!"

He laughed. The sound rolled across my skin as sweetly as his kisses had only moments before. "I am so glad we ran into each other, Emberly. I'll see you in"—he paused and looked at his watch—"just over seven hours."

"I'll be waiting." I got into the cab, gave the driver my address, then twisted around to watch Jackson walking away, until we turned the corner and I could no longer see him.

The minute I stepped out of the elevator I saw the small red light situated discreetly above our doorway flashing. I stopped cold. That light said our security system had been breached.

Sam's warnings came back in a rush, and I stared down the bright but silent hallway to our door with some trepidation. I might be able to protect myself both physically and with flame, but neither was entirely foolproof. And the memory of what had been done to the professor loomed large, a warning of what might happen if I acted stupidly.

I spun around and stepped back into the elevator. Once in the foyer, I called the cops, then sat back in the shadows and waited for them to arrive.

Only the cops didn't. Sam did.

I wasn't sure whether to laugh or cry. After five years of living in the same city but never meeting, we suddenly seemed unable to get away from each other.

I pushed upright wearily. "I thought you were intending to let someone else deal with me?"

His expression was as remote as I'd ever seen it. "We have your phone tapped, and I just happened to be close when you reported the break-in."

Annoyance surged. I understood the reasoning behind tapping my phone well enough—as he'd said, I was the only connection now between the professor and whatever else his murderers might have been searching for—but that didn't mean I had to be happy about it. But all I said was, "I'm already being shadowed by one of yours—why couldn't he have handled it?"

"He's a vampire. He can't cross thresholds unless invited." His gaze raked me. "I seem to remember you once saying that you made a policy of never doing that."

I didn't particularly want *him* crossing my threshold, either, but it wasn't like I had a whole lot of choice right now. So I simply shrugged and followed him into the elevator. Which suddenly seemed entirely too small with his dark and brooding presence in it.

"Where's your key?" he said as we neared the floor.

I gave it to him, being overly careful not to touch him. If he noticed, he didn't say anything.

When the elevator door opened, I followed him out, but was promptly stopped by an abrupt, "Stay here."

I obeyed. He was the cop, not me. Not in this lifetime, anyway. I crossed my arms and noted almost absently that as lean as he was, he still filled out the rear end of his jeans rather nicely.

He carefully unlocked the door, then drew a gun from inside his coat and, with a speed that seemed almost unnatural, had the door open and was inside.

I waited tensely, shifting my weight from one foot to another, aching to know what was going on. There was no sound, no movement, nothing to indicate there was any sort of scuffle going on in there.

After about five minutes, he reappeared. "If there was someone in there, they're well gone. But you'd better check to see if anything is missing." He hesitated. "In particular, you'd better check those notebooks you mentioned."

I swore internally. They'd be gone; of that I had no doubt. "As long as you stay outside."

He frowned. "Red, don't be ridiculous—"

I crossed my arms, and no doubt my expression was as stubborn as his was frustrated. "I can be as ridiculous as I want, because it's my damn apartment."

"Fine," he growled. "I'll wait here."

I brushed past him and went in. At first glance, everything seemed perfectly normal. Nothing appeared to have been moved or touched.

Then my gaze fell on the coffee table. My laptop was gone. As were Mark's notebooks.

I closed my eyes. *Fuck!*

Almost immediately Sam said, "What?"

I took a deep breath and released it slowly. "My laptop and Mark's notebooks are missing."

"Damn it!" The darkness within him seemed to explode, and the sheer force of it had me stepping back. "I should have followed instinct and fucking forced you to hand over the papers earlier tonight."

"There's no saying they would have been here even then," I snapped, guilt and anger swirling through me. He was right. I knew he was right, but that didn't mean I was about to put up with him ripping me to shreds. Not again. "I've been gone for nearly twenty hours. That's plenty of time for someone to come in here and retrieve the notes."

"And what about Rory?"

He practically spat the name, and it made me even angrier. "He's out for the night. And he's probably enjoying himself a whole lot more than I am."

"Oh, I don't know," he growled. "You seemed to be enjoying yourself just fine with that Fae."

My eyes widened. "You were *watching* me?"

"I told you we were." His expression closed over sharply. The darkness within him didn't retreat, however. It was as deadly and as alluring as ever.

I shivered and walked over to the planter. "No, you told me Adam the vampire was watching me."

"Adam is my partner."

I paused and looked over my shoulder. "You? The man who thinks all nonhumans should be dead, with a vampire partner? Yeah, right."

"I *don't* believe that," he growled. "I never have."

"Then why *say* it?"

He snorted, his expression dark, angry. But deep in the unlit recesses of his eyes, there were also the stirring ashes of hurt. "Because when you discover the woman you love is fucking another man, you tend to say things you otherwise wouldn't." He paused, then made a sharp motion with his hand. "That, however, is the past, and totally irrelevant. Protecting you, and checking everyone you interact with, isn't. And that duty, unfortunately, has been handed down to me."

I finally found the USB and swung around. "And what did you find out about my Fae?"

"Nothing yet. But if there's anything to find, we'll find it."

"And if there's not?"

He shrugged. "Then you running into him like that really *was* nothing more than a coincidence."

I snorted softly and tossed him the USB. He caught it easily, then said, "What's this?"

"Notes from four of the five notebooks I transcribed. Mark's caution rubbed off, and I usually keep a copy aside just in case the files went missing in the system or something went wrong in the transfer."

"What about the fifth one?"

I hesitated, then admitted, "I didn't get around to copying that over."

"Well, at least you've done something that vaguely resembles smart," he muttered, studying the USB like a scientist might a bug.

I glared at him for a moment, then said, voice flat, "Get out of my doorway."

He glanced up, surprise flaring in his eyes. "What?"

"I said, get out. Leave this building. *Now*," I added, when he didn't immediately move.

He raised an almost mocking eyebrow and half turned away, then paused. His shadowed blue gaze met mine a final time.

"One thing you should know," he said softly. "I don't believe in coincidences. Trust me, Red. The Fae is up to something."

And with that warning hanging in the air, he left.

CHAPTER 5

Thankfully, by the time I got to bed, I was too goddamn tired to dream about anything. My sleep was long and blissful, and I woke refreshed and filled with anticipation for the day ahead.

And not even Sam's warning could dampen that.

Even the weather gods seemed to be on my side. After the rain and the cold of the past few days, they'd pulled something magical out of the bag, presenting Melbourne with clear blue skies and an almost springlike ambience.

Given I wasn't exactly sure where Jackson was taking me—and to be honest, didn't really care—I went with a swirly, flowery skirt and tight-fitting shirt and teamed them with gorgeous leather boots with heels just high enough to flatter my calves while still being comfortable enough to walk a fair distance. Rory still wasn't home by the time I was ready to leave, so I left him a note, then happily made my way down to the foyer.

Jackson was waiting for me, looking decidedly sexy in faded jeans that emphasized the muscular length of his legs and a black, short-sleeved shirt that made the most of his shoulders and arms.

His gaze skimmed me as I walked toward him. "You," he said, wrapping an arm around my waist and pulling me close, "look fucking amazing."

And then he kissed me, not sweetly, not gently, but with a fierce hunger, as if he intended to make love to me here in the middle of the foyer.

To say we were both more than a little breathless when we finally parted was an understatement.

"If breakfast is anywhere near as good as that kiss," I said, my breathing erratic and my voice little more than a husky whisper, "I'm going to be a mighty happy woman."

He smiled, caught my hand, and led me out of the building. Just for a moment, awareness prickled my skin. It wasn't sexual in any way, but rather the sensation of being watched. I glanced around casually, but couldn't see anyone obvious. But then, I hadn't last night, either.

Jackson's mode of transport wasn't exactly what I'd been expecting, but it did totally suit him. It was a big red pickup truck whose nose and tail had been decorated with flames, and it looked as powerful as its driver. I couldn't help grinning. "And here I was thinking flame decorations were so last century."

"Only for those not Fae." He opened the door, ushered me into the passenger seat, then ran around to the driver's side.

The engine came to life, loud and growly. As he reversed out of the parking spot, I said, "Where are we headed?"

"Seeing it's such a lovely day, I thought we might picnic in the hills."

"But not at a popular tourist spot, I gather." My hopes of seduction would certainly take a tumble if that were the case. Although with the Fae, you could never be entirely sure. According to Rory, they had a tendency toward exhibitionism.

He grinned. "Oh, trust me, we're headed where few tourists go."

Again Sam's warning nudged my consciousness, and again I stoutly ignored it. It wasn't like I couldn't protect myself—I just needed to keep aware. To *not* get so carried away by desire that I ignored any warning signs of trouble that might inadvertently be revealed.

"And am I allowed to know the whereabouts of this mysterious, empty spot?"

"I own some land that runs alongside the state forest not far from Woodend."

I raised my eyebrows. "Why would you own land up there? It's not like you could create any sort of fire up there, especially in summer. The Country Fire Authority would be all over it in a flash, given how dry the state usually is. I would have thought the drier, hotter areas up near Mildura to be more your style."

"It is, and I do own land up there." He glanced in the rearview mirror before adding, "But it's also nice to own something within easy driving distance of the city. I might not be able to enjoy the pleasure of fire very often, but I *can* enjoy the wild peace of the place. I'm Fae first and foremost, remember."

"So you've built a home up there?"

He shook his head. "*That* would defeat the purpose. And before you ask, there's no toilet. But I do have plenty of trees. And loo paper."

I snorted softly. Talk about roughing it. He was looking in the mirror again, and something in his manner had my skin prickling. "What's wrong?"

"I think we might have someone following us."

I relaxed. "We do. My boss was murdered last night, and the police are worried that whoever did it might come after me."

"I noticed we were being followed last night. This isn't him."

He'd noticed? How? While I might have sensed the vampire named Adam when I'd walked to the bar, I'd certainly had no sense of him when we'd left. But then, the Fae's senses were pretty keen. "Well, no, because it's a different person doing the day shift."

He gave me a wry smile. "Yeah, I guessed that. But I don't think this is your official tail. He's way too close, and that suggests inexperience."

I flipped down the visor and looked behind us via the vanity mirror.

And what I saw was a red cloak.

Oh, *fuck*.

"Do you know who it is?" His sideways glance suggested he was very aware of the tension running through me.

Sam's warning swirled through my thoughts. How the hell was I going to explain this without giving too much away? "I ran across a couple of our follower's companions a few nights ago. Let's just say they're nasty pieces of work."

"I take it from *that* your meeting with said companions went rather badly—for them."

"Yes. I rather spoiled a party they had planned, and they didn't take it well." I studied the red cloak in the mirror for a moment. "I'm not sure why they'd be following me now, though."

Although the fact that they *were* meant that while they might be infected by a vampirelike virus, they didn't suffer the same restrictions when it came to sunlight. So why did UV lights affect them?

"What the hell is he?" Jackson asked. "Even in the rearview mirror he doesn't really look human, and he sure as hell can't be a vampire."

I hesitated. "I'm not sure what they're officially called, but I tend to call them red cloaks—"

"*That's* a red cloak? He looks nothing like the description I got."

Something in the pit of my stomach twisted. I closed my eyes for a moment, fighting the twin surges of disappointment and anger. Goddamn it, I didn't *want* Sam to be right. Didn't want to believe meeting Jackson was anything more than a coincidence.

"How do you know about the red cloaks?"

I said it softly, but there was an edge in my voice and he grimaced.

"Look, I haven't exactly been truthful—"

Anger won the battle over disappointment. "No *kidding*—"

"Emberly, just *listen*," he snapped, then took a deep breath, visibly getting himself under control. "I *am* Jackson Miller, but I'm a private investigator, not an engineer. Baltimore was someone of interest to my client."

Which was why he'd been so interested in *me*. It was as much the need for information as attraction. Lady luck, it seemed, really *had* decided to abandon me this life span—at least when it came to men.

"After running into you that first time," he continued, "I did some checking and discovered you worked for Baltimore."

"And what better way is there to keep an eye on him than to seduce his assistant?" I couldn't help the edge of bitterness in my voice.

"Yes." He scraped a hand across his chin. It sounded like he was rubbing sandpaper. "And no. That was my initial intention when I arranged our second meeting, but I discovered Baltimore was dead shortly after that. Theoretically, your usefulness as an information source was over at that point." His gaze briefly met mine. Those emerald depths showed little evidence of lying. "I didn't *have* to meet you at the bar. I wanted to."

I stared at him for several moments, then pulled my gaze away. I wasn't ready to forgive him just yet, and if I kept staring into his eyes, I would. "Prove that you're an investigator and you're just not spinning another line."

"My wallet is in my pants pocket." He glanced at me, eyes suddenly twinkling with mischief. "Of course, that means you'll have to reach in and get it. I dare not risk taking my hand off the wheel."

I snorted softly, then reached across the car and dug a hand into his pocket. Felt the heat of his skin through the thin layer of cotton, and again the hunger rose within me. *Later, later,* I whispered internally. *Maybe.* I grabbed the wallet, tugged it free, then opened it up. His driver's license was in a little window on one side and his private investigator's license on the other. He was who he said he was. I closed it and shoved it back into his pocket.

"Happy?" he asked.

"Satisfied that you're not actually lying about who you are anymore, yes. Happy, not so much." I paused, then asked, "Why is your client interested in my boss? And how do you know about the red cloaks?"

He hesitated. "Client confidentiality—"

"Be damned," I cut in. "In the last few days, I've been shot at, chased, my boss has been murdered, and, for a climax, I've been picked up by a Fae who's decided seduction is the fastest method to information. If someone doesn't start being honest with me, I'm going to get *violent*."

He grinned suddenly. "You're a bit of a firecracker, aren't you?"

"You have no idea," I muttered, and crossed my arms. "And to repeat my question, how much do you know about the red cloaks?"

"Not a lot more than the brief description of

them I got from several people who'd witnessed them murder someone."

"And who was that someone?"

He glanced in the rearview mirror again, then said, "How about we take out our tail, then have an information exchange?"

"There's one fatal flaw in that suggestion." Sam might have warned me against talking about these things, but I couldn't *not* talk about them, either. Not when Jackson was planning to attack one of them. "Those things are infected with a deadly virus that may affect nonhumans as much as it does humans. You can't let them scratch or bite you."

"Oh," he said. "Lovely."

He drove on without saying anything for a while, and I realized we were out of the city and on the Tullamarine Freeway, heading toward the Calder.

"Okay," he said eventually. "We'll let him follow us until we get to the exit. Once we hit the forest, we'll immobilize the bastard, then question him."

"Um, maybe you didn't hear me, but those things are deadly—"

"I heard." His gaze, when it met mine, was filled with a very *inhuman* hunger and excitement. Fae might be sensualists, but they obviously *weren't* averse to the excitement that came with danger—and that it could be deadly only made the chase all that much sweeter, it seemed.

I shook my head. "You're *crazy*." And so was I for even considering going along with his scheme.

"That's been said before," he agreed. "I am, however, still alive."

Silence fell. We continued up the Calder Freeway for a while, then swung left onto Lawson Road and up into the forest.

"Can you use a gun?" he asked, as he suddenly turned onto a dirt side road.

"I can, though I prefer not to. Why?"

"It's interesting that you appear neither shocked nor horrified by the thought I might be carrying weapons in the truck."

"Probably because my capacity to be shocked by anything has been erased by recent events. What are you planning?"

"Are you good enough to take out the tire of a car speeding past?"

"I think so." I'd certainly done it a few times in my past life as a cop, but that had been a while ago now, and not only were my skills rusty, but the guns were very different.

"God, where have you been all my life, woman?"

"I've been avoiding men like you," I said dryly. "Where's the gun?"

"Locked box under the backseat. Key code 3754."

I undid my seat belt and twisted around. Once I found the locked box, I typed in the code. A drawer popped out, revealing several guns cradled in foam. I chose the Glock semiautomatic simply because I'd used earlier versions. After checking that the internal locking system was engaged, I shoved in a single-stack, ten-round magazine.

"There's a blind corner just up ahead," he said. "I'll let you out just after it. Hide in the trees and shoot out the rear tires. I'll take care of the rest."

I nodded, throat suddenly dry and heart going a million miles an hour. Excitement, not fear.

He slid around the corner, raising a thick cloud of dust that hid his sudden stop. I opened the door, scrambled out, then ran for the trees as he took off again.

The red cloak wasn't far behind him. He came around the corner too fast and skidded sideways on the dusty road. I released the internal locking system, sighted on the nearest rear tire, and fired. The first two shots missed. The next two didn't.

The tire exploded, and the car—still going too fast and not under complete control after the semi-slide around the corner—reacted violently. The tire exploded, came off the rim, and fired thick bits of rubber in all directions as the car pulled savagely to the left. The driver's reaction was instant and totally wrong—he slammed on the brakes. This succeeded only in accentuating the car's reaction, and he spun completely around and then slammed into several trees along the side of the road.

Jackson's truck reappeared through the choking cloud of dirt and reversed straight into the undamaged side of the car, buckling both doors inward. For all intents and purposes, the red cloak was trapped.

I lowered the weapon but didn't slip the ILS back on. The red cloak might be trapped, but that didn't mean he wasn't still dangerous.

Jackson climbed out of the truck, a wide grin splitting his features and his enjoyment so strong it burned the air. "Shall we see how our captive fairs?"

I nodded and gave him the gun. He was legal to carry. I wasn't, and we did have a more official follower somewhere behind us.

He approached the broken car from the front and with caution, the gun held at the ready. The engine was screaming, the sound high-pitched and grating, and steam billowed out of the grille. The smell of gas stung the air, a potentially dangerous situation if there were any sparks or if the leaking vapor hit the hot exhaust or catalytic converter.

There was no movement inside the car. The air bags had all gone off, but were even now deflating, beginning to hang like loose white sacks from their moorings. The windshield had shattered, the bits of glass glittering like diamonds all over the crumpled front end. The red cloak inside wasn't moving. There was blood in his dark hair and he slumped half-sideways, as if the seat belt was the only thing holding him upright.

Jackson stepped closer, his nostrils flaring. Distaste spread across his face. "God, these things smell *rancid*."

"Well, they *are* diseased." I stayed where I was

and rubbed my arms. I'd been close to these things once before, and that was more than enough.

"This one is also human." He hesitated. "Or maybe that should be *was* human."

"Most vampires were human at one point in their lives," I reminded him. "That in itself is not an oddity."

"Yeah, but regular vamps smell like vamps. These things still have a human overtone. It's as if they're not quite turned."

Which would explain why they could waltz around in daylight when regular vampires could not.

As he took another step closer, flames began to lick the bottom of the car. "Jackson—"

"I can feel the fire," he cut in. "It's no danger, trust me."

"Meaning you're putting it out?"

He flashed me a grin over his shoulder. "What, and waste all that lovely heat?"

"That lovely heat," I said tartly, "will crisp our suspect, which is not such a good thing if you want to question him. Not that I think *that's* a good idea."

In the shadows crowding the rear seat, something moved. Tension and fear suddenly crawled across my skin. "I think there might be—"

Before I could get the rest of the sentence out, a seething, screaming mass that seemed more animal than human exploded from the car. Jackson swore and raised the gun, but it was flames, not bullets, that shot out at the red cloak. They encased the creature, but didn't stop him. It cannoned into Jackson, sending him sprawling, and came straight at me.

I swore and threw myself sideways, hitting the dirt hard enough to hurt but rolling back to my feet in one smooth motion. Fire erupted from my flesh, burning around me—through me—until I *wasn't* flesh, just a seething mass of flame. The creature lunged for me, his body afire and his red eyes glowing with both the reflection of my fire and his own madness. I retreated, trying to keep out of his way, but he was too fast and too close. His wickedly curved nails sliced through my flames, but there was no flesh left to rend and tear and possibly infect.

I loosed a long stream of fire at him. It lassoed his torso and snapped tight. My flames, stronger and more deadly than Jackson's, raced across the red cloak's flesh, but he didn't seem to care. He just kept coming at me even as his flesh blackened and began to peel away.

Two shots rang out, the sound barely cutting across the roar of my fire. The red cloak's head exploded, spraying blood and bone and brain matter everywhere.

I shuddered, suddenly glad I wasn't wearing skin. The last thing I needed or wanted was to be covered in red cloak goo.

The rest of the body continued to burn, the combination of Jackson's flames and my own quickly rendering flesh, muscle, and bone down to little more than ashes that the wind picked up and scattered through the forest.

I took a deep breath, then doused my fire and regained human form.

Jackson stared at me.

"I'd guessed what you were, but it's a totally different fucking thing to see it." His voice held a touch of awe. "I had no idea a phoenix could become nothing but flame."

"And I didn't know you could draw fire into your body and use it as a weapon. I thought fire Fae could only shape and control it." My gaze scanned him. He didn't seem to be hurt or bleeding, but I nevertheless added, "Did he scratch you at all?"

"No. He was too busy trying to get at you." He cocked his head to the side, listening intently. After a moment, he added, "Get in the car."

"What?"

"Our second follower is coming." He made the Glock safe and then strode toward his truck. "Get in the car, Emberly."

"But—"

"Do you want to be stuck all day in a police station being interrogated about this mess?" he snapped. "Because I certainly don't."

I stared at him doubtfully, knowing it was stupid to run, knowing that Sam would be madder than hell when he eventually caught up with us, and unable to deny the attraction of either.

"They'll just find us again, so what's the point?"

"The point," he said, opening the driver's side door, "is that you and I can at least talk beforehand."

I snorted softly. "What, and synchronize our stories?"

"You can say what you want. I certainly will."

"Then why run? It's not like we can't talk afterward."

"Yeah, but after this, their noose around you will be tighter, and I might not get close enough to ask my questions." His gaze met mine, grim but determined. "However much I desire you, Emberly, I still want information."

At least *that* was the complete and honest truth. Unsure whether to be happy or not, I climbed into the car, then stared out the side window as he took off.

We got back onto the main road and he hit the gas, steering the car through the twists and turns with ease. After a few more miles, he turned off again, then slowed down to cut the dust cloud. The trees closed in until it seemed we were driving along little more than a goat track.

"Where the hell is this place of yours?" I asked eventually.

He grinned. "You're in it. Have been for the last mile."

"You own a large chunk of forest?"

He nodded. "As I said, I need to be able to commune with nature on a regular basis."

We came out of the forest abruptly. The clearing was lush and green and sloped gently down toward a stream that was rock-lined and dotted with winter flowers.

He stopped and got out, then grabbed a basket from the back of the truck and motioned me to follow him. We walked down to the stream, where he set up a picnic on a grass verge near the cheerfully bubbling water.

"So," he said, flipping the basket open to reveal sandwiches, cakes, a bottle of wine, and a thermos. "Tell me about phoenixes. Are you creatures of flame or flesh?"

"Technically, neither. We're spirits who have three forms available to us—flesh, fire, and bird."

He raised his eyebrows. "Bird?"

I half shrugged. "A firebird. It's a form that's really only practical at sunset, because it's the only time our rather exotic red, orange, and yellow plumage doesn't stand out."

"Huh." He opened the wine and poured two glasses. "Is it true that a phoenix rises from the ashes of its death?"

I nodded. "We have a life span of one hundred years."

"Meaning you have to relive those shitty teenage years over and over?" He shook his head in mock sorrow. "That *has* to be the pits."

I grinned. "We only have to do it once. We're reborn into adulthood after that."

He handed me a glass, then raised his own. "To

never having to face teenage years more than once. And the hope that this sharing of information doesn't end here."

I snorted softly, but nevertheless clicked my glass against his. The wine was cool and fruity without being too sweet. "Speaking of information sharing, how about you start?"

He opened one of the foil-wrapped packages, revealing chicken and avocado on rye. "Have you ever heard of a Professor James Wilson?"

I picked up one of the sandwiches and shook my head as I bit into it. It tasted incredible, but I was always horribly famished after a flame up, and I demolished it rather than savoring it like it deserved.

"Ah," he said, eating the other half at a more leisurely pace. "He worked in the research division of Rosen Pharmaceuticals."

Who just happened to be one of our major competitors and was, coincidently, owned and run by Lady Harriet's ex. To say the two did not get along was like saying rain was wet.

"Wilson was murdered while on his way home two weeks ago," he continued. "According to witnesses, the killer had a scythelike tattoo on his right cheek and wore a red-hooded cloak."

What was the likelihood of Baltimore and Wilson—both of whom worked for privately funded research labs—being murdered within a matter of weeks of each other and the murders not being connected somehow? Realistically, slender to none. We might have no witnesses for

Mark's murder, and he might have been tortured rather than torn apart by a red cloak, but it still seemed too much of a coincidence. At least to my radar, anyway.

And yet something Jackson had said earlier niggled. I frowned. "Why did you seem so surprised to see our dead red cloak, given the description you were given matched the ones that chased us?"

"Because they really *don't* match. All the witnesses were close enough to note a marking on his cheek and yet made no mention of the way he smelled, his gauntness, or the red eyes. That seems rather odd to me."

"Witnesses to hideous crimes are often unreliable when it comes to providing solid information."

He grimaced. "I know, but it still strikes me as odd."

I wondered if Sam thought it was odd, too. Not that he'd ever tell me one way or another. "What happened to the red cloak? Did anyone try to stop him?"

"No, and you can't blame anyone for that, given Wilson was apparently sliced up pretty badly. The red cloak disappeared down a nearby sewer drain, and no one has seen him since."

And weren't likely to, I suspected, unless they were game enough to head into Brooklyn. Was that the real reason Sam had been there the night I'd saved his life? Had he been trying to find Wilson's murderer? It seemed logical—and it would also explain why the red cloaks had been so determined to get rid of him. Maybe he'd been close to uncovering their location.

"So was Wilson simply in the wrong place at the wrong time, or do you think there's something more behind his murder?"

"Personally, I think it's very likely the sindicati are behind it."

The sindicati were basically the vampire version of the mafia—only a hell of a lot more dangerous. I frowned. "Why would you think that?"

"Because the sindicati have a finger in every nasty pie in this city, so why couldn't they be involved in the murder of a scientist working on a top-secret project?"

"They're more likely to attempt to kidnap him and gain his secrets than kill him," I said. "He's no good to anyone dead. Besides, I can't imagine them working with the likes of the red cloaks."

"They'd work with whoever—or whatever—was best suited to the job they wanted done." Jackson's voice was grim, making me suspect he'd had dealings—or, at the very least, crossed paths—with the sindicati in the past. He added, "However, I haven't been hired to find Wilson's murderer. My employer is more interested in retrieving his research."

My eyebrows rose. "When was his research stolen?"

"The day after his murder. Whoever did it hacked into Wilson's computers at the research foundation and completely erased every note Wilson had made."

"They didn't have backups?"

"They did. Someone broke into the foundation the same night and did a hatchet job on the backup system."

All of which was a chilling echo of what had happened after Baltimore's murder. "Have they tried to retrieve the erased information?"

"Yes, but it wasn't successful."

Meaning whoever was responsible knew a thing or two about computers, because it wasn't easy to so completely erase information from a hard drive. "So who's your employer? And what does this have to do with Professor Baltimore's murder?"

He unwrapped another package, this time revealing thick slabs of corned beef on sourdough with a lavish helping of mustard pickle. Not my favorite, but given how much my belly was still rumbling, I wasn't about to be picky.

"Denny Rosen—the company president, not the gadabout son—employed me after getting little satisfaction from the team the investigation was handed over to."

Three guesses as to who *that* was, I thought, amusement running through me. "I don't suppose you know the name of the detective currently in charge?"

"Sam Turner." He paused, eyeing me. "You know him?"

"Used to." I shrugged and tried to ignore that tiny, insane fraction that wished I still did. "Good luck getting information about the case out of him. He's always been a clam when it comes to discussing any aspect of his work."

"I actually make a point of not talking to the cops. They tend to get antsy about private investigators snooping around their patch during an ongoing investigation."

"That's probably a good move." I licked the sweet pickle mustard off my fingers and said, "So why did Rosen point you in Baltimore's direction? I'm gathering he's not just doing it to piss off his ex."

"He's not." He picked up his wine. "Although I suspect there *is* an element of that. They sure do seem to hate each other."

Well, given the rumors suggesting infidelity and theft of research on *both* their parts, I could understand why. At least they had good reasons for the hate, unlike a certain cop I knew.

"Rosen wasn't very forthcoming about what, exactly, Wilson was working on, but I gather it's something to do with finding a cure for some new kind of virus." Jackson picked up the wine and filled my glass. "He inferred Baltimore might be working on a similar project and therefore could be behind the theft."

"What's the bet Wilson's project has something to do with the virus the red cloaks are infected with?" I said heavily. It had to be. It was too much of a coincidence to be anything else.

"Rosen simply called it the NSV01 virus—"

"And Baltimore's virus was NSV01A. I doubt it was a coincidence."

"Highly unlikely," Jackson said. "Rosen didn't say what it was or who'd employed him to work on it. I suspect, given how clammy he got, that it was a deep-level government initiative."

I frowned. "The government has its own labs—"

"Yeah, but it's not always easy to keep research a secret inside those labs. Too much red tape, too many management fingers in the pie. It's far easier to have a black slush fund and get it done privately."

"It doesn't explain why they'd be coming after me, though. If they were the ones who beat Baltimore to death, they must know I can't tell them anything more."

"What if it wasn't the red cloaks who beat him up? What if it was someone else entirely?"

I frowned. "Mark was the most harmless guy in the world. I can't imagine someone having a reason to kill him other than wanting his research. And as I said, I don't think he was onto anything monumental before he died."

"Maybe. Maybe not. Let me get something." He rose in one fluid movement and walked up the hill to his truck. His strides were long and easy but nevertheless filled with a sense of heated energy. Much like the man himself, really.

He came back with a manila folder. This time, he sat down beside me, his shoulders pressed against mine and the heat of him flowing across my senses, a siren call to the fires deep within. I took a shuddery breath, trying to concentrate as he flipped open the folder, rifled through some paperwork, then picked out a photo. "You ever seen this man before?" he asked, handing it to me.

The photo was grainy and speckled, as if it had been blown up from a much smaller picture. The man in it had half turned from the camera, but he was obviously a big man, bald, with heavy brows and a beaklike nose that seemed to jut out over thin, humorless lips.

He wasn't anyone I'd seen before, and I said as much before adding, "Who is he?"

"Sherman Jones, a thug for hire and petty thief."

I handed him back the photo and then picked up my wine. It didn't do a whole lot to quench the awareness surging through me. "You think he beat up Mark?"

"This was snapped by one of the street security cameras just up the road from Baltimore's apartment." His voice seemed suddenly deeper, edged with a huskiness that spoke of desire. "According to one of the waitresses in the café across the road, he'd been hanging around the nearby bus stop most of the day."

I frowned. "But if you know about this Jones person, the cops surely would, and they'd have interviewed him already."

"They would have, if they could find him. He disappeared not long after this picture was taken."

"Before or after Mark's murder?"

"After."

I finished my wine and held it out for a refill. Too much more and I'd get tipsy, but after the events of the last few days, that might not be a bad thing.

"And no body has been found, I take it?"

"No. However, Jones wasn't the type to completely freelance. I have it from a good source that he had several regular employers, including this man."

He held out another photo. This man had a thin, pockmarked face, small, beady eyes, and dark, greasy hair. He reminded me of a rat. "Who is he?"

"Marcus Radcliffe the third. He owns a chain of secondhand stores that are little more than a front for a roaring trade in black-market goods and information."

"You've talked to him?"

"Not yet. He tends to be surrounded by some rather large goons, has high-level lawyers on call, and he can smell a cop—or a PI—a mile away."

"Meaning you've hit a wall information-wise?"

"Not exactly. I've now got you."

"Maybe."

He grinned. It was sexy as all get-out, but also very confident. "Your turn, my dear."

I told him the little I knew, all the while trying to ignore the hunger in his eyes, the feel of heat barely restrained that flowed over my senses every time he moved.

When I finished, he said, "Given the research of *both* men has been taken, it suggests they might have had some sort of breakthrough."

"Yeah, but the question is, how would the people behind the murders have known?"

He shrugged. "Rosen told me Wilson presented weekly reports; it's possible someone, somewhere, talked."

"Maybe, but that doesn't explain what happened to Baltimore. Trust me. No one would risk Lady Harriet's ire by indiscreetly talking." I pursed my lips, my thoughts going a mile a minute. "Could the labs be bugged?"

Jackson shook his head. His auburn hair, I noticed idly, gleamed like fire in the sunlight. "Rosen apparently doesn't trust his ex as far as he could throw her. He has a team of specialists who sweep the labs weekly."

Well, at least Lady Harriet wasn't that paranoid. She had them swept only every other week. I downed more wine, then said, "So basically, we're as stuck for ideas as the cops."

His sudden smile was blinding in its intensity. "*We're* stuck? Does this mean you've forgiven my initial lie and are now intending to help me on my quest?"

Did it?

I hadn't meant it that way, but now that I'd said it, it was tempting. *Very* tempting. And it wasn't as if Sam was going to give me any answers.

"I don't know," I said, honestly enough. "I'm not sure it would be wise for either of us to tangle with the things that are carrying the virus."

"Can the virus affect nonhumans? Rosen gave me the impression it was human only."

I hesitated, but it wasn't like I hadn't already told him enough to get us both into trouble. In for a penny, in for a pound, as the saying went. Besides, he needed to know what he might be dealing with. "From the little I've been told, it very definitely affects humans and vampires. Some shifters seemed able to escape the virus as long as they shift immediately after being infected, but it's too new for anyone to be certain. Until we know for sure, I don't think you should be taking any unnecessary risks."

"Oh, I don't plan to when it comes to those things." He frowned. "What about phoenixes?"

I shrugged. "I'm spirit, not flesh, so any virus or drug that *does* get into my system will be burned away when I resume my true form."

"Handy trick."

"And one that doesn't stop me from getting hurt or dying before my time," I said, voice dry. "A phoenix making it through a full hundred years of life is something of a rarity."

"So how many lifetimes have—" He paused, listening intently for several seconds; then his gaze hit mine, sharp and intent. "Do you want to be found right now?"

Confusion swirled. "What?"

"There's a helicopter on the way. It's a fair bet that, given we've eluded your police tail, it's someone looking for you. So, make your decision. Come with me and not be found until you wish to be, or stay here and return to the safety of your police followers."

I stared at him, tossing between the insane need to know what was going on and the desire to stay safe.

"Decide, Emberly. We're running out of time."

What the hell? I thought, and fell on the side of insanity.

CHAPTER 6

We were deep in the trees by the time the helicopter clattered overhead. It swept over the meadow several times, then moved on, doing similar checks of nearby areas.

"You're not going to be able to hide a red pickup in the trees for very long. Sooner or later, they will spot it."

"I know." He was outside, leaning against the roof of his branch-covered truck, his gaze on the skies. "And I don't think we should evade them for long. I just wanted time to plan."

"There's no need to plan," I said bluntly. "Our next step is obvious. We have to find and talk to this Marcus Radcliffe the third."

He looked at me. The smile that teased his lips was decidedly sexy. "At the risk of repeating myself, where the hell have you been all my life?"

"Enjoying a peaceful life," I said. "And given they're probably trying to pinpoint us through our cell phones right now, shouldn't we get moving?"

"Yep." He jumped into the truck, started it up, then drove through the trees and out onto the road. Once there, he floored it. Within no time, we were back on the Calder Freeway cruising toward Melbourne.

"Okay, as I said earlier, Radcliffe is a hard man to get close to. He does, however, have two vices—gambling and women. He's a regular at Crown's VIP gaming lounges and always finishes the night with a lovely lady on his arm."

"I am *not* going to be one of those lovely ladies. I don't mind investigating bad guys, but I'm not going to bed them."

"And I wouldn't ask you to," he said, his annoyed tone softened by the amusement teasing his lips. "Especially not before I've had a chance to do so."

I smiled. "And here I was thinking *that* particular goal had gone out the window."

His gaze came to mine, and the rawness of desire so evident in those green depths had me struggling to breathe. Pinpricks of sweat broke out across my skin and the flames within surged, eager to taste the heat of him, to draw it deep inside and savor its sweetness.

"Trust me," he said softly. "That particular goal is stronger than ever."

I resisted the urge to fan myself and pulled my gaze away from his as I tried to get my breathing under control.

"So how are we going to separate Radcliffe from his people?" I hesitated, and grinned as I added, "Or should that be, how am *I* going to separate him?"

"I suspect all you'll need to do is wear some-

thing sexy and offer him a room number. It's happened before, from what the croupiers have said."
He grimaced. "Of course, the problem with that is that we first have to get you away from your police tail."

"Let me worry about that," I said, knowing our biggest problem wouldn't be me escaping a tail, but rather surviving the explosion of anger from the man who would undoubtedly be waiting when I returned home. "Let's just concentrate on the finer details of ensnaring Radcliffe."

Jackson pulled to a stop outside the Ascot Vale railway station and gave me a somewhat dubious look. "Are you sure you don't want me to drive you home?"

I shook my head. "I know Sam. He'll drag you away, lock you up, and interrogate the shit out of you. And that won't be at all conducive to our plans."

"But he can't legally retain me for too long, not without charging me."

"The law doesn't actually define what is a reasonable amount of time here in Victoria," I said, "and, as I said, Sam's not regular police. He's part of some sort of special unit. I suspect the restraints on what they can and can't do are somewhat lax."

Especially given they were apparently killing the red plague people willy-nilly and had threatened to do the same to anyone who knew too much about them.

Jackson still didn't look happy. I leaned across the seat and kissed him. It was meant to be just a short, friendly peck, but it turned into something a whole lot more fiery.

"Damn, woman," he said, his breathing harsh on my lips. "We really need to find some time for ourselves."

"Tonight." I quickly opened the door and got out of the truck before the urge to do more than just kiss him became too hard to ignore.

He drove off fast—as if he, too, needed to get away before he gave in to what burned unsatisfied between us—and I made my way home.

Sam was waiting near the front doors. No surprise there.

"Just what the *fuck* did you think you were doing?" he all but exploded the minute I got close. "Losing our tail was bad enough, but then to take out the red cloak like that—"

"Are we going to do this in the middle of the street," I interrupted calmly, "or would you at least like some privacy and a cup of coffee?"

"Privacy and coffee," he growled, and headed for the front entrance.

I stepped in front of him and pressed one hand against his chest, stopping him. Once, his body heat would have flowed through my fingertips as sweetly as a kiss. Now, though, there was nothing. It was as if all his heat had been sucked away by whatever had happened to him in the last year.

"I told you before, I don't want you near my apartment. Not any more than necessary." I nodded toward the semi-vacant Portside. "We go over there, or we go back to your station."

"Portside," he snapped, then motioned sharply for me to lead the way.

He followed me across, and it was all I could do not to rub my arms against the fear creeping across my flesh. It wasn't just the force of his anger; it was the intensity of the darkness within it. It felt like he was barely containing it.

And yet, once again, there was also a tiny sliver of emotion that *wasn't* dark or cold, but rather one that spoke of concern. Or was I simply feeling that because I so desperately wanted it to be true?

I selected a table away from the other patrons and we ordered our drinks when the waitress came.

"Okay," he said, once she'd gone. "Explain what the hell you thought you were doing."

"No," I said. "Not until you start answering some questions yourself."

"Emberly—" he growled, that darkness within him crowding even closer.

"No." I crossed my arms and met his gaze calmly, although I was far from calm on the inside. "I want to know what's going on, Sam. I want to know why those things are still after me. I want to know how the hell they can even *come* after me, given they're supposedly infected by a vampirelike virus and *should* have been crisped by daylight. But most of all, I want to know who the fuck you're working for."

He stared at me silently. Though there was little

change in his expression, I had a notion that a battle was being waged deep within him. I waited, hoping the right side won. Hoping that darkness *didn't*.

Eventually, he leaned back in his chair and blew out a breath. It was a sound of frustration and annoyance combined. "I work for the Paranormal Investigations Team—or PIT, as it is more commonly known. We sit between the police and the military, and we're sent in to deal with problems that involve the paranormal."

"Define problems."

He shrugged. "Any activity involving paranormal beings that sits either within or without the law and provides a potential threat to humanity."

Any activity? That suggested they had scarily wide-ranging powers. Even more than I'd suspected. "How long have you been with them?"

He hesitated. "Just over a year."

I smiled up at the waitress as she delivered his coffee and my tea, then, once she'd left, said, "But you're human. I would have thought a team designed to handle paranormal creatures and crime would consist mainly of paranormal personnel."

A human, even one as fast and as strong as Sam, wouldn't have much hope against a vampire—or most other nonhumans, for that matter—even if he was armed to the teeth. And while white-ash stakes and silver bullets *did* work, vampires moved so fast they could be on you before you were able to use a weapon—something I knew from experience.

"A good percentage of the team *is* nonhuman,"

he said eventually. "But there are humans on the team—although they are generally blessed with extraordinary abilities."

"So telepaths, pyrokinetics, stuff like that?"

He nodded. "They're mostly used in off-field areas, but they are sometimes placed in the less . . . tenuous . . . field operations."

"None of which explains why *you're* out in the field. You're human, but you certainly haven't any sort of psychic abilities."

"I'm there because I can be." His voice was flat. Obviously, it was a subject he wasn't about to get into. Not yet, anyway. And I very much suspected that if I pushed, he'd clam up totally, and I still had plenty of other questions. "So why are the red cloaks still after me?"

"That I don't know." He frowned as he dumped several sugars into his coffee—which was surprising given he never used to take sugar. "They obviously still want something, but what, I have no idea."

"But even that night I saved your ass, they came after me. And that was *before* Mark was killed."

He nodded. His gaze, when it met mine, held little of the recent darkness. All I could see was concern—not just about what was happening, but for my safety. It was gone almost as soon as I registered it, but it nevertheless had hope fluttering.

Which was stupid. Even if the man I knew *did* still exist somewhere beneath the cloak of darkness and anger, he'd certainly shown no desire toward me. Quite the opposite, in fact.

"But," he said, "we're not entirely sure Baltimore's killing is connected to his work on the red plague virus—the way he was killed is not the norm for them."

"Meaning if they'd been involved, he would have died the same way Professor Wilson died?"

His gaze suddenly sharpened, and again a tremor ran down my spine. Yet I wasn't entirely sure that tremor was all fear. Then he all but spat, "Jackson Miller."

"Yes." My voice was noncommittal. "It seems you were right. My meeting him wasn't a coincidence."

"I should break his fucking neck—"

"Touch him," I warned, "and I'll break yours."

He studied me for several long minutes. "So, it's like that, is it?"

"Yes," I said, though it wasn't. Not yet. "He's at least been honest with me, Sam. Unlike you."

"I'm being more honest right now than I fucking should be," he growled. "Don't push me, Emberly."

I didn't. "Why didn't those things burn up in daylight?"

"Because the earth's ozone layer blocks ninety-seven to ninety-nine percent of UV radiation from entering the atmosphere."

"But vampires still burn when touched by sunlight."

"Yes, but that's because there's three bands of ultraviolet radiation in sunlight—UVA, UVB, and UVC. It's the combination of all three that kills vampires, whereas the red plague victims seem only affected by UVA—or black light, as it's known."

I frowned. "But from what I understand, UVA is the main source of radiation hitting earth, meaning the red cloaks *should* burn in sunlight."

"It's the main source, yes, but for some reason, when it's combined with the other two types, the red plague victims are immune. That was the second part of your boss's brief—pinpoint what gave the red plague victims their immunity."

"I bet there are quite a few vamps in town who'd love to get their hands on that sort of research." Especially the sindicati—which was a point in favor of Jackson's suspicions they were involved somewhere along the line.

"Given he was killed at night, it's certainly an option we're exploring. The only flaw is that vampires can't cross thresholds uninvited, and that invitation has to be freely given."

I nodded. "Which doesn't preclude the possibility of vampires hiring human thugs to do their dirty work. Did you find any prints in Mark's apartment?"

"That," he said, somewhat dryly, "is not information I'm about to hand over to someone who is not a police officer. Why did you and Miller drive away from the accident?"

The darkness in him seemed to have receded, but my reaction to his closeness hadn't. It was a constant push-pull of fear and desire that was as confusing as hell.

"It wasn't an accident," I said bluntly. "And we both know it. We were intending to question them, but one came at us—"

"There were two?" he interrupted sharply. "We only found one."

I nodded. "The second one was shot and cindered."

He frowned. "Your flames shouldn't stop them."

"They didn't. The bullets in the head did. My flames just rendered his body to ash, which blew away on the wind."

"But why would your flames work in daylight but not at night?"

"Well, technically they *did* work; it's just that the UV lights burned them quicker."

"But Rochelle's flames can't render them to ash."

"That would be because a Fae doesn't create flames; they can only use and control them. And a regular fire, however hot, is totally different from the flames of a phoenix." I couldn't quite keep the sarcasm from my voice. "We're spirits and we burn far hotter, trust me."

Just for a moment, the past seemed to echo in the blue of his eyes. Him and me and the heat that had once burned unquenched between us. A heat that could *still* burn between us if the dying embers were given the slightest chance of rebirth. Then the echoes were gone, and all that was left was the anger of our final words. Words I doubted we could ever get past.

I pulled my gaze from his and drank some tea. "Did you find anything of interest in Baltimore's notes?"

"Not as yet."

"What about Wilson?"

"What about him?"

I frowned at him. "Well, why was he taken out by the red cloaks?"

"We don't know."

"And wouldn't tell me even if you did?"

He half smiled. Or maybe that should be quarter smiled, because it was little more than a ghost, barely there and yet breathtaking nonetheless.

"Jackson Miller is a private investigator who's been hired to investigate Wilson's murder. I'm not about to give him—via you—that sort of information." He paused, and that ghost disappeared. "You should keep away from him, Emberly. This case is far more dangerous than you know, and Miller is renowned for not knowing when to retreat."

"Which sounds a whole lot like someone I once knew." And it was what had made him such a good cop. But was it also responsible for the darkness I sensed in him today? Had he finally run into a situation that went way beyond his control? A situation far worse than having to shoot his own brother?

"Which is why I'm giving you a warning, Red. I know just how badly things can go." He half reached out, as if to caress my cheek; then his fingers clenched and he abruptly stood up. "Please be sensible. Don't stick your nose into the investigation, and don't skip out on your tail again."

I leaned back in my chair and met his gaze for several heartbeats. "Fine," I said eventually. "I'll be sensible."

Relief sparked in his blue eyes, but there was also a touch of disbelief—understandable, I guess, given he saw me as nothing more than a lying adulteress. "One of us will be in contact if we need anything else from you."

"What if I need to contact you for some reason?"

He hesitated, then reluctantly reached into his pocket and drew out a card. On it was a cell number. Nothing else, not even his name.

"Use that. It's a central number, unconnected to me or the team, but any message you leave will be shunted to me as a matter of priority."

Which was better than nothing, I supposed. I accepted the card and shoved it into my purse. "Thanks."

He nodded and left. No good-bye, no nothing. He just turned around and walked away. Like it was easy.

I rubbed my eyes wearily and wondered when the hell this stupid, irrational pining would stop. He might be the love of this life span, but that just meant he was the one destined to burn my heart to ashes. The sooner I accepted it and got over him, the better.

Which is always easier to say than do, my inner voice whispered.

I sighed, flicked out some cash for our drinks, then made my way home. Rory was getting ready for his evening shift at the fire station.

"Hey," he said, a smile on his face and a twinkle in his eyes. His night with Rosie had obviously gone well. "What's happening?"

"It seems the gods are still pissed off with me." I dropped down onto the sofa and gave him a brief update on everything that had happened over the course of the day.

"Christ," he said, handing me a cup of tea. "You've well and truly jumped out of your staid and boring existence, haven't you?"

"Yeah," I muttered, and lightly blew on the tea to cool it.

He sat down on the coffee table, his arms crossed on his knees. "I'm gathering you're intending to ignore Sam's warning and meet with Jackson tonight?"

And therein lay the difference between Sam and Rory—Rory knew immediately what I'd do. Sam, even after all that had happened between us, wanted to believe I'd keep my word. But then, what chance had Sam ever had to really understand me? I'd been too fearful of his reaction, too desperate to enjoy my time with him before fate stepped in to once again destroy everything, to tell him what I was. And by the time I'd tried, it was altogether too late.

"Sam's got people watching me, so I'm planning to sneak off at sunset. Is the roof code still the same?"

Rory nodded. He was more attached to his fire-bird form than I was and tended to risk evening flights at least a couple of times a week—some of them from the rooftop and some out in the country. "Just be careful. And if you and Jackson need some extra muscle, you know where to find me."

"Thanks."

He smiled, leaned forward, and kissed my forehead. "Have fun. And don't be surprised if Sam discovers your absence sooner rather than later. Whatever I might think of him otherwise, he's a very good cop."

"I know." I shrugged. "But I just can't sit around and do nothing."

"Well, you *could*. But you've always liked a challenge, and that's what this has turned into." He paused, then added, a wry edge in his voice, "And with this case, there's both a mystery *and* a man."

"I'm not interested in Sam—"

"Did I specify which man I was talking about?" he interrupted mildly.

"No." I tore my gaze away from the amusement in his. Damn him to hell for knowing me too well.

"As I said, just be careful. I'd hate to see him hurt you again."

"He won't." It was said with determination. After all, a phoenix's heart was supposed to break only once each lifetime, and I'd already had my turn.

"Good." He squeezed my knee, then rose and continued getting ready for work.

By the time I'd finished my drink, he'd left. I stripped off my clothes and had a shower, but as I was heading into my bedroom, my phone beeped. I walked into the living room and dug it out of my purse, noting in the process the glint in the window opposite. The old guy was watching again.

I shook my head at his persistence and looked at the text. It was from Jackson, and all it said was *Rubbish*.

Make of that what you will, Sam, I thought with a smile. I tucked the phone back into its pocket inside the purse, then went back into my bedroom, selecting a simple A-line dress for now and a more figure-hugging silk for later in the evening.

Once my shoes had gone into the backpack, I slung it over my shoulder and headed out. But I went up the fire escape to the roof, not down in the elevator to the lobby.

The evening air had grown cool, and the setting sun was beginning to render the sky with vivid splashes of color. I walked across to the cooling towers and waited for the splashes to grow, the breeze in my hair and excitement in my veins. I might not take firebird form very often, but it always made my blood sing when I did.

As the sunset began to reach its zenith, I unzipped the back of my dress so that the pack touched skin. It wouldn't be enveloped in the magic that allowed me to shift from one form to another if it wasn't. Then I closed my eyes and called forth the firebird.

She came in a rush that was fierce and frightening, a storm of energy that swept me from flesh to fire and then bird in quick succession, leaving me breathless and more than a little dizzy.

Damn, I obviously need to do this more often.

It was a thought that quickly disappeared as I raised glowing red-gold wings and leapt for the sunset-painted skies. It was a glorious sensation, and the urge to simply fly and enjoy not only the freedom but the power of the evening was a hard one to resist.

But Sam was down there somewhere and, as Rory had noted, he wasn't stupid. He knew I was a phoenix, and it wouldn't take him long to connect the appearance of a firebird to me.

So I swung around and headed into the city. Jackson and I were supposed to meet at the Crown Towers, but given I didn't have easy access to their rooftop, I flew around until I found a building within walking distance that had an external fire escape. I shifted form as I flew down, landing half-crouched but on two feet. After doing up my dress, I made my way down the metal stairs and walked to the Crown.

The woman at the rather opulent reception desk gave me a warm smile. "How may I help you?"

"I have a booking under the name of Tip."

"Just a moment." She tapped some keys, then gave me a key card. "Mr. Tip has already checked in. Room number is 15-8. Elevators are just along the corridor to your right."

"Thanks," I said, and headed up to our floor. I walked along the bright corridor until I found room

15-8, then swiped the card through the slot. The door swished open, revealing a large living area bathed in the remnants of the fading sunset. Jackson was standing near the wall of floor-to-ceiling windows. His auburn hair was damp, curling lightly around his ears and at the nape of his neck, and he wasn't wearing anything more than a towel wrapped around his waist.

He turned around as I entered, revealing a body every bit as lean and hard as it had felt under his shirt. But it wasn't so much his magnificent physique that had my heart slamming against the walls of my chest, but rather the raw hunger in his eyes. It radiated out from him in an all-consuming wave, and it momentarily snatched my breath and threatened to buckle my knees.

The fire Fae had finished waiting.

The door swished shut behind me. I slung my backpack onto the nearest sofa and walked across to the windows.

"Amazing view." My gaze was on the city vista laid out before us, but every other sense was attuned to the man standing so close.

"Isn't it?" His voice was little more than a deep rumble of sound. But I knew his gaze was on me rather than the view, and the heat of it had pinpricks of sweat skittering across my skin.

I swallowed heavily. God, I was a bundle of raw nerves and heady excitement—anyone would think I was a virgin on her first date.

"Would you like something to drink?" he asked.

I nodded. "A glass of red wine would be lovely."

I watched his reflection walk across to the minibar and tried to think of something—anything—other than the desire to rip the towel away from his waist and caress the body underneath.

"What time does Radcliffe usually get here?" I asked eventually.

"I'm told most nights it's somewhere between ten and midnight," he said, walking back.

He stopped and handed me a glass. The wine inside was dark red, its aroma rich and berry filled, with hints of chocolate and wood spices. I took a sip, but barely even tasted it. My senses were too attuned to the man now standing behind me.

"What about his guards? If he's so security conscious, I doubt he'd walk into the room of a stranger—however much he might want to fuck her—without first letting his guards do a sweep."

"I have prepared a hiding spot," he murmured. "But let's not talk about that right now."

The sound of my dress's zipper sliding down seemed abnormally loud in the brief silence. Expectation tumbled through me and my breathing quickened. I took a sip of wine and ignored the urge to just turn around and take what we both so obviously wanted. Sometimes, a slow seduction was infinitely better than the act itself—although I very much suspected that would *not* be the case here.

His breath brushed the back of my neck, and my nipples went tight. I gulped down some more wine, but it didn't do a lot for the sudden dryness in my throat or the tension thrumming through my body. For several minutes, nothing else happened. There was just his breath on my neck, the heat of him rolling across my spine, and the growing tremble of expectation.

"What happened to your back?" he asked eventually.

"I had a slight disagreement with a car fire," I said, half shrugging. "It won."

"Slight disagreement is something of an understatement." His fingers moved lightly over the ruined flesh. I could barely feel it, but even so, delight shivered through me. "But I would have thought a fire spirit would be able to control fire."

"I can, but there were too many witnesses to even attempt it."

"Damn shame." He slid his arms around my waist, his lips branding my neck as one hand slid downward and skimmed the front of my panties. A moan escaped. He chuckled softly but explored no further, his caress sliding back up, not down. He hooked his thumbs under my bra and pushed it up over my breasts; then he cupped them, pressing them together as his clever fingers began to tease and pinch my nipples.

I leaned back against him and slid my free hand behind me, tugging the towel from his waist. I tossed it to one side, then caressed his shaft. He was big, gloriously so.

"I don't think I should be the only one naked here," he murmured, then plucked my wineglass from my hand and placed it on the nearby table.

He slid my dress from my shoulders, and my bra and panties quickly followed. I was naked and standing in front of a window for all the world to see, and I couldn't have given a damn.

He pressed close again, his cock sliding between my legs, thrusting gently, teasing but not fully entering. My nostrils flared, and I drew in the heat of him. It slid through me as sweetly as his caresses, fueling the hunger, feeding the fires. His hands slid down my body, his touch so hot it felt like he was branding me. This time, though, he didn't retreat. His fingertips found my clit, his touch firm as he kissed my shoulders, my neck, my ear. My breathing sharpened, became moans of pleasure I couldn't control as the pressure built and built from within. But just as I was reaching boiling point, he pulled away, gliding his hands back up to my breasts, pinching and teasing and caressing until the tremors eased.

Then he started all over again. And then again, until I was so tightly wound it hurt.

Time, I thought raggedly, for a little revenge.

I spun around, dropped to my knees in front of him, and took him into my mouth. He shuddered, his fingers tangling in my hair as his body tensed and a groan escaped. Slowly, I moved my lips down his shaft, gradually taking in more of him, teasing him with my tongue, playing with him as he'd played with me, bringing him to the brink and then pulling away, time and again, until the heat of his desire was so fierce my inner fires were becoming drunk on the taste of it.

And suddenly tasting him wasn't enough. I wanted to claim *all* of him.

I rose and pressed a hand against his chest, pushing him back onto the sofa. His hands came to my waist as he sat down, guiding me down onto him but not allowing me to fully capture him.

"Kiss me," he growled.

So I did. With all the desire, all the need and hunger that burned within me.

After several long minutes, he finally released his grip on my waist. His thick cock speared me, going so deep it felt like he was reaching for my very core. Sheer, intense pleasure tore a gasp from my throat, a sound that was quickly swallowed as his lips crushed mine a second time.

I rode him slowly, trying to prolong the glorious moment. My clit rubbed against him with every movement, heightening sensation, intensifying pleasure, until I couldn't think, couldn't breathe, could only enjoy.

"Look at me, Emberly."

It was a demand, not a request, but my gaze fell into his green eyes nevertheless, and I drowned in the rising urgency there. His heat swirled around me, through me, fueling the inner fires to breaking point, making them rage and want. I gave in to need and sipped from the furnace of his soul, and god, it was glorious.

Our movements became more urgent, more frantic, until it felt like I would shatter into a thousand different pieces. Then I did, the intensity of my orgasm making me moan in pleasure as my body shook and shuddered. He came a heartbeat later, his body stiffening underneath me, his release a hot stream so very deep inside.

I slumped forward, the side of my face pressed against his chest as I battled for breath and listened to the frantic pounding of his heart—a rhythm that matched my own.

"Good lord," he murmured, after several long minutes. "I knew that as fire beings we would be good together, but that—"

"Was totally, fucking amazing," I finished for him.

His laugh was a rumble that vibrated through the very core of me. His fingers lifted my chin; then he claimed my lips, his kiss tender and yet filled with a fire that was banked but not yet quenched.

"We should go to bed," he said softly. "And mess up the sheets a little."

"A little?" I teased. "If we only mess them a little, I shall be sorely disappointed."

He laughed again, then swung his feet off the sofa and lifted me as he rose. "Then I shall make it my aim to ensure that over the next couple of hours you are not left disappointed."

Needless to say, I wasn't.

I smoothed down the sides of my silk dress with nervous fingers, then took a deep breath and leisurely entered the exclusive mahogany room. Normally, I wouldn't have been allowed anywhere near the place, but the same contact that had given Jackson all his information had also provided me with a VIP card.

I plucked a glass of bubbly from the tray of a passing waiter and kept walking, trying not to gawk at the plush surroundings and the heavy chandeliers that dominated the roofline. The tables were only half-full, and the bar and lounge area almost empty. Marcus Radcliffe III was easy enough to find—he was one of three men sitting at the second of the blackjack tables and the only one who had two rather stern-looking men standing at his back.

He was bigger than I'd thought he'd be, a thickset, muscular man who oozed confidence and power. There was a whole lot more arrogance in his thin, pockmarked features than had been evident in the photo, but his eyes were no less beady and he still reminded me somewhat of a rat.

I sashayed across to the lounge and selected a chair that was just within his line of sight. I sat, crossing my legs, allowing the side slit of my dress to fall open and reveal a long length of thigh.

It didn't take long for Radcliffe to notice.

He leaned back and whispered something to beefy guard number one. The guard nodded, walked across to the bar, talked to the bartender, then went back to his post.

Two minutes later, a waiter approached me.

"Compliments of the gentleman at table number two," he said, offering me another glass of bubbly.

"Thanks," I said, accepting it. I glanced past the waiter, found Radcliffe watching me, and raised the glass in salute.

He smiled. It was a hunter's smile.

A shudder went through me. I'd met men like him in the past, and they were always mean in bed. Mean and dominant. Thankfully, it was never going to get that far.

I remained where I was, sometimes watching him, sometimes not. His expression became more enamored, his eyes heavy-lidded with lust.

Eventually, I took a pen and piece of paper out of my bag, wrote my room number on it, then called the waiter over.

"Could you give this to the gentleman at table two, please?"

He looked across. "Mr. Radcliffe?"

Mr. Radcliffe was staring at the two of us, his body practically trembling in expectation.

"Yes." I placed the note and a tip on the waiter's tray.

As he left, I rose and sauntered toward the door. My gaze clashed with Radcliffe's a final time and, as the waiter approached him with the note, I blew Radcliffe a kiss and then left.

Once out of the mahogany room, I moved as fast as was possible in ultrahigh heels, needing to get to the elevator before he did.

I closed my eyes and released a breath as the doors closed and the elevator zoomed me upward. One part down. All we had to do now was hope that Radcliffe took the bait.

I walked down the hall to our room and opened the door.

"Okay," I said as I walked in. "All systems are go—"

The rest of the sentence froze in the back of my throat. It wasn't Jackson standing there waiting for me.

It was Sam.

CHAPTER 7

"What the fuck are you doing here?" The words were out before I could stop them.

"A question I was about to ask you," he snapped back. "I thought you'd agreed not to skip away from your tail and to keep your nose out of this investigation?"

"No. I agreed to be sensible. And I am. Where's Jackson?"

He wasn't in the living area—that was for sure—and I couldn't see any sign of a scuffle. I couldn't imagine he'd let himself be arrested easily, but then, I didn't know him well enough to be sure of that.

"Jackson has been immobilized and is in the next room. We appropriated it when we realized what you two were up to."

I eyed him for a moment. The darkness in him was very present, a dangerous energy that skimmed my skin and made it burn, but his anger—despite his tone—wasn't as fierce as I'd thought it would be. "And just how did you find us?"

"Did you really think we wouldn't have an eye on Radcliffe ourselves?"

"We knew it was a possibility, but we did have our fingers crossed that you didn't know about the tenuous connection between Sherman Jones and Marcus Radcliffe."

His smile held little humor. "If a private investigator can find out about it, why would you believe we wouldn't? We have resources Miller could only dream about."

There was nothing I could say to that, so I simply asked, "How long have you been watching him?"

"Since the murder. He's not a hard man to find, even if he is an extremely difficult man to pin down otherwise."

"So, basically, you saw both me and Jackson arrive."

"Yes." He shrugged. "We could have pulled you out then, but I was curious enough to see what you had planned."

And, obviously, he had no lingering sense of regret or jealousy, because he'd allowed me to come to this room and spend several leisurely hours with Jackson.

He'd totally moved on. It was a shame there were still pockets of me that couldn't and wouldn't.

"Meaning you couldn't get close to him, or that Radcliffe really *can* spot a cop a mile away, however delicious the bait."

He grimaced. "The latter. Rochelle tried several nights ago. He totally ignored her."

"So, despite the fact that you've warned me away from the investigation, you're not above using me if it suits a purpose."

"Totally." His cool blue eyes bored into mine. "In the end, the only thing that really matters is the investigation. Everything else—everyone else—is collateral damage."

Charming. I walked over to the bar and poured myself a large glass of red wine. "We were planning to drug Radcliffe via a drink. Is that still an option, or have you something better planned?"

"We have plans. And given Radcliffe will probably have his goons do a sweep of this room before anything happens, Adam and I will be waiting next door."

"Which doesn't exactly tell me if you still want me to administer the drug, or whether Adam is going to do his vampire-telepathic thing and render them all senseless."

He half smiled. Again, it was a fleeting thing, but it nevertheless stirred an ache deep in the heart of me. "He will do his telepathic thing and implant appropriate memories as necessary, both before and after we have the information we need from him."

I nodded. "You realize that he's going to have to include memories of Radcliffe messing around with me."

"Yes." He studied me for a moment, his expression closing over. "How were you going to get around that problem? I didn't think you were telepathic."

"I'm not. Jackson and I were going to make a little noise once Jones was completely out of it." I shrugged, my gaze on Sam's, watching for a reaction, any reaction. There was nothing. Why the hell I was expecting one, I have no idea. I really, *really*, needed to get past this. "He would have come to in the morning with a sore head and no memory of the night's events, but his guards would have had plenty of action to report."

"There's one flaw in your plan—Miller would never have gotten past the guards' pre-seduction search of the room."

I flicked a hand toward the sofa positioned near the minibar. "If you'd care to tilt that up, you'll see it's actually been stripped of all its stuffing and springs, providing enough room for a man to hide." And given Radcliffe's guards were both human, they shouldn't have been able to sense or scent Jackson. Whether Radcliffe would have was another matter entirely.

Sam grunted, then touched his ear lightly. For the first time, I noticed he was wearing an earpiece. "Okay," he said after a moment. "Radcliffe is on his way up. Adam and I will be next door."

"Just make sure you don't leave it to the last moment to capture their minds and render them harmless," I said. "I do not want Radcliffe's grubby paws anywhere near me."

He snorted softly. "Should have thought of that before you started all this."

My gaze narrowed. "Fine. Just remember, I literally *can* play with fire, so if you'd like a crispy suspect, just take your time."

"A crispy suspect is not going to help either of us," he retorted. "So don't make empty threats."

My sudden smile held little humor. "Oh, trust me, my threats are rarely empty."

He eyed me for a moment, then shrugged and made for the door. "We'll wait until the guards check before we move. Adam can only cope with a couple of minds at a time."

I leaned a hip against the minibar and watched him leave. Two minutes later, there was a knock at the door. My mouth went suddenly dry. I might have once been a cop, but I'd never been undercover. This was a whole new level of danger to me, and as much as I hated to admit it, it was both scary and exhilarating.

I took a sip of wine, then walked across to the door. "Who is it?"

"Marcus Radcliffe." His voice was low and rough with excitement.

I shivered in distaste, but forced a smile and opened the door. "Well, hello there," I said, in what I hoped was a suitably sultry voice.

His gaze swept me up and down, and his expression became predatory. "Do I get to know your name, mysterious lady?"

"Oh, I don't think so." My gaze went past him. "And I'm afraid this is a party for two, not four."

He smiled. It was all teeth and falseness. "Of course not. However, I hope you don't mind if they come in and do a security check of the place. I'm afraid a man of my wealth does have to be careful."

He placed a heavy emphasis on "wealth," and I raised my glass to hide my smile. He might have been trying to impress me, but over the many centuries I'd been alive, I'd probably lost more money than he could ever hope to have. Rory and I were not the greatest money managers in the world, but we always had enough squirreled away to live comfortably each life span.

I stepped back and opened the door wider. "Please, be my guest."

The two men came in. I watched them search for a moment, then said, "Would you like a drink?"

"That red wine you're drinking looks good."

I walked across to the minibar. He followed me a little too closely, his nearness burning across my skin like an unpleasant rash.

I poured him a glass and then topped off my own, all the while aware of just how closely he watched my movements. He really *didn't* trust anyone. Drugging him, as Jackson and I had planned, would have been difficult.

I turned around and offered him the glass. He smiled and took mine instead. "One can never be too careful," he murmured. He ran his tongue across the lipstick that smudged the rim, then licked his lips. "Raspberry. Nice."

My gaze narrowed slightly. He could taste the flavor of my lipstick from a smudge on the glass? Maybe he *was* a rat—a wererat. Just because all the ones I'd seen over the years had been lowlifes who tended to infest the bottom rungs of the criminal ladder didn't mean they all did.

I lightly clicked my glass against his. "To tasting more than just raspberry."

Hunger flared deep in his beady depths. I shivered again and hoped like hell he took it for desire rather than distaste.

The two men came out of the bedroom. "All clear, boss," the beefier of the two said. "No other people, no bugs."

Radcliffe nodded. "Then please wait outside."

They retreated. The door closed behind them with an ominous click. Radcliffe stepped forward and placed his glass on the cabinet beside me. "Now, let's—"

I neatly sidestepped his grab and gave him a smile. "There's no pleasure in rushing, Marcus. Let's sit on the sofa and get to know each other a little more intimately." I gave him a sultry smile. "Before we actually do get intimate."

I cast a hopeful glance at the wall that divided this room from the one Sam was in, although I wasn't sure why, given they couldn't see me and wouldn't know I was more than ready for this charade to be over.

But, as Sam had said, I'd made this bed, and now I had to lie in it. Although if it came to *that*, I sure as hell *wouldn't*. I might want to solve the mystery of Mark's death, but I certainly wasn't willing to bed a rat to do so. If things got too heavy, I'd start a freaking fire and have the hotel evacuated.

I sat on the sofa and patted the spot beside me. As he sat, his leg brushed mine. His closeness made my stomach turn, but I resisted the urge to move away. "So, tell me a little about yourself."

He shrugged. "I own several secondhand businesses."

"They obviously do well," I said. "That's an Armani suit, isn't it?"

He raised a hand and lightly touched my neck. I once again resisted the impulse to pull away and took another drink of wine.

"A lady who knows her suits," he murmured, his gaze becoming distracted as his fingers slipped down my throat and came to rest on my pulse point. It was hammering—hopefully he'd take it as excitement rather than disgust.

"Of course. The suit makes the man." I paused, then asked, "And is the man married?"

"Of course not." It was smoothly said, but his gaze flickered briefly from mine.

His fingers were on the move again, slipping down toward my breast. I held myself still, even though the flight urge was becoming stronger and stronger.

God, what the hell were Sam and Adam doing?

Just as his fat little fingers were about to splay over my breast, he froze. A heartbeat later, the door opened. Sam and a tall, thin man with gray eyes and blondish hair walked in. The vampire Adam, presumably.

I scrambled clear of both the sofa and Radcliffe, then swung around to face the two men. "You took your damn time."

Sam shrugged. "Caution is always better than carelessness."

He glanced at Adam. A look passed between them, and unease swirled through me. Something was going on. Something that meant bad news for me.

Sam walked toward me. I watched him approach, my wariness increasing and my heart racing with increasing speed. Something was wrong. Something was *very* wrong.

"I'm sorry, Red, but you can't stay here."

"Why the hell not?" My throat was dry and my stomach was beginning to churn more thoroughly.

"This is our room, not yours."

"That's true, but this is *our* investigation. You and Miller were warned not to interfere."

Alarm ran through me. I stepped away from him. Fire flickered across my fingertips, little sparks ready to explode at the slightest notice. "What the hell are you intending to do, Sam?"

"Catch you," he said.

As if his words were a trigger, my head began to spin and my knees buckled. He caught me one-handed, retrieving the wineglass with the other.

The wine, I thought. He'd drugged the wine. "Bastard."

"Totally," he agreed. "But it's not like you didn't already know that."

The room began to fade in and out of focus. It took me a few moments to realize we were moving, and by the time I did, we'd stopped again.

Cool hands touched my forehead, and an odd

sort of buzzing ran around my brain. Vampire Adam was attempting to access my mind. *Good luck with that*, I thought, and wasn't entirely sure whether I said it out loud or not.

Then the touch was gone, the room was gone, and all that I was left with was darkness.

Waking was hell.

There was a madman armed with a vice intent on squashing the hell out of my head, and my stomach seemed determined to lodge itself somewhere in my throat.

I groaned and rolled over onto my back. My *bare* back.

I was naked. In bed.

The thought had me lurching upright, but the movement was too sudden and my stomach rebelled.

"Whoa," a familiar voice said. "Aim for this."

A bucket appeared under my nose, and I promptly lost everything I'd previously eaten that day into it. When there was nothing left, it was whisked away, and I lay back down on the bed, flinging an arm over my eyes and groaning lightly.

After a moment, footsteps approached. "Where the hell are we?"

"Still at the Crown." Jackson's voice was grim. "Just in the room next to ours."

"Did they drug you, too?"

"Yeah. It was in the wine, apparently."

Bastards. "Did they also try to erase your thoughts?"

He laughed softly. "They certainly tried, but the mind of a Fae isn't as easily influenced as a human's, and mine less so than most."

And a phoenix couldn't be influenced at all. We were spirit, a totally different life-form from human, vampire, shifter, or were. I scrubbed the back of my hand across my eyes, wondering whether I had enough energy to go find my bag and grab some aspirin out of it.

"I'm guessing they put us into bed together?" I asked, wondering who'd undressed me. And why it even mattered.

"Yeah." The bed dipped as he sat down next to me.

"Here, take this."

I opened my eyes. He was holding out a glass of water and two white pills. *Aspirin*. "God, I think I love you."

He laughed softly. "I'm a Fae. We don't do love, just plain old lust."

I downed the painkillers, swishing some of the water around to take away the lingering bitterness. "I know, but you'd be quite safe from me emotionally even if you did."

"Good." He plucked the glass free from my hand. "But I just wanted to make sure we both understand where we stand. Hate for either of us to want what they couldn't have."

"What I want is sex. But not," I added hastily, as a lusty gleam appeared in his eyes, "right at this particular moment."

He laughed and rose. I noted in amusement

that he was more than half-ready for action. I resisted the temptation and dragged myself into a sitting position. "I don't suppose you gleaned any information from them before you were knocked out?"

He shook his head as he dumped the glass back in the en suite. "Those two were clams. What about you?"

I grimaced. "Not really. The drug took effect before they began questioning Radcliffe." I hesitated, remembering my brief conversation with him. "Is he married?"

Jackson plopped down next to me and stretched his long legs out beside mine. "Not that I know of. Why?"

"Because when I asked him, he said no, but his body language said yes."

"Why would he lie about something like that?"

I shrugged. "Given he's into the black market, maybe he doesn't want anyone to know about her. Maybe he fears she could be used as leverage against him."

"Possible." His expression was contemplative as he began to run his fingers idly up and down my leg. My head might be locked in pain, but the rest of me seemed to be in fine working order. "Did either of the cops hear him say that?"

"Not that I know of." I hesitated. "But Adam— the vampire—would have read his thoughts. He'd surely know."

"Not necessarily." His touch was slowly moving around to my inner thigh. Anticipation began to thrum through me. So much, I thought wryly, for the headache. "Despite what humans think, not all vampires are telepathic, and the ones who are usually need to be very specific in what they're looking for. They haven't got carte blanche access to the mind, especially when it comes to weres."

"Yeah, but knowing Sam, he'd have someone on his team who was one of those few who did." I paused. "So Radcliffe *was* a wererat?"

He glanced at me, his expression surprised. "You couldn't tell?"

"I thought he was, but the senses of a phoenix aren't that specific."

"But they're very prettily packaged."

I smiled at the compliment. "So our next course of action is looking for the wife?"

His hand slipped between my legs and the caressing continuing, running up and down my inner thigh, sending shivers of delight racing through my body.

"Either that, or we attempt to find out who else Sherman Jones worked with. He's our only other lead."

"He's missing."

"Someone on the streets will know something. They always do."

His fingers lightly brushed the junction of my legs, then moved away again. I resisted the urge to growl in frustration. "We do have one other option, although I daresay the cops have already checked it."

"What's that?" His voice was becoming more

and more distracted. This time, his fingers didn't brush. They slid through my slickness, caressing and teasing.

I took a somewhat shaky breath and somehow managed to say, "The waitress."

"The waitress?"

"The one my boss used to chat with every morning."

"Then she's definitely an option." He shifted, grabbed my hips, and tugged me down the bed. "However," he added, as he slid his body over mine. "There's only one woman I want to talk to right now."

Except there wasn't a lot of talking from that moment on, just a whole lot of loving, until an hour had passed and we were both replete and exhausted.

"Best cure for a hangover ever invented," he said, his breathing a harsh rasp as he finally lay down beside me. "Unfortunately, we now have less than half an hour to be out of here."

I glanced at the clock. It was nearly ten fifteen, which meant I was more than a little late for work—if I had a job left, that was. I shifted onto my side and propped my head up with my arm. "I need to go to the lab and report in."

"I'll drive you there, then walk across to the café and apply some Fae charm to the waitress." He hesitated. "She got a name?"

"Sandy, I think. But there was also a Michelle he often talked to. One of them reported Sherman Jones lurking about, but I'm not sure which."

"Good. As you said, the cops have probably gotten everything out of them, but it doesn't hurt to double-check."

I nodded, then swung my legs off the bed and headed for the shower. Unsurprisingly, he followed; exhaustion in a Fae was apparently a rather short-lived state. It meant my shower was rather longer than intended, and we barely checked out of the hotel in time.

We parted company just down the road from the Chase Research Institute and, as I headed inside, the awareness of being watched again rose. It seemed my official watcher was still very much on the case.

"Hey, Emberly," Ian said, his brown eyes somber when they met mine. "Heard you had one hell of a weekend."

"You could say that." I picked up the pen and signed in. "I don't suppose Abby has left a message for me?"

I hadn't received anything on my phone, which was slightly odd, given everything that had happened.

"Yeah, as a matter of fact, she has. Lady Harriet wants you upstairs ASAP."

"Upstairs? As in, her office?"

He nodded gravely. " 'Fraid so."

"God, that *cannot* be good," I muttered. "Wish me luck."

"Luck," he stated cheerfully, making me smile as I headed for the elevators.

Lady Harriet's offices were on the top floor of

the Chase building. I'd never actually been there before—when they'd employed me, I'd gotten as far as the personnel offices two floors down. Plebs were rarely invited any higher, so it was with some trepidation that I stepped out of the elevator and walked along the plushly carpeted corridor to the double doors that presumably led into her offices.

They swished open as I approached. Abby looked up from the landing-strip-sized desk she sat behind. "Emberly," she said, her voice oddly distant. "Ms. Chase has been expecting you."

"Yeah, sorry, but it's been one hell of a weekend and I slept—"

"That is not important right now," she interrupted. "Please go straight in."

She pressed a button on the control panel to her right, and the doors directly in front of me opened. The room beyond was both huge and shadowed, and it suddenly felt like I was stepping into the den of an ogress. Unease stirred, and I had to force my feet forward. The floor-to-ceiling windows that ran the full length of the room should have flooded it with light, but the heavy curtains were drawn, making me wonder if Lady Harriet had a vampirelike phobia about sunlight. She wasn't one, of course, because she was often out and about during the day, going to meetings and doing interviews, but the utter darkness was still odd.

A huge bank of bookcases lined the wall to my right, and to the left there were two doors, both of which were closed. Harriet Chase sat impassively behind a mahogany desk, which dominated the center of the room. Only she wasn't alone.

A man lounged casually in one of the visitor's chairs in front of the desk. Even seated he looked tall, and he had gray hair and old-fashioned rimmed glasses that perched precariously on the end of his nose. He had the air of a professor, but, as my gaze met his, the image that rose wasn't scholarly. It was of Death herself; she was standing close by his shoulder, waiting for her chance to reach out and take my soul.

I stopped, my heart hammering and my mouth suddenly dry. "You wanted to see me, Ms. Chase?" I said, my gaze still on the man in the chair rather than Harriet herself.

"Yes," she said, her voice almost mechanical. "Professor Baltimore's death is both unfortunate and untimely, but his work is far too important and must be continued."

I didn't say anything. I couldn't. Fear of the man in front of me had frozen over my throat.

"Luckily, Professor Heaton here is available to jump on board at short notice." She beamed at the man. It was a false thing, and hard to believe. "We are extremely lucky to have him."

"I'm the one who is lucky." His voice was a low rumble of sound and surprisingly pleasant—the total opposite of what I'd been expecting. "Baltimore was someone I admired greatly. I'm honored to be picking up where he left off."

Where Mark left off was being dead. I somehow doubted he'd find *that* such an honor.

"Of course, given you worked with Professor Baltimore for so long, Emberly," Harriet continued, "and you are already familiar with his research, it is in everyone's interest for you to continue your position as an assistant to Professor Heaton."

Work for Death? Not if I could help it. I wasn't *that* desperate for a peaceful job this life span.

"But—" It came out croaky. I swallowed heavily, then added, "I'm technically not a research assistant. I rarely did more than transcribe his notes."

And she knew that, so why the pretense?

She half shrugged. Again it was an almost mechanical gesture. "That doesn't alter the fact that you're more familiar with his work than most. So, could you take Professor Heaton down to the labs to familiarize himself with the work space?"

"What, now?" I squeaked.

"Now," she said firmly. "It is more than two hours into your workday, after all."

Heaton rose from his chair in one long, fluid movement, and I resisted the urge to step back from him. He reached across the desk and shook Harriet's hand. "I cannot wait to get to work, Ms. Chase."

His words sent another chill down my spine as visions of Mark, tied to a chair and beaten to death, rose like ghosts to taunt me.

He swung around and swept a hand toward the door. "Shall we go, Ms. Pearson?"

No, my inner voice said. *No!*

But I forced my feet to turn around and walk out of the office. He followed, a somber, forbidding presence who seemed to loom over me. He drew close the minute we left Abby's office, until every breath seemed filled with the nonscent of him and my skin crawled in distaste. Only, he didn't just have no smell; there was no heat in him, no sensation of life.

I remembered Abby's lack of life, Lady Harriet's mechanical responses, and my heart suddenly lurched.

He was a *vampire.*

And he'd been controlling them both.

I closed my eyes briefly and battled to remain calm. One thing was abundantly clear—I couldn't get into the elevator with him. I couldn't go *anywhere* alone with him. If he'd been controlling them to get at me, then he certainly couldn't intend anything good.

The urge to run was hard to ignore, but if I moved too soon, didn't plan my escape, he'd have me. Vampires were fast. Superfast.

My gaze swept the corridor almost frantically and came to rest on the fire escape down at the far end. I took a long breath, gathering courage, then strode forward, punching the elevator call button and hoping like hell the one closest to the fire escape answered. It was the one I'd come up in and—given how little time had passed—there was a good chance it was still sitting on this floor. The light above the doors flicked on, and I moved toward it with relief.

"Such prompt service," Heaton said, as if to make conversation. Maybe he sensed the tension in me and was trying to calm me.

Maybe I was overreacting and he *was* just a professor who intended me no harm.

But if that was the case, why mind-control the two women?

I clenched my fists against the flames fighting for release. I had to time this precisely if I didn't want to provide the security cameras with more of a show than they were expecting. I might not want to work for this vampire, but I wasn't about to out myself as something other than human, either. Of course, that was presuming the cameras were actually working. Heaton's appearance had all the hallmarks of a well-planned raid, and I doubted he'd chance the police using security-cam images to track him down if something went wrong.

But would he know that Lady Harriet had a separate system working in her office? Few people did. I knew only because I'd been working late the night it had been installed. It might have been a secret installation, but no one had informed the workmen, and they hadn't minded telling a curious female what they were up to.

As the elevator doors fully opened, I pretended to stumble. Heaton was following so close that not even his vampiric speed could prevent him from running into me. As he did, I caught his arm and yanked him forward with every ounce of strength I had, so that he sailed over my back and crashed into the rear wall of the elevator.

Then I spun and ran like hell for the stairs.

I flung the door open and called to the fires as I raced downward. They came in a rush, sweeping through my body like a maelstrom, flinging me from flesh to flame in an instant. No longer restrained by physical form, I leapt over the railing and surged downward, until the sound of the door above opening again echoed across the silence. I swept back over the railing, keeping to the wall and out of his sight as the race downward continued. As I neared the exit, I switched back to human form, and suddenly the awareness of him surged. He was only a couple of floors above me, a dark and forbidding presence that swamped my senses and snatched my breath. I crashed out into the foyer and ran like hell for the doors.

"Hey, Emberly," Ian called, as I raced past his desk. "Everything okay?"

"Yeah," I yelled, not wanting to say anything and risk the vamp getting into his head. "Just got an urgent errand."

The doors swished open and I raced out into the sunshine. I didn't immediately stop, but ran down the street to put some distance between me and the main entrance.

Finally, I stopped and turned around. Heaton had halted on the cusp of sunlight, his face impassive but his fists clenched. The darkness in him rolled out in waves, battering my senses, making me gasp.

I dragged my phone out of my purse and took a photo of him as he turned away. I doubted he'd seen me do it, but I also had no doubt that I *hadn't* seen the last of him. I might have escaped him this time, but that didn't mean they wouldn't try again. And if they knew where I worked, then they knew where I lived.

I grabbed my phone and called Rory.

"Hey, babe," he said, his voice cheery. "What's happening?"

"Don't go home," I said, the words coming out in a rush.

"What? Why?"

"Because a vampire intending me no good just made an appearance at the Chase Institute, and I don't think I can risk going home. I don't think you should, either."

"Are you okay?" Concern swirled through his voice. "Do you want me to come pick you up?"

I hesitated. I always felt safer with Rory around—he was my rock, the one person I could always turn to. But I also didn't want to drag him into this mess any more than necessary. "No. I'll have to report it to Sam, and I daresay he'll arrange a tighter security net around me. I just wanted to warn you, in case they were also watching the apartment."

"Get Sam to send his people over there. Vamps can't cross a threshold uninvited, so if there are people there, they'll be human or weres."

"I will. I just wanted to warn you first."

He grunted. "Be careful, and call me if you need help."

"I will. Thanks."

I hung up, then dragged Sam's card out of my pocket and dialed the number. A mechanical voice answered, telling me to leave a message.

"Sam, it's Emberly," I stated, and gave a quick rundown of events. "You might want your people to check both Harriet Chase and Abby to uncover just what other information he might have dragged from their minds. And Lady Harriet has a separate security camera system operating in her offices, so grab those tapes."

I hung up and jogged the rest of the way to the café. Jackson was talking to a dark-haired waitress at one of the outside tables, so I simply brushed past and continued on to the Magenta. Early morning or not, I needed a drink. A very large, very alcoholic drink.

Jackson slid onto the stool beside me about fifteen minutes later. He ordered himself a beer and another double vodka and orange for me.

"I'm gathering," he said dryly, "that things did not go well at work."

"You might say that." I finished my second vodka in one long gulp that had my head buzzing pleasantly, then got my phone out and found the photo I'd taken. "Do you know this man?"

He studied it for several seconds, then shook his head. "Why?"

"Because he claims to be a Professor Heaton,

and he's just been employed to continue Mark's work. Only he's a vampire, and he not only had Harriet Chase and her assistant under full mind control, but he got madder than hell when I made a run for it."

He took the phone from me and studied the image again. "Definitely not someone I know." He scrolled back to the main page, hit several buttons, then attached the photo and sent it off somewhere.

"I have a friend who might be able to help us pin down his identity," he explained, handing me back the phone.

I shoved it away and then smiled at the bartender as he delivered our drinks. "A cop friend?"

"Sort of."

"A secret source you fear to reveal, huh?"

"Yeah." He half shrugged and looked slightly embarrassed. "Thing is, your friend Sam and his partner seem ready and willing to roll over everyone and everything to get their answers. I'm not going to waste a valuable source by telling you, and have you willingly—or unwillingly—reveal it to them."

And I couldn't fault him for that—even if I'd already said my mind couldn't be rolled. "The only trouble is, Sam is undoubtedly keeping an eye on everyone I contact, and that will include anyone I contact via phone. He'll trace your source's number and probably shut them down."

Jackson smiled. "Well, no, because I actually forwarded the pic to one of *my* e-mail addresses.

It just happens to be one my source has access to and checks regularly."

"So your source is a female you're intimate with?"

He raised an eyebrow. "And why would you think that?"

"Because I can't imagine a man would be bothered checking for e-mails from you every day. A woman you're bedding, however, is an entirely different matter."

He grinned and didn't bother denying it.

I added, "Did either of the waitresses reveal anything exciting?"

"I'm afraid only Sandy was there, and she none too subtly suggested she was up for being taken in the storeroom."

I just about choked on my drink. "Really?"

"Truly," he replied somberly, though his eyes were twinkling. "Sadly, I had to inform her I already had my hands full when it came to catering to the needs of a woman."

I grinned. "And a Fae can't cope with more than one woman? I'm shocked!"

He laughed, the sound warm and rich. "Not even the Fae have unlimited stamina. Had it been later in the afternoon, it might have been a different story."

No doubt. "So did she reveal anything other than a high sexual drive?"

"Yeah. She and Baltimore were fuck buddies."

For the second time in as many minutes, I just about choked on my drink. Jackson slapped my back, his grin huge. "Your boss was old, not dead."

Which was exactly what Rory had said a couple of days ago. "But he's old enough to be her dad!"

"So?"

I studied him for a moment, then shrugged. I'd certainly lived long enough to know that men only ever stopped thinking about or wanting sex when they were dead—and sometimes not even then—but for some reason, Mark's predilection for much younger women really *did* surprise me. "Did she say how long it had been going on?"

"Ah," he said, with a knowing grin. "Therein lies the rub. They became lovers in June last year."

"That's the month Mark started his current project," I said with a frown.

"Coincidence, hey?"

I eyed him for a moment. "You obviously think not—why?"

"Because she was trying to read me." He tapped his head. "Felt the buzz of her telepathy, but she didn't have any more luck than that Adam fellow last night. As I said, I tend to rate rather highly when it comes to telepathy resistance."

"So did she offer the storeroom adventure before or after that?"

"After. I rather suspect I would have gotten a whole lot more than a tasty bit of ass."

I snorted softly. "So we have lead number two."

"Maybe. I mean, that cop friend of yours would no doubt be as aware of her connection to Baltimore as us."

Probably. And he'd no doubt had Adam covertly read her mind and pick out any information. "But if she was working for whoever is behind this, why is she still working there now that Mark is dead?"

"Probably for cover. It'd be too obvious if she quit right away."

"Yeah, but Adam's also telepathic, remember, and he—or someone with similar skills—would have interviewed her by now. She wouldn't be working there if Sam's people thought she was involved."

"Not necessarily. It's not unusual for strong telepaths to be unable to read each other. That might be the case here."

Meaning, if they'd been unable to read her, they'd undoubtedly have a watch on her. Which also meant Sam would be aware that Jackson had talked to her this morning and that we weren't letting the case drop as advised. "What about Michelle, the other waitress?"

"Interestingly, she hasn't come into work since Baltimore died."

That raised my eyebrows. "Has anyone contacted her?"

"Yeah. She's sick, not dead."

"Is she worth talking to?"

He shrugged. "It can't hurt."

No, I guess it couldn't. I downed the drink quickly, then rose. "Shall we go, then?"

"What, now?"

Getting up so quickly had my head spinning. I

had to grip the bar to steady myself. "You did get her address, didn't you?"

"Yes." He rose and threw some cash on the counter. "Might be worth waiting to see what we get back from my contact, though."

I frowned. "Why?"

"Because if he came after you, they might also be going after anyone else who had *any* contact with Baltimore." He rested his hand lightly against my spine, guiding me toward the exit. "And that could be a reason for her disappearing act."

"You said she was only sick."

"Doesn't mean she actually is."

True. I studied the sunlit street as we walked toward his pickup. For the first time that morning, there was no immediate sensation of being watched and, for some reason, concern stirred. My watcher had been nearby when I'd entered the institute less than an hour ago, so where was he now? And more important, where the hell was Sam? Why wasn't he answering my phone call? Frowning, I added, "What about Professor Wilson? Did he have similar liaisons?"

"Wilson was married."

"If a man is inclined to stray, being married certainly won't stop him," I said dryly.

"True. And to be honest, it never occurred to me to check. I've focused more on Baltimore and you, simply because that's where all the leads seem to be."

Not to mention the sex, I thought with amusement. "Meaning you haven't talked to the wife?"

"I have, but she was in a rather distraught state, and I couldn't get anything useful out of her. But if Wilson was having an affair, I don't think she'd know about it. She seemed pretty clueless about what he did for a living."

"She may have been clueless about his job, but if he was having an affair, or was otherwise in trouble, she *would* have had some sense of it—even if she didn't want to confront or admit the situation."

"Maybe." His expression suggested he didn't agree.

I shrugged. "Then we need to talk to his friends. If there's one thing I've learned over my many lifetimes, it's that men boast."

He grinned. "Well, when it comes to a tasty bit of ass, can you blame us?"

"When you're married, yes."

"I'm not married, and never will be."

"But if you were, I'd have to punch your lights out."

His grin grew. "Fae don't marry. We don't even do serious commitment."

"Which is a very good thing for both of us. But I merely meant that I don't believe in fooling around with a married man."

"You're perfectly safe with me, I assure you."

"Somehow, I'm doubting that."

My voice was wry, and he chuckled softly as I got into the car. "You could be right in that."

Once I was seated, he jogged around to the driver's side and got in. As he pulled out into the flow of traffic, I flipped down the sun visor and adjusted the vanity mirror to look behind us.

"Looking for anything in particular?" he asked.

"Just wondering where my official follower is. I've never really spotted him, but I've generally sensed his presence. I didn't when we left the bar, and it just strikes me as odd."

"Maybe they've been pulled off your tail since events at the Crown."

"Surely they'd only do that if they'd solved the case, and the vampire at the institute suggests this case is far from solved."

"True." He contemplated the rearview mirror for several seconds, then shrugged. "The only way to know for sure is to ring the cop."

"Tried that. No immediate response." I grimaced, then thrust the worry from my mind. There was nothing I could do about it, after all. "Where are we headed?"

"Braybrook. Michelle apparently rents a small house not far from the Braybrook Plaza."

Which didn't mean a whole lot to me as I really didn't know the area. We cruised on in comfortable silence, and it wasn't long before he was slowing in front of a small double-fronted house whose facade had been "beautified" by a wash of white concrete that made it stand apart from its orange-bricked neighbors. Two green rubbish bins stood on the lawn next to the concrete path that led up to the front veranda, and a white station wagon sat in the shared driveway.

"All the curtains are drawn," I commented,

peering past him. "But the wire screen door is open."

"And the front door is slightly ajar." He studied the house a bit longer, then parked several doors up. "She might be getting ready to leave."

"Could be."

We climbed out of the car and walked back. But as we neared the front gate, something shattered inside the house; then the screaming started. It was a woman.

"Back door," Jackson said as he bolted for the front door. I ran down the driveway, my sneakered feet making little sound on the concrete. A large metal gate divided the front yard from the back, but I leapt up, gripped the top, and hauled myself over.

Behind me came the sound of a door crashing back against a wall. Jackson, inside the house already. The screaming stopped abruptly but not the noise. Whoever was inside was on the move—toward me.

I bent and ran past a window, then stopped just to the side of the back door. The footsteps came closer—two men, not one.

I flexed my fingers, and fireflies danced across my fingertips. Timing was everything.

The door was flung open. I stuck a foot out as the first man appeared, tripping him and sending him stumbling; then I lunged around the doorway, grabbed the second man before he could realize what had happened, and sent him flying into the first man. They went down in a tangle of arms and legs, their heads smashing against each other, knocking each other out cold. They fell in a heap, one pinned beneath the other.

More steps approached. I tensed, the fireflies becoming flames inches high, then caught the warm, sunshiny scent and relaxed.

Jackson appeared a heartbeat later, his gaze sweeping me, then moving to the two men. "Good work," he said, then nodded back toward the house. "Call the cops and an ambulance. I'm afraid they made a bit of a mess of the woman."

"Then don't be gentle with them," I said as I stepped inside the house.

"Oh, I won't be."

His voice was grim, and I realized why a moment later. A dark-haired woman lay sprawled unconscious across the sofa in the living room. Her lip was split, her face bruised and bloody, and her dress was shucked up around her armpits. I doubted they'd had the time to rape her, but that had certainly been their intention.

I resisted the urge to march outside and punch the shit out of the two men and moved closer to the woman, carefully checking her pulse. It was fast but strong, and she didn't seem to be having any trouble breathing.

I stepped back and called the cops, telling them what we'd found and requesting medical assistance. Then I spun around and went looking for a blanket. I couldn't move her or tidy her clothes without the risk of disturbing any DNA evidence that might be present, but I couldn't bear to see her sprawled out like that, either.

I found a closet in the small hallway and opened it up. Blankets, sheets, and towels sat in neat little stacks inside. I reached for one of the blankets, but as I did, something stung the side of my neck.

I swiped at it irritably, but a hand caught mine and something cool and sharp pressed against the side of my head.

"Make a sound," a soft voice whispered, "and you die."

CHAPTER 8

Fire howled through me, thick and angry, but I couldn't focus and everything seemed fuzzy. The fire dancing around my fingertips seemed to be fading, and the roaring in my head was getting louder and louder, but it *wasn't* flame.

My knees buckled, but before I could slump to the floor, someone grabbed me. They ripped my purse from my shoulder, but everything after that became hazy. I wasn't knocked out, not entirely, but what I heard and saw seemed to be coming from a very great distance and didn't have a whole lot of impact.

Something was thrown over my body; then I was carried like a sack out of the house. Wind. Sunlight. Darkness and metal vibrating underneath me. Then nothing for a long period of time.

Rising to full consciousness seemed to take forever. My head was back to throbbing with an intensity that suggested it was about to tear apart, and there was a bitter, metallic taste in my mouth. My shoulders burned, and there was something tight around my wrists and ankles. It took a few minutes to register it was rope. I was tied.

Which was better than being dead, I guess.

As awareness grew, I remained still and listened to the sounds around me, trying to discover where I was and who might be near.

I was lying on something cold and hard. Not concrete, but smallish rectangular shapes. Bricks, I thought. Bricks that were slick with moisture. In the distance water trickled, the sound echoing lightly. The air that swirled around me was stale and heavy with the scents of excrement and rubbish. Either I was in a very old, not-often-cleaned lane or I was in a sewer.

My vote was on the latter option.

After a few seconds, I became aware of footsteps. They were barely audible, and I could hear only one set. But until I knew whether there *was* more than one person nearby, I wasn't about to give any indication that I was awake.

Time seemed to creep by. The pain in my shoulders flared downward until it felt like my arms were locked in agony. And the ropes around my legs were so damn tight they were cutting into my skin and making my toes numb. It was just as well I could take another form, because if I had to rely on *this* one to react with any sort of speed, I'd be in serious trouble.

A phone rang sharply into the silence and I jumped. Thankfully, whoever was out there didn't seem to notice.

"Got your parcel," a gruff voice said. "You were right—they did go for the waitress."

God, I thought, the waitress had been a trap. I

should have known that it had all been a little too conveniently timed.

"She did get a call off to the cops," he continued, "so I didn't get the chance to kill the waitress. And the Fae took out my two men."

He didn't get the chance? He'd had plenty of time to kill the waitress before we got there, if simple murder had been his intention. I wasn't close enough to hear the other side of the conversation, and that was irritating. I cracked open an eye and peered around. My captor was standing near what looked like a sewer's edge ten feet away. He was tall, broad shouldered, and thickset, with a bald head that seemed to gleam even in the thick shadows that surrounded us.

Even though I couldn't see his face, I knew who he was, having seen a photograph not so long ago. It was Sherman Jones, the man who'd mysteriously disappeared after Mark's murder.

"Don't worry. They can't tell anyone anything," Sherman said. He swung around, and I quickly shut my eye. "So there's no problem with the cops interrogating them. What do you want me to do about the waitress, though?"

He listened for several seconds, then grunted. "And this one?"

Again silence fell; then he said, "Fine. See you then."

He walked toward me and bent down. Even though he was close enough that I could feel the wash of his breath across my cheek, I couldn't really smell him. It was as if something had completely erased his scent. Maybe that was why Jackson hadn't realized he was in the house—either that, or the scent of the other two had been so strong he simply hadn't had the chance to look beyond it.

"So," he said softly, his rough fingertips trailing across my cheek. "It seems we have an entire afternoon to fill in before I have to hand you over."

"Well, you're not passing that time with me," I spat, and flamed. The force of it threw him backward even though he was barely touching me, and it cindered the ropes holding me captive in an instant. I let the flames take me fully into spirit form, then flowed forward. Sherman scrambled backward, his sharp face twisted with fear and his mouth open, though if he was screaming, he made no sound. I reached out and grabbed him with one molten hand. My flames danced across his clothing, setting them alight but not actually burning them. Not yet, not until I intended it. I slammed him against the slick brick walls and held him there.

"Tell me who you're working for," I said softly. "Or the flames that surround you *will* consume you."

He made several attempts to speak and eventually croaked, "What the hell are you?"

"Something you don't want to mess with." I shook him lightly. "Now, answer the question."

He licked his lips, then said, "I don't know his name. I was contracted through an intermediary."

"Marcus Radcliffe?"

He shook his head violently. "No. Haven't worked for him in weeks."

"Then who?"

I directed the flames up toward his face, letting them tease his chin and lightly burn. He gulped. "Lee Rawlings. I was supposed to hand you over to him this evening."

The timing suggested that Lee Rawlings was a vampire—the same one that had pursued me, perhaps?

"When and where?"

"Under the bridge near the red zipper sculpture in the Flemington Canal. Eight p.m."

"And is Rawlings the one who hired you to watch the professor?"

He shook his head. "Radcliffe did."

"Why was he interested in the professor?"

"I don't know. I was just asked to see who he interacted with on a daily basis."

Did that mean we had two different parties interested in Mark's work? "What about Professor James Wilson—was anyone following him?"

"How the fuck do I know? I was just employed to follow Baltimore. When he was murdered, I made scarce."

I guess that was no surprise. "What does Rawlings look like?"

Sherman shrugged, so I let the flames leap a little higher and singe his whiskers. He yelped and said, "Christ! He's tall and thin, like most fucking vampires. Dark hair, brown eyes."

"And what was the delivery deal?"

"Half before, half later."

"Half being . . . ?"

He licked his lips. "A thousand."

I was worth only a paltry thousand dollars? That sucked—or Sherman was simply cheap. "And what about the waitress?"

He frowned. "What about her?"

"Why were you employed to kill her?"

"I don't ask why," he all but whined. "I just take the job and do it."

"So you were told to beat her up and then rape her before you killed her?"

Sweat beaded his upper lip. He quickly licked it, his gaze darting away from mine. "Not exactly."

Disgust stirred, and it took every ounce of effort not to burn the bastard to a cinder right there and then. He might have been employed to the kill the waitress for whatever reason, but *he'd* been the one who decided on the more savage method. Because he enjoyed doing it.

"What's the security code for your phone?" I asked brusquely.

Confusion flitted through his eyes, but he rapidly spat out a number.

"Thank you," I said, then regained flesh and hit him as hard as I could. He went down like a sack of potatoes, hitting the ground with a sharp crack that suggested something had broken.

For several minutes I did nothing more than wince and curse as the pins and needles in my arms and feet made the mere act of holding hu-

man flesh sheer agony. As the pain began to sub-
side, I checked that Jones was unconscious, then
rifled through his pockets, discovering in the process he'd landed awkwardly on his left arm and
had indeed broken it. Feeling little in the way of
sympathy—especially given what he'd intended
to do to both me and the waitress—I plucked his
phone free. Mine was with my purse back at the
waitress's house, and I wouldn't have used it anyway. Not when Sam had it bugged. I flipped the
case open, typed in the security code, and saw the
time. I'd been missing for more than an hour,
which no doubt meant that not only would the
cops be at the waitress's house but Sam and his
people would be as well. Jackson would have
been interrogated, but had enough time passed
for him to have been released? Or was Sam holding him somewhere?

I guess there was only one way to find out.

I hit the text button and typed, *Hey, babe. I left in
such a hurry that I forgot to arrange another date. Ring
me when you're free.*

Once it was sent, I walked around gingerly until the pain in my feet eased, then rang Rory at the
fire station and updated him on events.

"Do you need help?" he said once I'd finished.

I hesitated. Rory and I had long ago made a
pact not to pull each other into dangerous situations, simply because if both of us happened to be
killed at the same time, it would be the end of us.
While the spirit of a phoenix always rose from the
ashes of its death, it was only with the assistance

of a ritual performed by their life mate that we were able to regain adult flesh and become whole. Otherwise, our spirits moved on, uniting once more with the great mother, never to know life and love and feeling ever again.

We'd come close to that once. I had no intention of risking it in either this lifetime or any other future lifetime. And I had a suspicion that this case would get a whole lot deeper and darker before we got any real answers.

"No," I said eventually. "I don't think we can chance it."

He swore softly. "Damn it, Em. Be careful. You know I'll be there if the worst happens, but I'd really rather just get through more than one life span without one or the other of us dying before our time."

I smiled. "Says the man who is currently a fireman."

"Hey, I'm not the one who has chucked in the staid life to go chasing after bad guys." He paused. "And that's two lifetimes in a row for you."

"Yeah, but last time I was official. This time I'm just pissed off."

He snorted. "I still want you to be careful."

"I will. I promise."

He grunted. He'd heard that statement from me almost as many times as I'd heard it from him. "Keep me updated, Em."

"I will," I repeated, then hung up.

It took several hours for Jackson to get back to me. Sherman rose to consciousness several times while I waited, and each time I knocked him back out—although I didn't hit him again, just used pressure points instead. If there was one good thing about living through so many centuries, it was an accumulation of knowledge. Rory had taught me the points after he'd learned the art during his time with an old Chinese kung fu master.

The phone rang about four o'clock, but the number that showed up on the screen wasn't Jackson's. I hesitated, then hit the answer button and cautiously said, "Hello?"

"Emberly? Is that you? Are you okay?"

Jackson's voice. Relief slithered through me. "Yes to all three questions." I hesitated. "I'm gathering you can talk freely?"

"Yeah. I've borrowed a friend's phone. Thought it would be safer."

I winced at the undercurrent of anger in his voice, even though I suspected it wasn't aimed at me. "How bad was the interrogation?"

He snorted. "Let's just say I'm surprised that detective friend of yours actually released me. I was sure the bastard was going to lock me up and throw away the key."

"I'm sure he would have, too, except he no doubt wants to follow you."

"Well, I wish him luck with that. He's not the only one with a few tricks up his sleeve."

"He doesn't need tricks. He has vampires and psychics, and he apparently has the right to use and abuse the law as he desires."

"Which is why I won't stay on the phone for long. If they did manage to follow me here, they're no doubt scrambling to find and lock onto this number."

Which was my cue to get on with it. "Are you able to track my location via the GPS on this phone?"

"I can't personally, but I know someone who could."

I smiled. "You must have some very interesting friends."

"And if you play your cards right, I might just introduce you."

I snorted softly. "Except when they're a source you don't want exposed."

"Exactly," he said cheerfully. "I'm gathering you don't know where you are?"

"Well, yes and no. I'm in a sewer somewhere, and I have Sherman Jones lying unconscious at my feet. He's arranged to hand me over to a vampire going by the name of Lee Rawlings this evening. I want to go to that meet and talk to him."

"That might not be a great idea." There was doubt in his voice. "Vamps can be tricky to deal with at night."

"They can't shadow when there's light," I commented. "Remember what I am, Jackson."

"Can one phoenix raise enough light to stop a vampire shadowing? A Fae sure as hell can't."

"I can."

"Ah, well, that's a different story." He paused.

"It may take me a little while to get to you—will you be okay?"

"Well, I've been in better-smelling places, but I'll be fine." I hesitated and glanced down at my captive. "Bring something that'll keep a wererat bound. I want to hand Jones over to Sam, but not before we get to that meeting."

"Will do," he said, and hung up.

I walked around a bit to ease the lingering remnants of the pins and needles, then sat down next to my captive and played solitaire on his phone to pass the time.

It was close to six p.m. by the time I heard footsteps. I shoved the phone into my pocket and silently rose, clenching my fingers against the flames that instinctively danced across my fingertips.

"Emberly?" Jackson said softly, as his form began to emerge from the darkness. "Don't flame. It's me."

Tension slithered from me. "I'm glad you're finally here. If I had to play solitaire too much longer, I would have gone stir-crazy."

He grinned and shoved a coffee container at me. "Thought you might need this. It's green tea, not coffee."

I took a sniff. Not just green tea, but mint-green tea. "You," I said, dropping a quick kiss on his lips, "are a darling."

"And you," he said, the amusement on his lips crinkling the corners of his bright eyes, "stink."

I snorted. "Not exactly surprising given I've been sprawled all over a sewer tunnel."

"But unattractive all the same. A shower is required before we go anywhere near that meeting this evening." He pulled a coil of metallic rope from over his shoulder and squatted beside Sherman. "Did you ask him about Baltimore?"

"He said Marcus Radcliffe hired him to watch Mark and take note of who he talked to on a regular basis."

"Did he say why?"

I drank some tea, then shook my head. "Which is not surprising. It didn't take much to get him to talk, so he wouldn't have been trusted with anything vital."

"Wererats are never trustworthy," Jackson muttered. "It's the nature of their beast."

I raised my eyebrows. "So what is the nature of the Fae? Besides being randy sensualists, that is?"

He glanced up and grinned. "You struck it lucky. Unlike most of my kind, I'm more beta than alpha. Which means I generally ask for opinions before I do whatever the hell I want."

I laughed. "Yep. That about sums you up."

He finished trussing Sherman up and then rose. "I'm pretty sure I got in here without a tail, but just in case, let's exit via a different sewer cover."

As he tucked a hand under my elbow to guide me forward, I said, "I'm going to need somewhere to shower and change."

He nodded. "I've booked a room in a hotel not far from where we'll exit, and I borrowed some clothes from my friend's wife. She's about your size. Oh, and I retrieved your purse from the waitress's place."

"You've thought of everything, haven't you?" I teased.

His grin was bright and cheeky. "Trust me, I do expect payment in kind."

I laughed. "Of course."

We wound our way through the tunnel system, following the little GPS map he had on his phone. Where the hell he managed to get an app that showed the sewers I had no idea, but I wasn't about to grumble. Not if it got us out of this stinking place sooner rather than later.

After about twenty minutes, I'd finished my tea and we'd finally reached our exit point. Once he'd checked that there was no one close, we climbed out. I took several deep breaths of air unfouled by rubbish and excrement, then looked around as Jackson replaced the cover. "Where are we?"

"Dorcas Street, South Melbourne. The hotel is just down the road." He caught my hand and tugged me forward.

"If I know Sam, he's probably got an electronic eye on all the hotel bookings, so he's going to discover our location sooner rather than later."

"He would, if I were using my own card. But I'm not."

"Another friend?" I said dryly.

He smiled at me. He really did have a nice smile. "He owes me several large favors. I saved his wife once."

"From what?"

"From a rather nasty kidnapping and extortion attempt." He shrugged. "The police weren't happy about my involvement, but who fucking cares when there's a life at stake?"

"That," I said with a smile, "is the alpha speaking, not the beta."

He glanced at me, eyes twinkling. "And also the reason the cops in this city and I don't see eye to eye."

He tugged me through the hotel's lobby. I blinked at the vibrancy of the red feature wall, but didn't get much of a chance to see more than that as we strode quickly to the elevators. In no time at all we were zooming up to the eighth floor. As it turned out, we didn't have a room, but rather a suite with a generous living area, separate bedroom, and a small kitchen.

"The shower is in the en suite," Jackson said, "and the fresh clothes are on the bed. What would you like to eat?"

"A big steak with lots of potatoes and another mug of green tea." I stripped off and headed for the shower. He was right—my clothes stank.

"A woman after my own heart. Except for the whole green tea bit."

"I've had enough coffee over the centuries. Time for a change."

"You know, I always wondered what being with a much older woman would be like. I have to say, it's better than I imagined."

I laughed as I shucked off the remainder of my

clothes, then headed in to clean up. Twenty minutes later, the luscious aroma of roasted meat told me dinner had arrived, so I hurriedly finished dressing. Though there was no underclothing—a fact for which I was grateful, because I drew the line at wearing cast-off bras and panties—the rest of the clothes he'd borrowed fit me nicely. My butt was obviously a little bigger than the wife's, because the jeans were rather tight, and the shirt fit like a glove, exposing more than it covered—a deliberate choice, I suspected. Thankfully, he'd also borrowed a coat—I could cover up and keep warm when I needed to.

His gaze skimmed me as I walked out, and a grin split his face. "Nice," he murmured, his gaze coming to rest on what the shirt wasn't covering. "Shame we haven't got time to peel off that shirt and explore what lies beneath."

"You know what lies beneath," I said, amused. "You've explored them once or twice already."

"Ah, but a good explorer is never afraid to retrace his steps on the off chance he missed something vital."

I snorted. "Let's concentrate on the business at hand, shall we?"

"Oh, I was," he murmured. But he sat down and uncovered the two plates—steak, mashed potatoes, and several helpings of vegetables.

"Right," he said as he picked up his cutlery and began to tuck in. "While I was twiddling my thumbs, waiting for your former boyfriend—"

"And just how do you know he's a former boyfriend?" I inquired mildly.

He waved a fork. "It's obvious given the way you talk about him. I'm guessing it ended badly, but some part of you isn't quite over it."

He'd guessed entirely too much. I waved him on irritably.

Amusement danced in his bright eyes as he continued. "My friend got back to me about that pic I sent her. She couldn't find a match."

"So, our mysterious Professor Heaton hasn't got a criminal record."

"Nor a driver's license."

"Inconvenient."

"Yeah." He munched on some steak for several minutes, then said, "Said friend is going to do an overseas search to see if anything comes up, but that may take a while."

"Which leaves us with the vamp tonight. Hopefully, he'll be able to enlighten us more than Jones did."

"If not, we go back to the waitress who tried to seduce me and do a little backroom interrogating of our own."

I nodded. "We also need to talk to Wilson's wife. And the friends."

"I really don't think the wife will be able to tell us anything more."

"Doesn't hurt to be sure."

His expression was dubious, but he didn't disagree any further. We finished our meals in companionable silence; then I grabbed my purse and borrowed coat and we headed out.

Though it was after seven, the rush-hour traffic

lingered and it took forever to cut across town. Along the way, I rang the number Sam had given me, telling him the GPS coordinates for Jones's location and letting him know what had happened— but not what Jones had said. He'd be pissed—I knew that—but having made the decision to see this thing through to the end, that was exactly what I intended to do. And while I knew it probably wasn't the smartest decision I'd made in my many lifetimes, it would hardly rate among the worst, either. That honor went to the time I'd decided to become a nun. The vows of poverty, chastity, and—worst of all—obedience had not sat well.

Darkness had well and truly settled in by the time we reached the park. As Jackson paid the driver, I climbed out and studied the huge wrought-iron struts that jutted out of the ground at an angle. How anyone could call it a sculpture, I had no idea. But then, I'd lived through some of the greatest eras when it came to sculpture and painting. When compared to the sculptures Rodin and Bernini—both of whom I'd known—had produced, this might as well be scrap metal randomly stuck in the ground.

Jackson shoved his hands into his pockets and stopped beside me. "The last four spikes are unlit. I'm thinking that's not a coincidence."

"Probably not."

He glanced at me. "You realize I'll have to carry you over my shoulder to the meeting—he'll be jumpy enough when he realizes it's not Sherman."

I nodded. "It's probably the only way of getting me close enough to encircle him with fire anyway."

Jackson glanced at his watch. "Eight minutes. I'm betting it'll pay to be early."

"I'm betting you're right."

He touched my elbow, lightly guiding me across the road, then, in the shadows of the bridge, hauled me over his shoulder fireman's style.

"Play dead," he said.

"As long as you don't play with my ass," I retorted.

He chuckled softly, the sound vibrating through my body. "As tempting as it is to have such a lovely ass so close to my hand, I suspect shifting my grip and risking dropping you would not be a wise move on my part."

"Too right," I muttered. "And can we please move? Despite what the literature says, this is not the most comfortable way of being carried."

"It's supposed to be more comfortable for me rather than you."

"Just get on with it."

He laughed softly and headed under the bridge and down to the canal. It was fenced off with high wire but had been cut in several places, so it was easy enough for Jackson to squeeze through, even carrying me.

He walked along the banks of the concrete canal, following the line of red-painted metal until he neared the shadowed section.

There he paused. "Lee Rawlings?" he said, not

raising his voice. If the vamp was out there, he'd hear us. "I have a parcel delivery for you."

For several seconds there was no response, then, "You're not who I was expecting."

The voice was smooth and urbane, but it wasn't the voice of the vampire who'd claimed to be Professor Heaton.

"Jones decided he couldn't risk being seen," Jackson said. "The police want to question him about some murder, and he'd rather not talk."

"And who might you be?"

"Let's just call me a subcontractor," Jackson said. "Now, do you want your delivery or not? She may look light but trust me, she ain't."

I resisted the urge to dig an elbow in and remained still. While we had no idea just how well the vamp could see, he *would* be able to hear the beat of blood through my body. I had to keep my pulse rate slow for this to work.

"You may leave her there and go," Rawlings said. "I shall pay Jones himself when I catch up with him."

Jackson snorted. "Hardly. The deal was half before, half after. Cash on the line, buddy, or no delivery."

Rawlings was quiet for several seconds and I wished I knew what the hell was going on. But with my nose stuck in Jackson's back, I couldn't see a damn thing.

After several moments, Rawlings said, "Very well. You may approach."

"So generous of you," Jackson muttered, making me smile.

He carefully navigated the steep canal sides, then splashed his way through the thin layer of water lying at the bottom.

"Far enough," Rawlings said.

Jackson stopped slightly sideways, and suddenly, I could see. And what I could see was feet. Jackson's. It wasn't a lot of help.

"Money first," Jackson said. "If you think you can throw twenty feet, that is. I don't appreciate wet cash."

Thank you; thank you, I thought, and called to the fire. Only this time, instead of using the flames that burned within me, I called to the heat of the world around us—the fire of the earth and the energy in the air—gathering it, weaving it, then casting it out to form a circle that was bright and fierce but also surreal. This wasn't normal flame; this was the flame of the mother herself, and she burned with a fire that danced with the colors of all creation.

"What in Hades . . . ?" Rawlings said, even as Jackson said, "Holy fuck, *that's* impressive."

"You can lower me now," I said, and he hastily did so.

Even in the vivid brightness of the flames that surrounded him, Lee Rawlings was a tall, thin shadow of a man. His eyes were as dark as his skin, and his thick glossy hair glinted with blue highlights. He was also very, very angry. It poured off him like sweat, stinging the air and making it hard to breathe.

Not telepathic, but empathic, meaning he could not only sense the emotions of others, but—as he was doing right now—use them as a weapon. Although in this case, he was amplifying *his* anger rather than ours.

"Stop projecting and remain still," I said flatly, "or the flames *will* burn you."

That thickening sensation eased, and suddenly I could breathe again.

"What trickery is this?" Rawlings's hands were clenched, and the anger that no longer burned through the air vibrated through his body.

"What this is," Jackson replied evenly, "is an information exchange. You tell us what we want to know, and you can walk away with your skin unburned."

His gaze flickered between the two of us. Him walking away didn't seem to be on his agenda right now.

"Trust me," I said softly, "any attempt to do anything more than walk away would *not* be wise."

I flicked a finger, and a slither of flame danced apart from the main ring of fire, shimmering softly as it curled toward Rawlings and almost lovingly wrapped around his ankle. His pants instantly began to melt away, but I withdrew the flame before it did any real damage.

Rawlings didn't scream, didn't react in any way, really. And, oddly enough, the anger in him seemed to fizzle away. But old vampires were very good at that sort of thing, and I very much suspected Rawlings was one of the old ones. His speech was too formal for him to be a more recent recruit into the vampire ranks. "What do you wish to know?"

"Who do you work for," Jackson said immediately, "and why do they want Emberly?"

He studied us for several moments, then said, "I work on a commission basis. You can threaten me all you like, but it would be far easier if you simply paid me for the information."

That raised my eyebrows. "You'd risk ratting out your employer?"

He half smiled. It was not a pleasant thing to behold. "*That* shows how little you know about the vampire sindicati and how they work in these matters. As I said, I merely accepted this commission and I can give you nothing more than the next person in the chain. I do not know the person behind the order. I will never know."

"Well, the next person is better than nothing." Jackson glanced at me and, at my nod, added, "How much will it cost?"

"One thousand. That is the fee I will lose."

"I seem to be going rather cheaply if you ask me," I muttered, resisting the urge to rub at the ache beginning to form just behind my eyes. The fire encasing Rawlings might not be mine, but it still pulled at my strength. I couldn't keep it going indefinitely—not unless I wanted to become little more than ash and flame myself. And that would *not* please Rory.

Rawlings's gaze flicked briefly to me, and in its

dark depths, amusement briefly glinted. Despite that he hired himself out to the vampire crime syndicates, I had a suspicion he wasn't intrinsically bad. "Having witnessed your rather extraordinary skills, I would agree that you most certainly *are* going cheaply." His gaze went back to Jackson. "Do we have a deal?"

"Yes."

"Wire the money into my account immediately."

Jackson drew his phone from his pocket and, as Rawlings recited the number, made the transfer.

Rawlings nodded. "The vampire who employed me for this parcel pickup was one Henry Morretti. I cannot give you his address, and I suspect the phone he called on is either generic or untraceable." He reeled off a number, then added, "And I was not told why he wished you collected, only that I was to be here at this time to collect you and then deliver you to an address in Laverton North."

"Why would you deliver me to what is essentially an industrial area?"

He raised an eyebrow, the movement rather eloquent. "Where else could you question someone without suspicions being raised? Most of the warehouses around that particular address are not twenty-four-hour."

Charming, I thought with a shiver. "What address?"

He gave it to us, then added, "I have lived up to my part of the bargain. I now expect you to live up to yours."

"Do not try to attack us," I warned.

"We made a deal. I will not go back on that."

An honorable criminal. Amazing. I glanced at Jackson, who nodded. I took a deep breath and released my hold on the flames. They shimmered for one brief moment longer; then their heat dissipated, retreating to the realms of earth and air.

Rawlings bowed slightly. "Thank you," he said, then promptly disappeared.

Jackson's nostrils flared. "He retreats, as promised."

"Good." I rubbed my temples wearily, wishing I had some aspirin.

Jackson frowned at me. "You okay?"

"I will be. Creating those sort of flames takes a bit out of me, that's all."

"Do you need tea? Painkillers?"

"Yes, but I'm guessing you don't have either right at this particular moment."

"No, but there's a 7-Eleven not far down the road. If you think you can walk there—"

"The only place you two will be walking," a sharp, all-too-familiar voice said, "is straight into two goddamn jail cells."

I looked up quickly and my stomach sank. Sam and Adam strode toward us, and to say neither of them looked particularly happy would have to be one of the understatements of the year. Sam's body practically vibrated with anger.

"Ah, Detective Turner," Jackson said equably. "How nice of you to join us."

Sam barely gave him a glance. He was too intent on glaring at me. "What the fuck do you think you're doing, Emberly? This isn't some sort of game, you know."

I bit back the instinctive smart-ass reply that rose to my lips. "I know."

"Then, to repeat, what the hell are you doing here, waiting for some criminal?"

Meaning he hadn't seen Rawlings, which put us one up on him—although what good it would do us if he threw us in jail, I had no idea.

"I told you—"

"You told me you were going to be sensible. This is not what I call sensible." He planted himself in front of me, his hands clenched near his sides and a blanket of darkness emanating from him. "You were both warned to stay clear of this investigation—"

"I'm being employed to investigate Professor Wilson's death," Jackson said flatly. "And if that means I also have to investigate Baltimore's, then so be it."

Sam's gaze flicked to Jackson. The darkness in him sharpened, even as his control seemed a little more tenuous. Fear skipped lightly into my heart. I had a bad feeling we did not want to see his control slip.

Sam took a half step forward, leaving me sandwiched between the two men. I don't think he even realized he was doing it, because he was so focused on the Fae at my back—a Fae who was more than ready to give as good as he got, if the coiled readiness I could feel in his body was anything to go by.

"You had better"—Sam's voice was little more than a harsh whisper, but the force of it seemed to shudder the air around us—"start listening, or else—"

Adam placed a hand on Sam's shoulder, as if in warning. Sam growled, the sound animalistic, then drew in a breath and released it slowly. He glanced down at me, and awareness flared. Awareness and hunger. It was thick and sexual and it stormed through me, making me ache even as the dark heart of it had fear stirring again.

After a moment, he stepped back. The darkness in him receded, but not the awareness. Not the hunger. "Adam, get both their asses out of here. Take them to headquarters."

Adam raised a pale eyebrow. "That will not please Henrietta—"

"Right now, I don't fucking care. Just do it."

Adam hesitated, then said, "And you?"

"I'm going to the hospital to question Michelle Rodriguez." He glanced at me. It wasn't a pleasant experience. "I'll interrogate them when I get back."

Adam studied him for a moment, then nodded. "You two, follow me. And please, do not attempt to run. It would be a fruitless waste of all our time."

I glanced at Jackson. He just shrugged and tucked his hand under my elbow, both guiding me forward and offering support in case I needed it. We were shoved into the back of a waiting van, which had no windows and no seats, forcing us to hunker down on the metal floor. The rear door slammed shut, and darkness closed in. After a few minutes, the engine started and the van drove off, taking us god knew where.

"Well, this is the first time I've been arrested in quite a while," I muttered, drawing my knees up to my chest. Flames flickered across my hands, but given the energy store was very low, they barely lifted the darkness. Jackson's eyes were little more than a pale glitter.

He raised his eyebrows. "Meaning this lifetime or past?"

"Past." I gave him a lopsided smile. "You'd be surprised at some of the things I've done."

Amusement tugged at his lips. "Actually, I wouldn't. I daresay a being who keeps getting reborn has more than her fair share of tales to tell."

"Yeah." I paused, then added, "Although being burned at the stake as a witch was not the punishment they thought it would be."

He laughed, but his attention wasn't really on me. I contemplated his intentness and realized he was listening to the sounds around us—a tram rattling by, the peal of a church bell, the heavy bass thump of music—normal noises that meant nothing unless you needed to retrace your steps.

Jackson was planning just that, I suspected. Or, at the very least, wanted to be able to should the need arise. So I watched him quietly, sensing we'd moved through the city and out the other side. Not too far, but somewhere close to the ocean. The distant call of seagulls ran under the night's stronger sounds.

St Kilda, I thought. There was a major police hub there, but I wouldn't have thought it'd be a suitable location for a specialized task force. But maybe that was the whole idea.

Eventually, the van dipped downward, then stopped. Doors slammed, and then the rear doors opened. Adam motioned us out and, with two other men, escorted us through a series of tunnels that were cold and bleak. PIT, it seemed, didn't believe in making their guests feel welcome.

Jackson was placed in one room, me in another. It was little more than a concrete box and was sparsely furnished—just a couple of long benches divided by a table, all of which were concrete. They obviously didn't believe in comfort, either.

I scanned the walls, looking for mics and cameras and finding none. That one fact chilled me more than my bare surroundings, simply because it meant they kept no formal record of what went on in these rooms. They really *weren't* tied to the rules of the regular police force.

I shivered and began to pace, half wishing Sam would hurry up and get here, but fearing what would happen if he did. Outwardly, at least, he wasn't the person I'd known—that darkness . . . Another shiver ran through me, and I rubbed my arms. Something had happened to him—something bad enough to change his very essence.

It was more than an hour before he did arrive, by which time I was practically climbing the walls. But as my gaze met the blue of his, I realized that was precisely what he wanted. Me on edge, desperate to get out. *Bastard*.

He stepped into the room, a paper coffee cup in each hand and what looked to be a BlackBerry tablet tucked under one arm. The darkness—or whatever it was I'd sensed earlier—had retreated. How far, I had no idea, but in its absence, he seemed a whole lot more . . . human. Which seemed the wrong word to use, given that was what he actually *was*, and yet it oddly fit.

"Thought you might like some tea." He slid one cup across the table and kept hold of the other. His voice held none of the cold abruptness that had been a constant in most of his dealings with me, instead hinting at warmth.

But it was a warmth I couldn't afford to believe. I made a short, somewhat humorless sound. "Last time I had a drink in your vicinity, I ended up drugged."

"Oh, for god's sake, Em." He picked the cup back up and took a drink. "Happy?"

I somewhat gingerly picked up the cup and sniffed the contents. It smelled like ordinary, every-day green tea. There was no weird scent that I could detect, but that didn't really mean anything—these days they had all sorts of drugs that were odorless and tasteless. I cautiously took a sip. It *did* taste like ordinary, everyday green tea.

"Now that we have that little drama over with," he said, voice a weird mix of annoyance and amusement, "will you please sit down?"

"Sorry. I prefer to stand." Besides, sitting would bring me far too close to him. I had a hard enough time resisting his presence when he was being a bastard—there was no way I'd cope being near this less-frosty version.

Don't let him hurt you again, Rory had said. It was a warning that was very much uppermost in my mind at the moment.

Sam shook his head and made a sharp "whatever" motion with his free hand. "Fine. Your choice. Tell me about Lee Rawlings."

"Why? It's not like you haven't found out all you need the same way we did—via Sherman Jones."

"Adam is interviewing Jones, but I haven't received the report yet."

I took a drink of tea, then said, "And you'd also like to cross-check information, just to make sure we didn't get anything extra."

"That, too."

I snorted softly. "Why am I here, Sam? We've done nothing illegal."

"You're interfering with an ongoing case. That in itself is enough to confine your ass in jail if I so desire it."

"And do you? Desire it, that is?"

His gaze swept me. The twin fires of need and fear stirred in its wake. The desire was echoed in his eyes. "That depends."

"On what?"

He slammed the BlackBerry on the table, then sat down on the concrete bench. "Your answers. And you staying away from this case as ordered."

"Jackson is a legal private investigator, and he's been employed by Rosen Pharmaceuticals to uncover who murdered James Wilson." Which wasn't exactly the truth, given what they wanted was his research rather than his killer. But Sam probably knew that. "You can't legally prevent him from doing his job."

"I can if he gets in the way, and he is." Just for a moment, the darkness resurfaced, staining his eyes and expression, making me wonder yet again just what had happened to him. What was *still* happening to him. But it disappeared as quickly as it had appeared. Fierce self-control, or had something else happened in the hour or so since I'd last seen him? "But that doesn't explain why you're involved—other than the fact that you've always been bloody stubborn."

"These people *killed* my boss. They've also made several attempts at snatching me, one of them successfully—"

"None of which would have happened if you'd just done as you were told," he cut in.

"You don't believe that any more than I do," I retorted. "So can we just cut the shit and get down to the questions? I want to get out of here."

He studied me for several seconds, and my heart began to beat just that little bit faster. Because there was hunger in his eyes—a hunger that had nothing to do with the deeper darkness within him and everything to do with desire. He still wanted me. After all that he'd said, after all the anger and hurt and sense of betrayal—a betrayal both us felt, for very different reasons—he still wanted me.

I didn't know whether to laugh or cry. Because if there was one certainty in this life, it was that he and I would never end happily.

I turned away to break the spell of his gaze and took a gulp of tea. It didn't do a whole lot to ease the fires that had begun to burn low down in my belly.

"Fine," he said abruptly. "What, exactly, did you get out of Lee Rawlings?"

I looked at him sharply. "Nothing. He wasn't there. You guys turned up and no doubt scared him away."

He gave me a long look. "We both know that's not the truth. Adam picked up the resonance of another life as we approached. Someone else *was* there."

"Adam was wrong." I started pacing again. The coldness in the room was beginning to get to me—it crawled across my skin like a live thing and made me shiver.

"Adam is a vampire. He's never wrong when it comes to the resonance of life."

"Well, I guess that naturally means I'm lying, then, doesn't it?"

"I guess it does. The question is, why? We're both after the same thing—we want the people behind these murders brought down."

"I want answers, Sam, and I'm not likely to get them from you, am I?" I downed the rest of the tea and tossed the cup toward the table. He caught it reflexively, his actions so fast they were almost a blur. I frowned. "What is going on with you? You've changed, and I don't just mean emotionally—"

"We're not here to talk about me," he said, voice still surprisingly mild despite the flicker of annoyance in his eyes. "Stop changing the subject and start answering questions."

I continued pacing but crossed my arms, trying to ward off the growing chill. "I have nothing to say to any of you. You can leave me in this cell to rot if you want, but I can't tell you what I don't know."

"Sadly, I knew you'd say that."

I gave him another sharp glance. "And what does that mean?"

"It means you were right. The tea was drugged."

Blood drained from my face and I stopped abruptly. "What?"

He shrugged and rose. "I figured you wouldn't cooperate, so we dropped a little something into the tea to ensure that you would."

"But you drank some of it."

"Only a sip. It wasn't anywhere enough to affect me." He hesitated. "I *am* sorry, but it was a necessary step. We need answers, Em, and we need them now."

I stepped away from him. But that chill in my body was growing, making my feet go numb, and I stumbled. Sam caught my right elbow and directed me backward, until my back was pressed against concrete. He placed his other hand under my left shoulder, effectively pinning me.

"Tell me what Lee Rawlings said."

He was close. *So* close. His breath teased my lips and his warm, woody scent filled every breath, making my nipples pucker and sending slivers of desire curling through my belly. The desire in his gaze sharpened a caress of heat that rolled over me, making me tremble, making me yearn.

I opened my mouth, then closed it again. Took a deep breath and released it slowly. "Go fuck yourself, Sam."

Anger flared, deep and fierce. Its intensity was frightening. But once again it was just as swiftly smothered. "Trust me, I was fucked a *long* time ago. Now, just answer the damn question, Red."

I closed my eyes and battled the need to obey. It would have been far easier to give him what he wanted, but something within me just wouldn't allow it. He was right. I could be bloody stubborn when I wanted to be. Stupid, even. Because really, what was I gaining by resisting? Nothing, absolutely nothing.

I licked my lips, saw his gaze drop to follow the movement. Heat rolled over me, thick with desire, fanning the flames within to greater heights.

"What is the drug you gave me?"

"N41A. It's designed to restrict certain paranormal powers and also acts as a truth serum of sorts. What did Rawlings tell you?"

That he was just another delivery boy, that the real meet was with a Henry Morretti in Laverton. But somehow, I kept the words inside. "Define what you mean by restrict."

"It means you will not be able to flame. It was created for those with talents such as telekinesis and pyrokinesis, but we figured it would probably work on rarer creatures such as yourself and the Fae."

"I'm not human, Sam. You have no idea how that drug will affect me."

"When you're in this form, human drugs will affect you the same way as they will affect any other human. In this case, it means you won't have full use of your flames for forty-eight hours." He studied me for a moment, almost seeming to lean in closer, as if he intended to kiss me. But his gaze was on mine rather than my lips, and the fires of desire were banked in his eyes.

I wished I could say the same about mine.

"The Paranormal Investigations Team has a long history of studying nonhumans, and while phoenixes might be rare, they are *not* unknown to us."

Meaning *if* he was right, I was without my one major form of protection. But they obviously didn't know everything. Any drug introduced into my system in flesh form would burn away in spirit, and no drug, no matter how strong, could stop a return to my true self. Only a lack of strength from within could do that and, right now, thanks to everything that had happened, I was running low on reserves. "They were unknown to *you* five years ago."

"That was before I joined PIT. I've learned a whole lot in the last year or so."

"Shame you never learned it's impolite to drug

the people you want cooperation from." And it was a shame the words came out a whole lot huskier than I'd intended.

"We don't. It's only those we can't read and who won't cooperate we drug. Tell me about Rawlings, Emberly."

I did. I couldn't help it. The words vomited from my mouth—Rawlings, his orders, the meeting details, even how much we'd paid for the information.

At the end of it, Sam grunted. "He said nothing else?"

I glared at him. "No."

"Good." He hesitated, his gaze sweeping my face and his lips suddenly closer even though he hadn't moved. "There's one other thing about the drug I forgot to mention."

My stomach did a strange flip-flop, but I wasn't entirely sure whether the cause was his words or the brush of his breath against my lips as he spoke.

"Gee, color me surprised." I intended sarcasm, but it came out far more breathless than that, and the desire in his blue eyes sharpened abruptly. It ran around me like a storm, and all I wanted was for it to sweep me away.

But that would be a very *bad* thing to happen. I had enough trouble now forgetting his kisses. I didn't need a refresher to make it all that much harder.

"That drug," he said softly, his lips so close to mine I could practically taste them, "is also something of an enforcer. You *will* obey what I say now that it is in full effect."

But thankfully, only until the moment I have the strength to take on my fire form. "Damn it, Sam, don't do this."

"You give me no other choice—"

"There's always a choice, Sam. You just have to want it enough."

Again his gaze swept me, and I knew in that moment I wasn't mistaken, that he *did* want me. Badly. I was in a whole heap load of trouble if he actually acted on it.

"Emberly Pearson," he continued softly. "You will not go anywhere near Henry Morretti or the meeting in Laverton. You will stop pursuing all leads pertaining to the murder of your boss."

"Bastard."

"Totally," he agreed; then, a heartbeat later, his lips met mine.

It was a fierce thing, this kiss, both familiar and yet not. It was everything we'd once shared, and yet so very raw and different. It was hunger and desire, darkness and desperation, and it reflected all that we once were and all that had changed.

It proved how much I still wanted him—and he me—but it also confirmed just how different he now was. Because where once I'd tasted nothing more than joy and desire, heat and passion, there was now also ash and anger, fierce and barely restrained, and it spoke of the night and even darker urges. I'd never kissed a vampire, but I imagined they would taste something like this.

But Sam wasn't a bloodsucker. He'd been out in the sunshine often enough to prove that. I had no idea what had happened to him, but the mere fact I could actually taste the changes scared the hell out of me.

He broke away with a suddenness that tore a gasp from my throat and left me dizzy and breathless. His gaze, when it locked on mine, was hot—hungry—and yet also very angry. With me, with himself, and with the world in general, I suspected.

"Stay away," he growled, leaving me wondering if he meant from the case or from him.

Then he pushed away from the wall, away from me, and I collapsed into a heap on the floor. The last thing I remember seeing were his boots as he walked away.

They were the boots I'd given him as a birthday present six years ago.

CHAPTER 9

As consciousness resurfaced, I realized I was no longer in the cell. Hard concrete still lay underneath me, but the chilled air was now filled with noise—the hum of traffic, the rumble of a tram rattling past, distant voices rising over the heavy bass beat of music. Obviously, we were no longer at PIT headquarters.

So where the hell had they dumped us?

I rolled onto my back only to discover there were madmen in my head armed with hammers they were not afraid to use. I groaned loudly.

A familiar voice said, "Yeah, I know exactly how you feel."

I cracked open one eye. Jackson sat a couple of feet away, his back propped up against a huge wrought-iron strut that jutted out of the ground at an angle.

I frowned. "How"—the word came out scratchy and I paused, swallowing heavily in an attempt to ease the dryness in my throat—"the hell did we get back to the zipper sculpture?"

"I'm guessing your charming ex had us dumped

here." He shrugged, his gaze sweeping me critically. "You okay?"

"Other than feeling like I've had far too much to drink without the fun of the alcohol, you mean?"

He laughed softly, then groaned. "God, don't make me do that. It hurts."

"Meaning they drugged you, too? Or did they get a little more physical?"

"They drugged me." He paused and added with a wry smile, "Though I wouldn't have minded getting physical. My interrogator was that Fae babe I've sensed a few times but never seen."

Meaning Rochelle, no doubt. "How long have we been here? Do you know?"

He shrugged. "Five minutes or so."

I slowly—carefully—pushed myself into a sitting position. It felt like my head was about to explode and, for several minutes, it was all I could do to keep breathing and not throw up. One thing was certain—I was not going to take fire form anytime soon. Not until I got to Rory, anyway.

Eventually, I said, "Did they order you way from Morretti and the Baltimore investigation?"

"Yeah." He grimaced. "But the drug won't stop me from at least trying to head over to Laverton the minute we get in the cab."

I didn't say anything, just watched as he took a deep, somewhat shuddering breath, then pushed to his feet. He stood there for a moment, body wavering and face green, then carefully shuffled toward me. "Come on. We need to get out of here."

I accepted his offered hand and let him haul me upright, but I wasn't entirely sure in the end who was holding whom upright.

"I'm not going to be able to walk far in this state," I muttered.

"There's a taxi stand down the street."

I frowned. "What about your truck?"

"I don't think it's wise to be driving in this state. I'll retrieve it later." He tucked his arm through mine, and we made our way slowly out of the canal and back onto Flemington Road. It was late, but there were still plenty of cars on the road, their headlights pinning us briefly in brightness before sweeping on.

Two cabs were waiting at the stand. We climbed into the first one, and the driver gave us a somewhat dubious look. "Where to?"

Jackson opened his mouth, but no words came out. He glanced at me, his expression suddenly furious. He really *couldn't* say the Laverton address. I licked my lips, picturing the address in my mind, determination high.

"We need to go," I said, but got no further. The words really *wouldn't* come out.

Jackson swore violently, then said, "Sixty-five Stanley Street, West Melbourne." When I glanced at him, he added, "My office. And home."

I nodded and relaxed back in the seat as the cab took off. It didn't take all that long to get across to Stanley Street. Jackson paid the cabbie; then we both climbed out.

"Wow," I said, looking around. The street was

wide but divided by center parking and pretty flowering trees, and the buildings lining either side of the road were a mix of light industrial and old Victorian. "Close to both the Queen Vic Market *and* Flagstaff Gardens. The rent here must be horrific."

He shrugged, then cupped his hand under my elbow and directed me across the road toward a double-story Victorian building that was little more than two windows wide and squashed between a blacksmith's workshop and an electrical store. "I can write it off, and having the residence above it actually saves me money."

He dug his keys out of his pocket and stopped at the pretty, blue-painted building, opening the wrought-iron gate before ushering me through. I walked up the two steps and leaned against the adjoining wall.

"Hellfire Investigations?" I said dryly. "Really?"

He gave me a weary grin as he brushed past to open the door. "I'm a fire Fae—any business I'm involved in is always going to have a name relating to fire."

"But surely even a Fae could think of something more imaginative."

"Oh, we can and often do." He ushered me inside. "But it usually involves sex. Or sexual positions."

I smiled and studied the long, thin room. It wasn't your traditional office—there was no reception area, just a couple of desks, a half-dozen comfortable chairs, and a line of filing cabinets along the left wall. At the far end of the room, there was a lounge area with several couches and one of the biggest espresso machines I'd ever seen outside a café. Jackson obviously had a serious love for coffee. A spiral staircase sat to one side of this area.

"How many people do you have working for you?"

"No one," he said, relocking the door. "Hellfire's a one-man operation."

"Why? Is it because you're a Fae, and Fae tend to be solitary creatures?"

He hesitated. "If I'm being honest, that *does* play into it. I've certainly been thinking about bringing someone in for a while, but I haven't found anyone I could stand to be with eight hours—or more—a day."

I raised my eyebrows, amusement teasing my lips. "What? Not even a female?"

"Oh, there are plenty of females I could stand being with. I just wouldn't want to work with them." He shrugged. I had a feeling he didn't really care one way or another. He added, "Would you like a cup of tea?"

"Please." I trailed after him as he walked across the room. "So what do we do now?"

"Given the restrictions they've placed on us, we've got no choice but to concentrate on Wilson's murder and somehow find the link to Baltimore."

"But if we *do* find a link, you won't be able to act on it." I sat on the thickly padded arm of one of the couches and crossed my arms. There was a weird mix of fire and ice in my veins, a result of both Sam's kiss and the drug.

Damn it. I could have resisted. I *should* have resisted. But I'd wanted that kiss too much.

And the result?

Confusion. Complete and utter confusion.

While there was no denying the desire that still burned within me, I had to wonder how much of it was fueled by memories of what we'd once had. Because the man I'd tasted in that kiss was very different from the man I'd fallen in love with. *My* Sam was undoubtedly still there, if buried deep. The problem was, I wasn't sure I even *liked* the man he was most of the time, so how the hell could I love him?

I scrubbed a hand through my hair and wished like hell I could travel back in time and erase the events of the last few days. My life had been a whole lot easier, and I hadn't appreciated it enough.

"No, but we can at least pass it on to your cop friend." Water spluttered as Jackson filled a teapot. He glanced over his shoulder. "I take it you're still intending to pursue this?"

"Hell yeah. The bastard's not going to get the better of me."

"Attagirl." He brought the teapot and a cup over to me and placed it on the nearby side table. "You want something to eat?"

"If you've got something sugary, that would be good."

"Iced doughnuts coming up." He returned with a large box of doughnuts, then made his coffee and plonked down on the seat beside me. "Tomorrow we'll start talking to some of Wilson's friends."

I nodded, too busy munching on doughnuts to speak. Between us both, we demolished the entire box of twelve as well as several hot drinks in very quick time.

"And now," he said, collecting both the cups and dumping them in the sink. "It's time for bed."

A smile teased my lips. "Oh, really?"

"Yes, really." He offered me a hand. "To sleep. Nothing more. I promise."

"A Fae going to bed with a woman and actually intending to sleep? Damn, that has to be one for the record books."

He laughed softly, tugged me up into his arms, and dropped a sweet kiss on my lips. It went some way to removing the taste of ashes and darkness.

"Trust me," he said softly, his forehead resting lightly against mine. "It saddens me greatly that I cannot raise anything more than the desire to hold you in my arms. I wish it were otherwise."

"Sleep," I said softly, "is all I really want."

"Good," he said, and tugged me up the stairs.

By the time I woke up, the sunshine flooding the far end of the room was bright and warm, suggesting it was closer to lunchtime than to breakfast. I rolled onto my back and realized I was alone in the bed. A quick look around provided no clue as to where Jackson was, which meant he was probably downstairs.

I stretched the kinks from my body, then scooted upright, hugging my knees as I looked around. Like the floor below, the upper living area was really nothing more than one big, open space. The kitchen was centrally located, and had all the latest mod cons as well as a sink filled with dishes. The living area was on the left side of the room and contained a TV that dominated an entire section of wall, while the bathroom—or at least, the shower and the bath—were in the opposite corner to the right of the bed. An open closet was situated nearby, filled with an untidy mess of clothes. Beyond that was a door, which led into the only separate room on this entire floor—the toilet.

My stomach rumbled a fierce reminder that I really had to feed myself if I wanted to regain the strength I needed to burn the drug out of my body, so I bounced out of bed and padded across to the kitchen. A quick investigation of the fridge provided a can of Coke and half a dozen cold cuts of chicken. I consumed several of those, then grabbed the Coke and went in search of my clothes. After retrieving my phone from my purse, I walked across to the windows. Sunshine caressed my skin, warm and intoxicating. I closed my eyes and let the heat infuse me for several minutes before I dialed Rory.

He answered on the second ring. "How did things go last night?"

"Good and bad." I updated him on all that had

happened, then added, "The drug he gave us was N41A. It not only restricts psychic abilities, but acts as some sort of enforcer. Until it's out of our system, we can't pursue Mark's murder."

"But the minute you burn into spirit form, it'll lose effect."

"Yes, except right now that's not really an option. I'm running rather low on reserves."

"Em, that's a dangerous state to be in with all this shit going down. I can get time off work if you want—"

"No," I cut in. "I mean, yes, we will have to meet later today, but don't take time off. You can't afford it."

"You're far more important to me than any damn job."

I smiled, warmed as much by the caring so evident behind the words as the words themselves. "I know, but given the drug's restrictions against following our one good lead, it's not like we can get ourselves into too much trouble before tonight. I'd like to get ahold of an antidote if there is one, though. I have a feeling the drug will leave Jackson incapacitated longer than either of us might desire. He may be a fire Fae, but it's not like he can become flame and burn it out of his system."

"That may not be a bad thing. I mean, it's Sam's job to catch the bastards behind Mark's murder, not yours or Jackson's."

"I know that. Jackson knows that."

"And neither of you care." He sighed softly. "If

a government department is using that drug, then there's got to be an antidote for it somewhere."

"Which is exactly why I called. Do you think Mike might be able to get his hands on it?"

Mike was one of the teenagers who attended Rory's kung fu classes at a run-down community center in Newport on the weekends. He'd been on the streets since he was eight and had survived by selling his body, stolen goods, and, these days, information and drugs. Not just any drugs, but the hard-to-come-by, black-market kind. The kind a kid his age should never be able to get ahold of.

He and Rory had formed an odd sort of friendship—probably, I think, because Rory accepted rather than judged. He could hardly do anything else when we'd both traveled Mike's path more than once in our lifetimes. You do whatever it takes to survive, and sometimes that "whatever" is neither pleasant nor on the straight and narrow.

"I'll ask. If he doesn't know about it, he might be able to point me in the direction of someone who does."

"Just tell him to be careful. Sam's people tend to play rough. Oh, and don't go back to the apartment yet. Not until we're sure it's safe."

"We'll have to go back there if you want to renew."

"I know. I just don't want to risk either one of us being caught alone at the moment." I paused. "Although to be honest, I wouldn't mind going for a drive to find somewhere remote."

After all, before flameproof rooms had come along, that was exactly what we'd had to do.

"It would be a nice change." I could hear the smile in his voice. "You'll ring?"

"I will. Just don't go home in the meantime."

"I won't. I'll bunk down at Rosie's for a couple of days."

"Good. But if they know as much about phoenixes as they claim, they could well be watching the fire station and you."

"I'll be careful. Just make sure you are. Remember, I want us both to live to old age this time around."

He hung up. I tossed the phone back onto the pile of my clothes, then finished the Coke and went in search of Jackson.

I found him at one of the desks downstairs. "Do you often work at your desk naked?"

"Only when I think it might induce a pretty lady to come sit on my lap." He caught my hand and tugged me toward him. "I was, however, beginning to think said pretty lady was intending to sleep all day."

I sat astride him and wrapped my arms loosely around his neck. Need stirred within, need that was both sexual and something stronger. Fiercer. "Hunger got the better of me."

"So it seems." He dropped a quick kiss on my lips. "Sadly, it seems to be for chicken rather than me."

"Hey, I'm here now, aren't I?" I shifted, and his breath hitched. The heat within him rose several notches. I flared my nostrils, drawing it in, allowing his warmth to slither through me, refueling the ragged edges of my soul. I was careful, though. He might be a Fae, but I couldn't take too much of his heat for fear of weakening him. But then, all I really needed was enough to keep the edge of utter exhaustion away. "So what dragged you out of a warm bed?"

"Thoughts about Mrs. Wilson." He brushed his thumbs across my nipples. Delight skittered through me.

"Not erotic thoughts, I hope."

"Hardly. Although I'm having a few now."

So was I. "What kind of thoughts were you having about her, then?"

Rather than answering, he shifted one hand, gripping the back of my neck to hold me still as his lips claimed mine again. The kiss became a long, slow dance of exploration and pleasure. Neither of us was breathing very steadily by the time he broke away.

"It's your fault."

I ran a fingertip down his abs. "What is?"

The question was absently said. Right now, I wasn't really caring about anything more than the tension that lay between us. I slid back on his lap to expose his erection, then played my fingertips across it. His cock leapt with every light caress, as if begging for more.

"Me being down here instead of in bed." His voice, little more than a low growl, made my senses hum. "You suggested Wilson's wife would have had some sense of him being in trouble—even if she didn't want to confront or admit the situation."

"So?"

"So," he murmured, his concentration seemingly more on caressing my breasts than what he was saying. "It just got me wondering whether Mrs. Wilson was as clueless as I'd thought, so I came down here to do a little investigating."

I slid my fingers down the length of his shaft, then gently cupped his balls. His breath hitched again. I smiled impishly and began massaging him, the rhythm of my movements echoing his. "And what did you discover?"

"That she is not as clueless as she appears."

"Surprise, surprise." I removed my fingers, then slid myself over his shaft, letting my wetness coat him as I slowly moved up and down the length of him.

"Yeah," he said, voice a little strained. "Seems she and Wilson hadn't known each other very long before they were married."

He ducked his head and caught one nipple in his teeth, teasing it lightly. Shivers of delight skittered through me. He released me abruptly, then swirled his tongue around the puckered, aching nipple, his touch light and erotic. I closed my eyes and simply enjoyed. But as my movements against his shaft got ever stronger, he groaned, gripped my hips, then thrust inside me.

For several moments, I didn't speak, didn't move, didn't do anything more than simply enjoy the sensation of him being so very deeply inside. "How did you discover that?"

"Our Mrs. Wilson has a Facebook page. She announced she'd met the man of her dreams in May of last year, then declared they were getting married a month later."

"Wow. One of them is a fast worker."

"Hmm," he agreed; then his lips caught mine again, and there was no discussion about Mrs. Wilson *or* her Facebook page for many, many minutes—just a whole lot of passion and heat. Heat that ran through me, fed me, even as I fought the urge to take all that I needed and leave him depleted. We came as one, our groans echoing through the large room as our bodies shook and shuddered. He made one final thrust, then briefly rested his forehead against mine, his breath warm against my lips.

"That," he said eventually, "is a fine way to start the morning."

"Except," I noted, brushing the sweaty strands of his hair from his cheek with my fingertips. "It is no longer morning."

"Let's not quibble over minor differences." He dropped a kiss on my lips, then said, "So, Mrs. Wilson. Not only did our loving couple have an extremely fast courtship, but they were married the same month as Wilson began his red plague research."

"What a coincidence," I said dryly. I was still sitting astride him, and I couldn't help but notice that while he might have only just come, he was more than half-ready to go a second round. Fae, it seemed, were insatiable.

"I'm gathering this led you to dig deeper into our Mrs. Wilson's past."

"It did indeed." He slid his hands down to my butt and then lifted me up and deposited me feet-first onto the floor. To say I was surprised was an understatement. He grinned. "You need to turn around and look at the computer."

I did so. On the screen was an image of a pretty blonde with pale blue eyes and a cherub's face. "Easy to see why Wilson might have fallen hard for her, although a pretty face doesn't mean she was up to no good. And if Sam suspected that she was, he would have already investigated her."

"Indeed," Jackson agreed. He reached around me and clicked open another screen. "Especially since dear Amanda has been married a number of times before."

I raised my eyebrows. "And did those unions all end in a bloodthirsty manner?"

"If you're asking if she killed them, then no, apparently not. One husband died in a car crash, two were divorced, and I haven't been able to track down the other, simply because she married him overseas and it apparently didn't last past the honeymoon."

"Four—five—husbands?" I blinked and studied the blonde. "She doesn't look old enough to have had that many already!"

"She doesn't keep them very long. She's been married to Wilson the longest."

I studied the blonde in the picture for a moment, knowing there had to be something else here. I could feel the excitement thrumming through Jackson, and while part of that was undoubtedly sexual, there was definitely more to it than that.

"So," I said slowly, "it begs the question, what was she after? Money, or something more?"

His lips brushed my neck. "I do so love the way your mind works." He reached past me and opened another screen. Information scrolled up. "Husband one was a biochemist, hubby two a bioengineer, three worked in the weapons department for the military, and four is a black-market fence, from what I can gather."

"So, aside from that one blip, it seems she has a thing for researchers."

"Or a thing for the information or items she could get from them."

Which we wouldn't know until we uncovered more about her. Even so, she was looking less like a clueless blonde and more like a schemer. I swung around and faced him. "So what happened to the husbands after she left or divorced them?"

"Ah, that's where it gets *really* interesting. Husband one was sacked two days before his accident. Husbands two and three also lost their jobs and were found dead a few days later. Suicide was the coroner's official verdict. As I said, I'm still trying to uncover what happened to four."

"Meaning our Mrs. Wilson is something of a latent black widow?"

"Possibly."

More than possibly, I suspected. "Why did the first three lose their jobs?"

"It seems there were . . . discrepancies . . . in their departments."

I raised my eyebrows. "Discrepancies?"

"Labs being broken into, research going missing, that sort of stuff."

"And the husbands were blamed?"

"They took the fall because they were in charge."

Uh-huh. "We *really* need to talk to her."

"We do." He dropped a kiss on my nose, then caught my hand and tugged me toward the stairs. "But not before I've ravished you senseless."

"I really think talking to Mrs. Black Widow could be a little more important than sex."

"Well, yeah, but Mrs. Black Widow is currently at the hairdresser, and that usually takes at least an hour, doesn't it?"

I followed him up the stairs. "How do you know this? Facebook?"

"Nope. I read her calendar when I was interviewing her."

"How do you know she's not just getting a quick trim?"

He gave me a long look over his shoulder. "Anyone would think you were looking for an escape clause. All you have to do is say no, you know."

I grinned. "I'm just worried that Sam will get there before we do and that he'll somehow ensure we lose any clues we might otherwise have gained."

"If he were investigating the wife, he would have done so by now."

We reached the top of the landing but continued toward the shower rather than the bed. He was obviously intending to combine two necessities. "Now, how about we quit the questions and just concentrate on the business at hand?"

I grinned as he tugged me closer. "Concentrating as ordered, sir."

And I did.

"So," he said, stopping his truck several doors up from Mrs. Wilson's house. "Who were you talking to when you first woke up?"

He had good ears, because I hadn't been talking that loud. "Rory."

"And who's Rory when he's home?" He shifted in his seat to look at me, but his expression was nothing more than curious.

"Every phoenix is one of a pair. He's mine."

His eyebrows raised. "He's your *mate*?"

"Not exactly." I half shrugged. "He's my lover, my friend, the other half of my soul, and the only man I can ever have children with. But we cannot, and do not, love each other. Not in the romantic sense."

"Really? What the hell did your people do to earn that sort of curse?"

"*That* is a million-dollar question, I'm afraid."

He shook his head. "Does that mean you're unable to fall in love at all?"

"No. We can and do, but it's part of the curse

that our relationships end badly. I don't think I've heard of one phoenix having a happy ending in all the centuries I've been alive. Certainly, I've never had one."

"But just because you haven't heard about it—or experienced it—doesn't mean it *can't* happen."

"Well, no. And I certainly keep hoping every time I'm reborn that *this* will be the one time it's different." I shrugged. "But I know for sure it's not *this* lifetime."

He eyed me for a moment, then said, "Because of Sam."

"Another one loved and lost, I'm afraid."

"That sucks. *Big*-time."

"Living forever always has a drawback. This curse is ours."

"Vampires don't seem to have many drawbacks."

"They live on blood and they can't ever walk in sunshine." My voice was dry. "Those are pretty big drawbacks in my book."

"Neither would worry me—especially if it meant more time chasing luscious ladies." He paused, looking thoughtful. "So have you and Rory had any kids?"

"We've only had five, because we aren't fertile every rebirth." I shrugged. "I haven't seen any of our children for a generation or so. Phoenix offspring don't tend to linger near the family nest once they find their mate."

"And how does *that* happen? I take it there's a

bit more involved than dating until you find the right one."

I smiled. "We don't date. At the age of sixteen, a ceremony is performed and our mates are revealed. From there on in, you're bonded for life."

He frowned. "What if you happen to hate your bonded partner?"

"That would totally suck, but it's never happened. Fate's not *that* cruel."

"I wouldn't bet on that." He glanced at his watch and his frown deepened. "How long does it normally take to get your hair done?"

I blinked at the sudden change of topic. "Around two hours if she's getting it dyed." Not that I actually knew for sure, as I never got anything other than a cut. Phoenixes aged normally through each cycle, but I'd grown rather fond of the gray over the years. "Why?"

"Because she should have been back by now."

"Maybe she went shopping or something afterward."

"Maybe." His frown deepened. "I've just got this itchy feeling something's not right."

"I didn't think intuition was a Fae thing." My gaze swept the street. There was a white car parked several doors up from Wilson's place and a woman cutting roses in a garden farther along the street, but neither pricked any sensation of wrongness.

"Generally, it's not." He frowned at the house for several moments longer, then dug his phone out of his pocket and made a phone call.

"Your secret source *has* to be a copper," I noted

in amusement once he'd finished. "Very few other people would be able to get you the location of a car via its GPS *that* quickly."

"Maybe." His voice was noncommittal. "But apparently, her vehicle is sitting in the driveway of her home."

I glanced at the empty driveway. "Someone's removed the GPS system."

"Which suggests the itchy feeling may have been spot-on." A devilish light entered his eyes. "Shall we go investigate?"

"If you break and enter, Sam *will* throw you in jail."

"Only if he catches us. Come on."

I shook my head, but climbed out and waited while he fidgeted in the back of the truck for several minutes. The day was bright and warm, and I tugged off the light sweater I'd borrowed from Jackson, allowing the sunshine to caress my skin and continue the refuel of my inner fires—although soon I'd need more than just sunshine and the threads of energy I could steal from Jackson, and that meant getting back to Rory.

Jackson shoved several items into his pockets and then headed up the driveway. I followed, then watched from several steps away as he knocked on the door. It was loud, but had an oddly hollow sound, which, for some reason, had visions of death stirring.

I rubbed my arms lightly. I was no stranger to the variations of death, but that didn't mean I ever welcomed its appearance.

Jackson stepped to one side and peered in through the window. "Not a lot to see—other than dust."

"Given her husband just died, dusting would be the last thing on her mind."

He gave me a wry look. "Remember we're talking about a potential black widow here."

"I know, but she'd at least want to stay in character until the inquest into her husband's death was over."

"True."

He stepped back, gave the front of the house a once-over, then stepped off the veranda and moved around to the backyard. He peered in a few windows, then gripped the back door handle and hit the door hard with his left shoulder. The lock gave way with very little fuss.

"Remind me to get our locks replaced with stronger ones when I get home," I said.

He gave me a somewhat absent grin. "There is no such thing as a Fae-proof lock."

"Then I shall coat the door with silver or something."

"Which would not stop me or anyone else from getting into your home if we were determined enough." He took two cautious steps inside, then stopped abruptly and swore.

"What?" I said immediately.

"Blood." He put a hand into a pocket and pulled out some rubber gloves, handing one pair to me. "Wipe the door handle with your sweater, will you?"

"How bad is the blood scent?" I tugged the sweater free from my waist and gave the handle a thorough wipe-down.

"Bad enough." He hesitated and lowered his voice. "But there's something else here, a scent I can't quite put my finger on."

"Something you've smelled before?"

"Or *someone*."

Sparks flickered across my fingertips, bright but not dangerous. I wasn't sure whether it was a result of the drug or my own lack of strength, but either way, it meant that if we *were* attacked, I'd be relying on my earthier skills rather than my elemental ones. I licked the trepidation from my lips and said, "Is that someone still here?"

"I don't know. I can't smell anything that suggests he is, but then, I didn't last time, either." He glanced over his shoulder and added, "Close the door behind you. We don't want the neighbors seeing the open door and reporting it."

I pulled on the gloves, then closed the door and drew in several deep breaths. The scents he could smell so clearly weren't evident to me.

We moved quietly from the laundry room into the kitchen. It was small but neat, but there were dishes draining on the sink and fat congealed on the top of the water. I dipped my gloved fingers into it. Stone-cold. Much like the house, really.

I followed Jackson into the next room. Again, it was as neat as a pin, and other than the light coating of dust over the wooden surfaces, there was nothing out of place. But the living room was even colder than the kitchen, and as I rubbed my arms, I realized why. The AC was not only on, but set to near freezing.

Jackson moved into the shadowed hallway beyond the living area. A cautious check of several rooms that led off it revealed neither our black widow nor anyone else, yet the tension in Jackson seemed to be growing. Whatever he smelled was obviously getting stronger. The final room turned out to be the main bedroom, and it was in here that we found Amanda Wilson. She lay on her back, one hand tucked under her neck and her long hair streaming across her pillow. If not for red splatters across the nearby pillow and the paleness of her skin, it would have been easy to believe she was asleep. She looked at peace. Happy even.

But maybe *that* was because she hadn't been alone in the bed before her death. Not if the indent in the other pillows and the state of the sheets and blankets were anything to go by. Obviously, the vampire responsible for this had taken his pleasure both physically and through her blood—although judging by the blood on the pillow, he was one messy feeder.

Jackson stepped over the bundle of bedsheets dumped on the carpet near the end of the bed and carefully gripped her chin, turning her head to one side to reveal a deep and ugly bite wound. I closed my eyes briefly and took a deep breath, but it did little to calm the instinctive rush of distaste and fear. Though I was more than aware that not all vamps got off on vicious blood taking—that indeed it was usually an orgasmic experience for *both* parties—my encounter with the vamp who'd sucked me dry had left me more than a little wary of them. Not to mention a total unwillingness to get anywhere near them sexually.

Obviously, though, Amanda had shared no such unwillingness.

"Oh fuck," Jackson said suddenly. "She's *alive*."

"What? How? Her lips are blue and she's not breathing—"

"She *is*, but it's so shallow it's practically unnoticeable. Call an ambulance before we lose her."

I dragged out my phone as he pulled the covers up and spread them over her.

But before I could dial, something solid hit the back of my head and sent me flying.

CHAPTER 10

I hit the wall face-first and pain exploded. For several seconds I saw nothing but stars dancing happily in black space; then hands grabbed me, pulled me around, and threw me again. This time, when I hit, there was a splintering sound, and I came down in a shower of wood and glass.

Dressing table, I thought fuzzily, and instinctively reached for my flames. Nothing happened. Nothing more than a slight fizz of heat that faded as quickly as it rose. I swore and groped for something, anything, to use as a weapon. There was blood in my mouth, my vision was blurry, and there was a roaring in my head.

But I still heard the heavy approach of footsteps.

My fingers found wood, but it was too small, too thin, to use as a weapon. I swept my fingers around desperately for something better and hit glass. A long, thick shard. I wrapped my fingers around it and gripped it tight. The ragged edges sliced into my skin, but I made no move, no sound, as those steps drew closer.

Feet appeared in front of my face. Big feet encased in heavy black boots. The kind that could do serious damage if they stomped down on my head. Tension slithered through me, the need to move warring with the need to be still and play helpless. Whoever this was, he was strong. Without my fires, all I had was surprise. My grip on the glass tightened. Blood began to ooze past my fingers and soak into the carpet.

He bent down, grabbed the back of my shirt, and hauled me upright. Heat rolled over me— heat and the pungent musk of man and sweat— and I realized my attacker was a werewolf rather than a vampire. Which explained the strength. It was a thought that quickly vanished as he held me at arm's length and gave me a toothy grin.

"You should have done as the cop suggested," he said. "Because now you have to die."

Shock rolled through me. Sam had been the only cop to warn me away from the case, but surely even *he* wouldn't resort to this sort of violence.

But he's changed, the internal voice whispered. *He's not the man you once knew.*

No, I thought, he wasn't, but I still refused to believe he was behind this attack. I battered away the lingering uncertainty and said, through puffing lips, "I've done the whole death thing more than once, and I have to say, I'm not quite ready to do it again."

With that, I plunged the shard of glass as hard as I could into his gut.

He released me instinctively and screamed—

but it was a sound that held fury rather than pain. I landed in a heap at his feet, but I didn't stay there. I twisted, swept my leg around, and knocked him off balance. He half fell, and I threw myself forward, knocking him back and sideways.

But he was a man *and* a werewolf, and that meant fast reflexes and greater strength. The advantage I'd gained in unbalancing him lay in seconds, not minutes, and he was up almost as fast as I was. I hastily wiped at the blood gushing from my nose, then ran at him again. I hit shoulder first, and the jagged edge of the shard sliced into me even as I drove it deeper into his gut. He flailed backward and crashed into the closet doors. With a howl that was still more fury than pain, he ripped the shard from his flesh and flung it away.

And in that instant, I knew my time was up. If I didn't drop him now, it'd be me on the floor, not him.

I leapt at him, feet-first. He saw me coming and twisted sideways, but his gut wound had at least slowed him enough that it didn't matter. I hit his left knee side-on, and there was a loud crack. His leg collapsed from underneath him and he went down hard to one knee.

But the bastard just wouldn't *fall*.

I hit the carpet yet again, sucked in a shuddery breath, and half turned. Saw his fist arcing toward me and flung myself desperately out of the way. The punch missed, but the heavy rings on his fingers gouged my skin. It hurt. God, how it hurt. But I thrust the pain aside and scrambled away from him.

Hands grabbed my right leg and dragged me back. I half yelped, then twisted around, kicking at his face with my free leg. It missed and he laughed, the sound fierce and cold. His gaze met mine, and all I saw was death.

Flames flared across my fingertips. They contained little in the way of heat, but it was all I had left, so I flung them at him. His eyes went wide; then he released me and threw himself out of their way. Another roar escaped his lips as he came down on the knee I'd broken; then the flames hit him, and he screamed again as they shimmered up his legs.

I didn't wait for him to realize they contained no heat. I lunged at him, slipped my hand under the cuff of his jeans, and grabbed his ankle. The minute my fingers wrapped around his flesh, the fires within responded, sucking in the heat of him, feeding on it. I drank it fast, robbing him of warmth and energy, until his skin was gray and shivers racked his body. It wasn't enough; I wanted—needed—more, but if I took it all, I'd kill him. And as desperately appealing as that thought was, we needed answers more.

I unlocked my fingers and peeled them away from his flesh, leaving the imprint of my hand on his skin—a lasting reminder of our fight—then took a deep, shuddering breath. It did little to quell the urge to finish what I'd started.

But as my breathing calmed, I became aware of the sounds. Grunts and the smack of flesh against flesh.

The werewolf hadn't come alone.

Jackson.

I scrambled to my feet, lunged for the biggest piece of splintered wood I could manage, then ran for the door. Jackson fought a man who was little more than a shadow. The two of them appeared evenly matched, going blow for blow, their bodies shuddering under the impact of each hit. Jackson had the mother of a bruise forming under his eye and slashes along his cheeks and arms. The vamp obviously wasn't afraid to use his nails.

I took a step toward them. The vamp hit Jackson hard, sending him staggering, then spun and ran for me. He was lightning fast, and I really had no time to do anything more than raise the wood.

He didn't see it. He just ran straight into it.

The jagged edges rammed into his body just below his ribs, and blue fire instantly exploded from the wound, consuming the wood as it rolled across his body.

He screamed, burned, blackened. Fell.

I stepped back and rubbed my arms, my stomach rolling as the pungent scent of burning flesh and meat filled the air. He stopped screaming, stopped writhing, but still the fire consumed him, until there was nothing left but ashes and the cindered remains of the carpet underneath him. At least it was a quick death, and that was probably more than he deserved.

"Damn it, Em," Jackson growled. "I wanted to question him."

My gaze shot to his. "It wasn't like I *meant* to do that. It was more luck and instinct than thought."

"Yeah, I know. It's just damn annoying that every step forward in this case is followed by two steps back."

"In this particular case, it's only one step. The other one is still alive."

"Really? Well done, you." He thrust a bloodied hand through his hair. "We'd better check Amanda before we interrogate him, though. You want to make that call to the paramedics?"

I followed him into the bedroom to retrieve my phone. Jackson glanced at the werewolf and then back at me. "Damn, that's a mountain, not a wolf. *Very* well done, you."

"The bastard very nearly got the better of me." I bent to pick up my phone, but that just made the blood oozing from my nose flow faster, and half the screen was covered in an instant. I walked over to the bedside table and grabbed some tissues.

"He didn't, and that's all that matters."

I guess. I shoved the tissues up my nose to help stop the bleeding, then called an ambulance.

"How is she?" I asked when I'd finished.

"She's still alive." He tossed me a handkerchief. "It's clean. You might want to use it on your hand."

I quickly wrapped it around the cut, but it didn't do a whole lot. "Let's hope she remains that way. If the wolf can't tell us much, she could be our only hope."

"I can't imagine your ex is going to allow us to talk to her once he finds out about our adventures here."

He was right. Sam would close out this avenue of investigation just as surely as he'd closed off Morretti. He might not use a drug to do it, but he didn't need to. All he had to do was place Amanda under protective custody.

"We could always ring the police rather than him. It might only delay the inevitable confrontation, but it would at least give us *some* time to question her."

"It's worth a shot. But when you *do* talk to the bastard again, give him a fucking earful about drugging us. Not having our fires could have gotten us both killed today."

I raised an eyebrow. "And do you think he'd care?"

"Probably not." He walked around the bed. "Ring the cops. I'll tie up our thug and do a quick search through the house."

"It might be a good idea to drag him into another room. If the paramedics arrive before his healing fully kicks in, they'll want to treat the bastard."

And while I wasn't against scum getting medical help when they needed it, after what he'd helped do to Amanda Wilson, a little bit of pain and suffering was the least he deserved. Besides, his wounds were already showing signs of healing.

"*That* is another good idea."

"I'm full of them today," I said, voice dry.

"My usual response to a statement like that is 'full of shit, more likely.'" He sent a cheeky grin my way. "However, I sincerely desire you in my bed tonight, so I shall restrain the urge."

"Oh, I'm *so* glad to hear it."

He laughed, then grabbed the wolf's arms and none too gently dragged him into the next room. While he tied up our captive with some wire coat hangers he found in the closet—which, under normal circumstances, wouldn't have held him for long—I called the cops. With that done, we searched Amanda's house.

Unsurprisingly, we didn't find anything useful.

As the distant wail of the approaching ambulance began to cut through the air, Jackson said, "We're out of time. Let's go question that wolf."

I followed him into the back bedroom. The wolf hadn't moved, but his skin had lost its gray pallor and his breathing seemed easier. If he wasn't yet conscious, he was damn close to it.

Jackson grabbed a fistful of the wolf's shirt, pulled him partially upright, then slapped his face. Hard. The sound reverberated through the stillness. "Stop foxing, you furry bastard."

The wolf made a low sound that seemed to rumble up from the depths of his boots. It wasn't a particularly dangerous sound, but that he was conscious enough to even do it meant he was a whole lot stronger than I'd presumed. I could have drained him more. *Should* have drained him more. I crossed my arms and tried to ignore the somewhat angry thought.

After another slap from Jackson, the wolf's eyes opened into slits and he all but growled, "What?"

"Who sent you here?" Jackson said, voice sharp.

"Sindi—" The wolf's voice petered out, and he coughed. Blood speckled his lips. I wondered if the cause was internal damage or Jackson's slap, but I didn't really care either way.

Jackson shook him. "The sindicati?"

The wolf groaned. Jackson's expression showed very little in the way of pity. "Why would the sindicati want Amanda Wilson dead?"

"Connected—"

"She's working for them?" I cut in, though I wasn't entirely surprised. If Amanda had been an ordinary black widow, surely she would have aimed for millionaires rather than researchers. She certainly had the looks to snag one. And researchers, while very well paid, didn't make *bundles* of money, especially those who worked for the military or the government. Or at least, my boss hadn't.

Unless, of course, it was the thrill of the chase she enjoyed more than anything else.

"Not just them. Subcontractor." His answer this time was stronger. Clearer.

Angrier.

Jackson's gaze met mine. "A black widow who subcontracts her services? *That's* a new one."

It certainly was. I returned my gaze to the werewolf. "So the sindicati employed her to keep tabs on Wilson?"

"And report on his research, yeah." He took a shuddering breath, and I could almost see the tide of strength flush through his body.

"But if that's the case," I began, letting sparks dance across my fingertips. It couldn't hurt to remind him he wasn't the only nonhuman in the room, even if the sparks were as dangerous as I got right now. "Why were you sent here to kill her?"

If the look the werewolf gave me was any indication, I was dead meat the next time we met. "Because Wilson's dead and they have no further use for her."

"But why not give her a new victim?" Jackson asked. "Surely she's too valuable an asset to waste?"

"Don't ask me—I'm just a subcontractor. You're lucky I know as much as I do."

"Meaning we obviously need to talk to the man who employed you—his name?"

The wolf hesitated. Jackson shook him. Hard. Breath hissed through the wolf's clenched teeth and his eyes narrowed even further—and yet again promised death.

After a moment, he said, "Henry Morretti."

"Surprise, surprise," I muttered.

Jackson's expression was as grim as mine undoubtedly was. "And how were you supposed to contact Morretti after the job had been done?"

"Phone call. Payment is cash, sent by courier."

Which was all very clinical and efficient. No face-to-face contact, no paper trails to trace. I was betting even the courier who delivered the cash wouldn't tell us much—especially given we were dealing with vamps who could easily erase or re-arrange memories. It made me wonder whether Henry Morretti even existed. It was more than possible it was just a cover name.

"I've given you what you want," the big wolf growled. "The least you can do is let me go before the cops get here."

Jackson looked at me, eyebrow raised. "What do you think?"

I paused, as if considering the request, then shook my head.

"I totally agree."

And with that, Jackson threw a punch so force-ful the wolf's head snapped back and his body went limp. Jackson checked his pulse, made a satisfied-sounding grunt, then released his grip on the wolf's shirt. The big man hit the carpet with a heavy thump. Jackson stepped over his legs and met my gaze. "The ambulance is almost here. It might be worth you going to the hospital with Amanda, just in case she wakes and feels the urge to talk."

"I'm not family, so they're not likely to let me sit in her room with her." Besides, I hated hospitals and tended to avoid them unless there was abso-lutely no other choice.

"Lie and say you are. It's not like they'll ask you for ID. They rarely do in emergencies." He handed me his car keys. "Besides, your hand needs stitches if the state of the handkerchief is anything to go by."

I glanced down to see blood dripping from the sodden handkerchief. "What are you going to do? Wait for the cops to arrive?"

"I'd better, if only for the sake of the cops. Wounded or not, our wolf could take out two humans without blinking an eyelid." He cocked his head, expression intent. "There are two sirens approaching. The cops were obviously close."

And wasn't Sam going to be happy that we'd rung the police rather than him. By the same token, our reluctance shouldn't really come as a surprise given what he'd done to us. "I'll give you a call if there's any news."

Jackson nodded. I headed for the front door to let the paramedics and the cops in.

Several hours later, sporting a freshly stitched and bandaged hand, I somehow managed to convince the hospital staff I was Amanda's sister and was allowed into her treatment room.

"How is she?" I asked, as the nurse checked Amanda's charts and made some notes.

"She's been stabilized and given blood, and we've treated the nasty bite on her neck, but otherwise, she's fine. She might want to stop playing around with vampires, though. This was a close call."

It should have been *more* than close. If Jackson and I had been a few minutes later, our black widow would have been well and truly dead. "If she's got any brains, she will after this."

"I'd be *making* her if she were my sister. I wouldn't let any of them damn leeches near the neck of someone I loved." The nurse's smile was grim. "She's just lucky you found her in time."

"That she was."

The nurse hung the clipboard back on the end of her bed. "I'll be back in twenty to check her again."

Once the nurse had left, I walked over to the lone chair sitting to the right of the bed and dug my phone out of my purse as I sat down. I hit Jackson's number, intending to give him an update, then realized there was no reception in this part of the hospital. I cursed softly and moved the phone around in the vague hope it might make a difference. Still nothing.

"And who the hell might you be?" Amanda's voice was low, but it held a surprising amount of strength for someone who had been hours—if not minutes—from death.

"I'm the person who saved your life, as you no doubt heard the nurse say." I relaxed back into the chair and pushed the record button on my phone as I put it away. "And you really should be more careful about who you go to bed with."

The confusion that flickered across her face actually seemed genuine. "What do you mean?"

"I mean, you shouldn't go to bed with a vampire and a werewolf. Especially when you've reached the end of your usefulness to your employer."

"I'm hardly likely to have bedded a man, let alone a wolf and a vamp. That wouldn't have—" She cut herself off with a cough.

"Wouldn't have looked good to the cops who are still investigating your husband's death," I finished for her. "How long will it take them to make the black widow connection, do you think?"

"I have no idea what you mean," she said, with such sincerity that I was almost tempted to believe her. Almost.

I crossed my legs and regarded her steadily for several seconds. If she was at all unnerved, she didn't show it. Eventually, I said, "I noticed you ignored my jibe about your employer. That might not be wise, given what's happened."

"Look, as I've already said, I have no idea what you're talking about. If you don't get out of here, I'm going to call security."

"You do that," I agreed. "And the minute I'm outside, I'll ring Henry Morretti and tell him exactly where you are. I bet this time he'll send a better grade of executioner."

Her eyebrows rose and her expression remained one of mild confusion. She should have been an actress rather than a black widow—she could have won an Academy Award with performances like this. "I still have no idea what you're talking about."

"I'm talking about the vampire who almost bled you dry and the werewolf who fucked you while the vampire drained you. Both were sent by Henry Morretti." I shook my head, my expression one of mock sadness. "Seems Morretti thought you'd reached the end of your usefulness."

"Look, as I've already said—"

"Fine." I thrust to my feet. "I'll just go make that phone call, then."

I was almost out of the treatment room when she said, "No, wait."

I turned and crossed my arms. "Why should I, when you apparently don't know what I'm talking about?"

She waved a hand, the motion elegance itself. "If what you're saying is true about the vamp and the wolf, why, then, did you save me?"

"Because I'm investigating the death of your husband, and it would be hard to question you if you were dead."

"But you wouldn't mind me being dead otherwise, if your tone is anything to go by."

"Totally wouldn't mind, but that's beside the point."

"At least you're honest." Her brief smile held very little in the way of amusement. "Are you a cop?"

"No. Personally, I would rather avoid involving the cops at the moment. I'm thinking you might want to, too."

"Possibly." She pursed her lips. "And just to put things straight, I didn't go to bed with either a vamp or a wolf."

"Perhaps not knowingly, but you must have let that vamp into the house. He couldn't have crossed the threshold uninvited."

"I let a plumber in—" She paused. "Guess I need to check credentials a little closer, huh?"

"If you're going to keep playing with pond scum like the sindicati, then, yeah, that might be wise."

"The sindicati pay in good, clean cash and, for a subcontractor like myself, they're a viable business option."

"Except when they believe you have come to the end of your usefulness to them."

She frowned. "That's what I don't understand. This is not the first time I've worked for them, and I'm very good at what I do. I cannot understand why they would wish to end my services in such a permanent manner."

I didn't really understand it, either, but then, I wasn't a vampire crime boss. "Did the sindicati order the hit on Professor Wilson?"

We already knew it was the red cloaks who'd killed him, but it never hurt to double-check.

"No. Why would they? They needed him alive to keep working on his research, as he hadn't pinned down all the enzymes that are apparently responsible for a human becoming a vampire."

So much for Jackson's theory that the red-cloaked figure had been nothing but a ruse. "Are you sure? Because another professor who was undertaking research similar to your husband's was murdered this week, and it seems very likely it was ordered by the sindicati."

"Perhaps it was, but I do not know or care about the sindicati or their plans for other researchers.

My job was to keep tabs on Wilson and his research, and that's precisely what I did."

"And ethics be damned?"

She shrugged. "Men and women have been using sex to get what they want for eons. I merely use it to get information for my clients." Her smile was cool. "And trust me, the men I bed get the better end of the deal. They have me at their beck and call."

"But afterward, they're left behind to take the blame."

"If they live," she murmured. "Not all of them do."

Which made me wonder just how many other "husbands" she'd had and how many of them were still alive today. I had a bad feeling there was a whole lot more dirt swept under this woman's carpet than what we'd already uncovered.

"So how do you get the information? Pillow talk, or by breaking into his computer and copying his files?"

"Nothing so crass. I'm a telepath with a photographic memory. I might not understand what I steal, but I never forget it."

A handy talent for a thief to have. "How do you get the information to the sindicati?"

She smiled again. A blond-haired shark with perfect white teeth. "You came here wanting information in exchange for saving my life. Why don't we make a deal?"

"What, saving your life isn't enough?"

"Well, no, because I need to be alive for you to

get your information. Therefore, I have leverage and you do not."

"And contacting the sindicati isn't a good enough form of leverage in your eyes?"

"Oh, it's a great form of leverage, but there is one major problem. You can't get reception here in the hospital, and the minute you leave, I'm gone. You'd lose not only me, but any additional information I might hold."

All of which was true, damn it. I eyed her warily. "What sort of deal?"

"In return for answering your questions, I want your help in removing myself from the sindicati's reach."

"I'm thinking there's probably not going to be many areas in Australia that meet that criteria." And maybe very few overseas.

"I agree, which is why I intend to flee overseas once I'm out of this state. I have passports and clothing at a safe place ready to go. All I need is transport there and then on to the airport."

"A deal that certainly gives you more than it gives me."

"Unless, of course, the information I might have also includes a hard drive containing not only every scrap of information I stole from Wilson, but every detail of anyone I ever dealt with in the sindicati."

I blinked and her shark smile got bigger.

"It always pays to have some form of backup plan."

"So why don't you use said backup to exchange for your freedom?"

"Because, as you said, they have obviously—for whatever reason—decided it is safer to be rid of me than use me again. Therefore, they will merely agree to the exchange and then kill me anyway." She raised an eyebrow. "I am fully aware of what my employers are capable of. Do we have a deal?"

I hesitated, but I had no real choice and we both knew it. Not if I wanted the answers that might well be hidden somewhere in those files. Besides, given Morretti was currently off-limits investigation-wise, it couldn't hurt to have a secondary option in the sindicati to chase down and question.

"Okay. Deal."

She held out her hand. "Shake on it."

I leaned forward and clasped her hands. Electricity buzzed across my senses, and I smiled. "Sorry, but I'm one of those people who can't be read telepathically."

"Well, damn." She didn't seem too put out, however. She pushed upright in the bed and pressed the buzzer for the nurse. "Let's get out of here first; then we'll play twenty questions."

I raised my eyebrows. "I doubt they'll release you that quickly."

"They can't actually stop me. Besides, we both know that my only chance to escape unscathed is in the next few hours. Once the sindicati realize what has happened to their assassins, more will be unleashed."

Undoubtedly. The nurse came in, and for the next half hour, Amanda argued her case about being released. Eventually, the hospital staff gave up and brought in an Against Medical Advice form for her to sign. She did so, then, still in her hospital gown and wearing my coat, followed me into the parking lot.

"Right," I said, starting Jackson's truck. "Where to?"

"Southern Cross Station."

I raised my eyebrows. "You hid passports and clothes at a train station?"

"Best place," she said. "And close to public transport should I need a quick escape."

At least she wouldn't be escaping quickly in her current getup. Not when she wanted to avoid notice, anyway.

"Okay," I said, once we were headed into the city. "Time to start upholding your end of the deal. What have you been told about Wilson's death?"

She shrugged. "Not much. The police simply said a man in a red-hooded cloak all but sliced him to pieces."

"And his body? Has it been released by the coroner yet?" If it had been, then maybe Jackson could use his contact again and get us the coroner's report. It might not help, but it couldn't hurt, either.

"No, it hasn't, simply because there was no body."

I blinked. "What?"

"There was no body." Her expression was amused. This time, the emotion was real. "The thug in the red cloak took his body with him when he ran off."

"But that makes no sense."

Why kill him in broad daylight and then snatch his body? Were the red cloaks making some kind of statement? Or was there something else going on? Something that was far bigger than this investigation—bigger, maybe, than even Sam realized?

I had a *bad* feeling that might be the case.

And was it possible, I thought with a chill, that they'd snatched Wilson's body to ensure *they* had him when he came to?

Sam had said the red plague virus was spread through either cuts or bites, which meant that if Wilson hadn't been killed, he would have been infected. So what if the virus reacted to death the same way sharing the blood of a vampire reacted in the human body? That is, on death, it put them into a coma while the body made the change from one form to the other?

Maybe he'd merely *looked* dead. Maybe he'd simply slipped into a form of suspended animation while he went through the change to becoming something more than human.

If that *was* the case, then one of the men who'd been employed by the government to find a cure for the red plague virus was now under the control of the red plague victims themselves.

And while *that* was a scary thought, an even scarier one was, if that *was* the case, then there *had* to be someone behind these things, controlling them. The red cloaks I'd seen hadn't seemed intelligent enough to do anything more than hunt and kill; nor had they appeared to *want* to do anything more than that. So either there was more to the cloaks than first appeared, or there was something deeper going on.

Either way, with Baltimore dead and his research in the hands of god knew who, Wilson was the only one left who had any hope of finding a cure anytime soon. Sure, other people could pick up the pieces, try to replicate and move on, but the reality was, it could take them years to even get back to where Wilson and Baltimore were.

But why would the red cloaks—or whoever was behind them, if there was someone behind them—want to control any possible vaccine? Did they hope to use the cure for themselves, or was there a more nefarious plan? I very much suspected the latter, though I wasn't entirely sure why.

"Given witnesses said he used talonlike fingernails to rip Wilson up," Amanda commented, drawing me from my thoughts, "maybe they simply took the body to prevent any possible DNA evidence from being found. That's what the cops appeared to think, anyway. They seemed pretty certain they'd find his body dumped somewhere in the sewer system."

I wished them luck with the search, because I seriously doubted they would find anything beyond rubbish, rats, and the occasional dead animal. "Did Wilson seem on edge before his death? Had there been any break-ins at either the research foundation or at your house?"

She shook her head. "Why?"

"Just trying to uncover any links between the two murders we're investigating." I tapped the wheel for several seconds. "What about friends? Did he confide in anyone besides you? Was there anyone new in his life, someone perhaps he was reluctant to talk about?"

"A lover, you mean?" Her expression was amused. "No, there was no one like that. It's rather hard to keep such things secret from a telepath."

Undoubtedly. I glanced in the mirror and noticed a white Ford following us. Nothing unusual given white Fords were a dime a dozen on the roads these days, but there *had* been one parked down from Amanda's, and after everything that had happened recently, I was a little wary of coincidences. I flicked on the blinker and went into the left lane. The Ford remained where it was.

I slowed as the lights ahead changed to red. "Did the police mention anything about Wilson's research notes?"

"No, but I know they're missing. I had a visit from Denny Rosen two days after Wilson's death." She pursed her lips, her expression thoughtful. "Shame this has all gone down as it has. He might very well have been my next target."

"Once Wilson was finished with, you mean?"

"Oh no." Her expression was amused. "During.

Wilson is work. Rosen, as head of a major research foundation, would have been a delightful—and undoubtedly profitable—sideline."

"You really don't have any morals, do you?"

She snorted. "You should check out Denny Rosen if you really want someone untroubled by morals. That man has not gotten where he is by playing nicely, let me tell you."

"Meaning?"

"Meaning, while Rosen Pharmaceuticals might have held a government contract for research on that damn virus, he wasn't above sharing the information in order to line his own pockets."

I frowned. "Why would Rosen risk doing something that could destroy not only a very lucrative contract, but possibly his own company?"

"Greed," she replied. "It's a huge motivator. Especially when you're heavily in debt."

"And Rosen is?"

She nodded. "To the tune of nearly a million dollars. Apparently, he has a very nasty gambling problem—he's the type who would bet on two flies walking up a wall if the odds were good enough."

"And you discovered all this in the brief time he came to see you?"

"Of course." Her smile was fleeting but smug. "Rosen may be very adept at hiding his problems from government scrutiny, but—as I have said— I'm *very* good at what I do. And I don't always have to fuck them to do it. Rosen, unlike Wilson, is an easy read."

Which made me wonder why the government wasn't working on some sort of device to prevent the minds of people in such important positions being read. Or maybe they were and, like the red plague virus, it just wasn't common knowledge.

I glanced in the rearview mirror again. The white Ford wasn't visible, but that niggling sense of unease refused to abate.

"Have you any idea who Rosen is indebted to?"

Amanda frowned. "That I couldn't quite catch, as he was trying not to worry about it." She waved a hand. "But it was a long, titled name that had something to do with a rat."

"Not Marcus Radcliffe the third?"

"That sounds about right." She studied me for a moment. "I gather you've come across him in your investigations?"

"You might say that." Unfortunately, Radcliffe was now in Sam's hands, and he no doubt now knew about Rosen's debt problems. Of course, that didn't preclude the possibility of us talking to him. Who knew? We might uncover some morsel Sam had missed.

And at midday tomorrow, vampires would start walking the streets.

I turned onto Spencer Street and said, "Okay, where in Southern Cross have you stashed your bags?"

"It's locker number ninety-two in the train concourse."

I grunted and swung into the station's parking

garage. After finding a spot on an upper level, I said, "Do I need a locker key or code?"

"Code. Nine zero five seven."

I opened the door, then hesitated. "Be here when I get back."

"I can't go anywhere without passports or clothes," she said, expression amused. "I'll be here."

I studied her for a moment, not convinced, then half shrugged and got out of the car. But I didn't go all that far. Once I was out of immediate sight, I stopped the phone recording, ducked down behind an old four-wheel-drive, and waited.

Sure enough, five minutes later, Amanda walked by, my coat fully zipped up so that only the ends of the hospital gown were visible. Unless you looked really close, it simply appeared as if she were wearing a light summer dress. I waited until she'd stepped inside the elevator, watched it descend until it was obvious it was going straight to the ground floor, then ran for the stairs. I called to my spirit form as I did so, felt the fires within surge to life, but—just as quickly—splutter into nothing. Goddamn it, I was still too low in energy to become fire. I ran down the stairs as fast as I could and prayed like hell the parking garage's elevator was as slow as most of them seemed to be. I was almost at the bottom of the stairwell when the door opened and a mom and two kids stepped in. Only fast footwork on *her* part saved us all. I gave her a quick apology, then dashed out. The concourse was packed. I paused and scanned the crowd heading to and from the retail center above us.

After a second or so, I found Amanda. I tagged along after her, remaining at a distance but nevertheless keeping her in sight. Unsurprisingly, she didn't head for the lockers in the main train station, but rather the ones located at the bus interchange terminal.

I waited until she'd opened the locker; then, phone in hand and Sam's number on the screen ready to call, I walked up behind her and said, "Just as well I wasn't inclined to take the word of a thief and a whore."

She jumped and turned around, but her expression was one of annoyance more than surprise. "Well, it was worth a shot." She grimaced. "I guess you're not as gullible as you seemed."

"No." I showed her the phone. "Give me one reason not to hit this number and hand you over."

She raised an eyebrow. "Go for it. I know for a fact that is neither Henry Morretti's number nor anyone else who provides a contactable front for the sindicati."

"No, it's not," I agreed. "It's actually the number of someone I think might be much worse where you're concerned."

"And who might that be? The cops? They're hardly likely to be concerned about a widow deciding to take a holiday."

"Maybe not, but I'm betting the police might be interested in our little conversation—which, by the way, I recorded. However, this isn't a direct line to any cop." I watched the amusement flee her face. The fury that took its place was an ugly thing to behold. Finally, I was glimpsing the real Amanda Wilson. "This is the number of a PIT detective."

"And what is PIT?"

"They're the Paranormal Investigations Team, and sit somewhere between the police and the military." I plucked the duffel bag from her hands. She resisted, but only briefly. "Basically, they have carte blanche to do whatever it takes to investigate and solve paranormal crimes. I'm afraid your husband's death falls under that umbrella."

"And this should scare me because . . . ?"

"Because they are not bound by the same rules as the police." I slung the bag over my shoulder, then stepped back and waved her ahead of me. "I was in their hands recently. They gave me a drug that not only forced me to answer their questions, but restrained my psychic abilities, leaving me unable to defend myself for several hours afterward."

Her gaze shot to mine. "And what abilities might you have?"

I gave her a smile that held very little humor. "Run again without holding up your end of our bargain, and you just might find out."

Her gaze lingered on mine for a minute, as if to assess whether I meant what I said; then she sighed. "There's a USB in the side pocket. That holds all the promised information."

"Conveniently, I have no computer to check this fact." Nevertheless, I found the USB and shoved it in my pocket. Then I searched the rest of the bag, found two more, and took those, too.

Her expression became even more sour, and I hadn't thought *that* was possible. "And now it's my turn to demand you uphold your end of the bargain."

It was tempting—very tempting—to tell her to go to hell, but I'd learned over my many years that karma had a way of biting you on the ass. Breaking a deal—even if it was with someone like Amanda—was never a wise move.

"You know where the car is, so lead the way."

She did so. Five minutes later, we were driving out of the garage and heading down Spencer Street.

A casual look in the rearview mirror revealed we were once again being followed by a white Ford. This time, that niggling sense of wrongness became a rock.

"What's wrong?"

I glanced at Amanda. "We're being followed."

She lowered the sun visor and slid open the vanity mirror. "White Ford?"

"Yes. How did you guess?"

"I noticed it parked down the street and re-membered the plates." Her smile held very little in the way of humor. "You tend to notice details in my line of work."

I bet you did. "Do you still want to head for the airport?"

She hesitated. "Yes. Once I'm through screening, I can acquire someone's ticket, get out of the state, then disappear overseas."

A statement that just made me want to stop the car and toss her out. "Then let's see if we can lose them."

I didn't immediately alter my speed, just kept cruising down Spencer Street until we hit a set of lights that were changing. I slowed, as if to stop, then, at the last possible moment, hit the accelerator and shot through the intersection. Car horns blared and I had to swerve around the pedestrian who'd already started crossing, but we got through unscathed.

A glance in the rearview mirror revealed the white Ford pulling out onto the wrong side of the road with the obvious intent of repeating our actions. If another truck or a car didn't take them out, we had—at best—a couple of minutes. And I wasn't sure that was going to be enough time given Jackson's truck was bright red and orange and rather easy to spot among the more mundanely colored vehicles.

I swung onto a side street. The tires screamed and the truck swerved dangerously. I fought for control, then hit the accelerator again. At the end of the street, I made a sharp left and belted down a narrow lane.

Up ahead, someone flung open the door of a parked car.

"Fuck!" Amanda slapped her hands against the dash to brace herself. "Watch out!"

I hit the horn and kept my foot planted. I had a brief glimpse of the driver's rear end as he dove back inside the car; then I hit the door. The force of the impact wrenched the door free and flung it up and over the truck's roof. Thankfully, it didn't appear to touch Jackson's shiny paintwork, but rather hit the road behind us and bounced into another parked car. I swung right onto another road and didn't slow as I made my way through the maze of side streets, all the time heading toward the airport.

I eased up only once we turned left onto Mount Alexandria Road. Amanda released a long breath and said, "I'm guessing we lost them?"

I studied the cars behind us. No white Ford, but—given who we were dealing with—that was no guarantee that we were safe. Especially given Jackson's truck had been parked in front of Amanda's place for quite a while.

"Maybe." My voice was grim. "It just depends who was actually following us and whether they placed a tracker on the truck at either your place or at the parking garage."

Her gaze widened. "Do you think that's likely?"

I shrugged. "As I said, it depends who we're dealing with."

She swore. "You might want to keep breaking speed limits."

I snorted. "Not on Mount Alexandria Road, I'm not. The last thing we need is to be pulled over by the cops, and they tend to be a little thick on the ground in these parts."

She swore again and flexed her fingers, making me wonder if she was intending to punch me out and take the truck.

We made it down Mount Alexandria without incident, and I could almost feel the tension slither from Amanda's body as we swung onto the Tullamarine Freeway. Which was stupid, because we weren't exactly home free yet. There was still a ten-minute drive before we got to the airport. Maybe I was being fatalistic, but anything could happen.

As it turned out, I wasn't being fatalistic.

Just as we'd crossed the Mickleham Road overpass, a big black van came out of nowhere and smashed into the rear side of Jackson's truck, sending us into an uncontrolled spin. I pulled my foot off the accelerator and fought the wheel, trying to drive out of the spin, only to be hit a second time. Amanda screamed, the sound almost lost to the roaring of the engine, the squealing of the tires, and my own cursing.

I saw the tree coming, but there was nothing I could do to stop us from hitting it.

The air bags exploded on impact, and Amanda's scream abruptly died. For several seconds, there was no sound other than an odd ringing in my head. Then I became aware of creaking metal, the hiss of water, the sound of an engine roaring. Of warm liquid pouring down the side of my face.

I looked up, saw the black van stop and two blurry figures get out. Wondered whether they were coming for Amanda or me.

The information, some still-aware part of my

brain whispered. *They can't get Amanda's information.*

Somehow, as the world started going black around me, I dragged the USBs from my pocket and slid them under the seat.

Then everything *did* go black, and I knew no more.

Chapter 11

Waking was a slow and agonizing process. As I climbed toward full awareness, various bruised and battered bits of my body came to life, and they all seemed overly determined to make consciousness a living hell.

I tried to shift position and ease some of the pain, but quickly discovered I couldn't move. It took several minutes to realize why—my hands and my feet were tied so tightly that red-hot lances of agony were shooting up my limbs. To make matters worse, a herd of people wearing hobnail boots were stomping about inside my head.

Waking, I decided, just wasn't worth it. But try as I might, I couldn't slip back into the peaceful bliss of unconsciousness. I took a deep, somewhat shuddery breath and forced my eyelids open. To be greeted by nothing but black.

But one thing was obvious immediately—wherever the hell I was, it was no longer in Jackson's truck. I had no idea how much time had passed, but surely I hadn't been unconscious long enough that day had turned into night. And even if it *had*, night wasn't usually *this* dark.

Thinking maybe there was something wrong with my vision, I blinked. It didn't help. Everything was still black.

But it was a blackness that was *not* uninhabited. Out there in the darkness, someone was watching. I couldn't hear him, I couldn't smell him, but I was nevertheless aware of him. The energy of his presence skittered across my senses, powerful and yet oddly repelling.

"I know you're there." The words came out little more than a husky whisper. I cleared my throat and tried again. "Show yourself."

For several minutes, there was no response. Tension crawled through me, and it was tempting— very tempting—to reach for whatever fire remained within and let it loose. But it was never a good move to reveal your trump card too soon— especially when that card wasn't up to scratch. The first thing I was going to do once I got out of this place—*if* I got out of this place—was reenergize with Rory so I could shift shape and burn the remnants of the drug from my system. I couldn't afford to be powerless—not when our investigations kept taking such nasty turns.

I flexed my fingers, desperate to get some life into them as much as trying to uncover what I'd been tied with. It didn't feel like rope. It was cool and smooth against my skin rather than rough, and there was odd warmth to it.

Silver, I realized. They'd tied me with silver. Which, under normal circumstances, wouldn't have been much of a problem, as silver didn't actually restrain or hinder those of us who were spirits.

But the fact that my captors had tied me with silver suggested they suspected I was a nonhuman, even if they didn't exactly know what.

"Look, whatever it is you want, just get on with it." Though I kept my voice low, it nevertheless spurred the hobnailed idiots in my head into greater action. Tears stung my eyes, and I blinked them away furiously. "I really haven't got the time to be playing games."

As I half expected, it was a comment that finally got a response.

"And yet," a cool voice replied, "we have."

It wasn't my watcher who spoke, but someone I hadn't sensed until now. Someone who stood behind me. I didn't bother twisting around to try to spot him. Not only would the hobnailed folk be unappreciative of such an action, but the utter blanket of darkness made any hope of spotting him nigh on impossible. Phoenixes weren't blessed with the extraordinary eyesight of werewolves and vampires.

And that, I thought with a chill, was who held me now.

Vampires. And not just any old vampires, but the sindicati.

Fuck.

"Well, good for you," I said, trying to keep my voice even despite my heart hammering so hard I swear it was attempting to jump out of my chest.

"But, as I said, I have things to do. Can we please just move this along?"

"It is odd that you do not question who we are or why you are here." He'd moved to my left, though I'd heard no footsteps.

A tremor ran through me. Only the very old ones could walk so silently. I licked my lips and tried to shove old fears back into their box. That I was still alive meant they had some use for me. Whether they'd let me go after I'd fulfilled those uses was another matter entirely.

"I don't question who you are because I already know that. As to why I am here—" I paused, then shrugged. I might not be able to see them, but I had no doubt that the two men in this room—if they *were* vamps—could see me as clear as day. Vamps were blessed with night sight very similar to infrared. Even if he couldn't taste my fear or hear the pounding of blood through my veins, he'd be able to see it. "I'm gathering it has something to do with Amanda Wilson."

"Then you would gather wrong."

Meaning I was in even deeper shit than I'd thought.

The voice, however, hadn't quite finished. "And just who do you think we are?"

"Sindicati, obviously."

"Ah," he said, his cool voice still giving little away. But then, if my guess was right and he *was* a very old vampire, that was no surprise. They had a tendency to become more remote—and far less human—the longer they were alive. "Dear Amanda obviously talked far more than was wise."

"Dear Amanda had little other choice given it was either talk to me or I'd leave her to the tender mercies of whatever goons you decided to send after her next."

The speaker was silent for several minutes. I closed my eyes and tried to get some sense of him. But all I could feel was the man whose presence was beginning to scratch at my skin like some foul disease. *He* was the real power here, I suddenly realized, not the man who spoke.

"Ah, so you *are* the reason no one has heard from either of the subcontractors."

"Well, I might be responsible for one being incommunicado, but not the other. He is, as far as I know, still in the hands of PIT."

This news finally got a reaction. It was little more than a hiss of annoyed air, but it was nevertheless there. It made me wonder if the werewolf we'd questioned was more closely connected to the sindicati than just being a mere subcontractor. While wolves and vampires generally weren't overly fond of one another, there were certain elements within each society that happily coexisted. I suspected the sindicati and whatever the werewolf equivalent was would be one of those.

"And you are responsible for this?"

"Well, he did try to kill me."

"An unfortunate mistake on his part," was the response. "Especially since we still have need of you."

And if they didn't, would I now be dead? The answer, very obviously, was yes. I flexed my hands, felt the surge of heat across my fingertips, but resisted the urge to let it show. I might have little more than sparks, but those sparks might yet save my life.

"Which leads neatly back to my original question," I said. "What the hell do you want from me?"

"Ah," the vampire said. "You are a being who obviously does not appreciate the complexities of bargaining."

"It's hardly bargaining when you have me tied up tighter than a mummy in a pyramid."

Amusement slid around me, its touch as foul as the silent presence in the corner. Who the *hell* was he? I had a vague feeling it was something I should know—that *not* knowing could prove very dangerous in the future.

Or was that merely fear speaking? Was it a combination of the uncertainty of the moment and the knowledge that my end in this lifetime might very well come at the hands of either of these men, and there was nothing, absolutely nothing, I could do to stop it?

"You are tied up for your own protection as much as ours." He'd moved around to the right side of my body and was close enough that his breath whispered past my ear.

I shivered and couldn't help wondering whether perhaps he was tempted to have a little taste . . . I swallowed, forced the thought away, and said,

"Yes, because one lone female of unknown heritage is such a danger to two very old vampires."

Again surprise rippled across the darkness. "Interesting that you know there are two of us. You should not have been able to sense my colleague."

"And why is that?"

"Because he is . . . not what I am."

Meaning he *wasn't* a vampire? Then what the hell was he? And how was he connected to the sindicati?

"And that, of course, makes perfectly good sense."

"Indeed." Amusement laced his tone. "Let's just say he and his kin are something society will see far more of in coming months."

Meaning another race of supernaturals was coming out of the proverbial closet? Or was it something more sinister? I didn't know, but I had a bad feeling it would be in my best interest to find out—and sooner rather than later.

"So why doesn't he show himself? In fact, why the darkness at all?"

"Because neither of us has any desire to reveal our identity." He paused. "However, this is all beside the point. Let's, as you have requested, get down to the reason you are here."

He'd moved again and was now standing directly in front of me. I couldn't see him. Couldn't even see a vague outline. It was an unnerving sensation.

"Excellent," I said. "And to repeat . . . What do you want?"

"An exchange."

Obviously, getting to the point was not one of this vampire's strong suits. "What kind of exchange?"

"You have something I want. I will exchange it for something you want."

I raised an eyebrow. "If you're talking about Amanda, then forget it. There's nothing I have that I'm willing to exchange for her."

It might have been a harsh thing to say, but it was nevertheless true. If Amanda was still alive, then I'm afraid it was time for her to lie in the bed she'd made. I'd done what I could to uphold my end of the deal. I wasn't about to do anything else. Not given what she was and how many lives she had already destroyed.

"Dear Amanda," he replied, "is not the asset we hold."

"Meaning she *is* still alive?" I couldn't help the surprise in my voice. Given that they'd sent two goons to kill her, I'd have thought completing the task would have been their first priority.

"Yes, she is, but only because my colleague has decided he has some use for her talents."

I remembered the way his goons had tried to kill her and knew with a chill the talent he was speaking about was not *just* telepathy. Amanda would undoubtedly die, but it only would be *after* the dark presence was done using her—in bed and out.

It was a shitty way to go, but I still couldn't muster much in the way of sympathy. Amanda had known what the sindicati were and what they were capable of when she'd thrown her towel in with them—she could hardly complain now that things had gone sour.

"If Amanda's not the card you're holding, then who is?" I asked.

"A very pertinent question," the vampire replied. "And one that will be revealed in the fullness of time."

I rolled my eyes. It was just my luck to be captured by a vampire who would *not* be hurried—although I guess that wasn't necessarily a *bad* thing if what lay at the end of this was my death. "Then what do you want in return?"

He didn't immediately answer, but I could feel his gaze on me, a weight that was both judgmental and condescending. "What we want is what you have hidden from us."

I blinked. "How could I have hidden something from you when I've never had any contact with the sindicati up until now?"

"That is not entirely true," he replied evenly. "And what we require is Professor Baltimore's missing notes."

"I haven't got them. They were stolen—a fact you're no doubt aware of."

"Yes," he said. "But the set was not complete. There's a notebook missing."

Meaning the sindicati *had* been behind the thefts. But did that also mean they'd killed Baltimore? It seemed logical and yet . . . my gaze drifted to the unclean presence hiding within the deeper darkness of the room. He wasn't a vampire, and that meant he could cross thresholds uninvited. Maybe I was clutching at straws, but I had a suspicion that even if he hadn't killed Baltimore, he'd at least been there.

"Why in the hell would you think there's a notebook missing? You've not only stolen all the information the professor had on either the foundation's computers or his own, but the notebooks I had as well."

"That is the problem. As I said, we do not possess all the notebooks. There's one missing."

I frowned. "No, there's not. I had five; you took five. End of story."

Again amusement swam around me. "You may have been given five, but we hold only four. You will find that missing notebook, and you will return it to us."

"In exchange for what? We're hardly bargaining here, because, as far as I can tell, you have nothing to give me in return."

"You do not consider your life good enough?"

"Well, no, because you actually need me alive to find the notebook. And trust me, you wouldn't want to try to kill me *after* the exchange, because that could go very badly for you."

"So says the woman who—as she noted herself—is trussed up tighter than a mummy and reliant on our goodwill to remain alive."

"And yet," I replied, keeping my voice level despite the surge of both fear and fire—though the force of the latter suggested that while I wasn't anywhere near full flame, I might yet be able to defend myself from at least one of them. "As you yourself noted, you have me so tightly contained because you're aware that I represent a very real danger to both you and your watcher."

"Perhaps," he conceded. "And perhaps we merely prefer to be prepared."

Well, it worked for the Boy Scouts, so why not the sindicati? "Look, enough with the word games. Play your trump card and let's be done with it."

"As you wish." It was said so formally, it wasn't hard to imagine him bowing as he spoke. "Please, pay attention to the screen on your right."

As he spoke, a bright light cut through the darkness, taking me by surprise and making my eyes water. I blinked furiously to clear my vision and saw, on the small TV screen, Jackson.

He'd been placed on a sturdy metal chair concreted into the floor, his limbs tied separately to each leg of the chair and by silver, if the gleam along the wire was any indication. There was another strand of much finer wire looped around his neck, which was connected to the ceiling. It wasn't choking him, but if he tried to move—tried to escape—it would slice into his neck and perhaps even decapitate him. The thin trickle of blood around his neck suggested he'd already tested the boundaries of the noose.

But he obviously hadn't gone down without a fight, because his face was bruised, his lips cut, and his left eye swollen shut. His torso was in little better shape, with his clothing torn and blood splattered, and cuts scattered across his chest and upper arms.

Anger surged through me, but again I controlled my fire. Now was *not* the time to reveal my hand. But Sam was certainly going to get more than an earful if I ever ran into him again. *He* was the reason this had happened. If not for that damn drug he'd administered, there was no way known the sindicati could have gotten the better of a Fae. Not when he could use the tiniest spark to create a bonfire strong enough to take out an army.

But they *had* gotten the better of him, and he was now one hell of a trump card. I could not— *would* not—let him come to harm for the sake of some damn research notes.

"A decent enough play," I said, "but there is one sticking point—what guarantee do either of us have that you'll let us free once I've found the missing notes?"

"You have my word," the vampire said. "You will both walk free once we have the final notebook in our possession."

Yeah, but just how far would we get before they tried to take us out?

"Forgive me if this sounds insulting," I said, as politely as I could manage and yet unable to help the slight edge of cynicism, "but the word of a vampire afraid to reveal himself is not something I'm inclined to put a whole lot of faith in."

Anger surged, so fierce and thick it momentarily snatched my breath—which was pretty scary given I wasn't usually *that* sensitive to emotions. I held my breath, my fires an invisible force ready to explode from my body. What good it would do me when I was so well tied up, I had no idea. If I'd been able to shift form, it would have been a different matter. But I couldn't. Not yet. Not until I got back to Rory.

The vampire didn't attack. In fact, he didn't do anything more than shut down the TV and plunge us back into utter darkness.

"You have twenty-four hours," he said, voice clipped and colder than hell itself. "If you have not contacted us in that time—or if we suspect police or PIT presence—we will scatter bits of the Fae from one end of this city to another."

Twenty-four hours didn't seem anywhere near long enough to find the missing notebook. Not given I had no idea where the hell it could be. But I kept my doubts to myself. Twenty-four hours at least gave me time to look. And time to figure out not only how to free Jackson, but to stop these bastards from getting what they wanted.

"And how do I contact you once I've found the notebook?"

"We have placed a number on your phone," he said. "Ring it once you've found the notebook, and we will arrange an exchange."

"The Fae had better not sustain any more wounds," I said, voice as cold as his. "Or there will be hell to pay."

"Do *not* threaten us." He was so close that his breath whispered across the nape of my neck. My breath caught somewhere in my throat and my stomach began to churn as I waited for that moment when teeth pierced skin. For several seconds, nothing happened; then he chuckled softly. The sound jarred uneasily against the ink surrounding us. "It would not be wise."

"I *didn't* threaten." My voice was little more than a croak of fear, but I couldn't help it. He might not smell as bad or radiate the desperation of the vampire who'd killed me several lifetimes ago, but he was still a vampire. And his hunger was so palpable I could have touched it had my hands been free. "I merely made a statement of fact."

"As, indeed, do I." His breath continued to brush my neck. "There is no place in this city we cannot get access to should we desire, and therefore no place that is safe from our ire. Remember that the next time you are tempted to make a statement of fact."

And with that, something pierced my neck. Before I could flame, before I could even scream, the ink descended and I knew no more.

Waking the second time was no easier than the first. I groaned loudly and rolled onto my back— and the mere fact I could do that had my eyes springing open. It was immediately obvious that I was no longer in the hands of the sindicati. The utter darkness had gone, replaced by thunderous skies and a drenching mist of rain—and I have to say, I've never been so happy about getting soaked in my life.

I was free and I was alive. It was definitely my lucky day.

The ground underneath me was slushy, meaning it had been raining for some time before I'd been dumped here—wherever the hell "here" was. There was no traffic noise and no industrial noise. In fact, there was nothing more than the occasional squawk of a bird and the mooing of cows. Meaning they'd dumped me in the country rather than the city. But why do that, given the twenty-four-hour time frame? It didn't make any sense.

Unless, of course, the black room itself was somewhere in the country rather than the city.

I carefully propped myself up on my elbows, but even that small movement had the hobnailed idiots in my head starting up again. I winced and tried to ignore the pain as I looked around. I was, as I suspected, in the middle of a field. Several cows were giving me the evil eye from under the cover of nearby eucalypts and, beyond them, kangaroos grazed near the banks of a decent-sized dam. Farther down the hill, sitting in a small hollow, the tin roof of either an old farmhouse or barn was visible through the trees surrounding it.

I shifted position, waited for the idiots in my head to calm down, and studied the land above me. There were tire marks coming into the paddock from a road that disappeared around the left of the hill, and, if the size of those tracks was any indication, we'd come here in a four-wheel drive. Which really didn't help all that much, because there were a million and one four-wheel drives on the road these days.

There was no sign of Amanda in either direction, but I guess that was no surprise. After all, my cool-voiced kidnapper had stated they had other plans for her.

I pushed fully upright. Almost instantly, a dozen different aches fired into action, and for several minutes I did nothing more than breathe deep in an effort to keep my stomach from leaping up my throat. When I could, I did a quick body check—bruised ribs, cuts on my left arm and right leg, and wrists that were rubbed raw by the thick wire that had bound me. Nothing truly incapacitating—a miracle in itself given the force with which we'd hit that tree. Air bags really *did* save lives.

But what about my neck? Had it been teeth or a needle that pierced my skin? I tentatively felt around and wasn't entirely surprised to find two neat, round wounds. The bastard *had* bitten me, though I very much doubted he'd taken all that much. It was more a reminder of what he was and what he could do if he so desired. But what about the man in the shadows? I checked the other side of my neck, knowing from my time as a cop that vampires rarely used the same entry point even if they were sharing a victim. Luckily, it appeared as if I'd been spared the horror of my unsavory watcher taking a sip—though why I should be more scared of being bitten by *him* than the vampire who'd done all the talking, I couldn't really say.

I took another deep breath that did little to ease the various aches and pains, then went through my pockets. All empty—not that I'd had much in them to begin with. Thankfully, there was a suspiciously familiar brown shape half-hidden in the grass ten feet or so away and, with any sort of luck, my phone and wallet would still be inside. I pushed upright. The paddock did a mad dash around me, and my knees briefly buckled. I swore loudly and fought to remain upright, knowing that if I went down I'd more than likely stay there. The cows, it seemed, were unimpressed by my language, because they now had their butts to me.

I glanced down at the valley, then up at the road, and decided to go up rather than down simply because it involved less distance and far fewer fences to climb over.

I walked across to my handbag. A quick look inside revealed both wallet *and* phone. But then, it would hardly make sense for them to take either of them—stranding me in the middle of nowhere with no way to communicate and no cash or cards to grab a taxi wasn't going to get them the notebook any quicker.

I turned on my stolen phone and discovered that it was nearly four in the afternoon. I'd been in the hands of the sindicati for more than five hours, even if I couldn't remember more than half an hour of it. I scrolled through the contacts list, looking for the number I was supposed to ring once I'd found the notebook, and discovered it under the name of Mr. Dark and Dangerous. Someone in the sindicati had a warped sense of humor.

The next thing I did was take a couple of photos of the tire tracks. Who knew? Jackson's secret source might be able to uncover what type of four-wheel drive used these type of tires. How that would help us find the vehicle, I had no idea. With the way our luck was running, it'd turn out to be a tire used by most of the major four-wheel drives found here in Australia.

That was presuming, of course, Jackson got out of this alive and in one piece. God, I hoped he was okay.

Hoped the sindicati weren't dining on him as they had on me.

I squished down the worry and contacted Rory.

"Thank god you're okay," he said without preamble. "I heard over the radio that there'd been a major crash on the freeway involving a red truck and a van, and I was worried it was you and Jackson."

I hesitated, knowing he'd be madder than hell given my promise to keep safe, then quickly updated him on all that had happened.

"Damn it, Em!" he exploded. "They could have killed you!"

"Not until they get what they want," I said. "Trouble is, I have no idea where that notebook is, and though there was a copy on my laptop, it also went missing."

"Well, no, it didn't. I have it."

I blinked. "You what?"

"The damn battery on mine died, so I borrowed yours. It's sitting in my locker at work as we speak."

I closed my eyes and rubbed my forehead wearily. Even if I couldn't find the notebook, I still had a chance of saving Jackson.

"Em, you okay?"

"Yeah. Listen, can you meet me at home? Before I can do anything, I need to recharge. It's just become too damn dangerous to run around as I am."

"Can do, but if you're intending to confront the sindicati, you are *not* doing it alone."

"Rory—"

"No," he cut in. "Not this time. I don't trust vampires at the best of times, let alone ones as steeped in crime as this lot. They won't see or hear me, Em, but I *will* be there, just in case."

I opened my mouth to protest, then closed it again. He was right. It was infinitely better to be safe than sorry.

"Okay. I'll meet you at home." I hesitated, then added, "Oh, and don't bring the laptop. It's safer where it is for the moment."

"No problem. See you soon."

I hung up, then slowly made my way up the hill. The clean air and exercise didn't make the hobnailed folk any happier, but it wasn't like I had much choice.

The road at the top was little more than a thin strip of gravel, and I hesitated, undecided whether to go left or right. Neither direction appeared particularly promising, given there was little more than trees and scrub to be seen either way. I tossed a mental coin, then headed right—at least it was downhill. Hopefully, it would lead somewhere. Even some sort of street sign would be handy right now; then I could call a cab.

After what seemed like ages, an odd sound began to cut across all the birdsong. I frowned and stopped. After a moment, I realized it was a car coming up the hill toward me.

Relief filled me, but it was quickly followed by wariness. This road didn't look particularly well used, so what were the odds of someone coming along at the precise moment that I needed them?

None. Not the way my luck had been running of late.

It couldn't hurt to be cautious. Even if it turned out to be a coincidence, as Rory had already noted, it was far better to be safe than sorry. I headed off the road, pushed my way through several feet of thick scrub, and sheltered behind the trunk of a big old ghost gum.

A dark blue car soon came into view. The windows were heavily tinted, so I couldn't see who was inside, but it slowed as it neared my tree. I resisted the urge to step closer to the trunk, knowing any sort of movement just might capture their attention.

If, of course, they were actually looking for me and not just slowing down for the corner.

The car crawled past, then stopped.

My breath caught somewhere in my throat. Damn it. What else could go wrong today? Wasn't being rammed into a tree and becoming an unwilling guest of the sindicati enough?

Apparently not.

Because the door opened and a man climbed out. It wasn't a stranger and it wasn't a vampire.

It was Sam.

CHAPTER 12

Silently cursing my luck, I stepped out from behind the tree and said, "What the fuck are you doing here?"

"Rescuing your stupid ass, obviously." His voice was clipped, frosty. "Why else would I be out here in the middle of goddamn nowhere?"

I crossed my arms and glared at him. "And just how do you know I need rescuing?"

He snorted, his gaze sweeping me. Though his expression remained hostile, there was the tiniest spark of relief in his eyes when his gaze met mine again. "Anyone with half a brain can see that you need help, even if you're too stubborn to admit it."

"And *why* might that be? Care to take a fucking guess?"

He raised an imperious eyebrow. "Because you didn't step away from the investigation when you were told to?"

My fists clenched and, for the first time in hours I was glad I didn't have much in the way of flames. It would have been entirely *too* tempting to burn his arrogant ass to hell and back.

"And maybe, just maybe, it was the drugs you gave me that all but handed me over to the sindicati."

He stiffened abruptly. "When did you land in the sindicati's hands?"

"Like you didn't know." Sarcasm rode my voice. "Isn't that why you're out here, to gloat and say I told you so?"

"No. I'm out here because the tail we'd placed on you reported the incident with the van, and we've been searching for you ever since."

"And you *just happened* to be assigned to the very area I was dumped." I snorted. "That suggests either dumb luck *or* connection to me, Sam."

"If," he said, voice low and barely controlled, "you're suggesting I'm connected to the sindicati, you would be well advised to take it back."

The darkness and fury in him was so fierce, the blood drained from my face and I couldn't help retreating a step. "So it was dumb luck?"

He hesitated, then shrugged. "It was just an odd hunch."

An odd hunch. Very convenient. And yet I *did* believe his statement that he wasn't involved with the sindicati. Had it been Luke saying those words, it would have been another matter.

I frowned, wondering why Luke had even entered my thoughts, then said, "And why would you and PIT even bother looking for me, given I'm nothing but a nuisance getting in the way of your investigation?"

"Because," he said, voice tight, "you're a key

player in that investigation—and one we certainly *don't* want in the hands of the sindicati."

"Yeah, well, shame you didn't think about that *before* you gave me the drug and left me defenseless."

He snorted. "You could still use that tongue of yours. It's sharp enough to cut glass, after all."

"Just fuck off, Sam," I said. "I don't need—or want—your help."

With that, I marched through the scrub and headed down the road again. After several seconds, a door slammed and the car continued on up the hill. Surprise flitted through me. Despite my words, I really *hadn't* expected him to go.

The surprise was short-lived, however. A few minutes later, the car pulled up alongside me. Obviously, he'd left only to find somewhere to turn around.

"Red," he said as the passenger-side window slid down. "Get in the car."

"What, are you going deaf or something? Didn't I just tell you to fuck off?"

"And we both know I'm not going to. *Get* in the car."

I stopped. So did he. For several seconds we simply glared at each other. But the truth of the matter was, I *did* need help, and it was stupid not to accept his just because I was madder than hell at him at this particular moment. Besides, being stubborn wouldn't help Jackson, but Sam just might.

I opened the door and got in. He planted his foot on the gas and the car took off.

"So," he said, once we were on a main road again. I could see the city skyline in the distance but had no idea where we were in relation to it. "What did the sindicati want?"

"What do you think they wanted?" I couldn't help the annoyance in my voice because, well, it *was* a stupid question.

"Obviously, it was related to Baltimore's research, but all indications suggest they have that already." The darkness in him briefly rose, touching his eyes and sending chills down my spine. Thankfully, it disappeared as quickly as it had appeared. I wished I could say the same about the desire that always stirred when he was this close. He added, "Unless, of course, you're holding additional information you haven't told anyone about."

"I'm not. Baltimore gave me five notebooks to transcribe the night he was murdered, and that's all the information I had."

"Well, they didn't snatch you for the hell of it, so what did they want?"

"The fifth notebook."

He frowned. "But they snatched all the notebooks from your apartment, didn't they?"

"Well, *someone* did. There's no evidence it was actually the sindicati."

"I can't imagine it being anyone else."

I shifted slightly in the seat and studied him for several seconds. He didn't react in any way to my scrutiny, though I had no doubt he was aware of it.

Eventually, I said, "Can't you?"

He frowned. "Can't I what?"

"Imagine anyone else wanting the research?"

"Well, yeah, the government. But the government wasn't involved in the raid of your apartment." He paused, giving me a dark look. "And before you say it, neither were we."

"Of course, I have only your word on that." It probably wasn't the wisest comment in the world, but it was out before I could stop it. The inner bitch, it seemed, was alive and kicking, even if the rest of me felt like doing nothing more than rolling over and having a good sleep.

"Of the two people in this car," he growled, "there's only one with a history of lying—and it's *not* me."

"I didn't lie," I snapped back. "I just didn't tell you the entire truth."

He snorted. "*That's* a cop-out, and you know it."

"What *I* know," I said, voice icy, "is that I believed you couldn't and wouldn't understand the situation with Rory. I still think that. Hell, you can't even hear his name without exploding in anger."

"*And* for a damn good reason."

"Did it never occur to you that I might also have had a good reason?"

"You were sleeping with *another* man," he growled, "even as you were professing to *love* me. What more is there to understand than that?"

"Far more than you will now ever know," I bit back. "Life isn't black-and-white, Sam. Not when you're dealing with someone who isn't human."

"But you live in a human world, and you were with someone who at the time held very human beliefs. How the hell did you expect me to react?"

There was anger in his voice, but there was also hurt and pain. It was a reminder that while his reaction had hurt me to the core, it was *my* actions that had truly ended our relationship. It was my refusal to trust, to share what I was and what that meant, to believe that someone could love me once they knew, that had doomed us from the very beginning.

Even so, I couldn't help saying, "What I expected was a *chance*. But you couldn't even look me in the eye once I told you what I was."

"Because when I looked at you, all I saw was a *lie*. You, me, everything. It was all a lie."

I closed my eyes against the sudden sting of tears. It wasn't a lie. Not then, not now. "If you believe that," I said quietly, "then you're an even bigger fool than I thought."

"Well, *that*, at least, is something we can agree on." His voice was bitter. "Who else do you think could have taken the notebooks, if not the sindicati or us?"

I took a deep, somewhat shuddery breath and fleetingly wished I could turn my emotions on and off as easily as he seemed able to. "It could be the very same people who took Professor Wilson's body."

A lone muscle along his jawline ticked, but other than that, I might as well have been staring at a blank canvas. "And why would you think that?"

"Well, it's hardly likely the red cloaks snatched Wilson's body for the sole purpose of getting rid of any DNA evidence that might be found on it. An attack as public as that one suggests it was a very deliberate choice—and *that* means there's another reason. One that's a whole lot scarier."

"That Professor Wilson is alive and now one of the red cloaks." He briefly met my gaze. "We are aware of that possibility."

"Then why not at least mention it when you knew Jackson and I were investigating Wilson's death?"

"Why would I, when fruitlessly pursuing information on Wilson at least kept you away from Baltimore's investigation?"

"What? You didn't trust your own drugs to do the job for you?"

"I ordered you away from Morretti, and for a damn good reason. He's not someone you want to tangle with, in *any* way, shape, or form. *Especially* now."

I frowned. "Why especially now?"

He took a deep breath and released it slowly. Obviously, he hadn't meant to add that little tidbit. "Because the sindicati is on the verge of a factional war, and it's not something you want to be caught in the middle of."

No, it certainly wasn't. But if that was the case, which faction had questioned me? Morretti, or the other? And did it even matter in this particular case?

"Yeah, well, I'm not exactly defenseless," I muttered. "Or at least I wasn't until you snatched any recourse I had of self-defense."

"Let's not get overly dramatic," Sam all but growled. "The drugs only dampen psychic capabilities and shape-shifting for forty-eight hours. I'd foolishly hoped that you might come to your senses within that time and leave the investigation to the experts, but I should have known better."

"It's kind of hard to walk away from something when vampire goons and their werewolf buddies seem intent on either tracking me down or beating me up." I shook my head. "But that's not the only reason drugging me was dangerous, Sam. I'm spirit, not flesh, and no matter how much you and your organization think they know about phoenixes, trust me, it's little more than a drop in the ocean."

"And *I* will do whatever is necessary to protect the people I work with against forces that could destroy us, Em. And if that means risking the effects of a drug on an unknown entity to prevent an attack, then so be it."

But that entity was someone you'd once professed to love. The words echoed through me, bitter and filled with hurt. Damn it, *no.* I wouldn't go there. *Couldn't* go there. This man might be the love of *this* lifetime, but that love was now a part of my past. It needed to remain there, no matter how much pain, regret, and anger lingered in the present.

No matter how much the occasional glimpse of the old Sam fanned the embers of hope.

"You know what? This is getting us nowhere. Just stop the car and let me out. Rory can—"

"Your damn lover can *wait*." The darkness within him was suddenly so close to the surface it was a living thing that crowded the car's cabin. "You've got a notebook to find and hand over first."

I somehow resisted the urge to inch away from him. In this confined space, that darkness—whatever the hell it was—was far too close, far too real, and *far* too dangerous. And, oddly enough, it reminded me a little of the man who'd silently watched me from the shadows.

"Rory is as vital to my life as the air I breathe in this form," I replied, the bitterness within me evident in my voice despite my best efforts of control. "And the very least *you* could have done was listen. What we had deserved—"

"Enough." It was an order and a warning, all in one. "We've studied your building's security tapes. It wasn't red cloaks who broke into your apartment, but a thief with a long history of subcontracting to the sindicati."

I took yet another of those deep, steadying breaths, but it had as much of an effect as the rest of them. "I gather you've a warrant out on him?"

"Of course."

He flicked on the blinker, and I realized with a start that we were now on the Tullamarine Freeway. Whether Sam was heading to PIT's headquarters or my home was very much up in the air, but I suspected the latter given he wouldn't want to risk me finding the notebook and handing it over to the sindicati.

"Unsurprisingly," he continued, "he's made himself scarce, but we have people checking his usual hangouts, just in case. The question, however, is why—if the sindicati have all the notebooks—do they now believe they are missing one?"

"That I can't tell you."

"Were there four or five on the USB you gave me?"

"Four, as I told you when I handed it over. I'd typed up the remaining one, but hadn't gotten around to transferring it."

I still had those notes, thanks to Rory. But I wasn't about to tell Sam that. Not yet. I might need it as a bargaining chip for Jackson's life.

"And you have no idea what happened to the final notebook?" Sam said.

"No. As I've told both you *and* them, as far as I was aware, all five had been stolen."

His gaze narrowed, and just for a moment it felt as if he were trying to read my mind and unpick truth from lies. Eventually, he said, "Well, obviously *not* by the sindicati if they were willing to go to such lengths to secure it."

"I think they saw me with Amanda Wilson and decided to kill two birds with one stone, so to speak." I hesitated. "You do know that the sindicati tried to kill her, don't you?"

He shrugged. "To be honest, good riddance. But why the hell didn't you report the attempted murder to us rather than the police?"

"Because I was—and still am—pissed off at you."

"Yeah, well, *that's* a two-way street," he muttered. "How are you supposed to get the notebook back to the sindicati?"

I crossed my arms and looked out the side window for several seconds. It was tempting—very tempting—not to answer, but I'd already seen the lengths he was willing to go to get what he wanted, and I wasn't about to risk another such debacle. Not with Jackson's life on the line.

"They've given me a number to call."

"What number? I'll have it traced."

"Why? It'll undoubtedly be a burn phone."

"Perhaps, but we might be able to get GPS positioning on it."

"And how does that help, exactly? Whoever is currently holding the phone will be a subcontractor. The sindicati haven't shown any real propensity to place themselves in the line of danger."

"Exactly, which makes the fact that they took such a risk to grab *you* in broad daylight even odder."

"As I said, I think I was merely an opportunity too good—"

"And what," he bit back, "if you're wrong? What if you were the target all along, and they were merely waiting for the right moment?"

"If they were going after me, they could have done it a whole lot sooner. Hell, I was next to useless for hours after you dumped us."

"Except that they must have known we were

watching you. That accident was not only very well timed, but executed in an area from which they could get away very fast—and they took our people out along with Jackson's truck."

Another chill ran through me. To do something like that took time and planning, and that could only mean he was right. But it also meant Amanda might not now be in the hands of the sindicati if she hadn't insisted I uphold my end of our deal. And that, I thought grimly, was karma at its finest. "Are your people okay?"

"Yeah. The same cannot be said for Jackson's truck, however. I'm not actually sure how Amanda Wilson survived that crash—there was a lot of blood on the seat."

Seat. Damn, the USBs. "Where's the truck now?"

"It was hauled away. I believe the police have been trying to contact Jackson." He gave me a look that sat somewhere between annoyance and disgust. "Wouldn't happen to know where he is, do you?"

"Yeah, I do. And thanks to you, he's in the same place I was."

Sam's eyebrows rose. "Why in the hell would the sindicati want *him*?"

"As insurance. I give them the notebook, they free him."

"Well, that ain't going to happen."

I stared at him for a moment, unable to believe he'd actually said that. "What the hell is that supposed to mean?"

"What do you think it means?" His expression was grim. "You've seen the red cloaks. You've seen what they can do. The life of one Fae is *not* worth the lives of the millions who could be affected if this thing gets out of control. We need the cure—or at the very least, a vaccine. To get it, we need those notes."

"If you think I'm going to let you sacrifice Jackson's life—"

"You haven't exactly got a choice here. You're in this car, with me, and you're not getting free of either anytime soon."

"What? You're going to chain me? Because that's the only damn way you'll keep me captive."

"Well, there *is* the drug option. Or I could simply take you back to headquarters and lock you in one of our flameproof cells." He half smiled, but it was a cold thing, holding little in the way of amusement. "It was designed to hold pyrokinetics, so I'm thinking it should be fine against the fires of a phoenix."

I snorted. It might well be capable of withstanding the fires of a pyro, but he was forgetting one thing—I was a fire *spirit*. Of course, at this particular moment I was a fire spirit stuck in flesh form, but under normal circumstances, a cell of any sort wouldn't have held me. Not unless they'd employed witches to create magical barriers.

But I wasn't about to tell him that—why give him a heads-up? Hell, even if I didn't find myself in that cell, another phoenix might. While there was generally only one pair per city, it wasn't unusual for youngsters to linger in an occupied city for a few weeks or months while they were looking for a place to call their own. And there were always free cities—no older pair could ever remain in one place their entire lives. Sooner or later, it paid to move on—especially in places where hatred for nonhumans was high. Melbourne was pretty mild compared to some cities, but even so, Rory and I would risk only a few more rebirths here before we went searching for somewhere new. Personally, I was voting for *any* city that had more warm days than it did cold. Somewhere with bigger, wider sunsets where a firebird could enjoy the freedom of the skies every single night.

"For god's sake, Sam," I said, shoving away pleasant thoughts of warm skies and freedom, "when did it suddenly become okay to sacrifice even *one* life? You're still a cop, even if the department you work for has a fancy title. Didn't you swear to protect and serve? To—as the force's motto says—uphold the right?"

He didn't answer. Didn't even look at me. But that lone muscle along his jawline was back in action. My words were hitting home, even if he wasn't responding. But would they make any difference? Once, maybe, but whatever had happened in the years since we'd parted had obviously altered at least *some* of the core beliefs and values of the man I'd once loved.

Would always love, no matter how much I fought it.

I sighed. "Look, I know we can't give the sindicati what they want, but, by the same token, you cannot seriously be saying you're going to let Jackson die. If you do, then you and PIT are no better than the things you hunt."

"Sometimes," he said, his voice holding a deep edge of bitterness, "you have to become the darkness if you're to have any hope of hunting it."

And he *had* become that darkness. It was in him, around him. But it hadn't yet totally consumed him. He wouldn't be arguing with me like this if it had. "The minute any society starts *that* sort of thinking, it dies. Trust me. I *know*."

He gave me another of those dark glances, blue eyes glinting fiercely in the gloom of the car. A tremor ran through me, fear and desire combined. "Just how old are you, Red?"

"Didn't your mother tell you it's impolite to ask a woman's age?"

"Meaning, I take it, you've had more than a few rebirths."

"Yes. I've seen Death in all her forms, and I have no desire to see her visit anyone I care about." I met his look evenly. "Hell, I don't want to see her visit someone I *used* to care about, which is why I saved your useless ass in the first place."

"Bet you're regretting that decision now," he muttered. "Look, I'll do what I can, but if it comes down to the notebook or Jackson, the Fae is a goner. We need those notes to have any hope of gaining ground on this virus. The sindicati—or anyone else—are not getting their hands on it."

"Unfortunately," I said, "they've already warned that the minute they *suspect* PIT or police involvement, Jackson is dead."

"Then he dies. We have no other choice."

"There are *always* choices, Sam. You've just got to be open to them."

He made a short chopping gesture with his hand. "There *is* no alternative in this case, Red, and you know it."

The time had come to reveal the ace up my sleeve. And, hopefully, it *would* be an ace and not another brick wall.

"That's not exactly true," I said. "You know how we'd presumed they'd taken my laptop along with the notes? Well, they didn't. Rory has it."

"And you've known this how long?" he said, voice remote and all the more scary for it.

"Since about five minutes after I woke up in that field."

"And you didn't think to mention this earlier?"

"I did *think* about it, but I decided to see how reasonable you were going to be first."

He shook his head, his expression a mix of annoyance and frustration—which was infinitely better than that dark and scary anger. "And this alternative of yours?"

"We find the notebook," I said, "and you take it. In return, you let me keep the laptop so I can exchange it for Jackson."

"Haven't you listened to a single word I've said? The sindicati are not—"

"Getting Baltimore's notes," I interrupted.

"Heard it, understood it. But I'm not intending to give them the notes. Not in their original condition, anyway."

He raised an eyebrow. "You intend to alter the formulas?"

"I may not understand what I type, but I'm familiar enough with Baltimore's work that I could fudge a couple of formulas and no one would be the wiser."

"Unless, of course, they check when the file was last accessed. I would."

"Yeah, but it'd be natural for me to open it to ensure it was still there."

"You don't have to open it to ensure that." He paused, expression thoughtful. "There is another option, however."

"What?" It was warily said, but I supposed I should be thankful he wasn't threatening to grab everything and lock me up. Not yet anyway.

"We insert a Trojan into the computer. One that will destroy all files the *second* time it's booted up."

I frowned. "Why the second time?"

"Because they will undoubtedly want to check that the file is present—and not obviously tampered with—before they hand over Jackson."

"Oh." I bit my lip for a moment, then added, "Can you access such a Trojan, though?"

He gave me the sort of look one would give a particularly thick child. "I wouldn't have suggested it if I couldn't."

"Meaning if you put this thing on the laptop, you'll let me meet with the sindicati? Alone?"

"If that's the way you want it, then yes. But just remember, the sindicati are *not* to be trusted. They are just as likely to kill you as release Jackson."

I remembered the vampire's promise. Remembered his anger at my doubting his word. They *would* let us walk away. Just how *far* we got—particularly now that I'd pissed him off—was anyone's guess.

"They wouldn't want to try," I said quietly.

His gaze met mine. After a moment, he nodded. "We'll head to your place first—"

The ringing of a phone cut him off. He picked up the earpiece sitting in the cup holder and slipped it on. "Yes?"

I couldn't hear what was being said, but if Sam's expression was anything to go by, all was not well at PIT.

"When did this happen?" he growled. Darkness crowded the car's cabin again, its caress sending goose bumps down my spine. And yet the element of sensuality was perhaps even stronger, attracting as fiercely as the darkness repelled.

I really, *really* wished I knew what the hell it was.

"Many fatalities?" The reply was obviously yes, because the darkness became so fierce it was suddenly hard to breathe. "Keep me updated. Oh, and, Adam? You want to e-mail me that doc file Trojan? I need to set it up on a laptop."

With that, he pulled the earpiece out and threw it into the cup holder.

"Problems?" I said, a little breathlessly.

"You could say that." He shot me a glance that was pure fury—but this time, at least, it wasn't aimed at me. "It seems your boss just walked out of the morgue."

CHAPTER 13

"That's impossible," I said automatically.

"Obviously not, given it just happened." He planted his foot, and the big car leapt forward. "It would appear Baltimore was somehow infected with the red plague virus. He woke up, broke free of the morgue, killing two people and injuring four others in the process."

"Fuck." I hesitated. "What will happen to those who survived now?"

"Now," he said, voice grim, "the waiting begins."

I frowned. "I thought you were killing anyone infected with the red plague."

He hesitated. "Not immediately. It often depends on what happens."

My confusion grew. "What do you mean? You said any scratch or bite would transmit the disease, and that it was all downhill from there."

"It is, but if you actually *survive* the infection, there appears to be two levels of degeneration."

I raised my eyebrows. "Meaning what?"

"The majority of those infected *do* become red cloaks, simply because that is who they are infected by. But it appears that there are some humans who have a natural resistance to the infection. While they still turn into vampirelike beings, they do not descend into utter madness. If you're infected by one of these, then you also have a greater chance of avoiding madness."

"What percentage are we talking about?"

"About ten percent of the cloaks, as near as we can figure, have avoided the madness."

Meaning it was more than possible for someone to be controlling the rest of the cloaks. "Then why not use the blood of those who have shown resistance to make a vaccine?"

"It's being tried; trust me. But not only is the virus constantly mutating within the body; it also reacts very differently in each person, depending on the race."

"Could that also be the reason some shifters are immune?"

"Possibly." He shrugged. "As I've said, we still don't understand a whole lot about this virus."

I snorted. "Tell me again why everybody thought it was a good idea to develop this thing?"

"Discovering the secret to immortality could very well help cure some of man's greatest diseases."

"Or it might just create more damn problems." It certainly had in this case. "What happens to those who don't fall into madness?"

"Whether they do or not, the result is generally the same. They head into Brooklyn."

"Why would they all go there?"

He shrugged. "We suspect there's something in the virus that produces a hive mentality in survivors."

As I'd noted the night I'd saved his ass. "Which would suggest that everything they do is for the greater good of the hive. And that means the question that has to be asked is, who is the queen of this particular hive?"

"*That* we don't know."

"Meaning there *is* someone in control?"

The look he gave me was fierce. I thought for a moment he wouldn't answer, but he surprised me.

"Yes. But we have no idea who and no idea how he or she gained control."

"Well, you'd think it would have to be someone who had natural resistance to the drug. Perhaps someone who was one of those initial infections."

"No. All the initial infections resulted in death or madness."

I wondered if the deaths were a result of the infection or PIT's intervention. I suspected the latter. "How many people have been infected all told? Have you any idea?"

"Outside the initial twenty or so, no. We estimate there's close to a hundred, though, if what we've seen in Brooklyn is any indication."

One hundred red cloaks. Fuck, that was a scary thought. "Why isn't the army involved? Why don't you all just go in there and shoot the shit out of the bastards?"

"That was tried. It ended very badly." He swung

off the freeway and onto Footscray Road. We were obviously going to my apartment rather than PIT headquarters. "Fifty men dead, another twenty infected, most of those now also dead."

I stared at him. "How in the hell did you keep a toll like *that* secret?"

"We didn't. Remember the reports of the two Chinook helicopters crash-landing during secret maneuvers?"

"That was a cover story?"

"Afraid so."

"But surely to god someone in Brooklyn witnessed what happened. I mean, it's not only the red cloaks who hide there, but all sorts of thieves and felons. How could the story of so many deaths *not* get out?"

"Thieves and felons are thin on the ground in certain parts of Brooklyn these days. Most of them have gotten the hell out of the sections the red cloaks control."

I hesitated, then said, "Is that when your brother was killed? During the military raid?"

"No. As I said, Luke was one of the first people killed by a red cloak. The military were sent in not long after that."

Again the edge of anger and guilt ran through his voice. "Was the scientist at work when the virus took full effect?"

"Yeah. He was working in one of the solo labs at the time, so no one noticed the changes until it was too late."

"And are you sure he's dead? Is it possible *he's* the hive leader?"

"No. He was riddled with bullets. Even if he *could* have survived the body shots, his brains were splattered all across the pavement. There was nothing left, and certainly no chance of any sort of rebirth."

"So the virus *is* capable of rebooting its host in much the same manner as a vampire's body is rebooted?"

"We had been hoping it wasn't possible, but your boss walking out this evening suggests otherwise." His expression was grim. "Future victims will have to be burned immediately after their deaths, it seems."

I scrubbed a hand across my eyes. "So what happens with Baltimore? Are you even going after him, given what happened to both the scientist and the military?"

"We're planning to try."

"God, be careful, Sam. I'd hate to have to come and rescue you again."

He snorted softly. "Thanks, Red, but next time you might be better leaving it in the hands of fate."

"Sorry. I've tried to do that over the years, but I just can't seem to stop sticking my nose into fate's business." Especially when fate was sticking her claws into someone I'd once cared about.

Someone I *still* cared about, despite every mean and nasty thing he'd said and done.

The whole trouble was, the man I'd loved *wasn't* gone. He'd just been buried very deep—at least where I was concerned.

"Or anyone else's, for that matter," he noted, voice dry.

I half smiled. "What happens next? Do you have to run off and join the hunt?"

"Unfortunately, yes. Baltimore has been tracked to Brooklyn, and there are only a few of us capable of hunting within that place."

"What about the notebook?"

"We find it. That's a priority right now. The hunt for Baltimore won't start until dusk anyway."

I frowned. "But that gives him time to find a hideout or join up with the rest of the crazies."

"That's presuming he *is* crazy. I actually suspect he might be one of the second-tier survivors."

"Why?"

"Because he'd be of little use to whoever is behind the hive if he were a mindless worker. For whatever reason, it appears the red cloaks are as desperate to get their hands on the cure as the sindicati. Why else would they have turned the head scientist of both labs involved?"

"It's not *that* surprising," I replied. "I mean, surely even the second-tier survivors must fear an eventual descent into madness?"

"It is certainly an ever-present threat." He glanced at me. "Survivors have told us it's like a black curtain they constantly have to push back."

"Have you got any survivors working at PIT?"

He hesitated. "We have people who were attacked. Whether all those who survived are still working, I couldn't say."

"If they are, isn't that a risk, given what you said about the black curtain?"

"No, because all our survivors are tagged and tracked. If they go off the reservation—in any way—they're killed."

I blinked. PIT didn't seem to hold a lot of belief in the sanctity of human life. "How, if they're off the so-called reservation?"

"It's done via a form of suicide pill that can be activated remotely. Every survivor has one implanted. They stray, and they're dead."

"Nasty."

"But better than killing survivors outright."

I guess. I studied the road ahead and realized we were close to my apartment. And that Sam was intent on coming in with me.

I took a deep breath and slowly released it. "You should wait in the car while I go search for the notebook."

"Why? So you can run off with it?"

"Sam, I promise—"

"And we both know how much weight your promises hold, don't we?"

It took every ounce of strength I had not to bite back, not to give in to all the anger and hurt that surged at his words. "When we split," I said, voice even, "I sold or burned every single thing that reminded me of you and our time together. *Everything*. Even the damn ring you gave me."

"That was my mother's—"

"And now it's a lump of metal sitting at the bottom of a rubbish dump somewhere. As I've already said, I was a little pissed off." And really not thinking with all that much clarity. If I had been, I probably wouldn't have melted the ring, because I knew it had been in his family a long time. "I was determined to start fresh, and I have. I don't want you in my apartment, Sam."

"In case it's escaped your memory, I've already been in your apartment."

"Yes, but I stayed outside. Big difference."

He snorted. "If there's any sort of logic in that statement, then I'm not seeing it."

No, he wouldn't. But then, he wasn't the one who'd see him surrounded by my things. Who'd later have to touch the same items he'd touched. Who'd once again see him in the room every time I closed my eyes. I'd freed myself from that sort of anguish when we'd moved. I didn't want to return to it, even if Sam was doing nothing more than helping me search for the missing notebook.

"You can wait outside the door if you like. There's only one exit—"

"Bullshit," he cut in. "You have a patio. And even *I* know phoenixes can take winged form."

"Yeah, but it's the middle of the day and there's a pervert in the opposite building who constantly has his telescope trained on our building in the hope of catching nakedness. I'm not about to out myself as something more than human to him or anyone else. Not for the sake of a damn note-book."

"Look, I have no desire to invade your privacy any more than necessary, but I will not—"

"I'll keep the door open," I said. "Or you can go in and search. Either way, there is no way known you and I are going to be in that apartment at the same time. I couldn't take it."

"The woman I"—he hesitated, looking away briefly before adding—"once loved is stronger than that. Besides, memories aren't deadly."

"Unless you have too many of them."

And I did. Many lifetimes' worth, in fact. It never got any easier to ignore them. Starting afresh, in a place that held none, was the only way I'd learned to cope with lifetime after lifetime of disappointments and heartache. I liked where we were currently living. I didn't want to have to move just yet.

"There's no such thing as too many memories, Em." His voice was soft, distant. Wistful, even. "Especially when it's only memories that stand between you and utter darkness."

I frowned and shifted slightly in the car seat to study him. "And is that what you're doing, Sam?"

His gaze met mine. There was no darkness in those blue depths, no anger. For the first time since we'd been reunited, there was just him, me, and the echoes of all that we had been and all that we could have been. And I knew in that moment that he felt the loss of our relationship as keenly as

I did. That he missed it—missed me—as keenly as I missed him.

But I also knew that it was *because* of the darkness more than everything else that had happened between us that he would never admit to either.

"Who said I was talking about myself?" He pulled his gaze away from mine and turned the car onto a side street.

Frustration swirled through me, even though I wasn't entirely surprised he'd backed away from the moment. He hadn't been overly forthcoming with general information, so it wasn't surprising he was even less so when it came to whatever was going on with him. Because something very definitely was.

We drove around my building several times before we found a space a block away. Once he'd parked, he held out one hand and said, "Apartment key. Sorry, Red, but that notebook is too damn important for me to trust that you'd hand it over once you've found it."

"Fine," I muttered. I went through my handbag, found my keys, and slammed them into his waiting hand. "The notebooks were only ever in the living areas. They were never in the bedrooms."

"Don't worry," he said, amusement in his voice. "I had no intention of going through your underwear drawer."

I didn't bother replying. It wouldn't have been of much use anyway—he'd already left the car. I watched him walk across the road. And with every step away from me, that darkness seemed to wrap around him again, as if it were some sort of private storm.

It made me wonder if I still would have fallen for him if we'd met now rather than years ago. Fate could be a bitch at the best of times, but even she wasn't often *this* cruel. The men slated to become heartbreakers each rebirth were generally decent enough in and of themselves. It was mostly outside circumstances—and the inability to either accept what I was or the situation with Rory—that caused the problems. Although there *had* been one or two who were either outright bastards or utter psychos . . . The serial killer had been one of those. Not that we'd realized *that* until it had been far too late for both me and his other victims.

I crossed my arms and stared out the window. Heartbreak might be our destiny, but it would be a whole lot easier to deal with if only fate would clear out our memory banks at each rebirth. At least it would have allowed hope to burn bright. But after all this time, there was little enough of that left.

And yet, somehow, it survived—even if the flame was growing smaller and smaller.

It wasn't long before Sam returned. In fact, little more than ten minutes had passed. I frowned and watched him approach, a slender, powerful figure that moved with the grace of a predator. He didn't appear to be carrying anything and his expression gave little away.

"Well?" I said the minute he slammed the driver's door closed.

"Your place is being watched," he said. "It's lucky for the both of us I parked so far from your building; otherwise your presence in my company would be immediately reported."

"The sindicati?"

"Yes."

Meaning it wasn't just lucky for us, but lucky for Jackson. I had no doubt they'd kill him if they had the slightest inkling I'd talked to Sam. And though it wasn't at all surprising that they were watching me, it was damn inconvenient.

"I'm gathering you didn't bother doing anything about him?"

"No. They'd simply put another in his place. At least we're now aware of this one."

I frowned. "He can't be very good if you picked him out so easily."

"A comment that suggests you think my policing and observation skills aren't up to scratch."

"No, that's not what I meant—"

He waved the rest of my comment away. "As it turned out, I didn't spot him. Not at first. It was his brief attempt to read me that gave the game away."

"So was he a vamp or a psychic?"

"Vamp. He was wearing too many layers for a warm building."

I raised my eyebrows. "Why would a vamp be pulling watch duty during the day? Surely a wolf would be more suited?"

"They would, but telepathic wolves are rare."

"Even so, there's twenty-four-hour security in the foyer. I can't imagine any of the guards—"

"It *was* the guard," he cut in.

"No—"

"Yes." He raised an eyebrow. "Or are you saying you know them all personally?"

"Well, of course not, but after so many years of seeing the same faces, I have formed a casual, how're-the-kids-type friendship."

"And yet you noticed neither the new guard nor that he'd appeared one day after your boss was killed. Which doesn't say a lot about *your* observation skills."

No, it didn't. But then, why would I be on the lookout for something like that? It wasn't until very recently that I'd even become *aware* of the sindicati's involvement in all this crap.

"I'm not the cop in this little game. You are," I snapped back. "And I would have thought—given your goons are still following me about—that background checks would have been performed on all those I interacted with."

"They are. Unfortunately, that vampire is using an assumed name—Michael Venton. And Venton checked out."

He might have checked out, but he wasn't one of the guards I was familiar with—and I probably wouldn't have any chance to do so now, given the remains of the real Venton were probably buried deep in the countryside somewhere. Maybe even the same countryside in which I'd woken.

I scrubbed a hand across my eyes again. The hobnailed folk had calmed down a little, but I was still in serious need of some painkillers. And a hot shower. And several decent mugs of green tea followed by the biggest block of chocolate I could buy. It had been that sort of day. Unfortunately, it wasn't over yet.

"So how did you explain your presence there?"

"I didn't. I simply flashed the badge, said I needed to talk to you, and asked if he knew whether you were home. When he said he wasn't sure, I went up and banged on your door. Naturally enough, you didn't answer."

I half smiled. "A fact he would have seen on the security cams."

"No doubt. It does mean we have a problem, however. I can't get in there to get that notebook and—if you do—you can bet your life that vamp is going to find a way to relieve you of it."

I frowned. "Why would they do that when we've already made a deal to exchange the book for Jackson?"

"They're a *crime* syndicate." Sarcasm filled his voice. "They don't give a rat's ass about convention or rules, and they *always* stack the odds in their favor."

They might be the biggest, baddest things out there—other than the red cloaks, that was—but that didn't mean they were without their own rules and laws. Hell, the vampire who'd been sent to collect me from Sherman Jones had been courteous to a fault, and even the vamp who'd tasted me in that darkness had been nothing other than polite.

But being polite didn't mean they couldn't also be double-crossing bastards.

"Which has left us with only one course of action, and it means we're both going to have to take a bit of a risk."

"I'm not letting you go—"

"But you already have." Once again the comment was out before I could stop it, and it was filled with the bitterness that still lurked deep inside. I silently cursed myself and quickly added, "We both know you—or at least your department— could make my life hell, so the sooner this is over with, the quicker we can go our separate ways."

"But that vampire—"

"Look," I cut in, a touch impatiently. "The sindicati will be expecting me to go home. If I don't, it'll only raise suspicions and perhaps endanger Jackson."

He snorted. "That's not exactly a winning argument. Not given my already-expressed feelings where the Fae and the notebook is concerned."

"Maybe, but they're not likely to do anything until I've found the notebook and made contact. Until I do that, we have time to maneuver."

"And just how do you plan to get back here with the notebook? If you attempt to leave, you can bet your ass that vamp will try to grab it."

"Only if he sees me leave, which he won't. Security cams monitor the inside of the building, not the outside, remember. I'll simply take fire or firebird form and leave from the balcony."

"Which means exposing your true self to possibly hundreds of people in nearby buildings, as you said before."

"I'm well aware of that, Sam." But it was worth the risk if it saved Jackson's life.

He studied me for several seconds, then tore his gaze away. The muscle along his jaw had gone into serious overtime, but there was little other emotion to be seen.

"Okay," he said, voice flat. "We do it your way. But if you're not back in twenty minutes, I'm coming in."

"Make it an hour, because I need a damn shower." I got out. It was pointless to do anything else, and arguing with him wasn't going to get me anywhere. It never had.

It didn't take me long to get home, but it took every ounce of willpower I had to do nothing more than give the guard a polite nod in greeting as I walked by.

But I could feel his gaze boring into my spine long after I'd entered the elevator, and I had no doubt his gaze was glued to the monitor screens as I headed for my apartment.

"Rory? You here?" I said as I opened the door.

"Certainly am." He appeared around the corner, his hair wet and a towel wrapped around his waist. "You didn't pass Sam on the way up, did you? He was here banging on the door a few minutes ago, but disappeared before I could answer."

"That's because it was a ruse for the guard downstairs."

He frowned. "Why?"

I locked the door and began stripping as I walked toward our flameproof room. "Because the guard downstairs is sindicati. If they see me with Sam, or believe he's working with me, they'll kill Jackson."

"And is Sam working with you?"

I half smiled. "No. Quite the opposite. He wants the missing notebook, as does the sindicati."

"So who are you giving the notebook to? Sam or the sindicati?"

"Sam's getting the notebook. The sindicati are getting the laptop." I grabbed his hand and tugged him into the room. "But right now, you and I need to flame."

"Your wish is my command," he murmured, as he wrapped his arms around me and swept us both into fire.

"So, let's retrace your steps," Rory said, half an hour later. "After you typed the notebooks up, what did you do with them?"

"Nothing. I left them all on the coffee table." I thrust my hands on my hips and glared at the room in frustration. It wasn't offering up any clues. "You didn't move them, did you?"

He raised an eyebrow. "Me? Tidy something up? Are you serious?"

"Okay, silly question." But if neither of us had moved them, what the hell had happened? Why would anyone steal four notebooks when five had been sitting there? It didn't make any sense.

"You didn't knock them over or anything, did you?" Rory said. "I have a vague memory of you running into something and swearing like a trooper one morning."

I blinked, suddenly remembering hitting the coffee table and scattering the notebooks the morning Sam had woken us early. I'd picked them all up and thrown them back on the table, but I certainly hadn't taken the time to count them. Had I missed one?

I scrambled over to the coffee table and began searching under both it and the nearby sofas. Rory joined in, and five minutes later, we found the damn notebook. It had somehow slid all the way into the kitchen and was resting under one of the cabinets.

Relief slithered through me, but it was tempered by the knowledge that the game wasn't over yet. Jackson was still in the hands of the sindicati, and who knew whether this new and darker Sam would uphold his end of the deal.

"So what happens now?" Rory said.

I tucked the notebook inside the waist of my jeans, making sure it was not only secure, but touching skin. "I go back to Sam, and you go get the laptop. I'll ring and let you know where to meet us."

His expression was dubious. "Do you really think you can trust Sam?"

I half shrugged. "I have no other choice."

He caught my hand, tugged me closer, and dropped a sweet kiss on my lips. "Be careful. And take flame form, not firebird. There's a chance people will think we've simply thrown something burning out of the window."

I nodded, stepped back, and called to the fire. In very little time, I was back on the street and walking back to Sam's car.

"So?" he said, the minute I dropped into the passenger seat.

I pulled the notebook out of the waist of my pants, but flipped it away from him as he tried to take it. "I want you to promise you'll uphold up your end of the deal once I hand this over."

"Red," he growled, eyes narrowed. "I said I would, and I will. Now stop playing stupid games when lives are at risk."

"It's the whole lives-at-risk bit that's making me play them," I replied. "We both know PIT is working on the bigger picture and wouldn't really care if the smaller elements—like Jackson—fall by the wayside."

"As I've already said, if you want to risk your neck saving Miller's useless ass, then go for it. Neither PIT nor I will interfere, as long as we can ensure the information on that computer is secure. Now, give me the notebook."

I hesitated, then shook my head. "*After* we meet Rory and you've put the virus onto the computer."

He glared at me, his expression so savage it was all I could do not to shrink back in fear. But fire flickered across my fingertips, touching but not burning the notebook. For several seconds, neither of us moved; then he tore his gaze away and I started breathing again.

"Fine," he said, voice clipped. "Where are we meeting him?"

I released a somewhat shaky breath and doused the flames. "Head for Spencer Street."

He started the car and did a quick U-turn, wheels spinning. I grabbed my phone and sent Rory a text, asking him to meet us at Black Sugar, a café a stone's throw away from Southern Cross Station. Putting Sam and Rory in the same small space probably wasn't a great idea, but it wasn't like I had much choice. Besides, I doubted Sam would start something in public—not given how much he and PIT seemed to value their anonymity.

Sam stopped in the parking lot near Southern Cross Rail Station, and in silence we walked down to Black Sugar. The place was packed, but we managed to find a spare table at the back of the room. Sam took the chair closest to the wall—a position that allowed him to see not only the entire room, but the entrance as well—leaving me either the chair opposite or the one to his left. Both were entirely too close to the man for my liking, but I chose the latter, simply because I didn't want to have my back to the entrance.

But as I sat, his scent spun around me, warm and enticing. And even the darker notes so evident within it couldn't stop desire from spinning through me.

I closed my eyes and fought the wash of useless regret. This was my life. This would *always* be my life. It was no use wishing for anything else, because—as far as I knew—no phoenix had ever been able to break the curse and live a happy life. Not with the love of their life. Not ever.

It certainly wasn't about to happen in this life, with this man.

You'd think after spending so many lives in the exact same position, I'd be used to it. But there was something about this man that called to me in a way few others had. Even with that darkness.

"Red," he said, voice holding a slight edge. "How long do we have to wait?"

My gaze met his. The edge, I realized, was desire, barely controlled. It made me want to lean closer, to see if it was possible to kiss away the ash and the darkness and unveil the man that still lay beneath them somewhere.

I didn't. I might be occasionally reckless, but even *I* wasn't that foolish.

"Not long." I leaned back in my chair, though it didn't really improve the distance between us or diminish the desire to kiss him. "Rory said it would take him twenty minutes to get here, so unless the traffic is hideous, he should only be a few minutes away."

Sam pulled his gaze from mine. After a second, he said, "When you meet with the sindicati, watch your back. They have a liking for sharpshooters perched up high."

"Thanks for the warning."

He shrugged. "I don't want you dead, Red, no matter how much I hate what you did to us."

I opened my mouth to argue, then closed it again. There was no point in trying to explain. Not anymore.

"I don't want me dead, either," I said instead. "It would be damnably inconvenient to die early in two consecutive lifetimes."

He glanced at me, eyebrows raised. "You get to live again, so why does it matter?"

"Because dying before your allotted time makes rebirth a bitch." I glanced toward the door and saw Rory. His gaze met mine, flicked briefly to the man sitting beside me, then returned. His expression didn't alter, but tension rode him. It was evident in the set of his shoulders, in the brief clenching of his free hand as he made his way toward us.

I cleared my throat, but before I could say anything, Sam murmured, "Well, well, the boyfriend arrives."

"And *that* statement proves just how little you understand about phoenixes—and Emberly." Rory came to a halt in front of us, bright sunshine against the darkness of the man beside me.

"So you deny you're her boyfriend?" Sam growled. "That you were—and still are—lovers?"

"I deny nothing."

Rory's voice was as even as Sam's, yet it hinted

at the anger that burned just beneath the calm exterior. The heat of it rolled over me, as fierce and as frightening as the darkness that lurked within Sam, but for a very different reason. I knew that anger, knew what it was capable of. Knew that if there was one flaw in the control Rory had over his fire, then it was me. Or rather, his desire to protect me from whatever life and fate threw at us. As much as he ever could, anyway.

And though he'd promised long ago to never again retaliate against those who were destined to hurt me, he'd been itching for a chance to confront Sam. Because he knew, just as I knew, that Sam had somehow been different. That the hurt this time had been deeper and harder to handle.

"But I *am* a necessity," he continued softly. "Without me, she cannot be, and vice versa. And if you cannot understand that, if you cannot accept that, then you are more of a fool than I thought."

Sam thrust to his feet, his fist clenched and very obviously close to losing control.

"Damn it. Get a grip, both of you!" I stepped in front of Rory, forcing him back with my body as I thrust my hands on my hips and glared at Sam. "This is neither the time nor the damn place to get into this sort of shit. Not when we have a deadline to meet and lives to save."

Sam didn't immediately move or react, but the muscle along his jaw was back in action. After a moment, he nodded and sat back down.

"Give me the computer."

I held out my hand. Rory placed the computer in it, and I handed it across to Sam.

"How do we get the Trojan onto it?" I said as Sam opened the laptop.

He didn't answer, simply fired it up and, after a few seconds, said, "Password?"

I told him. With the computer unlocked, he got onto the Internet, using his phone as a hot spot, and download a file from an e-mail account. After a few more minutes, he shut the computer down and handed it back.

"Now," he said, voice little more than a growl. "The notebook."

"You've installed the Trojan?"

"Of course." He held out his hand. "The note-book, Emberly."

I handed it over. He rose, his expression as still as stone but the darkness within thicker—more dangerous—than ever before. And again, it al-lured as much as it repelled, and I had to fight to remain exactly where I was. Though whether I would have stepped forward or back, I wasn't en-tirely sure.

"As I've said before, be careful when you meet the sindicati. They tend not to stick to deals made with the likes of you and me."

I raised an eyebrow. "Meaning?"

"Meaning, the honest, law-abiding types." His mouth twisted into a smile, but it was a bitter thing to behold. "Obviously, they don't know ei-ther of us too well."

And with that, he walked out. I didn't watch

him leave. I didn't need to. I could feel the deep gloom of his presence as surely as Rory's heat at my back. When he'd gone, I released the breath I hadn't even realized I'd been holding, then turned around and melted into Rory's waiting arms.

He kissed the top of my head and said, "At least it's over with, Em. At least you don't have to see him again."

"I can only hope." But I had a bad feeling fate wasn't about to let me off that easily. "But that's not what matters right now. We have a Fae to save."

"Well, I do agree with your bastard of an ex about one thing—the sindicati are not to be trusted. We need to meet them on our terms, not theirs, if we want any chance of pulling off this rescue."

I grimaced and pulled free from his grip as a waitress finally approached. After ordering a green tea for myself and a coffee for Rory, I sat back down and said, "I'm not sure they'll agree to a change of plans. They hold the cards, not us."

"If they want what we have, they'll play the game. At least until we hand over the laptop."

"Maybe." I wasn't too confident, but I guess we really had nothing to lose by trying. "Sam said they have a liking for marksmen placed on high, so we need to factor that in."

He pulled out a chair and sat down. "We could always go up to the rock. While it does provide plenty of places for a marksman to hide, I can easily keep watch from the sky."

The rock he meant was Hanging Rock, a recreational reserve that featured a large mamelon formation. Rory often went up there after hours for some flight time during the long golden sunsets of the summer months, because the surrounding areas were farmlands and the chances of being seen were few. While I did go up there occasionally, he was far more familiar with the area than I was.

I frowned. "Do you think they'll agree to meet that far out of town?"

"We're dealing with the vampire mafia, remember. Trust me when I say they won't want anything too public, especially if they're planning a few nasty surprises of their own." He smiled up at the waitress as she delivered our drinks, then added, once she'd left, "Our main problem will be getting them to agree to dusk rather than night."

"True." I dunked my tea bag into the mug of hot water and watched the bubbles rise as it sank. And hoped like hell it wasn't an omen for things to come.

Rory's hand slid across mine, his grip warm, comforting. "It'll be all right, Em."

I smiled, but it felt tight. Fake. "Will it? I have a bad feeling about all this, and it's a real risk for both of us to be there."

"Vampires can't fly," he said reasonably. "So as long as I keep to the skies, we'll be fine."

Yeah, we would, but we both knew that he wouldn't keep to the skies, not if things started going bad on the ground—just as I wouldn't, if the situation were reversed. It was one of the reasons we'd agreed that the two of us should never again get jointly involved in dangerous situations—the need to protect each other was so much a part of our psyche that we not only placed our very existence at risk, but the chance of rebirth. As he'd noted to Sam, one could not be without the other.

I leaned back in the chair and regarded him for several seconds. "Promise me you'll keep to the skies. That you won't get involved in the fight if things go to hell on the ground."

He hesitated. "I promise I'll keep to the skies unless I see a sharpshooter. Them, I'll take out. Fair enough?"

"Fair enough."

"Then ring them and make the meet."

I took a deep, somewhat quivery breath that didn't do a whole lot to calm the butterflies suddenly going nutso in my stomach. I might have lived many lifetimes, but I'd never been one to march boldly into dangerous situations. "Avoidance was the better part of valor" tended to be the code I lived by.

But I dug out my phone and made the call regardless. After all, this wasn't about me. It was about Jackson. About saving his life if it was at all possible.

"Well, well," a cool and familiar voice said. "You report in far earlier than any of us predicted."

"That's because I have no desire to prolong these proceedings any more than necessary." My voice was surprisingly calm given all I could suddenly think about was his teeth tearing into my neck. "I've looked for the notebook and I can't find it. I do, however, have the laptop on which the notes were typed."

"And is the file on said laptop untampered with?"

"I haven't opened it," I replied, and thanked the stars I'd listened to Sam and hadn't tried to tamper with the notes themselves. "You can check the date it was last accessed when we do the swap, if you want."

"Oh, I will," he murmured. "Now, as to the swap—"

"Not so fast," I cut in. "I want proof that Jackson Miller is alive first."

"I gave you my word that he would be."

"You did," I said. "But past dealings with vampires have left me a little less inclined to trust a promise given by one."

"That *is* unfortunate." Though there was still little in the way of emotion to be heard in the vamp's tone, trepidation stepped through me. He really *didn't* like having his integrity questioned in *any* way, and I had a feeling doing so was a bad, *bad* idea.

I reached for my cup of tea, but my hands were trembling so much that liquid splashed over the sides and scalded my fingers. Rory plucked the cup from my hand, discarded the tea bag, then, with a wry smile, brought it up to my lips. I took a sip, but it helped with neither the dryness in my throat nor the butterflies doing a tango in my stomach.

For several—very long—minutes, there was nothing but silence. Then came the sound of a click—the sort of sound that came from a light being turned on—and a muffled curse. The voice was Jackson's. But the surge of relief was tempered by the knowledge that while he was alive right now, it didn't mean he would be when the time for the exchange came.

"The lady of fire wishes to confirm you're alive, Fae." The vampire's cool tones echoed slightly over the phone. Wherever they were, it was somewhere cavernous. "Please assure her that you are."

His choice of words had alarm shooting through me. I glanced sharply at Rory and mouthed, "How the hell could they know what I am?"

But even as he shrugged, I remembered Rawlings, and the fire I'd encaged him with. Obviously, he'd reported events to the sindicati, something I hadn't counted on but surely should have. And while it meant the sindicati now knew some of what I was capable of, they didn't know it all. Didn't know I was a fire spirit and capable of a whole lot more than just calling forth fire from the earth itself.

Unless, of course, they'd beaten the information out of Jackson. He not only knew what I was, but he'd witnessed my transformation from flesh to fire.

"Emberly," Jackson croaked, "I'm alive."

"And you sound like shit," I replied, trying not to envision what had been done to him.

"I have had better days." Amusement briefly overrode the pain so evident in his gruff tones. "But it's nothing a good barbeque can't fix up."

"Except both of us know that controlling any sort of barbeque is not on the list of things you are currently capable of, Fae," came the amused comment. "So let us not wish for something that cannot be."

Once again his comment had alarm stirring. If the sindicati knew Jackson couldn't control fire, then that could mean only one thing—PIT had been infiltrated. There was no way they could have known that otherwise.

"And you, dear Emberly, have your confirmation that the Fae still survives," the vampire continued. "If you wish him to remain that way, you will meet—"

"No," I cut in. "Sorry, but we're back to that whole trust issue again. We meet at a time and a place specified by me, not you."

There was a long pause. "When and where?"

"Hanging Rock, central parking lot, at dusk."

After another long pause—during which I had no doubt he was consulting someone—he said, "As you wish."

His agreement only ratcheted up my tension. I'd expected at least *some* argument, especially given they were vamps and night would suit them better than dusk. That there was none could only mean the meeting point suited them just as

much as it suited us. Still, I had one advantage—
they didn't know about Rory.

Or at least I hoped they didn't. The shit could
really hit the fan if they did.

"Fine. I'll see you then."

"You will indeed," he murmured, and hung up.

I breathed a sigh of relief, then plucked my tea
from Rory's grip and downed it in several gulps,
hoping it would at least drown the butterflies. It
didn't.

I glanced at my watch, then met Rory's understanding gaze. "We have three hours."

"Which gives us time enough to eat before we
have to head up to Macedon." He caught my
hand and kissed my fingertips. "You need to fuel
this body, Em, not just the fire spirit."

"I know." I scrubbed a hand across tired eyes.
After everything that had happened, I felt like
shit, and I very much suspected it was a feeling
that wouldn't go away, even after I'd eaten. "It's
just that I'm—"

"Worried. I know. But it'll all work out. I'm sure
of it."

I hoped he was right.

Hoped like hell that things didn't go down as
badly as I suspected they would tonight.

Chapter 14

I drove past the locked gates that led into Hanging Rock Reserve, then came to a halt in the shadows of several eucalypts farther down the road and climbed out. Dusk was just beginning to weave red and gold fingers across the cloud-held sky, and the air had a charged, electric feel to it.

Or maybe that was just *me*.

Fire burned through my limbs, a force so eager to be used that sparks danced lightly across my fingertips every time I moved.

I clenched my hands and tried to control the fear that was leading to the fiery output. I might have serious doubts as to whether the sindicati would uphold their promises and let us go free, but I couldn't walk into this meeting so obviously ready for trouble. *Any* show of force, however small and bright, might just turn things down the wrong path.

I raised my gaze and scanned the sky. Rory was up there somewhere, but it didn't make me feel any safer. We might have set this meeting for a time convenient for us, but the cool-voiced vampire was one of the old ones, and dusk provided little impediment. And they'd had several hours to prepare their net—if indeed it was a net I was stepping into, and not just old fears and prejudices raising their ugly heads.

I blew out a breath, wished the nerves could so easily be released, then leaned back into the car and plucked the laptop—now safely secured in a backpack—off the backseat. After locking the car and shoving the keys under the rear wheel arch to ensure I didn't lose them in whatever mayhem might happen over the next half hour, I walked through the scrub that divided the road from the fence and climbed into the reserve.

It took about ten minutes to walk to the main parking lot, and sunset had taken full hold by the time I arrived. The power of it sang through me, a fierce, warm energy that—in any other situation—would have had me dancing.

I paused on the edge of the tarmac. There were several cars present, but no sign of the occupants. Given the reserve was closed for the evening, they had to belong either to the rangers or to the sindicati themselves. But if it was the latter, where the hell were they?

My gaze jumped to the ancient rock formation that loomed above the parking lot, but I couldn't see anyone there, either. Not that I would. I mean, we were talking about vampires, and those bastards were well able to conceal themselves in shadows. And even with dusk in its full glory there was still plenty of *those* lurking about.

I resolutely took four steps forward—and sud-

denly felt horribly exposed. Keeping my fingers
clenched, I said, without raising my voice, "I
know you're here. Reveal yourselves."

For several minutes there was no response.
Sweat began to trickle down my spine, and my
heart felt ready to tear itself out of my chest.
Which, no doubt, was precisely what they wanted.

Then, directly opposite me, a long stick of a
man shook free of the shadows lurking under the
trees and stepped into the sunset-bathed parking
space. He had dusty blond hair, a thick, handlebar
mustache, and was dressed rather like an old-
style cowboy—complete with boots and hat. The
telling thing, however, was that he didn't even
flinch when the waning sunlight hit him. He was
one of the old ones, and possibly *had* been a cowboy before he'd turned.

He was not, however, the man I'd been speaking to over the phone—the one who'd tasted me
when I'd been held captive in that place of darkness. Why I was so certain I couldn't really say,
other than the fact that the same sense of menace
wasn't emanating from him.

Although that didn't make him any less dangerous.

"You have the laptop?" His voice held the
slightest hint of a drawl and none of the cool re-
moteness of the other vampire.

"I do, but I'm not about to risk handing it over
to any old lackey. If the man I made the deal with
isn't here, then I walk away."

"Such an action would only result in the Fae's death."

"Kill the Fae, and you kill any chance of getting the notes." A flicker of gold caught my eye. I glanced up, saw a trail of fiery red-gold plunge from the streaked skies. Tension wound through me, and it was all I could do to remain where I was, to not step back to the shelter of the trees, where I was less of a target for a marksman. But I couldn't help adding, "Kill me, and you won't get the laptop's password."

His eyebrow raised almost imperceptibly. "That is hardly a consideration when we have more than enough resources to break whatever password you may have placed on the computer."

"Perhaps." My gaze swept the parking lot's boundaries, sensing movement but not seeing it. "But if you shoot me, you risk damaging the computer itself in my fall. Isn't it far easier for everyone involved if the man I made the deal with just stepped forward?"

"Why does it matter who you deal with?" the cowboy countered.

I smiled, but it was thin and forced. "Because my deal was made with him, not you. He gave me his word on our safety. You did not."

"A small but important distinction, I agree," a cool voice said to my left.

I jumped and half swung around as a shadow appeared out of the trees only yards from where I stood. God, I hadn't even sensed him—how many damn others were nearby? More than even imagination could conjure, I'd wager.

I swallowed to ease the sudden dryness in my throat and watched him walk—although to be honest, gliding seemed a more apt description of his method of movement—into the middle of the parking lot, where he turned to face me. He had what could be described only as classic male features—a wide, angular jaw, a square chin, a prominent brow, and a strong—almost Roman—nose. Both his eyes and his hair were a steely gray, and he was rangier in build than his whip-thin compatriot.

"Now, the laptop. I wish to see it."

"And I have the same desire to see Jackson Miller. You present your offering; then I'll present mine."

He sighed. "And still you don't trust me. This aggrieves me greatly, I assure you."

"I'm sure you'll survive my mistrust," I said. "After all, you are a rather high-ranking member of the sindicati. I would think mistrust comes with the territory."

"That, unfortunately, is very true." He paused, and a slight smile touched his lips. A chill ran across my skin, and I clenched my fists so hard against the surge of fire that my nails dug into my palms. "But also somewhat earned."

He raised a hand and made a quick "come here" motion with two fingers. Out of the shadows behind him, two more vampires appeared, Jackson gripped between them as they dragged him forward. His clothes were torn and his body beaten and bloody; he looked every inch as bad as he'd sounded on the phone. But his gaze, when it met mine, was filled with pain, fury, and fire.

It was the fire that caught my attention. It burned deep in those green depths, and it suggested he was more than ready to wield flames should the slightest spark arise.

Had the drug worn off?

God, I hoped so. Even if he wasn't at full strength physically, we had more of a chance of surviving this encounter if he at least had *some* fire capability. I returned my attention to the cool-voiced vampire.

"Your turn," he said evenly.

I swung the backpack around and pulled out the laptop.

"Start it up. I want to check that the file has not been touched." His sudden smile held a mocking edge. "I'm afraid the lack of trust goes both ways."

"You're welcome to check, but the laptop doesn't leave my hands while it happens." My gaze skated across the shadows haunting the tree-lined parking lot. The sense of movement was increasing, as was the sense of danger. I rolled my shoulders, trying to ease the tension, with little success. "But no tricks. I'm a lady of fire, remember, and flesh burns just as easily as trees."

"Oh, we forget *nothing*." It was a warning more than a statement, and it had my gaze darting across those shadows again. I had a bad, bad feeling that the "we" he was talking about was *not* those I could see or sense, but those I couldn't.

Who was out there, watching the proceedings from the shadows? That silent stranger again? Or someone else? And did they intend to do anything more than just watch?

I hoped not.

The vampires already in the parking lot and those I could sense moving around were more than enough to contend with. I didn't need any more shit added to an already overloaded plate.

A vampire came out of the trees to my left and walked toward me. I booted up the laptop, typed in the password, then held it up as the vamp stopped in front of me. He was tall and thin, as most tended to be, with thick brown hair, an aristocratic nose, and a mouth that seemed locked in a permanent sneer. He smelled of garlic and earth—an odd combination that didn't do a whole lot for the tremulous state of my stomach.

His fingers flew over the keyboard, his touch so light I barely felt the movement. After a moment, he stepped back and glanced at his boss.

"The file has not been touched."

"Excellent. Bring the laptop to me."

"Not so fast." I snatched the computer away from the grasp of the vamp. "An equal exchange, please. And you"—I added, glancing at garlic breath—"can go back to the shadows, if you don't mind."

The vamp glanced at his boss, then retreated as requested. It didn't make me feel any safer. "Now release Jackson."

The cool-voiced vampire waved those two fingers again. The vamps holding Jackson released him and stepped back. Jackson slapped to the ground like so much bloodied meat and, for several seconds, didn't move. Then, with a hiss of air that spoke of extreme pain, he rolled onto his back.

"I'm afraid," the cool-voiced vamp said casually, "that your friend has suffered a broken arm and leg. It is, unfortunately, a far easier way to manage captives than any regular means of restraint."

I swore under my breath. I should have guessed the bastards would do something like *that*.

"Then you need to step back." I shoved the laptop into the backpack and swung the pack onto my shoulder. "Once I have Jackson, you can have the pack."

After that, I could only hope that they *would* uphold their end of the deal. But even if they didn't, we had more of a chance against them if we could at least make a stand together.

The cool-voiced vampire raised his hands and all three stepped back to the edge of the trees. Their easy compliance only ratcheted the tension and the fire singing through me.

I studied the nearby tree line for several seconds, wishing I had the ability to look beyond the shadows, wishing I could see who was watching, who was waiting. But that was an ability—like the dreams—not often found in phoenixes. And I briefly wondered, if I'd dreamed that *this* would be the end result of saving Sam, whether I'd have actually saved him.

Yes, that insane bit of me whispered, *you would have.*

I took a deep, somewhat shuddery breath; then, my grip tight on one of the backpack's straps, I walked toward Jackson.

His gaze met mine as I neared, and the fury was richer in his bright eyes. "Damn it, Em, you shouldn't be here."

"If I were the sensible type, I wouldn't be." I stopped beside him, swung the backpack off my shoulder, and carefully placed it on the asphalt. As I did so, I sent the flames that sparked across my fingertips onto the pack, where they shimmered and danced but didn't burn. Not yet, anyway.

"Destroy that backpack," the cool-voiced vampire commented, "and you destroy any agreement we had."

"The flames won't destroy the pack. Not unless you attack." I squatted down, keeping my gaze on the vamp as I said to Jackson, "I'm going to need your help to get us out of here. You up for that?"

"You bet your sweet ass I am," he muttered. And I knew he was referring more to fighting the vamps than any toll the mere act of moving would have on him. Fae were a damn tough lot. He added, "Haul me up on the left side. It ain't broken."

To haul him up, I'd have to turn my back on the vampires—not something I was overly keen on doing, but it wasn't like I had a whole lot of choice. "Tell me if one of them moves or disappears."

"I will."

I changed position, then gripped his raised hand. My gaze met his again and he nodded, briefly. With very little ceremony—but a whole lot of effort—I hauled him upright onto his good leg. He gritted his teeth and hissed, the sound long and pain filled. Sweat broke out across his brow and his skin suddenly looked ashen—not a great look on a fire Fae. I quickly shoved my shoulder under his and took most of his weight as he wobbled about. I slipped my other arm around his body. His heart was beating so hard it felt like someone was thumping my hand, and he was trembling violently. How he was even conscious, I had no idea.

"Now," I said, just as much to the vampires as to Jackson, "we get out of here."

"And the flames on the backpack?" the cool-voiced vampire inquired.

"Will retreat when we're safe, not before."

"You have until the trees. Release it then, or we *will* attack."

"And what happens after I release the pack? We're hardly safe in the trees."

He raised an eyebrow, his expression mocking. "Would it matter if I promise that neither I nor any of those *I* brought to this meeting will attack?"

"It probably wouldn't, but I'd like to hear it, all the same."

"Then I so promise. *We* will not attack you."

The slight emphasis he placed on "we" had my gaze going to the trees again. The cool-voiced vampire and his cronies might not attack, but whoever was hiding in those shadows more than likely *would*.

Still, it was a risk we had no choice but to take.

I headed for the trees and tried not to jar Jackson's broken limbs too much—an impossible task given that he was forced to hop. After several minutes of doing so, he began to swear vehemently. I stopped immediately—which only caused another round of swearing.

"Damn it," he said, between gritted teeth. "Just keep going."

I did, moving as slowly as I could, trying to keep an eye on the vamps behind us as the awareness of the threat still hiding in the trees grew. To make matters worse, the dusk was fading and darkness would soon be upon us.

And darkness was the vampires' ally, not ours.

But I couldn't go any faster. Jackson was a big man, and it was taking everything I had to keep him upright. Sweat dribbled down my face and back, and the scent stung the sweet evening air until all I could smell was it and fear.

We inched along, slowly drawing closer to the trees. I glanced at the skies and hoped like hell Rory was watching. That he'd be ready.

The shadows reached for us, though their grasp was anything but comforting. Those shadows held dangerous secrets, and I wasn't looking forward to their revelation.

One problem at a time, I reminded myself fiercely. And that, right now, was the vampires at our backs.

I looked over my shoulder. The cool-voiced vampire remained in the middle of the clearing, his arms crossed and his expression sitting somewhere between amusement and contempt.

Something was very definitely about to happen—and it *wasn't* us getting free.

"That is far enough, Emberly Pearson. If you do not release the backpack from its flames, we will unfortunately be forced to attack."

"Don't do it," Jackson muttered. "They'll attack the minute they have the laptop."

"And they'll attack if they don't get it," I murmured. "But never fear. I do have a trick or two up my sleeve."

"I hope they're damn good ones, because we're not exactly in a great state here. Or at least, I'm not."

"You *do* rather look like shit." I came to a halt. Tension—or maybe it was pain—rippled through Jackson's muscular frame. "But the big question is, are you shit that can use flame?"

His snort was one of amusement, but it quickly became a groan. "God, don't make me do that. But yeah, I can."

"Good, because there's something in the trees and it's getting ready to attack." My gaze met the cool-voiced vampire's again, and I raised my voice as I added, "Remember your promise, vampire."

And with that, I waved a hand, the gesture grander than it needed to be, but I had to be sure Rory spotted it. The flames skittered away from the backpack and quickly faded into the ether of the evening.

The cowboy stepped forward, picked up the pack, and withdrew the laptop. The pack itself was contemptuously thrown to one side and skidded underneath one of the parked cars.

"Thank you for upholding your end of our deal. And now—"

I had no idea what else he said, because his words were lost in an explosion of flame. They sprang from the earth itself, a wild and tempestuous storm that burned with all the colors of creation.

Rory, connecting with the great mother to provide a barrier around the parking lot to keep the vampires contained.

"That," Jackson said heavily, "is one hell of a trick to have up your sleeve."

"Yeah, but it only accounts for one problem, not the other. Let's get out of here while we still can."

We moved on as quickly as Jackson was able. The power of the flames that danced at our backs rippled across my skin, drawing answering sparks that shot into the shadows like little tiny comets. Under normal circumstances, I would have tried to control the output, if only because such a show gave away our position. But it was pointless to do so here; whoever—*whatever*—was out there knew exactly where we were, sparkly show or not.

Besides, between the sparks and the fire at our backs, Jackson surely had enough fire to amplify and use.

Jackson's breathing became more labored the farther we went into the trees. He didn't say anything, but the trembling was far worse, and his body was drenched in sweat. I couldn't see him making it to the car. And while I *could* drag him, I certainly wouldn't be able to get him up and over the fence. And Rory needed all his strength to maintain that fire barrier.

"It's not that far now," I muttered. "You have to keep going, Jackson."

"Don't fucking worry about me." The words were little more than short, sharp expulsions of air. "Worry about the things—"

Something hit us side-on, with such force it tore Jackson from my grasp and sent me stumbling into the trees. I crashed into the trunk of a tree and crumpled to a heap at its base, seeing stars and fighting for breath. Heat exploded across the air, accompanied by the sharp smell of eucalyptus as the trees around me burst into flame. I groaned, rolled onto my back, and forced my eyes open.

And saw, in the dancing gleam of fire, Jackson—on his back, flames shooting from both his good hand and his body as he fought to keep a snarling, writhing, red-cloaked figure away from his neck.

Red cloaks . . . Holy fuck, the red cloaks were working *with* the vampires.

The thought quickly died as several of them appeared in my line of vision. Their unscarred faces were twisted, their mouths open, as if screaming, though no sound came out. I swore and scrambled upright, backing away fast and calling to the fire within. I was halfway through the change when they hit me and sent me flying. I crashed to the ground with a grunt—a sound I repeated as the bastards flung themselves on top of me and began tearing at whatever remaining bit of flesh they could find with wickedly sharp nails and teeth. A scream tore up my throat, but it was lost to the roar of flames as I became full spirit. The red cloaks burned, but they didn't seem to care, tearing and biting at flesh that no longer existed.

And they sure as hell weren't burning fast enough for my liking.

My flames became incandescent. The red cloaks screamed then, but the sound was quickly cut off as their flesh cindered and their bones became little more than ash, which the force of my fires blew away. I flowed upright and arrowed toward Jackson. The red cloak he held was little more than a fleshy torch, but again the creature didn't seem to care. Two others tore at Jackson's legs, taking little notice of his efforts to kick them away or the flames that were searing their flesh. I flicked a ribbon of fire around their necks, drew the noose tight, then ripped them away from him, rising up-ward and dragging them with me, high into the treetops. They kicked and screamed and fought my rope, but there was only one way they were going to get free—and that was when my noose burned right through their flesh and separated their heads from their bodies. I lashed my fiery rope to the trunk of the tree, then swirled back down and grabbed the other red cloak. Him I sim-ply flung at the nearest tree, then tied securely with another ribbon of fire.

More red cloaks came at us. I twisted away from them, the movement so swift my flames trailed behind me like a comet's tail. I threw up a wall of fire between them and Jackson, then reached for the earth mother. Felt the trembling in the ground underneath me as she responded. Then her en-ergy exploded through me, a wild force that this time would not be contained or in any way di-rected. But it wrapped almost lovingly around the five red cloaks and cindered them in an instant.

Then it retreated, leaving me shaken and back in flesh form. I scrubbed a trembling hand across my face, smearing wetness, then forced myself upright and staggered across to Jackson.

His arm was torn and bleeding, and there were chunks of flesh missing from his legs. But he forced himself upright with his one good arm and said, "Let's get the fuck out of here."

"No," I bit back, my gaze skating through the shadows. The red cloaks hadn't finished with us yet; of that I was sure. "Not before you take my fire into yourself and burn the virus from your body."

"Em, now is *not*—"

"You were bitten by *red* cloaks," I reminded him fiercely. "And no one knows if the Fae are affected by it. The only thing I'm sure of is that I'm *not*. As a fire Fae, you should be capable of taking in the fires of a phoenix without being cindered."

"I guess death by flame is a hell of a lot better than a descent into madness." He hesitated. "Have you ever tried anything like this before? Heard of anything like this being tried before?"

"No and no."

"That's what I was afraid of." He took a deep breath and released it. "You need to straighten my leg before we can attempt this. If I can chase the virus from my system through your flames, then I sure as hell can heal other wounds as well."

I glanced at his leg. It was sitting at an odd angle, with a ragged piece of bone protruding through bloodied flesh. It wasn't going to be easy to straighten it—for him or me.

But then, moving with it in this state couldn't have been pleasant, either.

I turned, but moved too quickly and had to slam a hand down to stop my face from planting itself into the dirt. I waited till the slight bout of dizziness eased, then, a little more cautiously, moved to the other end of Jackson's body.

"You ready?" I said as I gripped his foot.

He nodded, his expression grim. I didn't give him any warning, just simply did it. It ripped a scream from his throat, and the sound echoed through the trees. Somewhere in the distance I thought I heard laughter and wondered if it was the cool-voiced vampire or someone else.

I flamed, felt Jackson latch on to my fires, on to *me*, drawing all that I was into him, through him. Fire and flesh become one, and then there was no flesh, no him, and no me, just one united being of flame. And while it wasn't in any way sexual, it was nevertheless an incredible sensation.

Then the connection broke. The suddenness of it slammed me backward, and for several seconds it was all I could do to suck in air and remain conscious.

"Em?" Jackson's voice was as weak as I felt. "You okay? I didn't hurt you?"

"No." I felt like hell, and there was little more than ash in the storage banks right now, but I was alive. "You?"

"Same." He paused. "The leg and arm are only half-healed."

"You're lucky it did that." I pushed upright. "Phoenixes generally aren't capable of healing their wounds with fire. That's why I still have scars on my back."

"Yeah, but I'm Fae, and we *can* use our elements to heal."

"I'm not an element. I'm a being."

Behind me, to my left, a leaf snapped. I swung around, sparks halfheartedly dancing across my fingertips. Saw a ghostly, gray-cloaked figure watching me, the cowled hood deep enough to hide his face and yet, oddly, not his eyes. They glowed with an unearthly blue fire and were filled with such hate it shook me to the core.

"You," he said, the words soft, yet carrying easily on the evening air, "will yet be mine."

Then he was gone, leaving me not only shaking, but wondering what the hell was going on. Nothing we'd discovered so far was adding up, and the only thing we could really be certain about was that there was something a *whole* lot bigger than our investigation into the murders of the two scientists going on.

Something—if the stranger's words were anything to go by—that would drag me far deeper into this whole mess.

Red cloaks appeared and charged as one. I raised my hands and backpedaled fast—only to trip over something and fall ass over tit. I landed on my back, had a glimpse of claws thicker than my arm, and quickly glanced up. It wasn't trees that filled my vision; it was fire. Not mine, not Jackson's, but Rory's. I flung out a hand and added what little fire I had left to his. The red cloaks were hit by the joint wall and had little hope. In a very short time, they were ashen blobs on the forest floor—blobs that the wind picked through and scattered.

Silence returned to the forest.

For several minutes, I didn't move. I could no longer hear the crackle of Rory's containment circle, but I had no sense that anyone was near. Perhaps the cool-voiced vampire had indeed kept his word and retreated rather than attacked. But then, if he *was* working with whoever controlled the red cloaks—and I very much suspected that *that* person was the gray-cloaked figure I'd seen—he had no real need to attack. Not given that he obviously expected them to take us out.

I pushed to my feet, brushed sweaty strands of hair out of my eyes, and met Jackson's gaze. "You up to getting out of here?"

"Yeah." He raised his good arm, and I hauled him to his feet again. This time the effort left me panting.

"We're a damn fine pair, aren't we?" He wrapped an arm around my shoulders and leaned on me heavily.

"Seems we're perfectly matched when it comes to finding trouble," I agreed. My gaze swept the trees around us. That gray-cowled figure was still out there somewhere; his presence was like a canker in the fast-fading light of the sunset.

You will yet be mine, he'd said.

A shiver ran down my spine. I had no idea who he was—or even *what* he was. I only knew he was someone better avoided.

And why the hell would he want me? It wasn't like I had any special talent. Yes, I was a phoenix capable of taking several different forms, but that didn't make me any more special than Jackson—or any other nonhuman, for that matter.

So why me?

I had no idea—but it was very obvious some-time in the near future I was going to find out.

Trepidation trembled through me, but I thrust it aside. *One problem at a time,* I reminded myself yet again.

And that, right now, was getting the hell out of this forest.

CHAPTER 15

Rory met us at the fence line and, between the two of us, we managed to get Jackson over the fence and into the car without too much further damage to his half-healed arm and leg.

"Where to?" Rory said as he retrieved the keys from under the wheel arch.

"I don't know." I ran a trembling hand through my matted hair. "We need to go somewhere safe and regroup. This isn't over. Not by a long shot."

"No, it's not," Jackson said from inside the car. "But there's little we can do here. You might as well come back to my office, so we can decide where we go from here."

I glanced at Rory, who raised his eyebrow and shrugged. "Right now, it's as good an idea as any. But you and I will need to go home sometime this evening."

Yes, we would, if only so he could recharge. Though I'd called on the earth mother's power myself, it had been only briefly. Rory had drawn on her energy for a far longer period and, though he hadn't said anything, his skin was pale and the heat emanating from his body was muted.

We climbed into the car and headed back to the city. I flipped the vanity mirror down and kept an eye on the road behind us. But darkness was rapidly closing in, and it was damn difficult to distinguish cars that might be following us from cars that were simply going in the same direction. In the end, I gave up.

Thankfully, we arrived at Jackson's without further incident. Together we helped him inside. Though he didn't say anything, he was trembling by the time we deposited him on the sofa at the far end of his office.

"Right," I said, rolling up my sleeves. "We all need to eat before anything else happens. Rory, you arrange drinks for everyone, and I'll rustle up some grub."

I ran up the stairs and raided Jackson's fridge, ending up with a big platter of chicken, a variety of cheeses, and some bread that I'd roughly cut into thick slabs. I carried it down and placed it on the coffee table, grabbing a chicken leg and chunk of bread for myself before retreating to one of the chairs.

"So," I said, once everyone else had helped themselves. "What the fuck do we do now?"

"That," Jackson said heavily, "depends very much on what the sindicati decide to do next. They have the laptop, so maybe they'll walk away and leave us be."

"They may have the laptop," Rory said, "but they won't have the files they wanted. A Trojan will destroy all of them the next time it's booted up."

"Good move." Jackson finished his wine in several large gulps, then held it out for Rory to refill. "But it's one that will surely piss them off."

"Better to piss them off than give them Mark's notes." I grimaced. "But it may not mean anything, given Baltimore has walked out of the morgue and disappeared into Brooklyn."

Jackson raised his eyebrows. "He was infected?"

"Apparently. God knows when it happened."

"Damn it. That means the red cloaks have *both* of the scientists who were working on the cure for that fucking virus. That can't be a good thing for the rest of us."

"No," I agreed. "And it's made worse by the fact that—if tonight is any indication—the sindicati are now working with the cloaks."

"Which doesn't make sense. I mean, from what your ex said, vampires can be infected as easily as humans. Why the hell would they work with the people who cannot only give them the disease, but who now control the only two men capable of finding its cure? Wouldn't it make more sense to try to grab the research and scientists for themselves?"

"The sindicati are nothing if not opportunists," Rory said, voice grim. "They probably see more benefit in working with the cloaks to gain a cure than working against them and risk infection and possible subjugation."

"If that's the case," I said, "why the farce tonight? The cloaks have the scientists, so if they are working together, they don't need the notes. And if they simply wanted to kill us, they could have done so when they had us all tied up in that damn room."

"The sindicati may be opportunists," Rory said, "but they are also backstabbing bastards. If the cloaks trust them to uphold whatever deal they've made, then they're fools."

And whatever—whoever—that gray-cowled figure was, I doubted he was a fool.

Perhaps our next move should be trying to uncover *what*, exactly, those plans were—although that wasn't likely to be an easy task. If Sam and PIT were having trouble locating the people behind the cloaks, what the hell made me think we'd have any greater luck?

We wouldn't—except for the fact that the gray-cowled figure had revealed himself in the forest. I had a feeling *that* was something he'd not done before.

Of course, just because Sam had said they had no idea who was behind the cloaks didn't mean he'd actually been telling the truth.

"Sam did mention that the sindicati were having factional problems," I said. "It's possible that has something to do with the vamps working with the cloaks."

"Only if one of the factions has decided it needs help to oust the other, and that would be very rare," Jackson noted. "They tend to just slaughter one another and then start anew with whoever is left."

"But what would the red cloaks get out of the deal?" Rory asked. "As far as I can see, there's nothing the sindicati can give them that they can't just take by infecting them."

Jackson shrugged. "It could be something as simple as not having the manpower they need at the present time, thanks to the fact that the virus makes most of those infected mad."

"It only makes them mad if they're infected by one of the rotten ones." I tossed my chicken bone onto the platter and grabbed a bit of cheese to munch on. "Otherwise, it just wipes out free will and replaces it with a hive mentality."

"Whatever the hell is really going on," Jackson commented, "the fact remains that neither party is going to be happy with us after this evening's events. There *will* be reprisals. Everything else might be up for conjecture, but *that* is fact."

"Actually, they'll be coming after you two." Rory waved a bit of bread at the two of us. "Me, they don't know about as yet—and it might be wise to keep it that way."

"An emergency backup," Jackson commented. "I like it."

My gaze met Rory's, and he smiled. We both knew it was a bit more than that—him stepping back meant life could go on for the both of us if the very worst happened. I might have been re-born more times than I could now remember, but I wasn't tired of life just yet—even if I *was* getting more than a little pissed off with our whole "love will go sour" lot in life.

"What it does mean," Rory said, "is that you two may need to watch each other's backs."

"And I," Jackson said, a gleam in his eyes, "have the perfect way to do that."

"Oh, yeah?" I said, not trusting that gleam for an instant. "And that would be what, exactly?"

"This." He airily indicated the room around us.

I grinned. "I'm not moving in with you. As I explained, Rory and I need—"

"No, no, that's not what I meant." He paused. "Well, I wouldn't mind if you occasionally stayed here. No sane man is ever likely to reject the possibility of great sex—and certainly no *Fae* ever did."

"Then what did you mean?"

"I meant Hellfire Investigations." His expression was serious, the gleam giving way to determination. "As I mentioned earlier, I've been looking for someone to work with for a while, and if the last few days have proven *anything*, it's that we work well together."

I raised an eyebrow. "Didn't anyone tell you it's a bad idea to sleep with employees?"

"I *don't* sleep with employees. Well, I don't anymore—not after I ended up in court fighting harassment charges." He grinned. "Partners, however, are an entirely different matter."

"Only a Fae would think there's a difference," Rory commented, voice dry.

"Well, there *is*. We'd be on equal standing, rather than in a superior-subordinate situation."

I stared at him for a moment, then said, "Are you serious?"

"Totally." He leaned forward and caught my

hand. "I've got so much work, I'm having to turn potential clients away. I really *do* need help."

I had to admit, the thought of becoming an investigator certainly had my blood racing. As Rory had noted before this whole mess had begun, I wasn't usually one to put up with a staid life for very long. But this would be two lifetimes in a row I'd done something dangerous—and joining forces with Jackson against those who would hunt us down was certainly that—and it was supposedly Rory's turn to live on the edge this time around.

Not that he'd actually taken up the option beyond becoming a fireman.

I bit my lip and glanced at him. He smiled at my unasked question and said, "I'd feel a whole lot better if you were working here rather than off somewhere else where there's no one to watch your back."

I returned my gaze to Jackson's. "So, full partner? Done legally, with me buying a percentage of the business?"

"Fifty-fifty, and everything legal," he agreed. "With a cooling-off period of thirty days, just to be safe."

I hesitated, then grinned. "You have yourself a deal. And a partner."

Jackson grabbed the bottle of wine and refilled all our glasses.

"To Hellfire Investigations," he said, raising his glass. "Long may we prosper."

"To Hellfire," I echoed, and clinked my glass against theirs.

And knew, even as I drank the wine, that it wasn't prosperity we had to worry about.

It was survival.

Don't miss the last novel in
Keri Arthur's Dark Angels series,

DARKNESS FALLS

Available from Piatkus in December 2014

The Raziq were coming.

The energy of their approach was very distant, but it blasted heat and thunder across my senses and sent me reeling. But even worse was the sheer and utter depth of rage that accompanied that distant wave. I'd known they would be angry that we'd deceived them, but this . . . this was murderous.

Up until now, the Raziq had used minor demons to kidnap me whenever they'd wanted to talk to me—although *their* version of talk generally involved some kind of torture. This time, however, there would be no talking. There would be only death and destruction.

And they would take out everyone—and everything—around us in the process.

It was a horrendous prospect given we were still at the Brindle, a place that not only held aeons of witch knowledge but was also home to at least two dozen witches.

I reached for my sword. Even though we couldn't fight in this place of peace, I still felt safer with Amaya's weight in my hand. But she wasn't there. Just for an instant, panic surged; then I realized I'd left her behind, among the ruins of our home. In the aftermath of my father's destruction, I'd been desperate to see whether Mirri—who'd been under a death sentence, thanks to Father's magic—had by some miracle survived, and I hadn't given Amaya a second thought.

"We cannot stay here." The familiar, masculine tones broke through the fear that had been holding me captive.

My gaze met Azriel's. He wasn't only my guardian but my lover, the father of my child, and the being I was now linked to forever in both life *and* afterlife. When I died, I would become what he was—a Mijai, a reaper warrior tasked not only with protecting the gates to heaven and hell, but hunting down the demons who broke through hell's gate to cause havoc here on Earth.

Of course, reapers weren't actually flesh beings—although they could certainly attain that form whenever they wished—but rather beings made of energy who lived on the gray fields, the area that divided Earth from heaven and hell. While I *was* part werewolf and therefore flesh, I was also part Aedh. The Aedh were energy beings who at one time had lived on the fields like the reapers, and also had been the traditional guardians of the gates. My father had been one of the Raziq—a group of rebel Aedh who were responsible not only for the destruction of the Aedh but for the creation of the three keys to the gates—and he was also the reason they were currently lost.

Or rather, only one key was still lost. I'd found the first two, but both had been stolen from under my nose by the dark sorceress who'd subsequently opened two of hell's three gates.

Things hadn't quite gone according to plan for her when she'd opened the second one, however, because she'd been captured by demons and dragged into the pits of hell. I was keeping everything crossed that that's *exactly* where she'd remain, but given the way luck had been treating us of late it was an even-money bet she wouldn't.

"Risa," Azriel repeated when I didn't immediately answer him. "We *must* not stay here."

"I know."

But where the hell were we going to go that was safe from the wrath of the Raziq? There *was* nowhere safe. Maybe not even hell itself—not that I particularly wanted to go *there*.

I briefly closed my eyes and tried to control the panic surging through me. And yet that approaching wave of anger filled every recess of my mind, making thought, let alone calm, near impossible. If they got hold of me . . . My skin crawled.

It took a moment to register that my skin *was* actually crawling. Or at least part of it was. I glanced down. The wingless, serpentlike dragon tattoo on my left forearm was on the move, twisting around like a wild thing trapped. Anger gleamed in its dark eyes and its scales glowed a rich, vibrant lilac in the half-light of the room.

Of course, it wasn't an ordinary tattoo. It was a Dušan, a creature of magic that had been designed to protect me when I walked the fields. It was a gift from my father, and one of the few decent things he'd actually done for me since this whole key saga had begun.

Unfortunately, the Dušan was of little use here on Earth. It shouldn't even have been able to move on this plane, let alone partially disengage from my skin, as it had in the past.

"What's wrong now?"

I glanced at Ilianna—my best friend, flatmate, and a powerful witch in her own right. Her warm tones were rich with concern, and not without reason. After all, she'd only *just* managed to save the life of her mate, Mirri, from my father's foul magic, and here I was again, threatening not only Mirri's life but Ilianna's, her mom's, and those of everyone else who currently stood within the walls of this place. Because not even the magic of the Brindle, as powerful as it was, would stop the Raziq. It had been designed to protect the witches from the evil of *this* world. It was never meant to be a defense against those from the gray fields.

"The Raziq hunt us." Azriel's reply was flat. Matter-of-fact. Yet his anger reverberated through every inch of my being, as fierce as anything I could feel from the Raziq. But it wasn't just anger; it was anticipation, and *that* was possibly scarier. He drew his sword and met my gaze. If the ominous black-blue fire that flickered down the sides of Valdis— which was the name of the demon locked within the metal of his sword, and who imbued it with a life and power of its own—was anything to go by, she was as ready to fight as her master. As ready as Amaya would have been, had she been here. "We need to leave. *Now*."

Ilianna frowned. "Then go home—"

"We can't," I cut in. "Home's gone."

It had been blown to smithereens when I'd thrust Amaya's black steel into my father's flesh and had allowed her to consume him. And it was an action I didn't regret, not after everything the bastard had done.

"Yes," Ilianna replied. "But the wards your father gave us should still be active. I placed a spell on them that prevents anything or anyone other than us from moving them."

"Even from what basically resembled a bomb blast?"

She hesitated. "That, I can't guarantee."

"A half guarantee is better than nothing." Azriel's gaze met mine again. "If they *aren't* active, then we stand and fight. They still need you, no matter how furious they might currently be."

Yes, but they didn't need *him*. And they would destroy him, if they could. Still, what other choice did we have? No matter where we went, either here or on the gray fields, others would pay the price. I hesitated. "Will the Brindle's magic react if we transport out from within its walls?"

"Normally, yes," Kiandra—the Brindle's head witch—replied. She stood near Mirri and Zaira, Ilianna's mom, her gaze bright and all too knowing in the shadowed room. "But given the events of the last few days, I have woven specific exceptions into our barriers."

"Thanks." We were going to need it. I swallowed, then stepped toward Azriel.

"Call me," Ilianna said. "Let me know you're okay."

I didn't reply. I couldn't. Azriel's energy had already ripped through us, swiftly transporting us across the fields. We reappeared in the blackened ruins of the home I'd once shared with Ilianna and Tao—although to call them ruins was something of a misnomer. Ruins implied there was some form of basic structure left. There was nothing here. No walls, no ceiling, not even a basement. Just a big black hole that had once held a building we'd all loved.

I stepped away from Azriel and glanced up. The faintest touch of pink was beginning to invade the black of the sky; dawn wasn't that far off. I wondered what day it was. So much had happened over the past few days that I'd lost track.

Time appeared. The familiar, somewhat harsh tone that ran through my thoughts was heavy with displeasure. *Alone should not be*.

Sorry. I felt vaguely absurd for even issuing an apology. I mean, when it was all said and done, Amaya was a *sword*. But somewhere in the past few days, she had become more a friend than merely a means of protection.

I picked my way through the rubble and found

her half-wedged into the blackened soil. I pulled her free, and definitely felt a whole lot safer. Though it wasn't as if Amaya or Azriel—or anyone else for that damn matter—could save me if the Raziq really *had* decided enough was enough.

"The Raziq have split," Azriel commented.

Confusion—and a deepening sense of dread—ran through me. "Meaning what?"

The ferocity that roiled through the connection between us gave his blue eyes an icy edge. "Half of them chase us here. The rest continue toward the Brindle."

"Oh, fuck!"

"They plan to demonstrate the cost of misdirection, and there is nothing we can do to prevent it." His expression hardened, and I hadn't thought *that* was possible. "And before you say it, I will *not* let you endanger yourself for them."

"And I will *not* stand here and let others pay the price for decisions I've made!"

"We have no other choice—"

"There's *always* a fucking choice, Azriel. Standing here while others die in my place is *not* one of them."

"Making a stand at the Brindle will *not* alter the fate of the Brindle."

"Don't you think I know that?" I thrust a hand through my hair and began to pace. There *had* to be an answer. Had to be some way to protect the Brindle and everyone within her without either Azriel or me having to make a stand. Damn it, if only Ilianna had had the time to create more protection stones . . . The thought stuttered to a halt. "Oh, my god, the protection stones."

Azriel frowned. "They are still active. I can feel their presence."

"Exactly!" I swung around to face him. "You need to get them to the Brindle. It's the only chance they have against the Raziq."

"I will not—"

"For God's sake, stop arguing and just do as I ask!"

He crossed his arms and glared at me. His expression was so fierce my insides quaked, even though I knew he would never, ever hurt me.

"My task is to protect you. No one else. You. I cannot and *will* not leave you unprotected, especially not *now*."

Not when there is life and love yet to be explored between us. Not when you carry our child. The words spun through my thoughts, as fierce as his expression and yet filled with such passion that my heart damn near melted. I walked back to him and touched his arm. His skin twitched, but the muscles underneath were like steel. My warrior was ready for battle.

"I know it goes against every instinct, Azriel, but I couldn't live with myself if anyone at the Brindle died because of me."

"And I would not want to live without you. There *is* no where that is safe from the wrath of the Raziq."

"Maybe not—" I hesitated, suddenly remembering what he'd said about the Aedh temples and the remnants of the priests who still haunted that place. They weren't ghosts, as such—more echoes of the beings they'd once been—but they were nevertheless damn dangerous. I'd briefly encountered one of them when I'd been chasing the sorceress to hell's gate, and it had left me in no doubt that he could destroy me without a second's hesitation.

"*That* is not a true option," Azriel said, obviously following my thoughts. "And there is certainly no guarantee that the priests will even acknowledge you again, let alone provide any sort of assistance."

"That's a chance I'm willing to take." And it was certainly a better option than letting the Brindle pay the cost for my deceit. "Those who haunt that place weren't aware of the Raziq's duplicity, Azriel, but I think they might be now. And you're the one who told me that if they decide you're an intruder, they can cause great harm."

"But the Raziq were once priests—"

"*And* they're also the reason the Aedh no longer exist to guard the gates," I cut in. "This might be the only way both of us are going to survive a confrontation with the Raziq, and we *have* to take it."

He stared at me for several heartbeats, then swore viciously. Not in my language, in his. I blinked at the realization I'd understood it, but let it slide. Right now it didn't matter a damn how or when *that* had happened. All that did matter was surviving the next few minutes.

Because the Raziq were getting nearer. They'd breached the barrier between the fields and Earth and were closing in even as we stood here. I suspected the only reason they hadn't yet confronted us was simply that we had moved. But that wouldn't help the Brindle.

Azriel sheathed his sword, then caught my hand and tugged me toward him. "If we're going to do this, then we do it somewhere where your body is going to be safe while you're on the fields."

"Not the Brindle—"

"No."

The word was barely out of his mouth when his energy ripped through us again. We appeared in a room that was dark but not unoccupied. The scents in the air told me exactly where we were—Aunt Riley's. She was the very last person I wanted to endanger in *any* way. I wasn't actually blood related to Riley, but after my mom's death, she and her pack were the only family I had left.

But before I could make any objection about being here, she said, "I'm gathering there's a good reason behind your sudden appearance in our bedroom at this ungodly hour of the morning."

Her tone was wry, and she didn't sound the slightest bit sleepy. But then, she'd not only once been a guardian, but one of their best. I guess old habits—like sleeping light—die hard.

"The Aedh hunt us." Azriel's voice was tight. He didn't like doing this any more than I did, though I suspected our reasons were very different. "I need you to keep Risa's body safe while she's on the gray fields."

And with that, he kissed me—fiercely but all too briefly—then disappeared. Leaving me reeling, battling for breath, and more frightened than I'd ever been. Because I was about to face the wrath of the Raziq alone, even if for only a few minutes.

Not alone, Amaya grumbled. *Here am*.

Yes, she was. But even a demon sword with a thirst for bloodshed might not be enough to counter the fury I could feel in the Raziq.

And why the hell could I even feel that? Had it something to do with whatever Malin—the woman in charge of the Raziq and my father's pissed-off ex—had done to me that time she'd tortured me? I didn't know, because Malin had also erased my knowledge of the procedure to prevent my father from figuring out what she'd done. But with him dead, maybe it was time to find out.

"Risa?" This time it was Riley's mate, Quinn, who spoke.

He was the reason Azriel had bought me here. While Riley may once have been a guardian, Quinn was a whole lot more. Not only was he a vampire who'd once been a Cazador—who were basically the high vampire council's elite hit squad—but he was also what I was: a half-breed Aedh. One who'd undergone priest's training. If there was anyone here on Earth who could stand against the wrath of the Raziq for more than a second, it would be him.

I swallowed heavily, but it didn't do a whole lot

to ease the dryness in my throat. What I was about to do was the very last thing I'd *ever* wanted to do, but the reality was I'd been left with little other choice.

"There's no time to explain," I said. "I have to get onto the fields immediately. People will die if I don't."

"Then do it." Quinn climbed out of bed and walked to the wardrobes that lined one wall of their bedroom. "No one will get past us."

I hoped he was right, but it wasn't like I was going to be around to find out. I sat cross-legged on the thick, cushiony carpet, saw Quinn open a door and reach for the weapons within, then closed my eyes and took a deep breath.

As I released it, I released awareness of everything around me, concentrating on nothing more than slowing the frantic beat of my heart so I could free my psyche, my soul—or whatever else people liked to call it—from the constraints of my flesh. *That* was what the Raziq were following—not my flesh, but my spirit. I hoped they would follow me onto the fields and not wreak hell on the two people I cared about most in this world.

As the awareness of everything around me began to fade, warmth throbbed at my neck—a sign that the charm Ilianna had given me when we'd both still been teenagers was at work, protecting me as my psyche pulled free and stepped onto the gray fields. Here the real world was little more than a shadow, a place where those things that could not be seen on the living plane became visible. It was also the land between life and death, a place through which souls journeyed to whatever gateway was their next destination, be it heaven or hell.

But it was far from uninhabited. The reapers lived here, and so did the Raziq who remained.

And right now it was a dangerous place for me to be. The Raziq could move far faster here than I could. My only hope was reaching the Aedh temples that surrounded and protected the gates.

I turned and ran. The Dušan immediately exploded from my arm, her energy flowing through me as her serpentine form gained flesh and shape, became real and solid. She swirled around me, the wind of her body buffeting mine as her sharp ebony gaze scanned the fields around us. Looking for trouble. Looking to fight.

I had to wonder whether even she would have any hope against the Raziq. Because they were coming. The thunder of their approach shook the very air around us.

Fear surged, and it lent me the strength to go faster. But running seemed a hideously slow method of movement, even if everything around me was little more than a blur. I wished I could transport myself to the temples instantaneously, as Azriel had in the past, but I wasn't yet of this world, even if I was destined to become a Mijai upon death.

The Dušan's movements were becoming more and more frantic. I swore and reached for every ounce of energy I had left, until it felt as if I were flying through the fields of gray.

But even when I reached the temples, I felt no

safer. This place was as ghostly and surreal as the rest of the fields, but it was also a place filled with impossible shapes, high, soaring arches, and honeycombed domes sitting atop floating towers. Yet it no longer felt as empty as it had the first time I'd come here. There was an awareness—an anger—here now, and it filled the temple grounds with a watchful energy that stung my skin and sent chills through my being.

I stopped in the expanse of emptiness that divided the temple buildings from the simply adorned gates to heaven and hell. The Dušan surged around me, her movements sharp, agitated. I tightened my grip on Amaya as I turned to face the oncoming Raziq. Amaya began to hiss in expectation, the noise jarring against the watchful silence. But none of the priestly remnants appeared nor spoke. I had no doubt they were aware of my presence, but it seemed that, for now, they were content to watch.

Leaving me hoping like *hell* that I hadn't been wrong, that they *would* interfere if the Raziq got too violent.

But it wasn't like I had any other choice now, anyway. They were here.

Electricity surged, dark and violent. Without warning both the Dušan and I were flung backward. I hit vaporous ground that felt as hard as anything on Earth and tumbled into the wall of a building that stood impossibly on a point.

Amaya was screaming, the Dušan was screaming, and their joint fury echoed both through my brain and across the fields. The Dušan surged upward, briefly disappearing into grayness before she dove into the midst of the Raziq, snapping and tearing at the beings I couldn't see, could only feel. A second later, she was sent tumbling again.

If they could do that to a Dušan, what hope did I have?

Amaya screamed again. She wanted to rend, to tear, to consume, but there were far too many of them. We didn't stand a chance ... and yet, I couldn't give up—not without a fight. Not this time.

I pushed to my feet, raised Amaya, and spit, "Do your worst, Malin. But you might want to remember you still need me to find that last key. And if you kill me, I become Mijai and beyond even *your* reach. Not something you'd want, I'd guess."

For a moment, there was no response; then that dark energy surged again. I swore and dove out of the way, and the dark energy hit the building that loomed above me. Its ghostly, gleaming sides rippled, the waves small at first but gaining in depth as they rolled upward, until the whole building quivered and shook and the thick, heavy top began to crumble and fall. I scrambled out of the way only to feel another bolt arrowing toward me. I swore and went left, but this time I wasn't quite fast enough. The energy sizzled past my legs, wrapping them in heat, until it felt as if my flesh were melting from my bones.

A scream tore up my throat, but I clamped down on it hard, and it came out little more than a hiss. I wasn't flesh; I was energy. *This* was nothing more than mind games.

Mind games that felt painfully real.

Damn it, no! If I was going to go down, then I sure as hell was going to take some of these bastards with me.

Amaya, do your worst. And with that, I flung her as hard as I could into the seething mass of energy that was the Raziq. They scattered, as I knew they would, but Amaya arced around, her sides spitting lilac flames that splayed out like burning bullets. Whether they hit any targets, I have no idea, because I wasn't about to hang around waiting for another bolt to hit me. I scrambled to my feet and ran to the right of the Raziq. Amaya surged through their midst, still spitting her bullets as she returned to me. The minute she thumped into my hand, I swung her with every ounce of strength and anger within me. Steel connected with energy and the resulting explosion was brief but fierce, and would have knocked me off my feet had it not been for my grip on my sword. Amaya wasn't going anywhere; she had a soul to devour, and devour she did. It took barely a heartbeat, but that was time enough for the rest of the Raziq to rally. Again that dark energy swept across the silent watchfulness of the temple's fields, but this time the invisible blow was broader, cutting the possibility of diving out of its path.

Amaya, shield! I dropped to one knee and held Amaya in front of me. Lilac fire instantly flared out from the tip of her blade and formed a circle that encased me completely.

And just in time.

The dark energy hit the barrier, and with enough

force that it pushed me backward several feet. Amaya screamed in fury, her shield burning and bubbling where the Raziq's energy flayed her. She held firm, but I had to wonder for how long. Not very, I suspected.

Damn it, where were the remnants? The Raziq were the reason we were all in this mess—they were the reason the priests were dead. Did they not realize that? Did they not want to avenge that? I knew Aedh were supposedly emotionless beings, but they were not above pride and they certainly weren't above anger. Surely the priests had to feel *something* about their demise.

But what if they didn't know or care?

Maybe it was time to remind them of their duty to protect the gates.

"Killing me won't solve your current problem, Malin." I had to shout to be heard above both Amaya's screeching and the thunderous impact of the dark energy against her shield. I had no idea where the Dušan was, but she was still very much active if her bellows were anything to go by. "As long as there's one key left, you—as an Aedh priest—cannot be free from the responsibility of caring for the gates. If you so desperately want to close the gates permanently and therefore end your servitude to them, then you're better off trying to sweet-talk me."

"Sweet-talk?" The voice was feminine and decidedly pleasant. There was none of the malevolence I could feel in the dark energy, yet it nevertheless sent chills down my spine. Malin could charm the pants off a spider even as she dissected it piece by tiny piece. She'd dissected me once. That time, at least, she'd put me back whole, though not entirely the same. And while Azriel certainly knew what she'd done to me, he wasn't saying anything. This time, however, I suspected she would not be so generous. "You defy us at every turn, you do not take our threats seriously, and you expect us to simply accept your games of misdirection? Since when did insanity become a thread in your being?"

"I'm guessing it happened the day you lot entered my life." It probably wasn't the wisest thing to say, but hey, what the hell? It wasn't like she could get any angrier. Although the fresh burst of energy that hit Amaya's shield very much suggested I was wrong. And the fact that *she* was no longer screaming was an ominous sign her strength was weakening.

Is, she muttered. If there was one thing my sword hated, it was admitting she wasn't all-powerful. *Yours must draw soon.*

Her drawing on my strength was the very last thing *I* wanted right now, but again, until Malin and the rest of the Raziq calmed down a tad, it wasn't like we had another choice.

Presuming, of course, they *would* calm down.

"And insanity aside," I continued, "it doesn't alter the fact you still need me to find the final key."

"Not if we've now decided it would be better to destroy both the gates that are opened and the one that is not."

My body went cold. If they did *that*, then heaven

help us all. Hell would be unleashed on both the fields and on Earth, and I very much suspected neither world would survive.

But would the fates and the priestly remnants allow that?

The continuing silence—at least when it came to the Raziq—very much suggested they might.

"The mere fact you make such a threat shows just how far the Raziq have fallen." Azriel's voice cut across the noise and the anger that filled the temple grounds as cleanly as sunshine through rain. Relief made my arms shake and tears stung my eyes. I blinked them away furiously. It wasn't over yet. Not by a long shot. It was still him and me against all of them.

"You no longer deserve the name of priests," he continued, voice ominously flat. "And you certainly no longer have the umbrella of protection such a title endows."

"Do *not* make idle threats, Mijai." Any pretense of civility had finally been stripped from Malin's voice. It was evil personified; nothing more, nothing less. "We both know you would not dare to violate the sanctity of this place."

"Not without the permission of the fates," he agreed. "And *that* we now have."

With those words lingering ominously in the air, he appeared.

And he wasn't alone.

Do you love fiction with a supernatural twist?

Want the chance to hear news about your favourite
authors (and the chance to win free books)?

Keri Arthur

S. G. Browne

P.C. Cast

Christine Feehan

Jacquelyn Frank

Thea Harrison

Larissa Ione

Darynda Jones

Sherrilyn Kenyon

Jackie Kessler

Jayne Ann Krentz and Jayne Castle

Martin Millar

Kat Richardson

J.R. Ward

David Wellington

Laura Wright

Then visit the Piatkus website and blog
www.piatkus.co.uk | www.piatkusbooks.net

And follow us on Facebook and Twitter
www.facebook.com/piatkusfiction | www.twitter.com/piatkusbooks

piatkus